Table of Contents

Steve Trew

EIGHT KIDS FROM LONDON

An Olympic Love Story

AUSTIN MACAULEY PUBLISHERS®

LONDON * CAMBRIDGE * NEW YORK * SHARJAH

A CIP catalogue record for this title is available from the British Library.

ISBN 9781035852628 (Paperback)
ISBN 9781035852635 (ePub e-book)

www.austinmacauley.com

First Published 2025
Austin Macauley Publishers Ltd®
1 Canada Square
Canary Wharf
London
E14 5AA

For Chris Mawer, who read, re-read and edited. For Sue Jeffries, who sketched the book front cover and gave me so many ideas. For Dulcie, Christine, and Andy, who gently (and not so gently) made suggestions. Couldn't have done it without you guys.

Part One
A New Beginning

Chapter One
The Runner

He looked, and was, an athlete. Mickey Honey was an athlete, possibly one of the best in the world…Actually, probably one of the best in the world. Slim, muscle definition standing out (although not big, rather honed and toned) and tanned by the sun. What a life! Oh God, he loved what he did, where he did it, how he trained and lived!

He loved the sun, loved being out in it, loved training in it, loved just sitting or lying in it after training. Loved racing in it; when some of the other guys started to complain, he was right in there. "Oh man, I LOVE it! Bring it on, more sun the better, hot, hotter, hottest!" They'd laugh then, but in a way, it gave him a bit of an upper because they all knew that he really did love the sun and really did race better in it while they were cautious about being out there all that time.

He chose to do a lot of the run sessions when the sun was at its hottest, midday or thereabouts. Didn't matter where he was or where the training camp was situated; he'd be out there in the midday sun. "But why, why do you do that?" the others would ask. "Man, we got all day; we're professional athletes; we can choose what time's best."

"Yeah, and this time's best for me," he'd say, putting on his sun cap and adjusting the shades as he went out of the door. A couple of minutes and the sweat would start. Oh man, he loved that, loved that feeling of the moisture running from his forehead, down his face, even into his eyes; he knew that when that happened, he was working hard.

By himself, out on the highway and then turning onto the dirt trail that he'd run so, so many times. A little bit of sand and dust kicking up, but really it was a half rock, half stone surface, more like the edge of a desert where the cacti and the sparse green-brown plants started to recede, to leave only the sparse underfoot reflecting the heat and the sun back up onto the body, his body. It was the waves of heat, then; the glorious sun hitting the stone surface and then reflecting the scorched air upwards. Even his breathing was fine; the other guys would complain sometimes, "Oh man, feels like you're swallowing an inferno out there!"

He'd smile then. "Yeah, you got it, man; swallow that heat, make it hotter." The edge—that's what it gave him—that little bit of edge.

Rarely, very rarely, did he see anyone else out running in the midday heat; he pretty much liked it that way. And if there was an edge to be considered (there's always an edge to be considered...), he felt the solitude gave it to him. Sure, great to have the other guys around most of the time; he would always want them there when he was doing his swimming or biking as recovery sessions, although even on the bike he sometimes relished that loneliness in the middle of nowhere, the sun—as ever—beating down and he in his tucked time-trial position, just pushing and pushing and pushing.

But today was just running. What was that old British movie? Oh yeah, *The Loneliness of the Long Distance Runner*, that was it. He'd seen it once, wasn't at all what he'd expected—well, maybe just a little bit. That kid in the institution, the young offenders unit or something, and he took the power away from his captors, took revenge because he really could run, could run fast. And when they (the prison officers) wanted him to beat the posh boys, the public school that they were running against, he chose to do it his way. Well into the lead, coming into the home straight with victory assured...and he chose to slow down, chose to stick two fingers up proverbially, chose to lose...because by losing, he won. Yeah, he could understand that. Nice one.

But what he also totally understood was the freedom and the peace that the lonely kid, the lonely runner, had when he was out there running by himself; that tranquillity, that sense of invulnerability to be alone in the early morning, sometimes the mist, sometimes the sun just rising...Yeah, he got that all right.

On the edge of the desert now, focusing on his own peace and tranquillity in the heat, in the sun, in the sweat and grit of his own making. No one else around, no one. No cars, no sound, even bar that of his own breathing and maybe the slight, almost imperceptible scuffing of his shoes as they lifted and landed again and again and again. It was his life.

Chapter Two
Beginnings

It hadn't always been like that, of course. Jeez, it certainly hadn't always been like that! Growing up in East London, growing up poor. Growing up in what the social services called a 'dysfunctional family'.

"I'll show you what a fucking dysfunctional family is, you bitches!" He remembered his father saying on one of the many, many visits they had endured. "Fucking dysfunctional, my arse! Now fuck off out of here!" And indeed, the social workers had indeed—as his father had so eloquently phrased it—fucked off.

He would have been around eight years old then, two years before the millennium, maybe a little bit older or a little bit younger. A skinny little kid, always pale, always looking that bit unhealthy. Hollow, dark shadows under his eyes, cheeks seemingly pinched inwards. His dad was around then—not always, though. He'd been told that his dad was 'working away', the times that he wasn't there; a few weeks here, a couple of months there. And then a kid in his class at school had told him the truth, "Your dad's inside; he's doing time; he's in prison." It hadn't particularly shocked him; rather, it had all made sense then. It just 'was'. Life, his life, was like that.

He never thought of himself as being poor. What was poor? OK, sometimes there wasn't enough to eat, sometimes (if truth were told, often) he was hungry. But that wasn't particularly different to the other kids around where he lived. It was just a fact of life; sometimes you were hungry and, if you were lucky, sometimes you weren't. Life, his life, was like that. Get up, more usually get woken up by Mum, maybe get a slice of toast, maybe. Get to school, usually (make that 'often') late because Mum had been dealing with a hangover and hadn't got him to bed—actually hadn't got him to bed at all—he'd put himself to bed, like always. Get told off by the teacher; teacher didn't really care as she'd

17

been telling him off ever since she'd taken over his class. So, he didn't really care either; that was just life; his life was like that. School dinner was good; it was good because he actually got something to eat. Hang around for second helpings, maybe; that was good as well. It was the same kids always hanging around for seconds, always the same little group.

It was pretty much the same bunch of kids that he'd hang around with in the flats. They'd get in from school, maybe have something to eat or, if they were lucky, be sent up to the fish and chip shop. And if that happened, that was a good day indeed! Eat the fish and chips. Sometimes it was only chips, no fish. Actually, quite often, it was only chips, but who cared? No one ever seemed to go in early. Why would they want to do that? Get in, get shouted at by your parents, told off by your mum if your dad wasn't there, and, truth be told, there were a lot of kids whose dad was 'working away', and it wasn't really talked about at all; it just was. And they'd play, all the usual: football, of course, cricket in the summer, rounders, if the girls made them, or they wanted a change—and they'd run.

They'd run, of course, in all the games they played, but sometimes they'd just want to run. All the kids did, even the fat ones. And there was no political correctness in this particular group; if you were fat, you were fat. And you got told so. To be honest, there weren't a lot of fat kids at all. Street-level diet and food and continuous activity meant that there wasn't a lot of energy that didn't get used up.

There was a central core to their group; some kids drifted in and out or moved in or out of the area, but there was that little nucleus that stayed the same. The group was centred around the flats where they lived because that was their world. The thoughts of moving out of the area unless it was absolutely necessary never even entered their heads. It was a cosmopolitan group, and everyone had nicknames, which weren't always used, but if there were new kids around, then the nicknames were always used. Using their nicknames gave them just a tiny bit of an edge, a little bit of being part of something special. There was Mickey, of course. Mickey was white and nicknamed the Duracell Bunny. Epic Eric was black and did the worst West Indian accent you'd ever heard; the other kids loved it and would be getting old Epic to talk like that all the time.

Bobby Carter, 'Carter the Farter', didn't actually live in the flats because his mum and dad had a sweetshop just on the corner, and Bobby lived above the shop. Bobby had the ability, it seemed, to be able to fart on demand. "Urrgh Gross! Gross man!" they'd yell at him, but they loved him.

Bobby's dad was white, and his mum was black, and sometimes he'd tell them, putting on his most serious expression, "No, I'm not mixed race, I'm dual heritage." And then they'd all burst out laughing because it didn't matter a stuff to them who you were or what colour you happened to be.

And then there was Joshi. Joshi the Doc, they called him. Joshi was pretty serious; he was going to be a doctor, and he was the one who always paid attention in class, but the others forgave him that.

And then there were the girls; Lucy, "Lucy Lastic!" they shouted out. Even at ten years old, Lucy had a serious crush on Mickey but couldn't even rationalise it to herself. Lucy was petite and had the cheekiness of someone who was happy in her own skin, which just happened to be black. Shelley was nicknamed Jelly Belly. "We love Shelley with the big, fat belly!" Shelley would just smile because they were only words, and she loved, absolutely loved, being a part of their group, and Shelley had the slimmest waist. In some ways, Shelley seemed to be a little older, maybe a little more mature than the others. Shelley lived with her mum; she didn't have a dad, which wasn't particularly unusual where they lived. Shelley was white, as was Joanna, 'JoJo'. Sometimes one of them would make a poor joke and say, "Only Jo-king," but that wasn't particularly funny at all, so it was pretty much always JoJo.

Alisha was Joshi's twin sister, and Alisha was a rascal, an absolute rascal. Even the others would get worried when they knew that Alisha was on a mission. Alisha had this beautiful colouring that gave away her Indian heritage, but with Alisha, all those cliched statements about obedience, quietness, good student went right out of the window because they were just cliches. How and why do we expect someone to behave in a particular way just because of their particular race and heritage? Why? Because that's what we've been told to expect, usually by someone older and supposedly wiser.

In class, sometimes when everyone was quiet and supposed to be reading or doing their own work, Alisha would whisper so softly that only the kids at the desks near her could hear, "Willy."

"Bum Bum."

"Poop," and he would keep repeating softly until someone (never Alisha) wouldn't be able to keep it in any longer and would burst out laughing and get sent out of the room. And Alisha would sit there with the innocence of a thousand years on her face. They all loved Alisha, and Alisha loved all of them.

They called themselves 'TMRG', which pretty obviously stood for 'the multi-racial gang', but they liked to think that nobody else realised that, and it gave them that little edge of being special. That was life, their life.

They'd run around the block of flats. You could run all the way around or, if you cut in and out of the central area, it was pretty much a figure of eight. The figure of eight was the best one; you could start with one other kid and you'd run away from each other, and then, of course, at halfway on the figure eight, you'd be cutting into each other as you got back to the middle. That way, you could see who was winning. Mickey won a lot—not always, but pretty much.

"Mickey Honey, the Duracell Bunny!" the other kids would shout out, and Mickey liked that. He was good at something, actually got a bit of praise, and that was always nice, especially when it was from friends. Rarely did Mickey get any praise or attention from grown-ups—not teachers, not his mum, never his absentee dad. So, yeah, it was nice to get a bit of praise. So much better than a clip around the ear, the muttered swear word or, even worse, just being ignored.

"For fuck's sake, just give me a bit of attention!" he would quietly scream inside his head when he was sitting at his desk, but the teacher would just walk by. Why would she waste time on someone who was going nowhere, or if heading in any direction, likely to be following his father to petty crime and frequent prison time? The kid who couldn't even get himself to school on time, why waste time on him? Even when she saw him on TV so many years later and marvelled at what that particular athlete was achieving, she never once realised that it was the same lost little boy that she had had in her junior school class; she didn't even connect the name. Why would she remember—or even want to remember—the name of one of the lost souls?

None of the TMRG could really remember when and why they'd started running, especially the figure eight. Shelley Jelly Belly thought it was when they were being chased by an angry grown-up whom they'd been teasing when the scruffy grown-up had walked out of Bobby Carter's mum and dad's shop and they'd wanted to get away from him but not get too far away from the flats. The scruffy bloke had chased them a little way but had quickly given up. But the figure eight was soon established as the rat run, if and when they ever needed to get away from someone, maybe the big kids—the older ones, maybe mums and dads wanting them in right now. It was a secret escape, their secret escape.

Lucy was the fastest of all the girls; actually, she was the fastest of all of them, but if she and the Duracell Bunny were running around the figure eight together, she would never let herself beat him. She didn't rationalise why, just decided that it wasn't important enough to her, and she knew, deep down inside, just how important it was to Mickey Honey. It was a funny little world, but it was their funny little world, and as far as they knew, it would last forever. But forever is a long, long time, and nothing really lasts forever.

So, it was no wonder—no wonder at all—that this particular group— TMRG—and almost certainly other little groups wherever they happened to be stuck together. It gave them an identity, a reason, if you like. It was life, their life. Them against the world? Not quite, but sometimes it felt like that.

So, for Mickey Honey, the Duracell Bunny, and for many of his friends, school was a bit of a lost cause. You went to school because you had to go to school. You learnt some stuff because, well, if you sat there long enough, then at least something would be taken up. But for all of them—most of them—school was just another thing to endure. It was life, his life, their life. For these kids (apart from Joshi, who was going to be a doctor because his parents said so), talk of a career, talk of 'making something of yourself' was just that: talk. They knew that their working life—if indeed they were even to have a working life—would be one in a factory or shop work or casual labour, maybe working on the council if you were lucky enough to have a relative who could 'put in a good word for you'.

For many of them, it would drift into unemployment, starting with a few days away from work, then a week, a month and waking up to nothingness one morning to realise that they hadn't been in paid employment for six months. And then they would drift, drift into the well-worn path of petty crime or just slightly illegal work, being paid in cash. "Nothing to see here, Guv!"

And one day, things changed, changed a lot. Things were about to change for Mickey Honey, and things were about to change for all the TMRG. It was the first day of term in his final year at junior school, and for once, he was on time. It was a bit of déjà vu revisited when his mum had said the night before, "Things are going to change; you'll be on time; you'll do well at school." But Mickey had heard those same words before, pretty much on the night before every new term started at the beginning of the school year…and did things change? You're kidding, of course. Maybe one or two days, a couple of times, even a week or so…But then, they just relapsed. His mum lost interest, and so, naturally, did Mickey.

There are some teachers, educators and coaches who are simply born to be teachers, educators and coaches. No one is a lost cause to them, no one, not ever. And these very special people don't even know that they're special. For them, teaching is just the best thing to be doing. For them, there is no need for praise, acclaim, glory. No, for them, the only glory and acclaim that they want to see is in one of their (so, so lucky) pupils achieving. For them, that is all that is needed.

For Mickey Honey and the other (could-have-been) lost souls in that class, it was Mr Warren. Mr Warren was born to teach. Mr Warren had been in the armed forces; Mr Warren had seen the other side, the bad side of the world, in Afghanistan, Iraq, Iran, and other hellholes in the world that you and I don't really know exist. Sure, we see them on television; we read about the atrocities, the torture, the less-than-human day-to-day activities that we really can't accept because, you know, television isn't real.

Not properly real. For Mr Warren, they had been very real indeed, and for Mr Warren, his life's work was to ensure—or try to ensure—that the kids he taught would never, ever have to live even one tiny part of their lives like that. The kids in his class didn't know it on that first day, although they were soon to find out that Mr Warren was god.

Christopher Warren hadn't always been god, had never had any intention of being god. Would have laughed at you way back then if you'd said that to him. But it was those years out in the badlands that had made a life-changing impression on Chris Warren. He had seen things that he was cursed to remember forever; he'd tried to blank them out, tried to sterilise his mind and memory from the images that would still sometimes wake him in the cold sweat and silent screaming in the middle of the night and would keep him awake and remembering through the dawn of the new day. He had seen so much suffering out there—suffering, agony and death.

Adults, of course, servicemen like him. But he'd also seen the children suffer and die, seen the agony in their parents' eyes as they watched their children die, knowing that they were unable to help. For we all know that it is not right; it is not in the order of the universe that your children should die before you, before their parents, mums and dads, who wanted a lifetime of watching their children grow up.

It was those scenes that had changed Chris Warren, had given him that absolute determination to make things better. For the children, always for the children. And for TMRG, Chris Warren was to enter their lives and indeed make things better—so much better.

When Chris Warren resigned from Special Services to step back into civilian life, he knew exactly what he was going to do, knew without a shadow of a doubt that he was going to be a teacher. Chris had gone before the Special Services Board after his resignation and once the senior officers had quickly realised that they weren't going to be able to persuade him to stay on, to renew his commission, they asked what he intended to do and how they could use their powers to assist. There is always money to help ex-servicemen get back to civvy street.

"I'm going to teach, sir. I intend to be a teacher."

"Good show, Warren, good show. Physical education, I presume?"

"No, sir, I intend to teach primary school children, junior school." He hesitated. "I want to give kids the best opportunities before it's too late for them."

And so, it was done. A one-year placement to study for his PGCE, funded by the Services, of course. It included two periods of teaching practice: one was in a well-off middle-class area in the suburbs, and one was in a rundown, less than working-class area in London. There was absolutely no doubt where Chris Warren intended to teach—absolutely no doubt at all.

And that was how Mr Christopher Warren came to be standing in front of his new class, his new challenge, on that first Monday in September. He had been nervous the first time (make that every time) he came into conflict with opposing forces. He was just as nervous, but in a very different way, standing in front of thirty ten-year-olds beginning their final year in primary school. The eight members of TMRG and the other twenty-two kids looked back at him. Mr Warren smiled, opened his mouth and started the journey that would change most—if not all—of his young students' lives.

Chapter Three
New Term Starts

"Good morning, boys and girls. I'm your teacher for the year; my name is Mr Warren." Mr Warren turned to the whiteboard and wrote his name on the board. He turned back to them and smiled. "It's hard being the new boy here"—a pause—"especially with all you old hands"—another pause—"I'm going to need your help"—yet another pause—"to help me to make you—all of you—to be the very best that you can be." So, all the kids in class 6W looked around at each other…What the hell? This new geezer talking to them like they were OK? Not shouting and telling them to sit down? Oh man, this was going to be different— very different! Soft touch? Maybe, but maybe not. And he was different; just being a 'he' made him different. Not one of them had ever had a male teacher before through junior school, not that that was either good or bad; it just was.

Most of them instinctively liked him. Maybe because of the way he looked and presented himself and the way he spoke—a bit posh, they thought, but not silly posh—and there was a huge difference between posh and silly posh. But just because they liked him didn't necessarily mean they were going to give him an easy ride.

"It's an important year for all of you. Next year you start secondary school, and what happens there will have the biggest influence on your lives. My job is to make sure that you go to secondary school ready and prepared to take advantage of what your new school can offer you. How you decide to spend this year with me will also decide how you are going to live your lives and how successful you are going to be in your lives."

Mickey looked over at Shelley and Lucy…both of them raised an exaggerated eyebrow. This year looked like it might be a bit different.

"Now, some of you may not have liked school before, some of you will have loved it. For those of you who loved it, I want you to love it even more. For those

24

of you who didn't like it, I want to see if we—together—can make it more likeable. And how are we going to do that? Let's see how we go this week, yes?" Chris Warren looked at all the kids—his kids—again. His head moved slowly, his eyes looking over them all, still with a small smile on his face. If he didn't know himself better, he might even think he was falling in love.

That first day went well, went well for Mr Warren, went well for the kids in 6W, went well for the TMRG. When the final bell rang at 3:15, the looks of surprise were on many (make that most) of the faces. Where did that go? It didn't feel like they'd done any work, really. But then, yeah. Alisha had loved it; Shelley had loved it. Mr Warren was everywhere, desk by desk, pupil by pupil, just talking, advising, 'maybe look at that sum again', 'do you want to check the spelling?' Lots of 'That's really nice work, well done!' And then, "Thank you, class 6W; thank you for making my first day truly enjoyable." What the hell? A teacher thanking them! How did that happen?

"I know it's been a long day; first days back always are." It really hadn't felt like a long day at all to TMRG. "Now, I don't know if you've had homework before?" The shakes of thirty heads indicated that no, they hadn't had homework before. "Okay, I don't want to give you too much work to begin with, so just one piece of homework, and you can take all week to do it."

The looks went around the class…Homework? Really? And then, "The thing is, 6W, I can give you homework, but I can't make you do it. You have to choose to do it, and if you've never had homework before, then you might think, why do I need to do this? Well, when we started this morning, I said that my job is to try to help every one of you to be the best that you can be, remember?"

A lot of up and down shaking of thirty heads indicated that yes, they did remember. "The thing is—and I'd like you to try and remember this—the way you do anything is the way you do everything, so let's start with homework. I would like you to write me a story—let's call it an essay—about anything that you like to do. You can call it hobbies, seeing your friends or anything at all. I don't care how long your essay is, but I want to enjoy reading it. Deal? Remember, one week. Off you go, class; enjoy your evening."

And off they went into the real world; most of them said goodbye to Mr Warren. "Goodbye, sir."

"Thank you, sir."

"He's nice," Shelley said.

"Yeah, he's nice," Alisha said.

"I like him; he talked to me like a human being…"

"Yeah, he's all right, I s'pose. Are you going to do the homework?" A little bit of silence then, because what if you said you were going to do the homework and the others laughed? Bobby Carter took on the challenge.

"I'm gonna do the homework. He said he wanted to make us be the best that we could be; no one has ever said anything like that to me before. I'm definitely going to do my homework."

And just like that, it was settled. If Bobby said he was going to do the homework, they were all going to do the homework. They walked back to the flats together, talking about their first day, talking about Mr Warren.

"D'you think he's real?"

"Whad'ya mean 'real'?"

"Like, is he gonna be like that all the time, or is he going to turn out to be like all the rest as soon as he gets bored with us, you know, start shouting and telling us off for nothing?" TMRG considered that quietly.

"I think he's real; yeah, I do think he's real," Bobby said. The rest looked at Bobby and then nodded their agreement.

"What you gonna write about?" JoJo said.

"Dunno, he said that we could write about anything. I think maybe I'll write about us, what we do, where we live, I s'pose how we hang out together. Like you can't write about stuff that you don't know, can you? And this is what I know." Mickey Honey spread his arms and hands out wide, almost as if he were including them all in his statement, which, even if he didn't know it, he was.

"Mon, me gwan write 'bout my homeland, me gwan write 'bout Jamaica," Epic Eric said in his broadest West Indian accent.

"Eric, you never even been to Jamaica!" TMRG were falling about laughing, slapping each other gently. Bobby Carter was rolling about on the floor, kicking his legs up and roaring.

"Yeah, but teacher mon he don't know dat." The laughing got louder; even Shelley broke into a smile. Lucy smiled back at her and then stole a glance over at Mickey, who was already looking at her, and Lucy quietly and very gently blushed and found something fascinating at her feet to look at.

And then, "My mum and dad want me to be a doctor. I've told everybody that I'm going to be a doctor, told you lot." Joshi spoke quietly; the nodding heads were unanimous.

26

"But if I'm honest, I'm not sure that I've really believed it," Joshi went on. "But I'll tell you what, listening to Mr Warren today, I think maybe I really can. Could you believe that? Me, a doctor! Oh my god!"

Alisha smiled at her brother, went over and hugged him. The others were almost shocked. Like what! Displays of affection didn't normally happen too much in TMRG.

"Yes, you're going to be a doctor; trust me, I know you are." Joshi just looked back at his sister and couldn't say anything, couldn't say anything at all.

Mr Warren didn't stay too long in the staffroom after his class had left. There was a staff meeting, of course, but it was general administration mostly. He chatted with the other members of staff, all of them women, but very quickly they were gone. He was alone by himself. He reflected on the day, smiled and smiled again. He'd loved it—absolutely loved it. The kids? Well, they seemed to like me, listened, took it in, asked questions. Were they testing me? Of course, they were; they're kids; that's what kids do. And then, if they trust you? Well, if they trust you, then teaching is the best job in the world. Not really a job, then, is it?

He stood up, looked around the empty staff room, smiled again and walked out.

Chapter Four
That Night

He'd got home, changed into his running kit, went out for a solid hour. Came back, stretched, cup of tea (of course!) and relaxed. He loved running; it calmed him, chilled him out, all that stuff. He'd never been a great runner as a kid, did all the usual PE lessons, few clubs after school, ran for the school if he was asked, but that was all. He'd discovered running properly when he was in active service. The billet was underground, and he was a newbie, an officer, but still very much learning his trade. The day, every day, was split into three sections. Section one: sleep. Section two: out on patrol. Section three: free time. Eight hours, eight hours, eight hours. And it was section three that got him, section three that got to most of them. What do you do when you know that next time out there, out in the badlands, might be the last time? A very real threat. Dealing with it was what made the difference. Often made the difference between surviving or not. The sergeant went a long way to him making choices, the correct choices.

"Look around you, son, look around you." The sergeant was allowed to call him son or Chris; nobody else did, but the sergeant was a lifer; he could make the difference if you survived or not. Chris Warren looked around. "What d'you see, Chris?" Using the first name was unusual; it was one of the things that made Chris Warren listen, maybe a little bit harder than he might have done otherwise.

"Sarge, I see a load of guys sitting around resting."

"And?"

Chris looked again.

"Reading, smoking, drinking, some of the guys in the gym downstairs."

"Chris, when you start in this game, you have to make choices; one of the biggest choices is what you're going to do in your downtime. See these guys? Some of them won't make it out of this tour; they're not strong enough. Sure, physically, they're hard, hard men. But mentally? That's the difference, Chris;

that's the difference. So, the guys sitting around drinking and smoking, the ones who are going to nip out to the bogs, toilets if you want to be posh, to take the pills, a little bit of weed, maybe some smack, a little coke, perhaps?" The sergeant was shaking his head. "They're not going to survive, sir." Chris smiled at the 'sir'. "Not in the long run; they ain't gonna make it, ain't got what it takes…unless they change…and that's a big decision."

A pause. "You gonna make it, sir? You in it for the long run, sir? Sir, you can't; you mustn't sit around and feel sorry for yourself. You chose this, you deal with it."

And that was when Chris Warren started running, learnt to love it because it kept him sane and it kept him human. There were seventy-two servicemen on that command, three squads of twenty-four. While one squad was patrolling, the second was sleeping, and the third was relaxing. Going out on patrol should have been the tough one, eight of them in an armoured vehicle with the important two looking out or hanging off the back. Reinforced jackets, of course; metal helmets, of course; weapons permanently held and ready to fire, of course. And the seconds and minutes would tick off with interminable slowness.

Rarely anybody about, pure silence often, occasionally a figure in the shadows, always the worry and the stress. "Is this the one we don't come back from?" Not everybody did come back. Hidden snipers, concealed mines, rockets from the deserted buildings. Shit happens; deal with it.

But Chris Warren and his squad did come back. Maybe it was their caution, their awareness, maybe it was pure luck, but they always came back to the fortified subterranean safehouse. Chris would rip off his clothes and shower immediately. He knew that he always stank after a patrol, hated it and accepted it as a part of his present life because smelling your own sweat, your own body odour meant that you'd got back alive. Until the next time, maybe. He would head directly to the gym, switch on the power jog machine and start walking. After five minutes, he would start to jog, to run easily. He could feel the tension gradually oozing away out of his body, the headache diminishing. He wound up the speed, ramped up the gradient. He became human again.

Another shower, longer this time, then back into the living quarters that most of them still called the mess. He'd get something to eat, although eating did nothing for him; it was just a necessity to stay alive, to get through the next twenty-four hours. He'd look around, acknowledge everybody. There would be a short debrief, but the important briefing would be just before the next patrol.

He'd see the drinkers, the smokers, those who were always sniffing, rubbing their noses with backs of hands, going out to the toilets many times and coming back with that slightly dazed look with the sweet smell on them. He knew; everyone knew.

For some of them, that was the way through, the only way they could cope. "Nothing wrong with a little bit of weed, man! Gets me through it, relaxes me. I can handle it; not like I'm addicted or anything." The cry of the loser, the explanation, the justification for taking stuff. Always the justification. No one stood in judgement of the guys who took stuff. You took it or you didn't, your choice.

A six-month tour that seemed to go on for six years. Day after day after day of the same numbing boredom. But that boredom was the enemy; you get bored, you don't make enough effort to stay aware. You don't stay aware, then you die. You die, you die, you die.

Chris Warren had no intention of dying; he had too much living still to do.

Sometimes it went bad—very bad. The necessity was to anticipate that it would always go bad, and then, if you were lucky, you were able to deal with it. It would maybe be a mine exploding under a front wheel when the dirt roads were meant to have been checked. If the wheel was totally gone, disappeared, then it was full screaming reverse from the driver while everybody raised the guns, rifles, rockets...And waited for the attack that was sure to come. Usually gunfire, sometimes rockets. Shadowy figures would appear out of doorways, windows, rooftops. React, shoot, hide—whatever was needed to stay alive. Just do it. And Chris Warren stayed alive; he had too much living still to do.

*****

And now he was a teacher, one whole day done! Still running, still very much alive. Chris Warren spent the remainder of that evening reading through the profiles of his class, planning, taking notes, enjoying what he was reading. These kids—his kids—would never have to go through what he had gone through. He went to bed to sleep.

Sometimes the nightmare would come; sometimes it didn't. On that particular night after Chris Warren's first day's teaching, it didn't.

Chapter Five
Second Day of the New Term

Jelly Belly and the Duracell Bunny were sitting on the wall just outside their flats, waiting for the rest of the TMRG to arrive. They'd all decided the previous evening that they'd go into school together, and they'd most definitely be on time.

"Did you do the homework, Mickey?" Shelley said.

Mickey looked at her, and a slow smile started on his face. "Yeah, I did, Shelley. I did."

"Me too, it was like 'I have to do this!'"

Alisha and Joshi came around the corner, and Epic Eric and Bobby were doing a little dance together. "Get back to ma roots!" sang Bobby while Eric was mockingly applauding him. Lucy and JoJo were whispering to each other and smiling.

"D'you know what?" Alisha said. "I think this is the first time ever (Alisha had almost shouted out the word 'ever') that I've looked forward, that I've wanted, to go to school!" Everyone was nodding their heads, and when they saw that they were all doing it, they laughed.

They were pretty much the first in the playground, and that was a first for them. Kicking the tennis ball around, the girls as well as the boys, because they were the TMRG, and that was what they did. The whistle blew, and they walked over to stand in their class lines. And the first eight in the class line for 6W were entirely composed of members of TMRG.

"Morning, sir."

"Morning, Mr Warren."

"Hi, Mr Warren. How are you?"

"Hello, sir, I did my homework." Lots of nodding heads there.

"Good morning, girls and boys. I had a lovely day yesterday, and I thank you for that. I'm sure it will be another lovely day today."

There he goes again, thanking us, bloody hell! Mickey quietly shook his head. This guy wasn't like the other teachers. The day was similar to the first day of term, things and lessons progressed so smoothly, so positively, that any bell to signal breaktime, lunch, came as a surprise. The final bell sounded. The eight members of TMRG and three other students stood by Mr Warren's desk.

"We did our homework, sir." Eleven heads nodded along with the smiles. "Do you want it now, sir?"

"Oh wow! That's a surprise! I didn't think you'd have anything done on the first night! Yes, please, I'd love to have your homework in; it'll make me very happy reading through them all this evening." *And there he goes again, does the thanking us bit again. We're making him happy! Amazing.* The eleven students walked out of the school gates together; at the first corner, they split into two groups of three and eight students, the eight members of TMRG nudging and gently pushing each other.

"Mr Warren's really good, you know," Lucy said, and to the others, it sounded like the 'really' had been spoken in capital letters. And the muffled 'yeahs' and the forward nodding of eight heads indicated that, yes, Mr Warren was really good.

"So how come a posh bloke like that wants to teach in our school, then?" asked JoJo. "I mean, like he's not like us, is he?"

"The thing is, JoJo, that he might not be like us"—a hesitation then—"but these past two days have been the best I've ever had in school. I just loved being in the classroom with him, and I have never, never, never liked being at school before. And he might not be like us, but I'd really like to be like him. You know what I mean?" Mickey said.

Oh shit, what did I just say, 'I wanna be like him'? The thought sprung immediately into Mickey's mind. *Here we go, piss-taking starts right here.* But it didn't start, didn't start at all. All the members of the TMRG just looked at the Duracell Bunny.

Then, "I don't have a dad, don't even remember him, don't miss him, just me and my mum, and that's OK." As Shelley spoke, there was utter silence from the others. "So I don't really know what it's like to have a dad, but I tell you what? If I did and he was like Mr Warren, I reckon that would be pretty good. Sir treats me—he treats all of us—with so much respect and kindness. So, I do know what you mean, Mickey, and I think you're brave even saying it 'cause all of us can take the piss out of each other a lot." There were lots of smiles at this.

"There's nothing wrong with liking a teacher; he's the best one I've ever had, so yeah, Mickey, why not want to be like him? Look at us lot, we've only had Mr Warren as a teacher for two days and he's got us doing our homework and liking school and all of us talking about him."

Mickey the Duracell Bunny looked at Shelley Jelly Belly and smiled his thanks, and how it happened no one could remember, but it was one huge group hug before a slightly embarrassed removing of arms.

*****

Back in the school staffroom, Mr Warren sat with his cup of tea, chatted with the remaining staff still there, thought about reading and marking the essays, and then decided that, actually, he'd do it when he got home and could look through them all while he sat in his big, comfy chair. Just for a couple of seconds, Chris Warren closed his eyes and leant back, going through the day. *I love it—I actually love it! How lucky am I!* He washed his cup, said his goodbyes and walked out of the school building, looking forward to reading the kids' stories later.

The flat that Chris Warren had rented wasn't too far away from the school; he'd wanted to be near but not too near. It was close enough to take the bus rather than drive, even close enough to walk if he needed to, so, within fifteen minutes' driving time, he was home.

Having served in Special Services, Chris was used to changing accommodations whenever. Where he lived didn't really matter to him. What mattered to him was what he did while he was there. What he did right then was to put his kit on and go out running. As ever, he felt that it cleansed him, although after what he'd seen in his previous life, his life now in his classroom with his kids felt like El Dorado; yeah, he'd discovered gold. Maybe he didn't need the cleansing anymore.

One hour, just under ten miles. Not world-class, certainly not world-class, but not silly jogging either. He got back home, stretched, showered, changed and put on a microwave meal; he felt a bit like Steve McQueen in *Bullitt* then, supercop, no time to waste on cooking, just do it as a necessary part of existence and get on with real living. And his real living right now was to do what was best for his students, his kids…he already felt like they were 'his' kids. Just about six o'clock, he turned on the TV for the evening news, poured himself a glass of wine, opened his briefcase ('me, a fucking briefcase!') and pulled out the eleven exercise books.

And it was another 'fucking' revelation. All eleven kids had opened their hearts to him. The grammar, the spelling and the punctuation didn't matter; of course, he'd correct them, but it didn't matter, didn't matter one tiny part. They'd opened their hearts to him and showed him that they trusted him. Oh my God! And he'd even said that phrase to himself in capital letters. OH MY GOD! They'd told him everything about themselves. They'd told him about their homes, their parents, their existence, their lives. How they hung about together, how they naturally gravitated towards each other. And then the next bit was a little bit difficult because he'd started identifying with one group; there were eight in the group, and although he didn't yet know that they called themselves TMRG, he knew immediately that they identified with each other.

The names: Joanna (JoJo, they all called her), Shelley, Lucy, Alisha, Mickey, Bobby, Joshi, Eric (did the others really call him 'Epic Eric'?) kept recurring in all of their essays/stories. They did this together; they did that together; it seemed that they pretty much did everything together. Chris Warren was sucked in and blown out in bubbles. At their tender ages of ten and eleven years old, they had already established a rapport that he had experienced in Special Services. And— how silly this was!—he almost wanted to be a part of their group. And the other silly thing was that although Chris Warren didn't know it, he was already a part of that group. Because TMRG had chosen him, had trusted him.

A lot of their stories were sad, not to them, not to TMRG, but to Chris, to Mr Warren, to sir. Their lives were exactly that—exactly what they had. There were no outpourings of 'It's not fair!'. None at all; this is what it was, this is what it is. Do it, get on with it. And TMRG just got on with it because that's what you do. And there was one further little bit that had got to him; they did what he did: they went out running, and five of them had written about doing a 'figure of eight' run. It seemed that Lucy and Mickey were the stars, although it also seemed that it didn't really matter to any of them who were the stars; all that mattered was that they did it, and they did it together.

When Mr Warren went to bed that night, the nightmares didn't come. And that was good.

*****

Mr Warren was in the playground early the next day; he was early because he owed it to them, to his students. They were all over him. "Hi, Mr Warren!"

"Hi, sir." Now this was really weird because Chris Warren felt both humbled and honoured that the kids in his class were calling out to him. Once again, it was similar to the memories he had of Special Services, everyone looked out for each other because you had to; that was the way it was. And thank God for that! And some of the kids in the other classes said 'hello' as well.

"Hi, Mr Warren, my sister's in your class; she says that you're really nice!"

"Mr Warren, when we come up to Year 6 next year, will you be our teacher? I really hope so!"

The teacher on duty (not Mr Warren, even though he was there as well) blew on her whistle, and the kids scrambled to line up. Class by class, they went up the old-fashioned stairway in the old-fashioned school building into their modernised, but still old-fashioned, classrooms. 6W stood at their desks because Mr Warren had asked them to do that, and it just seemed natural to do what he asked; they would have done anything he asked.

"Good morning, children."

"Good morning, Mr Warren."

"OK, sit down, everyone." And they sat, of course. "Those of you who handed in your essays yesterday, I thank you. I read and marked them all last night…"

The class waited. Here it comes…

First bit of telling off…that wasn't good enough…

Oh no, please, not just like the others…

"And I have to tell you that every single one was excellent."

You could almost hear the sighs of relief, even though the silence was absolute. Then the smiles started and kept coming. "I look forward to seeing everyone else's homework when you've done it, and there's no rush; I did say you have a week. For the ones who have already done it, I'll talk to you all as we go through today, but I have to tell you that every single one of you has got an 'A'!"

So, one by one, Chris Warren talked to each of the kids who had handed in their homework after just one night, and every single one of those kids walked back to their desks with their hearts bursting with happiness. 'Praise! Praise! Praise! I did something good! Someone cares, really cares about me!' And every single one of the kids who hadn't yet finished their homework or had quietly decided that, no, they wouldn't be doing any homework, why should they, made a silent promise to themselves that it would get done and handed in.

TMRG stood talking in the playground at lunchtime after they'd had their (mostly) free school dinners.

"I got a fucking 'A', me, I got a fucking 'A'!" Eric said.

"Me too. I got a fucking 'A'!" Joshi said…and then you really could hear the gasps because Joshi never ever swore. They looked at him; he smiled a really big appreciative smile. "Yeah, I know, but I'm not swearing because I got a fucking 'A'. I'm swearing because we all got fucking 'A's!"

And then TMRG started dancing around and slapping high fives and screaming with laughter, and then all together, including the girls, said, "I got a fucking 'A'!" Which just started them off again.

Oh man, how good was school! How good was Mr Warren! And to prove exactly what a great day it was, Bobby Carter—ever the subtle one—dropped the loudest, biggest fart, which, of course, literally brought them to tears.

Chapter Six
Transition

That was how the year started, and that was how the year went on. The difference that a special teacher can make in kids' lives is nothing short of remarkable. And that was Mr Christopher Warren; he was quite remarkable. His pupils, his 6W class, idolised him, adored him, respected him. They all knew, just knew, that he was doing it for them, and if he was doing it for them, then they'd do it right back for him. He always had time for them, always. When the buzzer went for the morning breaktime, it was only fifty/fifty that Mr Warren would get to the staffroom for his coffee; there was too much to talk about, too much to discuss, too many new ideas to throw at the kids, who'd decided that, if Mr Warren chose to be available to them, they'd pretty much stay around. A volunteer would be dispatched to the staffroom; a knock on the door, then, "Would it be possible for Mr Warren to have his coffee in his classroom, please, miss? He's doing some extra work with some of the class." And the coffee would duly be poured and sent.

Sometimes Mr Warren would go down to the playground; the weeks that he was on duty, he would necessarily be there, but sometimes he chose to go down the stairs and join in whatever football match was being played. Sometimes it seemed that the entire school was playing, with the goals chalked into the concrete walls at each end of the playground and the goalie's throw sending the ball from one end right the way down to the other, barely skimming a frantic attempt at a headed ball in between.

"Who d'you support, Mr Warren?"

"Well, the local team's Leyton Orient, so I support them."

"But they ain't that good, sir. Why not Spurs or Arsenal in the premier?"

"That's the easy way, though, isn't it? I think it's right to keep supporting what you know rather than choosing the easy option of looking for a team that's already there." And that particular conversation continued into the next lesson back in 6W's classroom.

"Sir, you know you said that you should support your local team? Well, what team did you support when you were growing up?" JoJo said. JoJo was the best footballer out of the girls, so she was allowed to ask. "I bet it was some posh rugby team, sir, wasn't it?"

"JoJo (Mr Warren was allowed to call her JoJo, but if any of the other teachers called her that, she would say, 'My name's Joanna, miss.'), there weren't any posh rugby teams around where I grew up."

"Where did you grow up, sir? Bet it was nicer than here, bet it was pretty posh even if there wasn't a rugby team," Epic Eric asked.

Mr Warren knew that it was coming, knew that it was going to be very important for them to know so that they could take the next step. Chris Warren took a very deep breath; the entire class of thirty children stared at him.

"OK, you know Peabody Mansions just off of Archway Road?" Heads nodding, if anything, Peabody Mansions was even a little lower in social status than their flats and school area, just over half a mile away, but none of the kids would go down there or even be allowed to. Why would you want to go down there? The kids down there were nasty and really tough. Wouldn't be worth it; you'd probably get beaten up...

"Well, that's where I grew up. I was born in Leyton General Hospital and lived in Peabody Mansions till I was a teenager."

The absolute silence, apart from a lot of intakes of breath, lasted and lasted and lasted, then, "But, sir, like...like...oh man, sir, how come? Like you talk really nice, you dress in nice clothes, you're not like us...How come, sir? Really? You really grew up around here in Peabody Mansions?"

"Certainly did, Eric...Or may I call you Epic Eric?" Eight members of TMRG and the rest of the kids in the class gasped outright, and then a few chuckled and giggled. "I don't know if you remember, but when I started teaching you at the very beginning of this term, I said something like, 'I want to help you to be the best that you can be', d'you remember?" Everyone nodded again; they were spellbound. "I said something like you can choose how you want to be for the rest of your lives, yeah?"

Thirty heads all went forward in unison. "I was very, very lucky at junior school, my teacher always helped me out. My mum and dad didn't have much money, but it didn't matter. I didn't have many nice clothes either, but that didn't matter either. My teacher back then said to me that where I was and where I came from was much less important than who I wanted to be and where I was going. He cared about me, and I never forgot that. If I hadn't kept trying and just given up, it would have been letting him down; it would have been wrong. He told me that nothing has to be for life; he said that anyone can be who they want to be if they care enough and if they try enough. He said that stuff takes time, and that's what beats lots of people; they just stop trying. He said it doesn't matter where you come from; he said that what matters is where you want to go…Does that make sense?"

Every single one of the children in the classroom was spellbound. Mr Warren is like us! We just didn't know it. He started where we are now, and look at him! Just fucking look at him! They all looked at each other, eyebrows raised, heads shaking and nodding; they knew that they'd be sticking around together directly after school tonight.

Had he done the right thing? Had he said the right thing, or should he just have talked around the question and waffled? But no, he'd done the right thing— the correct thing. If he'd waffled, he would have been letting the kids ('his kids', he reminded himself) down. If he wasn't straight with them, then how could he go on teaching them what was important? He thought back to his leaving interview with Special Services. "To teach, sir. I want to give kids the best opportunities before it's too late." Yes, he'd done the right thing, he knew that.

Thirty heads were down for the remainder of that afternoon; everyone seemingly totally engrossed with their work. But every so often, Chris Warren would look up and he'd see one, two, three or more of his pupils just gazing at him. To be honest, he wasn't really that surprised.

He wasn't really that surprised, either, that when the final buzzer sounded, there seemed to be a reluctance for many of the students to go home. Desktops going up and down and up and down, books put in and taken out of bags and satchels, shoes being tied and re-tied. One by one, the kids drifted out of the classroom—some of them, most of them, nearly all of them.

Every one of them stopped to say goodbye. "Bye, Mr Warren."

"Night, sir."

"Thank you, sir. I really enjoyed today, sir." Mr Warren smiled and replied to every one of them, saying their name rather than just a short 'Goodnight'; it was a matter of respect. They all showed him respect, and they very much deserved to be shown respect by him. Most of the kids left in twos and threes, and they were already talking about the revelation; Mr Warren had been like them, oh man, can you believe that?

And then there were eight, and Chris Warren wasn't the tiniest bit surprised to see them standing there.

"Sir, Mr Warren? Sir, can we talk to you? Have you got time, sir?"

"Always got time for nice people, Mickey." There he goes again! Everything he says is nice, oh man!

"Mr Warren?" A slight hesitation. "Sir, what you said today, about growing up in Peabody Mansions, is that really true? I mean…I don't want to sound rude, sir, but, but look at you! Look at us." Mickey realised that he was slowly clenching and unclenching his hands; he made a conscious effort to stop.

"Mickey, all of you, I would never lie to you, never. I promise. I probably wouldn't have said anything about me growing up, but I was asked a very direct and respectful question and it deserved an honest answer. So, yes, I grew up around here just like you guys, and yes, I lived in Peabody Mansions." A short pause. "Doesn't actually look very much like a mansion, does it?" And that broke the ice. Mr Warren smiled, and TMRG all started laughing.

"Oh, sir, we all thought you were posh; like, you're a teacher and all teachers are a bit posh. Well, they are to us, anyway," Shelley said.

"I'm not posh, Shelley; I'm certainly not posh. Now everybody can choose how they want to live their lives, how they want to act and behave, how they want to speak, and if I didn't behave nicely and act politely to you, then I would not be treating you with respect…and is there any one of you who thinks they don't deserve respect?" Lots of agreeing and head nodding.

"And all you guys respect each other, don't you?" More nodding heads. "And you probably mess about and take the mickey out of each other?" Still nodding. "But that doesn't mean you don't respect each other, does it?"

"'Course not, sir, but we never think of it as having respect; it's more like we're all friends and we want to stay friends. Like, sometimes we do fall out, but it never lasts long…What would we do without each other?"

Probably the most heart-opening speech that Epic Eric had made in front of TMRG, and they all knew that it had taken real courage. And TMRG looked at each other, and that sudden, heartfelt knowledge that, yes, they respected each other and their friendship would last a lifetime. And maybe, just maybe, that might be true for them, but very little in life lasts a lifetime.

Lucy made a decision; she hoped it would be all right with the others.

"Mr Warren, you know all of us hang around with each other pretty much most of the time, don't you? Like, not just in school but when we play out in the evenings and after school."

"Yes, Lucy, I was pretty much aware of that. Your brilliant homework stories showed me that."

"And, sir, we have a name for our group. I'd say 'our gang', but that doesn't sound very nice. Our name is TMRG." and the other seven members of TMRG smiled at Lucy, and she knew it was OK. "Bet you can't guess what TMRG stands for, can you, sir?"

Chris Warren stretched his arms out behind his head, leant back in the chair, put on an exaggerated frown and started to stroke his chin. TMRG looked at him.

"Oh wow, that is a difficult one…" Still stroking his chin. "…It couldn't possibly stand for The Multi-Racial Gang, could it?" Absolute amazement! Mouths really did drop open!

"But, sir, sir! How did you know? Who told you?"

"Aah, Lucy, all of you, nobody told me, honestly, and I wasn't sure that I'd got it right. But maybe, growing up here, I'm a bit more like you than you thought."

It had been that sort of day.

"Did you tell him?" They were walking back home, back to the flats, together. Shelley was the one who dared to ask; she looked at Mickey, at Joshi, at them all. Everyone shook their heads.

"No."

"So how did he know? How did he guess?" Bobby was the one who answered.

"Shelley, look at us; look at us properly. We're black; we're white; we're Indian; we're mixed race." A pause. "What I meant to say, of course, was dual heritage."

Bobby grinned. "And Mr Warren's a teacher; he's pretty smart; he's from around here…I reckon you could say that he made an educated guess, don't you think?"

"I like him even more now, I really do," Shelley said.

"Me too," said Joshi and Alisha together, which made them all smile.

"I…just…feel…like, running!" shouted Mickey and started to run home. And, of course, all the rest did exactly the same.

41

"Mum (and sometimes 'Dad'), we've got this new teacher, and he's really good." The exact words might not have been the same, but the emotions were the same when the members of TMRG finally got into their homes that evening. "Mr Warren, that's what he's called; he just makes you want to get on with your work; he just makes it feel right that you work hard. He says that 'Anyone can be who they want to be if they try hard enough and keep trying.' He's nice, Mum; he really is, and he's not like a teacher…Well, he is like a teacher, but he's how you want a teacher to be." Heartfelt words out of the mouths of babes and innocents, perhaps? Eight noble souls and many other noble souls from class 6W slept soundly that night.

*****

But one member of class 6W didn't sleep soundly, and it was after that single member from whom the class took the initial 'W'. Chris Warren had the dream again—it hadn't visited him for a little while now, but it always came back, always. And it was always the same dream, except it wasn't a dream at all; it was a nightmare.

The shadow was dressed in black; they were always dressed in black. The face and mouth were covered, also in black. The shadow came out of a shadow, and the guns and faces of the squad on the jeep swivelled towards the dark shape immediately. Sometimes, mostly, it was nothing. Just one of the locals coming out to have a look, sometimes going directly back inside.

Sometimes spitting on the ground, sometimes shouting out something unintelligible, sometimes an arm raised in an obscene gesture. Man? Woman? Who knew? Who could tell? And sometimes, this time, it was something. Sometimes, this time, the men on the jeep sensed it. The guns were raised and aimed. And then…she/he was carrying something: a gun, a grenade.

Bomb? The shadow lifted the shape into the air in front of body and face. The shape made a noise, and the noise was a baby's cry. How the fuck could anyone do that? These men had seen everything, absolutely everything in their years of action and confrontation—or they thought they'd seen everything. But not this, no, not this. What to do? They knew that they were in serious danger, but what could they do? Fire and hit the kid? Not fire and get killed? Two-way radios, mobile phones were crackling. Seek advice, take an order, make a decision. The driver made the decision for them. He gunned the motor, slung the jeep into gear and drove like a man possessed, while behind them, the shadow lifted the child high in the air, and a barrage of machine-gun fire erupted from the windows.

Chris Warren screamed out of his troubled, shallow sleep. The cry was already on his lips: "No!" Absolutely wide awake, he fell back into his sweat-drenched bed. It had visited him once again. And although it was a nightmare—a well-remembered nightmare—it had happened in real life. It had changed his life. "To teach, sir. I want to give kids the best opportunities before it's too late." Yes, he'd done the right thing; he knew that. Eventually, he managed to get back to a semblance of sleep.

*****

The next day was a Saturday, and for the first time since he'd started teaching, Chris Warren was grateful that he didn't have to go into school. He felt as if he had a bad, bad hangover, and there had certainly been some of those over the years in the badlands. He did the only thing he knew to get rid of the feelings. While his tea was brewing, he changed into his running clothes and shoes. Thinking, thinking, thinking now while he sipped his tea—where to go, where to run? Of course! Hackney Marshes, that epicentre of East and North London football. But for Chris Warren, it had been the nearest that he could run in the countryside when he was growing up. "Back to my roots." He smiled to himself.

He parked the car by the changing rooms, early enough that there weren't yet any of the myriads of footballers who would arrive later. He was already in his running kit so placed the car keys under the rear wheel ('yeah, that'll fool them') and started jogging easily over towards the River Lea. Gradually, he increased his pace, still easy enough but a run rather than a jog 'til he hit the towpath of the river. He could feel the tension and the quasi-hangover slipping away now while the nightmare—still remembered—but now a fuzzy memory rather than the stark terror receded further. He upped his speed, felt the sweat beginning to flick away from his face and decided that he'd test himself out, just a little.

"We'll go thirty seconds at 90%, back to thirty easy and repeat ten times of each." He could hear the words of both his old PE teacher and his drill sergeant and smiled again by himself. How silly, yet how important that he could remember them. And off he went, loving the extra discomfort of every repetition, feeling the recovery thirty seconds seemingly get shorter each time. Nine reps done, easy, and into the tenth and final one. Saw another runner just up ahead on the towpath, and as he came to the end of the final hard effort and returned to his jog, he cruised past the figure.

"Chris? Chris Warren?" What the hell? Who could possibly know him here? He eased off and turned around, steadying to a walk. The runner with the startling red hair smiled at him.

"Hi, Chris. I didn't know you were a runner?" Gillian ('call me Gilly') Ring, Miss Ring, teacher at Chris' school. Chris smiled.

"Hey, Gilly. I'm not really a runner, not competitive anyway; it just makes me feel good sometimes. But I didn't know that you ran?"

"Yeah, I run for Victoria Park Athletic Club. 'Vicky Park' everyone says, but I like coming over to the marshes sometimes when I'm just getting my long run in rather than do everything in Vicky Park. Nice to run somewhere different sometimes, stops the boredom." She paused. "But I'd say you're a real runner, Chris, just watching you go through the reps just now, that's serious."

"Gilly, you finished your session?" The words just came out; he hadn't realised he was going to say anything.

Gilly Ring nodded. "So, fancy a coffee? Where are you parked?"

"I didn't bring my car, Chris, I ran up here from home to get a few extra miles in, but yes, I'd love a coffee. We haven't really had a chance to chat; you're so rarely in the staffroom."

"You know how it is, Gilly; sometimes the kids just want to talk, and I can't—actually, I don't want to—say 'no'." She looked at him and smiled.

"Yes, I do know; your class absolutely adores you."

They jogged back easily to his car.

*****

It had been a great way to spend a morning. Chris realised that, for the first time since he'd started teaching, he'd actually socialised with someone. Gilly had been superb company; she'd made him laugh by talking about her student days, about her initial problems in the classroom, about the runners she trained with at Vicky Park. She was just bloody good company, and Chris realised that he'd missed that adult interaction. It was with very little surprise that he'd agreed to go running with her again, maybe even to turn up at the running club and see if he enjoyed the more structured sessions. It was with even less surprise that they'd both decided that a drink and a meal that evening would be even better than the coffee they'd both drunk with each other.

They ended up in a small Indian restaurant in Walthamstow, very near to the tube station. Chris had had no idea of where to go. It made him realise once again that he'd become somewhat of an unsociable animal, so he happily agreed when Gilly suggested it. The restaurant was more than small; it was 'tight'. They were at a table for two but so close on both sides that it could have been a table for ten with them in the middle. After a couple of minutes of 'Excuse me?', 'Pardon?' and 'Sorry?' Chris and Gilly came to the conclusion that they needed to lean into each other if they were to have any sort of conversation at all.

"So why teaching, Gilly?"

"Always wanted to be a teacher; well, when I decided that I was never going to be good enough to be a professional athlete…And I changed my mind about being a policewoman!"

Chris laughed out loud.

"The mind boggles, Gilly! You, a policewoman!"

"My dad was a copper, Chris; you always think you're gonna do what your mum and dad do, don't you? And what about you, Chris? Not a lot of men going into primary school teaching right now, not a lot at all." So, he told her.

"OK, promise not to laugh?"

"I won't laugh; I'd never do that." She smiled back at him. "Go on then, how did Mr Christopher Warren appear in my life at Riverside Junior School?"

And so, bit by bit, slowly at first, but then—when he saw that Gilly was taking it all in—most of it, not all, but most…school, university, Armed Services Commission. He didn't tell her about the Special Forces Unit…not yet…but if this was going in the direction that he sensed it was—actually wanted and perhaps even believed it was—then he knew he'd tell her everything.

"And I saw some stuff when we were in action that was pretty awful; I saw just how unfair life can be if, through no fault of your own, you happen to be born, to grow up, in the wrong place, maybe the wrong country. Gilly, I know it sounds a bit over-the-top, but I just wanted to do something for kids, to help them…to help them be the best that they can be, to give them some of the chances and opportunities that I had."

And then he saw the tears just starting to glisten in her eyes.

"Gilly, what have I said? Oh God, Gilly, I am so sorry. I didn't mean to upset you."

"You have no idea what a lovely man you are, do you, Chris? No wonder your class absolutely adores you; some of their brothers and sisters in my class talk about you because their big brothers and sisters have come home with a 'Mr Warren said this, Mr Warren did this, Mr Warren made me understand the sums, Sir helped me with the spelling, Mr Warren stayed behind after school with my composition'. You've already made a huge difference for those kids. Please God they get someone like you when they go up secondary school this September."

She put her arm through his as they came out of the restaurant, then said, "Drink?"

They both said it together and laughed out loud. And then she turned directly towards him, stretched up onto her toes and kissed him on the mouth.

Chapter Seven
Middle-Class Values

"It's time to start thinking about secondary school, boys and girls."

But they didn't want to start thinking about secondary school, not one pupil of class 6W; they were Mr Warren's class, and they wanted to stay as Mr Warren's class until they finished school.

"Listen, class, I know it's scary to start looking at the future, but when we all started together at the beginning of last term, that was a new thing, wasn't it?" A few nods here and there. "And it hasn't been so bad, has it?"

"But, sir, Mr Warren, it's different now. You showed us what to do; you showed us that we were able to do so much more than before; everyone knows that!"

Mickey was breathing hard now. "You know what happens when we get to big school, to secondary school? Well, I'll tell you, sir. What happens is that no one cares about us anymore, not like you, sir. You know what the school we're gonna go to is like? Well, I'll tell you, it's a—" Mickey almost swore out loud but stopped himself just in time. Although he still thought it, *It's a shithole; it's a dumping ground.* "It's just not very good, sir."

If he was honest, and he certainly was, Chris Warren was expecting something like that response, and he was expecting it if not from Mickey Honey, then from one of TMRG. So, he had done his own homework on the local secondary school, and he'd looked at all other possible options for his class. He'd even discussed it with Miss McCarthy, the headteacher. Patsy McCarthy had looked at him and smiled.

"I see what you're doing, Chris, and I most certainly admire you for it, but I have to ask you: do you think that you're trying to impose your own middle-class values on the children in your class? How do you think the children's parents are going to react? It would almost be like heresy to them to suggest what you're saying to me."

He'd almost lost it then—almost, but not quite. Chris had planned out what he was going to say, planned it out like he'd planned many a military manoeuvre in a previous life. First, deep—very deep breaths—then: "Ms McCarthy—Patsy, just because we're teachers doesn't mean that our values are different from those of the kids we teach. OK, maybe where we teach isn't the nicest area in the world, but it's most certainly not the worst. And the kids who we teach are most definitely not the worst in the world. To be honest, to me, they're the absolute best kids in the world. I'd do anything for them. Surely, that's the reason we teach? To give all our kids the very best start in life that we can? To deny them any possible opportunity would just show that we're not doing our job properly, maybe that we don't care enough? I can't do that; I won't do that. These kids have changed my life these last six months; they've given me more than I could possibly give them. It's only right that at least we open up the possibilities, maybe even to show them not to be scared."

Patsy nodded and then smiled. "Of course, you're right, Chris. Of course, you are." She hesitated for just a moment, then said, "And I owe you a huge apology. I really do…go then, tell me."

He almost, but not quite, hugged her. "Oh, Patsy! Thank you so much!" And he started to outline his plan of operations.

*****

"Just because Grange Secondary is the nearest school to us doesn't necessarily mean that's where you have to go."

What! Here he goes again. Class 6W sat up in their seats and listened to Mr Warren.

"You see, actually, you're allowed to apply to whatever secondary school that you want to; the practicalities, however, are that it's going to have to be a school that's near to you, and sometimes it may not be fair, sometimes just because of where you live, that the local school may be better or worse than a school in a different area. The reality is that some schools will be oversubscribed because they're popular, and some schools will be undersubscribed because they're not so popular. So again, the reality is that most junior school pupils will go to their nearest secondary school." Thirty sets of ten and eleven-year-old shoulders slumped in unison. *Fucking letdown! Mr Warren built us up and now he's let us down. That's not fair; that's not like Mr Warren.* And, of course, it wasn't like Mr Warren.

A hand went up. "Sir."

"Yes, Lucy?"

"Sir, why are you telling us all this if we can't go to any other school?"

"But you can, Lucy, you can."

"But, sir, you just said that if we're not in the…" She struggled for the correct word.

"Catchment area, Lucy; it's called the catchment area."

"Thank you, sir. So if we're not in the right catchment area, then we won't get into a different school whatever we do." Lucy's hands spread out almost in desperation; it had been given and then taken away. But, of course, it hadn't.

"Not usually, Lucy, but sometimes if you want something hard enough, then there is a way. It might not be easy, but then most things in life that are worthwhile aren't easy, are they?" And they all looked at him again, waiting, just waiting.

"Who's heard of Stratford Academy?" A few hands went up. "And does anybody know anything about Stratford Academy?"

"Sir, it used to be called Stratford Grammar School? Like, only the really clever kids go there."

"You're right, Joshi; it used to be a grammar school, but it's not anymore. And you're right again, a lot of clever kids went there." He paused and held the pause. "And I truly believe that there are an awful lot of clever kids sitting right in front of me. I believe that there are an awful lot of kids in this class, in this wonderful class, who deserve to go to Stratford Academy."

It was an eye-opener; it really was a fucking eye-opener. Mr Warren had gone and fucking done it again!

They sat in the playground after school and looked at each other.

"He really does care, doesn't he? Mr Warren, I mean." But they all knew without needing to be told that it was Mr Warren who Shelley had been talking about. "I can't believe that he'd do all that for us, honest. I just can't believe it! He said that he'd do extra lessons with us; he said that he'd teach us about exam technique; he said that he'd do anything he could for us if we gave everything we could as well."

49

"Do you remember that thing he said almost at the end, just before the bell went?" They all looked at Bobby Carter, who was, for once, being absolutely serious.

"It was the one about that American poet; what was she called? Mary Oliver or something, I think. It was that bit of poetry that went…hang on a bit; I wrote it down." Bobby pulled his rough book out of his backpack and read it out to them: "Tell me, what is it you plan to do with your one wild and precious life."

"That is just fucking amazing; it really is amazing. It was like he knew we'd understand; he never ever talks down to us, not ever. Well, with my one wild and precious life, I'm going to try my absolute best." Bobby paused and went a little bit quieter. "I'm going to make Mr Warren proud of me; I really am. If Mr Warren thinks that we'd be OK, then we'll be OK. No, we'll be better than OK, much better!"

*****

"So, this is the situation: as Stratford Academy used to be a grammar school, it's allowed to allocate thirty per cent of its places for new pupils at its own discretion. The remaining seventy per cent is allocated on catchment area, and because it's almost always oversubscribed, even in the catchment area it will depend on how close to the school you live. I know it's not fair, but I don't really know how to make it fairer. It's a big school with a big intake; last year, they had two hundred new entries into Year 7—I still think of Year 7 as a new first year to secondary—and there seems to be a possibility that they may even increase that number for this academic year and have nine form entry rather than eight form entry. Listen, kids, it's not for everybody, but I think that if you want to give it a go, why not? I think you guys have been brilliant this year, and it's only halfway through. I've watched you all as you've improved in everything; you all work hard; you always give the very best of yourselves…

"You make me very proud to be your teacher. I know—I absolutely know— that everyone one of you will make a success of your life, whatever you decide to do. It's hard going up to secondary school; everything you've known so far feels different. I still remember when I was going to big school, I was pretty scared."

And if truth be told, there were a lot of scared, maybe anxious, children in 6W. "It was all right for Mr Warren to say all that stuff, but what about our parents? What's my mum going to say about all that?" Once again, TMRG were holding a council of war in the playground.

"I'm going for it; I'm definitely going for it," said Joshi, with Alisha nodding her head alongside him. "My mum and dad will be OK with that. I know they will…If they want their little boy, little me, to be a doctor, then that's what's going to happen. Mr Warren says we can, then we can. Has he ever let us down? No. Has he ever told us anything that wasn't true? No. I'm going for it. I'm definitely going for it."

"Yeah, but your mum and dad want you two to go there, it's obvious, isn't it? I'm not so sure that my mum will, really not sure at all…" Mickey trailed off as he contemplated his future. "I'll tell you something for nothing, though, wouldn't it be a laugh if we all applied and we all got in!"

And that was the statement that persuaded them all: they could be together forever! Now to persuade their mums (and dads).

"See, Mum, it wouldn't be any different. If I did get in and I'd have to work really, really hard just to stand a chance, then it would only be leaving for school ten minutes earlier, and if I did go there, it would be so much better for me getting a job when I leave school, a lot more money. Mum, I really don't want to work down the tip, on the market, on the council. Honest, Mum, I can do better than that." Epic Eric's words but repeated in one form or another by five other members of TMRG. Joshi and Alisha's mum and dad had needed no persuading at all. In the end, it had been easier than they'd expected. There had been questions about money—always questions about money—about uniforms, about everything. And almost all of the questions betrayed the fears of their mums and dads; it was something different, unknown, outside their areas of knowledge.

And then there was also a little bit of pride, perhaps. "Yes, my daughter goes to Stratford Academy; it used to be a grammar school, you know. Still is, really. They only take the brightest kids; my daughter got in; she's very bright, you know." And variations were repeated, if not aloud, then certainly in the minds of all those parents.

And so it started.

"There will probably be two exams, tests if you like; one will be maths, and one will be English. The school might wrap them up, disguise them if you like, and call them something else, but they'll still be maths and English, believe me. They might even give you a story, an essay, to write, and sometimes this is the one that can make the difference between getting in or not…if you want to get in, that is. And then one more thing…Sometimes they just want to talk to you, and this can really make a difference. They'll want to know why you want to go to Stratford or why your local school isn't for you. And this one I can't do for you. I can help you with it. I can listen and suggest. Actually, if we're going to do this properly, then everyone will listen and suggest, but it's going to be down to you. Listen, guys, don't do this for me, do it for yourselves. If you truly, truly want to be the best version of yourselves and you think Stratford Grammar—I mean Stratford Academy, of course—will be good for you, then we go for it, yeah?"

That very first night after school finished, it started properly.

"First thing is, you must read the test paper before you start, yeah? It might say that you have to do a certain number of questions rather than all of them; the English paper might give you a choice of questions to answer. It's not like they're trying to catch you out. What they want to do is find out what you know, what you're interested in, what you're going to be able to give to them. Thing is, guys, if you do get into Stratford or if you decide that you want to go to Grange, then you're going to be there for at least five years. And if you decide to stay on to the sixth form, you'll be eighteen years old before you leave. That's an adult, an adult! How crazy that you can be an adult, but you're still at school."

Mr Warren shook his head and laughed out loud. "Sometimes I don't feel very much like an adult even now!"

Three nights after school, every week for six weeks, there was the usual stuff: maths and English of course, but also Mr Warren getting each of the seventeen pupils who had decided to try for Stratford Academy to stand up and make a pitch, a speech, a presentation to the rest of the class. And then he encouraged the class to make positive comments on each other's presentations.

"We're not tearing you apart, guys. If anyone says anything, it's to try and help you. That's what we're here for, to help one another, not to break them down. In my mind, there's nothing better than reaching out and helping to lift up another person, a friend, a classmate. And remember, when you've said something, then people have the right to ask you why. So don't say anything just because you think it's the right thing to say or that it sounds good. Make sure that you believe in what you say, and you can back it up."

"Mum, I think I want to be a teacher," Shelley said. "Mr Warren says 'why not?'. Mr Warren honestly thinks I could be a teacher!"

"Mum, I'm going to be a teacher…can you imagine? Me, a teacher!" Lucy said.

"Mum, I could be a teacher. Honest, I could! I can. I really can. I know I can. I really do. I'm going to bust a gut trying. I can. I can be a teacher!" JoJo shook her head just a little and cried, just a little. But she believed she could.

And then it was time. All seventeen of them met up outside school and walked down to Stratford Academy together.

"No, Mum, no, Dad, you can't come with me. What are you gonna do? Come in for the exam with me…Durrrh! I don't think so."

One in the morning, one in the afternoon. And in between, they all stayed for lunch at the possible new school. Some of the big kids came over and talked to them. "It's good here; you'll like it here. The teachers care about you here; they really do. Good luck for this afternoon!"

They all walked back together and gradually split up and peeled away as they got to their flats and houses, until there were only the eight members of TMRG still there.

"Gotta go in, I s'pose. Let me Mum know how I got on," Epic Eric said.

"How d'you think you did, Epic?" Mickey said.

"All right, I think. What about you, Mickey?"

"Yeah, all right…I think. Lucy? Shelley? JoJo? Alisha? Joshi? Bobby?"

"Dunno really. I did my best. I really did my best." Anyone of them could have said it, anyone of them could have meant it.

*****

The letters arrived two weeks later. All seventeen in Mr Warren's class received the same identical letter. "Congratulations on an excellent first set of entrance exams. We would like you to attend an informal interview with the headteacher and head of Year 7."

"Mr Warren! Mr Warren! Sir! Look, sir, look! We've all got called back— every single one of us, everyone! Oh, Mr Warren, sir!" Shelley just couldn't help herself; she burst into tears and hugged Mr Warren. Politically correct or not, Mr Warren hugged Shelley right back, and it was absolutely the right thing to do.

"I am so proud of you guys. I really am so proud of all of you. Well done, everyone!"

And it had never happened before, but the entire class of 6W stood up and started clapping and cheering.

"Three cheers for Mr Warren, hip-hip…"

And for the first time in a very long time, Mr Warren felt the tears come to his eyes.

"Sorry, children, sorry. You just made me emotional for a minute there."

"But it was you, sir. You made us do it; you almost did it for us…I would never—no, we would never—have thought of applying for Stratford if you hadn't told us that we could do it."

Shelley stopped and slowly withdrew from the hug.

"Sorry 'bout that, sir, sorry." Shelley blushed. "Couldn't help it, just couldn't help it!" And after she had withdrawn from that first hug, the rest of TMRG and indeed the other nine children who had been called back for an interview went straight into a mass hug. And then it wasn't only Mr Warren with a few tears in his eyes.

*****

"Hello, Michael—or do you prefer Mickey? I am Dr Fisher, the head teacher of Stratford Academy, and this lady is Ms Hajisoteris, head of Year 7 for September. And our first question is, why do you want to come to Stratford Academy?" The head of Stratford Academy smiled at Mickey Honey.

"Sir, miss, I prefer Mickey if that's OK?" He hesitated, then said, "And, sir, do I call you doctor or sir?"

"Sir is fine, Mickey, absolutely fine." Dr Fisher and Ms Hajisoteris waited.

"To be honest, sir, miss, at the beginning of Year 6 I wouldn't even have thought of applying to Stratford Academy"—slight hesitation—"but we had a new teacher this year and…and…well, he's changed the way that I, and, well, all of our class, think and act. Mr Warren—that's my teacher's name—said that anyone can be who they want to be as long as they try hard enough. He said that most people will give up because they're not prepared to be patient, but you have to keep going. Well, I'm going to keep going. If things aren't easy, then I'll keep working hard until I make them easy. Because of Mr Warren, I actually enjoy working hard now. I think just about everyone in my class would say that. I get a real sense of satisfaction when I've done something that I wasn't sure I could do, and it turns out OK."

And Mickey Honey, the Duracell Bunny, continued, "I'm not sure what I want to do when I leave school, but I know now that when I do decide what I want to do, what I want to be, that I'll give it everything. So, you see, miss, sir, if I do get selected for Stratford Academy, then I'll give it everything here as well. That's what I've been taught; that's what I'll do."

A few more questions followed, but the head teacher and the head of year had already decided on one new entrant to Year 7 in September. Name and name of the school were noted down. It took until the end of that week for all the possible new kids to be interviewed. By the end of that week, there were seventeen mentions of Riverside Junior School noted.

"What d'ya talk about, Eric?" Bobby asked.

"'Bout school here, working hard, Mr Warren, getting a good job when I leave, 'bout my friends, all that stuff."

"Shelley?"

"Same, I s'pose, and then…" A really long pause. "Well, don't laugh; don't you dare laugh at me…I talked about wanting to be a teacher, maybe." Shelley glared at them, waiting for the reaction, any reaction.

There was a silence, then, "I said that as well!" JoJo and Lucy had both spoken at exactly the same time.

"But you never, you never said…!"

"Nor did you, Shell, nor did you."

"I would never have thought about being a teacher until this year, Mr Warren and all that. But you know what? Now, now I think maybe I could be…can you imagine that? Being a teacher like Mr Warren!" And yes, the three of them—and the others in TMRG—dared to dream; they could be whatever they wanted to be as long as they worked hard enough and as long as they didn't give in.

*****

The letter arrived the following Monday.

Dear Ms McCarthy,

Stratford Academy is delighted to offer places in Year 7 for the academic year beginning 1 September to all seventeen of your pupils who applied to Stratford Academy. Their written examination work was excellent, as were all of their interviews. They displayed a confidence and maturity that impressed myself and Ms Hajisoteris, who will be their pastoral head of Year 7 in September. From their interviews, it would appear that all pupils are in the same class group. Many of them referred to their teacher, Mr Warren. It was obvious how highly they regarded him and equally obvious how hard he must have worked to have inspired his pupils. Please do pass on our congratulations to him. We look forward to welcoming our new pupils from your school.

Yours Sincerely,
Dr D. Fisher
Headteacher, Stratford Academy.

The other seventeen letters had also arrived on that same Monday. Seventeen pupils from Riverside Junior School arrived at school, each holding their individual letters.

"D'you get in?"

"Yeah, got in. You?"

"I did, I did! Can't believe it! Me, going to grammar school!"

"Well, academy, but yeah, it is a grammar school, really."

"My mum cried this morning; no really, she was like sobbing. Says she can't believe how happy she is for me." Shelley was actually quite pale and kept shaking her head. "I got in; I actually got in, me…"

"Our mum and dad said that they were very proud of us, that they knew we could do it," said Alisha and Joshi.

"Me dun know all time, me know it ma natural Yamaican sense of rhythm dat got me into dat posh skool," Epic Eric broke into his reggae shuffle, swiftly followed by Bobby Carter, while the others just burst out laughing.

"Epic, hate to tell you, but you got NO sense of rhythm, none at all!"

But then they all started dancing around Bobby and Eric, laughing at themselves but so happy, so proud.

"Mr Warren! Sir! Sir! I got in! We all got in! All of us! Can't believe it, really can't believe it! Thank you so much, sir."

Mr Warren already knew, of course. Ms McCarthy had phoned him just after seven that morning, but being Mr Warren, well…

"No! Really! All of you? Oh wow, I am so proud, so pleased for you. You have all worked so hard; you all deserve this."

Not too much academic work got done on that particular day—not that much at all. But there was a lot of looking up, looking around, shaking of heads, smiles directed at sir, at 'their' Mr Warren.

Chapter Eight
Sports Day

They'd been an item for some little while now, Gilly Ring and Chris Warren. Actually, more than a little while, ever since they had met up that Saturday morning out running. It had been a slow process, but neither Gilly nor Chris minded because they both sensed that this would not be a short-term, 'slam-bam-thank you, ma'am' relationship, and for that, they were both grateful. Gilly had talked about her few previous relationships without going into detail; Chris had even fewer to talk about. They were comfortable in each other's company, comfortable in each other's silence sometimes. Comfortable in the other's nearness.

Gilly had encouraged Chris in his running, although Chris needed no encouragement. She had given him a little more structure to his sessions rather than him just going out and running as he felt like, although sometimes there was still the necessity of doing just that, just running free. Gilly had talked about her dreams of being a full-time professional athlete.

"Yeah, I was quite good, Chris. Went to English schools; that was brilliant! Made GB junior team a few times…but I was never the best, not ever. I trained hard. I really did. You know that; you've seen how I train now?" A quick nod of acknowledgement from Chris. "But I never had that little extra bit of magic that I saw in some of the other girls. I hung on in there for a long time, saw off a few of the others; they just weren't prepared to tough it out, yeah, that old cliché 'when the going gets tough, the tough get going', yeah, that was me…in spades!"

Gilly paused, then said, "I thought I could go to the Olympics, go to the Games, you know? And then one day, I just realised that I wasn't going, not ever. It didn't break my heart or anything like that. In a way, it was a bit of a relief. I wasn't planning my holidays and my future life around non-existent competitions; Olympics, Worlds, Commonwealths and Europeans. I still love running though, Chris. Honestly, I do. I feel better when I run, feel better straight after. Even when the session hasn't been that good, I go to myself, 'any session is better than no session'; it's a bit of a mantra for me, I s'pose."

And so, Chris told Gilly a little bit more of his previous life; told her about the underground life that he had lived for those tours of duty. Told Gilly about the release, the cleansing, the rebirth, if you like, that running had been to him.

"I needed it, Gilly. I so needed it. People don't understand; honestly, they don't. Stuff we did...well, it's there forever for me. Not nice, really not nice at all. But you tell the guys who weren't there, who didn't live it and they go."

"Yeah, must have been awful...But they don't understand; no one who hasn't been there would understand."

"I-I-I still have the odd dream about it, more than a dream actually; it's a nightmare, same one, same one every single time. And while it's happening, the dream, that is, it's real. Honestly, it's real."

Chris shook his head. "I've learnt to live with it; it's just a part of me now, but it's not nice; it's really not nice at all. That stuff I did, the way I lived, well, I don't regret it; honestly, I don't. It was part of me; it's very much still part of me. I told you about why I decided that I wanted to teach? Well, that's even truer now. Stuff these kids have shown me and taught me this year...unbelievable, totally unbelievable! These kids are the nicest, the best kids in the world. And just because of where they live, where they've come from, stuff they've had to deal with...people write them off, people say, 'well, you'd expect that from them, wouldn't you?'

"And they are so wrong! Give these kids a chance, just give them a chance! Every single one of the kids in my class who applied to Stratford got in! Every one of them! That is amazing! It really is! And you know what, Gilly? They started out doing it for me. I'm not stupid, I know that. But in the end, bottom line, they did it for themselves. They did it because they believed they could. And how good does that make me feel? Yeah, you got it, in the words of Mr Neil Diamond, 'So good! So good!'"

"You did it again, Chris; you just did it again. You made me cry. Sometimes I think you know how my heart works, and sometimes I think you have absolutely no idea!" She threw her arms around him. "Come on, we need to go to school...let's go and teach these unbelievable kids!"

So, Chris drove the car to school, and as always, he let Gilly out a couple of hundred yards before they got to the school gates. Maybe a bit stupid, maybe a bit too cautious, maybe just the right thing to do. Gilly started to open the door.

"Wait, Gilly, I've got an idea. Tell me if I'm being totally stupid, does the school have a sports day?" Gilly looked back at him.

"Don't think so, Chris. I've only been here a year more than you, but there certainly wasn't a sports day last year."

"I think that would be great for the kids. Let's see what we can do."

Lunchtime was D-day, a knock on the door, then, "Come in. Hello, Chris. Hello, Gilly. What can I do for you both? A two-pronged suggestion?"

She smiled at her two favourite members of staff. "Come on, I won't bite your heads off!"

"Well, the thing is, Patsy…we were wondering if the school has a sports day, and if it doesn't and you think it is a good idea, then we'd be happy to organise one."

One second's thought, then Patsy said, "That sounds like a brilliant idea, very happy to go along with that. When would you like it to be?"

"We thought perhaps the last week of term? Would be good to give Year 6 a send-off into secondary school."

"Brilliant! I'll leave it to both of you to set up. Let me know what you need and what I have to do."

*****

"Listen up, guys, listen up!" And so, all of class 6W listened up because Mr Warren had told them to. "It's getting near the end of term, near the end of the school year, and I know that some of you—make that most of you—have mixed feelings about going to secondary. That's fine, and it's totally understandable. But I want to tell you something. When you grow up, when you're working and the guys you work with ask about what school you went to, you know what you'll tell them? You'll tell them the secondary school." A few negative shakes of heads. "Yes, you will. You won't believe it right now, but trust me, what you've done this year is really the introduction, and secondary is the main act. It's where you'll focus your ideas a lot more; you'll find specialist teachers, teachers who are very good at their specialist subject. They'll be able to guide you in the right direction; they'll be able to help you to the best future for you."

"But, sir, Mr Warren, that's what you've done for all of us this year. Honest, sir, my mum can't believe how much I like school now, and that's because of you, sir," said Mickey Honey.

And the others joined in.

"It is, sir."

"Mr Warren, I've loved this year."

"Mr Warren, I don't think I would have stayed coming to school if we hadn't had you."

"Aah, Mr Warren, you've been great!"

"Sir, we want to be like you!" Nobody knew who had said it, but they all knew that it could have been anyone, and it would have been true. The class went quiet then.

"That is a lovely thing to say; it really is. It's a huge compliment. But I want you to know something important now; this really is important. Maybe of all the stuff we've done this year, the most important of all." A hesitation, the entire class froze. "OK, if you try to be someone else, you'll become nobody at all. There's nothing wrong with looking up to people, 'course not, the footballers, the singers, all that stuff. But if you want to actually be them, it won't work; really, it won't work. What you have to do is examine what they have done to get where they are, and then use that to get where you want to be. The only great person you have the possibility of becoming is the greatest version of yourself, and that is a pretty great person."

Mickey shook his head. Mickey was stunned, absolutely stunned. He looked at all the members of TMRG, really stared at them, one by one, and they all knew what Mickey was thinking because they were all thinking it as well: *Mr Warren's only gone and done it again! Oh man! He keeps on doing it; he's amazing. 'Greatest version of myself!' Oh wow! But it's true, isn't it? It's true. I just needed him to say it, and he did.*

Then, "Listen up again, 6W, remember that what you don't know yet is more important than what you do already know. OK, and this is important as well…how you are doing in life in six months' time depends on what you're doing right now, and how you're doing in life in a year's time depends on what you'll be doing in six months' time. Got me? Good! Now go out and do it!"

The bell rang for playtime. "They call it 'break' in big school," said Alisha.

"Ooooh, get you!" came back JoJo. 6W went out for playtime, although they were already thinking of it as 'break'.

"Dat man, teacha man, him dun talk de sense, him g'wanna give me da ideas; me gonna be da man in ma dreams, dat me de greatest in ma life." And Epic Eric broke into his little dance that the others had got used to when he made a statement. TMRG had a little chuckle at old Epic.

"Eric, d'you reckon you're Bob Marley or something? Like do I go, 'oh goodness gracious me'?" Joshi said in an absurd parody of an old Indian sub-continent accent. TMRG stood back. This wasn't like Joshi. Joshi never ever took a stance, never ever said anything controversial, so, what was coming next? "C'mon man, you black, me a dusky Indian shade." TMRG gasped out loud! "You white, you in between, does that matter a left-handed fuck?" They gasped again. Oh man, where was old Joshi going with this one?

This just wasn't Joshi. Joshi didn't swear, not ever. Joshi didn't look for controversy in anything. Old Joshi was happy just to swing along with the tide…so this wasn't Joshi. And then, Joshi grinned, and then, he laughed out loud. "Didn't think old Joshi would ever say anything like that, did you? Well, old Joshi has just realised how fucking lucky he's been to have Mr Warren as his teacher for the last year. Old Joshi has just realised that he's in control of what he wants to be, where he wants to go, old Joshi has just realised that he can be anything he wants to be!" A little pause, then he said, "Eric, Bob Marley? Really? How about Mr Rodney Stewart instead?"

And then, old Joshi started to sing out loud, and TMRG almost gasped again and looked at Joshi, and he was SO enjoying himself. He sang, "Ooh, ooh, ooh, ooh, ooh, hearts beating like a drum."

And immediately TMRG knew exactly where they were going with this one, and they all joined in with the (their) next line, "Hearts beating like a drum, stick your fingers up your bum!" And they burst out laughing, really laughing out loud because they knew exactly how lucky they were, how lucky they were to have Mr Warren—good old Mr Warren—as their teacher. And old Epic Eric went over to Joshi and put his arms around him.

"Love you, man, really love you!" And, of course, the entire TMRG didn't want to miss out, so they all joined in the group hug, and of course, Bobby Carter decided to drop the biggest, loudest fart that they'd EVER heard, and of course, TMRG fell about laughing.

"Aah, gross man, totally gross!" And of course, Bobby took it as a huge compliment.

"Well, thank you very much; it is so nice to have my particular talents appreciated." And then Bobby dropped an even bigger fart, which left Shelley, JoJo, Lucy and Alisha crying with laughter.

*****

"Miss McCarthy says that the school can have a sports day, 6W. What do you think of that?"

"That's brilliant, sir. What sort of sports day? What events are there? Is it during school time or after school? Who are the judges?"

"OK, OK!" Chris Warren laughed. "It's an athletics sports day; it'll be at school and during lesson time in the last week of term; the events are a sprint race of eighty metres, a hurdles race, high jump and long jump, throwing the cricket ball, and then the last event of the day will be a long-distance race of fifteen hundred metres. The judges will be the teachers, and we'll also have some help from the local athletics club, Victoria Park Harriers, because Miss Ring is a member of the club and quite a few of their athletes volunteered to help out. The events will be separate boys and girls except for the endurance race, the fifteen hundred, which will be mixed. The races will be separate for each year group and years three, four and five won't be allowed to do the long-distance race, only you guys in Year 6 and the other Year 6 class, of course. The athletes from the club said it would be better for them not to race that far just yet."

And that was when Mickey Honey, the Duracell Bunny, decided that he would win the endurance race. Mickey decided not to enter any of the other events; he was going to focus on the long-distance one. It was something that he knew he was good at, something that meant a lot to him. Mr Warren had said that if you wanted to succeed, then you had to keep going even when it was tough. Mr Warren had said that most people didn't succeed because they gave up too early, they got bored, it didn't mean that much to them anymore.

Well, that ain't gonna be me, thought Mickey, *that certainly ain't gonna be me.* That night, Mickey went out and ran around TMRG's figure eight course, then he ran it again, and again. And the next night, and the next, and the next. Mickey Honey had made his big commitment, and he wasn't going to take any chance, any chance at all that he wouldn't finish what he'd set out to do.

It was the day before sports day; three days before the end of term. Three days before a new life would start for all of Mr Warren's class, for TMRG. Mr

Warren had called the register; one hundred per cent attendance as was normal now. He started writing on the whiteboard while the class, his class, were getting their diaries up to date. He wrote:

1. Autonomy: Everybody has a need to feel that they are masters of their own destiny and that they have at least some control over their lives and behaviour.

2. Competence: Everybody has a need to build their competence and take control over the stuff that is important to them.

3. Connection: This is all about friends, all about the people that you connect with. You become like the people you are with most of the time. Choose your friends wisely. Everybody needs to have a sense of belonging and being connected.

Mr Warren stood back and read over his words.

"OK, guys, listen up, this is important. First of all, I want you to have a look at what I've written on the whiteboard, then I want you to have another look and read it through in your own minds. Then I want you to have another read through. There are some big old words here, but I reckon—'cause I happen to know that you are probably the most intelligent eleven-year-olds in the entire world—that after you've read them through to yourselves a couple of times that you'll understand exactly, exactly, what I've written."

And so, Chris Warren's class of the most intelligent eleven-year-olds in the entire world read through the words and read them again, and again. He waited, then, a hand went up. Actually, two hands went up, JoJo and Shelley.

"Who wants to be first, JoJo?"

"Sir, it's what you've taught us this year, everything that you've said. It's down to us. What we put in, we get back. You're right, sir; it makes total sense to me for sure."

"Shelley?"

"Oh, Mr Warren, JoJo's right. I don't really understand some of those words, 'Autonomy', 'Connection', but what I do understand is what they really mean. If you work hard, then you get it back, but you have to keep working hard even if it sometimes feels like you'll never win. And the other thing, having good friends that you can trust is just about the most important thing ever!"

"Thank you, Shelley. Thank you, JoJo, absolutely right, one hundred per cent."

There was an awful lot of thinking and talking amongst the (probably) most intelligent eleven-year-olds in the entire world for the rest of the day; an awful lot of thinking and talking. And Mr Warren thought quite a lot as well, *I love those kids; I absolutely adore those kids.*

And so, it was sports day, and it was a very, very good day indeed. It was a very good day for certain members of TMRG. JoJo won the sprint. Shelley was the star turn winning the hurdles and the high jump. Joshi, Eric and Bobby did fine but no wins. And then it was the last race of the day, the endurance race, the long-distance race, the fifteen hundred metres. The race that Mickey Honey had promised himself that he would win. Grass track, two hundred metres round, seven and a half laps in total.

"On your marks." A crack of the starting gun courtesy of Victoria Park Running club...And they were off! A huge starting field, Mickey Honey and Lucy in the leading group, half a lap done, seven laps to go. Two laps done, three laps done; leading group down to six runners; Lucy and Mickey, Eric and Joshi, Shelley and JoJo. Alisha and Bobby ten yards adrift, and then a big gap to the rest of the field. Five laps done, Mickey and Lucy; Mickey sensed that Lucy's breathing was suffering.

With one lap—the final lap—to go, Mickey Honey, the Duracell Bunny, accelerated, and within twenty metres, he was away! By himself, all the promises that he'd made to himself about to come true. He'd done it! And then...what had Mr Warren written and said? 'Everyone needs friends, choose your friends wisely.' Mickey Honey made an instant decision on what was important in his life...he started to slow just thirty metres from the tape. All the kids were screaming; all the teachers were screaming.

Lucy drew level with him. "Mickey, you all right?"

"Yeah, I'm good, Lucy, just remembered what was important to me. You OK with this?" And he stopped, held Lucy's hand and waited while Eric and Joshi, Shelley and JoJo and then Alisha and Bobby ran up to them. The eight members of TMRG kept holding hands and crossed the finish line together. And Mr Warren, lovely Mr Warren, sobbed his heart out.

And so did TMRG.

Chapter Nine
End of Term

"That was an amazing thing you did yesterday, Mickey."

Mickey had had to get up early to collect a parcel from the post office for his mum (and didn't they get on so much better now?) and so had gone to school early. Maybe some of TMRG would be there, and they could hang out in the playground. Last day! Last day! Mickey shook his head, but no, none of the other members of TMRG were there yet. But Mr Warren was, of course, he always got to school early. And, oh, look, there was Miss Ring as well…

"Sir?"

"Stopping and waiting for all your mates when you'd absolutely blasted that run—that really was an amazing thing to do. You made me cry, Mickey; you really made me cry. Not in a bad way, no, not in a bad way at all."

A silence, then while Mr Warren waited on the old stone stairs, he said, "Mr Warren, it was what you said, you know about having good friends who you trust is the most important thing ever. Well, all those guys have been my friends forever; they really have. And Lucy, well, I'm not stupid, Lucy's a really good runner. Honest, I did want to win this one. I even went out running, you know, like training, by myself so I'd have a chance of winning. Running's important to me, dunno why really, just makes me feel good about myself, you know?

"But then, when I was running and I managed to get away from Lucy, well, you know, I'd sort of done it. I'd done what I wanted to do. I was in front. And then I just thought, you know? These are my mates; these are the guys I've hung around with since, well, I dunno, since whenever, I guess. And I thought that we'd done everything together, always stood up for each other. Down our flats, our estate, it ain't pretty, Mr Warren; honest, it really ain't too nice. There's loads of drugs; all the big kids, well, a lot of the big kids get into it, dealing, you know.

"We haven't done that, like never. Been offered, of course. Big kid comes up to you and says, 'Take this over to that kid or to that kid', and like, you do it once, honest, just once, and they've got you forever. But me and Joshi, Eric and Bobby—not once. And same with all the girls, never done it. Honest, sir, you do it once, it's like forever. And the girls? Lucy and Alisha, JoJo and Shelley; can you imagine what it's like for them? We don't have much money, Mr Warren, to be honest. We don't have any money, and if and when one of us does, then we all do. And the girls, sir, they're like me, eleven years old, and the big kids are coming onto them already!

"Fucking perverts, sir! Sorry, sir, but they really are. Like Shelley, she looks like thirteen or fourteen already, and she don't like it too much. She's like my sister, sir, honest, don't wanna sound stupid, like, but me an' Shell, well, we just are. She tells me stuff that I don't think she tells anyone apart from the girls; like, when her body was changing, she was like, 'Oh, Mickey, I just woke up one day and I had all these bloody bumps and curves, kept falling over myself, just couldn't work it out!'

"Now, Mr Warren, can you imagine what guts that must have taken to even tell me? Man, if that was happening to me, I dunno what I'd do, but Shell, she just gets on with it. She's my mate, and just because she's a girl, well, don't matter to me; don't matter to Shell either. I know that. And these fucking big kids who think they're gangsters, you wanna hear them, 'Shelley, you wanna do this? Shell, come up to my place. Shell, I really fancy you.' Fucking hell, sir, they're just shit; they really are. Thank god, Shelley can handle herself. She just like looks at them, like down her nose. She'll even stare them out, and that ain't easy down where we live.

"Shelley's hard as nails, sir; she really is, but she don't want to be like that all the time. That's why she thinks so much of you, Mr Warren; honest, you must know that. And a lot of the big kids, the dealers, went here, to Riverside, same as us, and then as soon as they get to secondary school at Grange Comp, it all goes bad. Honest, sir, they think they're fucking gangsters, fucking big time! They reckon they're gonna make it, you know, flash cars, new trainers, big old watches, and the truth is, they'll probably end up inside like my old man, like of lot of dads around here, or they'll get taken out by the real gangsters, the real hard men, if they think the new boys are coming into their territory. Sorry, sir, didn't mean to say that again. Really sorry, sir."

"Mickey, that's fine, totally understandable. It wasn't quite as bad when I was a kid, when I was your age down in Peabody Mansions, but I'd be stupid if I didn't know what was going on, even back then…But you've made a big choice, no, a huge choice; you decided not to; that's absolutely brilliant; it really is!" The man and boy, the teacher and the pupil, stood there in silence.

"Sir, it was you. Oh man, hadn't been for you, sir, I reckon I could easily have got into all that. Easy money, easy money when no one's got a real job, sir; could so easily done all that, done it and thought it was right. You listen to some of the guys who think they're big time, and it's all, 'well, what else was I gonna do?' Like that makes it all right. Fuck that—sorry, sir—but fuck that, all the same. We didn't know! Honest, none of us knew! We all thought that what you had was all you were gonna get! Like you're born around here, you're stuck around here; you told us, sir.

"Sir, don't know if you know—not really—but you showed us. It's different now—different for all of us—actually different for everyone in your class, sir. It don't have to be like that! We can change things. You said it, sir, 'Anyone can do anything, you just gotta stick with it.' Well, that's all us lot now, all of TMRG. We know that we can do stuff, different stuff…Thank you, sir. Thank you, Mr Warren, really, really truly."

And then Mickey Honey did a most remarkable thing, a thing most unlike Mickey Honey. He went up to Mr Warren, put his arms around him and said, "I wish you was my dad, sir, honest. I wish you was my dad!" And then, "Sorry, sir, but I mean it, and you know what? It don't really matter because you've been like my dad all year—more than my real dad's ever been. He's never fucking been here! Same for all of us, Mr Warren; it's been special this year, just different from before." And then, "Sorry, sir, sorry 'bout all that; didn't mean to get all emosh, you know…Just between us, sir, yeah?"

"Yeah, you got it, Mickey, just between us, right? And Mickey, thank you, thank you so much…You just made an old man very happy!" And that was exactly the right thing to say because they could both pretend that they were joking, but deep down, well, actually not that deep down at all, they both knew that they weren't.

It was pretty 'emosh' for all the kids in 6W that last day; in fact, emotional was very much an understatement. Lots of tears, lots of nervous giggles and laughs, lots of going up to Mr Warren and saying, "Just wanted to say thank you, sir, loved having you as my teacher this year." And there were lots of cards, all addressed to 'Sir', 'Mr Warren', 'to sir, with love.' And good old Mr Warren held it together pretty well, didn't get too emosh at all…well, not until he opened and read the card from Shelley.

'Dear Mr Warren, dear sir, I want to thank you from the bottom of my heart for everything that you've done for me this year. For a start, you made me believe in myself; you made me believe that I was worth something, that I could be somebody; you said it—you can be anybody you want to be; just believe in yourself—and now I do, sir; now I believe in myself. I promise you that I'm going to work hard at Stratford Academy; truly, I promise you, I will be the best possible version of myself. And it's because of you, sir; it really is. There's never been a grown-up man that I could look up to in my life, not properly. And now there is. Thank you, sir, for everything, all my love, Shelley.' And, of course, there was a big row of Xs at the bottom of the card. And good old Mr Warren, for the second time in two days, just managed to hold on until breaktime, when he could disappear into the male toilet and once again sob his heart out.

But it wasn't over yet, not quite.

"OK, 6W, nearly time." And the whole class immediately went quiet. Was it really over? Not one of them could bring themselves to believe it. They were never going to see Mr Warren again, never! Oh man, that's not right! And Mr Warren began to write on the whiteboard, probably for the last time with this class, and he wrote in capital letters: 'SKILL SETS'. And then, good old Mr Warren started talking, and while he was talking, he was also writing some of the points he was making on the whiteboard.

"To be the best version of yourself, you don't have to be the best at everything you do, 6W. There aren't a lot of jobs that need you to be the best at just one thing. What you have to do is be near the best at a few things—things that you're going to need in your life—in your new school, at a university or in an apprenticeship, and then when you start working properly. You don't have to be the best at one particular thing. What you do have to do is be pretty good at the various skills needed for whatever route life takes you—or more likely, whatever route you decide to take in life—skills that are needed in your choice."

And the whole of Mr Warren's class sat quiet and spellbound.

"OK, as a very basic and simplistic example, for me to teach you, I need to know, say, about Maths and English, yes?" And all thirty members of Mr Warren's class nodded. "But that wouldn't be any good if I didn't know how to talk to you about them, if I wasn't able to explain, so that's just two bits of the skill set that I need to be, hopefully, a good teacher. If I was going to work in a shop, to be a salesperson, then I'd need to know about the products that we had in the shop, but I'd also need to be persuasive, to be nice to the customers so that they'd want to buy. In a way, what I'd be doing was selling myself as well as selling the clothes or machines or maybe even sweets!"

And 6W had a little chuckle then—could you imagine Mr Warren in a sweetshop!—but they all nodded again. "So, one of the sort of basic skills that everyone has to have is to be a good communicator, to be able to speak to people, to be nice to them, in a way to make them like you. That is a really valuable skill to have…does that make sense, you guys?" And yes, indeed, that made absolute sense to the (probably) most intelligent eleven-year-olds in the world. So Mr Warren went on, "Have a think about what particular skills you already have, and believe me, every single one of you has an amazing amount of skills already; have a think about what you might want to do with your life, and I know that all of you will have been thinking about that already, and then try to work out what particular skill sets you might need for that, and then—and this is the hard one— could you learn any new skills that will give you a bit of an edge over people already doing those jobs?"

And Mickey Honey, the Duracell Bunny, never forgot those words, never forgot what his 'wish you were my dad' had said then. "What will give you an edge?" And Mickey Honey and all of Mr Warren's class already had, even if they didn't quite know it yet, a bit of an edge.

"Last thing, my lovely class, I have absolutely enjoyed every single minute of being with you, teaching you this year. It's been my first teaching job, and I didn't know if I'd be any good at it, didn't know if I'd enjoy it at all, didn't really know if I'd last the year. And I did, so I want to thank each and every one of you. You've changed my life, you guys; you've absolutely changed my life. I know I'm the teacher, but I need to tell you something: you guys have taught me so much this year, really have, so much. Thank you. OK, last thing, and then I'll let you go." And not one single boy or girl in Mr Warren's class wanted to be let go, wanted to have that freedom because they'd found that freedom already in Mr Warren's class that year.

"I don't know what you guys are doing this summer holiday. Going away? Anything special? So, look, if you're at a loose end, the Borough is putting on an activities summer project. You don't have to pay anything; it's absolutely free. You even get a lunch there! It's a real full-on activities thing; lots of team games; football, netball and basketball. There's running and swimming—one of my old friends is looking after the swimming. My friend's name, the guy who's in charge of the swimming, is Dan Bullet. I used to work with him at my job before I decided to be a teacher. He's a really lovely man. Oh, and I'm going to be helping out as well. Miss Ring, you know Miss Ring who has the Year Three class? Well, Miss Ring is involved and has asked me if I'd like to help…And I need the money! Guys, the leaflets are here on the desk; take one when you leave if you're interested."

And all of a sudden, that was it. It was over. It was almost an anticlimax. Some of the pupils hugged Mr Warren as they walked out of Riverside Primary for the last time; some of them shook his hand; some of them cried. It was over.

But it wasn't really over…but you knew that, didn't you?

Part Two
That Summer

Chapter Ten
That Evening

They were sitting on the pavement down by the shops, sharing a pizza; make that two pizzas. They'd clubbed together, looked at the 'two-for-one' deals and had opted for the biggest and cheapest ones they could get. It was meant to be a celebration—all of TMRG still together at the end of the term, at the end of school, really. Next year, it was Stratford Academy, and although they were all going, it was unlikely that they'd all be in the same class; they knew that. But it didn't feel like a celebration, more like a wake, although they would have been hard-put to understand what a wake was. "It was good, though, wasn't it? No, it was really good; never thought I'd like school. I'm missing it already, even though it's only just finished. I s'pose what I'm missing is knowing that I won't be going back to school on Monday, won't be listening to Mr Warren anymore. I do hope that Stratford is gonna be good…Won't be as good as Mr Warren, though." Lucy had just verbalised the thoughts of every one of them.

"What you doing for the summer, Lucy? You going away anywhere? Like the Mediterranean or Greece or Italy." JoJo grinned.

"Naah, me neither!" And they all laughed, mocking themselves as if anybody like them could ever go on a real holiday.

"Well, I won't have time to go on holiday; my very rich and very posh boyfriend will be taking me out for meals and champagne up the West End. You haven't met my boyfriend yet. I'm not sure if any of you are posh or rich enough to meet him…His name is Tarquin, and he drives a Rolls-Royce." And Alisha stood up out of the gutter and pavement, with her left hand on her hip and her right hand with the imaginary cigarette up towards her mouth, shook her imaginary long blonde hair and slowly walked on the imaginary catwalk, swinging her oh-so-narrow little girl hips from side to side. And that broke them up—really broke them up.

"Tarquin! Fuckin' Tarquin! Nice one, Alisha! Sure his name isn't Marmaduke or Cyril?"

Epic Eric and Bobby (of course) were already lying on their backs, kicking their legs in the air. Alisha had lifted them; that was all that was needed.

"So, you're posh now, Alisha, are you? Well, that makes you posh totty!"

Bobby Carter had managed to lift himself off the floor and wipe the tears from his eyes just enough to get the words out, and that remark 'posh totty' got them all screaming out even more.

And then, "Gotta do something, though," Mickey was a little hesitant. "'Bout what Mr Warren said, you know, the activities programme. What d'you reckon? Might be a laugh."

"I'm definitely gonna give it a go. Mr Warren said there were team games, so there's bound to be football; that's what I'm gonna do," JoJo, of course, said.

"Yeah, me too; I loved sports day; doing the hurdles and the high jump gave me a real buzz, you know. See what it's like, and if it's crap, then just won't go again," Shelley said.

"Miss Ring said after sports day that I was a really good runner, and if I wanted, she'd take me down her running club to do some proper training. Can't say no, can I? I like Miss Ring, second best teacher in the school, if you ask me. Mickey, would you go too? I know how much you love running; could be really good, and Mr Warren's gonna be doing some of the training; he said so, didn't he?"

Lucy looked at Mickey and then looked down in case Mickey saw her blush. "What you did, Mickey, in the race, was pretty special, you know; that meant a lot to all of us." And all of TMRG put the backs of their hands to their foreheads and bowed towards Mickey, and, of course, it was in jest, but it was also with respect.

"Yeah, yeah, all right, 'course I'm going, free lunch every day! 'Course I'm going! Well, you know what I want to do? I want to do the running training if there is any, and I really want to be able to swim properly. I see some of the kids who go to swimming club, and they just look different in the water. I get in, and it looks like a hedgehog is having sex with a tortoise!" And Bobby and Eric were immediately back to laying on the ground and kicking their legs up.

"Hedgehog having sex with a tortoise! Oh man, you really crack me up, Mickey! Where d'you get that from? Brilliant! 'Course, if the tortoise didn't like it and they had a fight, then there'd only be one winner…" They all looked at Bobby.

"What d'you mean, a fight between a hedgehog and a tortoise? Naah, all right then, who would be the winner?" Shelley said.

"The hedgehog would win, of course, on points!" Epic Eric was literally in tears and kept shaking his head. "Hedgehog, on points, brilliant, totally brilliant!"

"So, Bobby, you coming to the summer camp?" Mickey said.

"Well, actually, not sure. I'd like to go even if it's just to be hanging out with you guys, but my mum and dad said they'd probably need me to work in the shop a bit, to help them out, and they said they'd give me pocket money as well. So, yeah, I'll come to camp if I can, but gotta help my mum and dad out." And both Shelley and Mickey thought how lovely it would be to have a mum and a dad; how lovely it would be to be able to just help out your mum when she asked, help out your dad when he asked. And both of them thought how lovely it would have been if they'd had a dad as well as a mum, a dad like Bobby's dad. Or a dad like Mr Warren.

"Me and Joshi might not be able to go either…"

All of them waited for Alisha to continue, then she said, "Well, got something to tell you; you know that chemist shop just outside the estate on the main road?" They nodded their heads, 'yeah'.

"Thing is, our mum and dad might be taking it over, so we'll be helping them with all sorts of stuff, you know, like moving and then getting everything set up properly. I mean, actually, it could be pretty good 'cause they've both wanted to run a chemist's for ages. Our dad was a scientist before he and Mum came over here to England…to good old England. Just think, if they hadn't left India, me an' Joshi would never have met all you 'orrible lot…wouldn't have had Mr Warren as a teacher either. Funny how things work out, innit? My dad was talking about maybe having to move away, like out of London even, to be able to get a chemist's, but now we can stay here, so it's all working out even if I and Joshi can't do the summer camp. Got loads of time later, anyway."

But sometimes loads of time isn't any time at all. And for the second time in those few minutes, both Shelley and Mickey thought how great it would be to have your mum and your dad around and to actually feel wanted by your mum and dad.

"Epic, what you doin' for the summer, mate?" And old Epic Eric didn't let them down.

"Me gwan back to my homeland; me gwan back to Jamaica; me gwan see Kingston, ma hometown." And as TMRG started to laugh, old Epic Eric did a most unlike Epic Eric thing; old Epic started to cry. And TMRG just didn't know what to do, what to say, how to react.

"Eric? Eric, what's the matter, mate?" And Bobby came over, put his arms right around his friend and dancing partner, old Epic Eric, and hugged and hugged him while Mickey, Joshi, Shelley, Alisha, Lucy and JoJo just stared at the ground.

"Sorry, Bobby, sorry, guys, didn't mean to do that, honest." Just a moment's silence, then. "Look, I didn't say anything before, but, but my mum and dad are splitting up." And old Epic Eric had tears in his eyes again. "I sort of thought that if I didn't say anything, then it wouldn't happen, but it is. So, my dad said that it would be good for me to go to Jamaica while it all gets sorted out and stay with his relatives. But I don't wanna go. I don't even know them properly! I just fuckin' don't want to go to Jamaica! All my fucking talk about my homeland, Jamaica, and I'm fucking terrified, to be honest." And then he added, "I'm on the plane on Monday…And I'm shit scared."

And JoJo came over, and first, she hugged Eric tightly, so tightly, then she stood back a little and held both his hands in both hers, and then said, "Oh, Eric, shit happens; it really does." And JoJo hardly ever swore, and so her words were the more powerful for it being a rarity. "Whatever happens, all of us will be waiting for you when you come back, you know that. I don't know what else to say really, but I promise you that every single one of us will be here for you…but I guess you know that."

And that was the sign for another TMRG group hug and also a few more tears from Eric and from all his friends. It was a realisation for all of them—the realisation that for the very first time since they'd known each other, since they'd become TMRG, since they'd started and finished primary school together that the whole of TMRG wouldn't be spending those lovely endless summer holidays all together. And that was a very big realisation indeed.

Chapter Eleven
The Bullet

Mickey met up with JoJo, Shelley and Lucy just outside the flats, and they walked together down to the Summer Activities Camp. It was a subdued walk, even though all four of them were looking forward to it. It just didn't feel right with only the four of them, the other necessary part of TMRG wasn't there, and that wasn't right at all. Shelley put her arm through Mickey's arm, and when Lucy saw that it was OK, she did the same on the other side. JoJo just grinned.

"Sorta feels a bit weird, don't it?" Shelley spoke for all of them. "Poor old Eric, never seen him cry, not ever. Totally understand, though; I mean, I'd love to go to Jamaica, really love to, even getting onto an aeroplane, can you imagine? But I'd want my friends or my mum with me if I did." And that started Shelley and Mickey thinking about Eric's mum and dad splitting up; now there were the three of them without dads; life really could be shit sometimes.

But it was the summer holidays, and when you're eleven years old and you're going to a summer camp that's free, you get a lunch every day and you have your best friends with you, then life ain't quite so bad. Crossing over to Hackney Marshes and continuing down over the main A12 trunk road, Mickey and the girls could see a bunch of other kids making their way down. It was busy but not too crowded. All of the other East End kids seemed and looked to be older than they were, and of course that brought a little bit of nervousness.

The four of them signed in at the desk and looked around. First, they saw a few other kids from their class, and then they saw Mr Warren and that gave a sense of relief; at least they knew one adult there! And also, Miss Ring was there. Two adults, yay! They smiled at them and waved, and of course they all waved back.

Mr Warren saw them and winked…and then put his thumbs up to them. "Good to see you guys; chat later, yeah?" he mouthed at them, his thumbs went up again, and that brought them a little bit more calmness. Mr Warren was there, so everything was all right.

A whistle blew and then, "OK, you guys, come and sit down." They went and sat on the grass and looked at the man, who was smiling and about to talk to them.

He was big. And he was black. And his face looked as if it was going to burst into laughter at any minute. No, wrong, he wasn't big, he was very big.

"OK, my name is Dan Bullet. I'm the camp organiser for the borough this summer. I'm not a teacher, so you can call me Dan, or Danny, or Mr Bullet, or even 'Speeding' when you get to know me." He waited, but that one went right over their heads. "And I'll be one of the instructors, one of the coaches for you guys who want to do some swimming this summer. So, this is how it works: you get to choose the activities that you want to do. There are two activities a day: morning and afternoon. My advice, for what it's worth, is to choose a different one in the afternoon from what you choose for the mornings. Yeah, that way you won't get bored and you won't get too tired. If too many of you choose the same activity, then it's first come, first served. After today, you get to choose in the evenings what you want to do the next day, got it?"

Every single head nodded. "There's a hundred of you here and ten instructors. A couple of our instructors—actually, I'm going to call them coaches from now on—are teachers in this borough. So some of you will know them; let me introduce all our coaches." And the Speeding Bullet called up the coaches one by one, and TMRG all quietly waved and smiled at Mr Chris Warren and Miss Gilly Ring.

"Do you think we can call them by their first names now?" Mickey asked.

"No, that wouldn't feel right," Shelley said.

"Well, at least not yet…Sort of be nice, though, sort of, but not sure."

"He sort of looks familiar, you know, that Mr Bullet; like, I'm sure I've seen him before but can't remember when or where." Mickey was searching his brain.

"Sure, I know him from somewhere," Mickey said.

"Yeah, know what you mean. He's a big 'un, ain't he!" Lucy said. "Tell you what, why don't we ask Mr Warren? He said that he knew him from his previous job before us lot."

But before they could find Mr Warren to ask, Dan Bullet blew his whistle and then clapped his hands.

"Listen up, you guys, we're halfway through the morning, so I'm going to ask one of our coaches, Gilly Ring"—Gilly stood up, smiled and waved—"to take us all through a mobility warm-up. I know we're all looking to do different sports, but if there's one thing that I've learnt from back when I was trying to be an athlete, it's that by doing a good warm-up, including mobility and flexibility, stretching, if you like, is one of the things that helps us avoid injury…All in favour say, 'Aye!'."

And just like Pavlov's conditioned canines, every single one of the kids shouted back, "Aye!"

And Dan Bullet laughed out loud and clapped his hands towards them. "Good stuff, guys; it's gonna be a great summer!"

And then it was Miss Ring's turn ('Gilly' would come later). Gilly smiled at the hundred or so kids in front of her.

"So here we go, guys, here we go." And Gilly led them all through a programme of stretching, flexibility, mobility, all the while encouraging, making small jokes, bringing every single one of the summer campers into the mix.

"Never done anything like that before, miss!" Lucy looked at Gilly Ring in what might have been interpreted as awe, but it wasn't, wasn't at all. It was just pure respect for giving something new, something that Lucy had never experienced before.

Lucy's eyes were shining. "Oh, miss, that just makes me feel good! Sort of ready for anything!" JoJo, Shelley and Mickey all looked at Gilly as well.

"Honest, miss, that was brilliant!" Mickey said the words, but it could just as easily have been JoJo or Shelley. Their eyes were shining—certainly something to think about and then to discuss with each other later on.

"Lucy, Mickey, that's great that you enjoyed it!"

"We all did, miss!" Shelley said. "Honest, that was brilliant! Miss, where did you learn to do all that stuff?"

"I guess it was somewhere like this; a summer camp when I was about your age, and I wanted to be, I dunno, a runner, or just something to do with sport, and the teacher said to all of us that if we were serious, we had to look after our bodies and that it wasn't just about the training for running or football or swimming or whatever sport. The teacher said that we needed to make sure that we didn't get injured. So, I did start to take running pretty seriously as I was growing up, and that stuff about 'looking after my body' always stayed with me;

I guess I just got into the habit of doing it, and here I am fifteen years down the line and still doing it!"

Danny Bullet walked into their discussion.

"Guys, we're ready to rock! You know the options, yeah? If you're not sure where to go, just check it all out on the whiteboard where we had the first meeting. Any swimmers here? OK, I'll see you at the pool in ten minutes. Bring a water bottle. If you don't have one, there are still a few where you signed in this morning; grab a bottle, maybe put your name on it—there are some marker pens on the front table—and then keep the bottle for the course—you even get to keep it afterwards!"

And then Danny Bullet was gone, getting over to the pool before any of the newbie swimmers could get there. First rule of the coach is to be prepared; second rule is to get prepared before your athletes arrive.

"You doing running, Mickey?" said Lucy, of course.

"Yeah, I am, Lucy…But not 'til tomorrow…I wanna have a real go at swimming while I can. Remember what I said about a hedgehog having sex with a tortoise?" Three heads nodded; three faces grinned. "So I am gonna run, but what I wanna do is to do one run a day and one swim session a day; I reckon then I won't get bored and I might actually learn to swim a bit and get better at running."

"Yeah, that's exactly what I'm going to do," Lucy said, and Shelley and JoJo just grinned inside. But JoJo had already known what Lucy was going to choose if Mickey was choosing swimming for the first session.

"No, not me, guys. I'm going on the football bit," JoJo said. "It's like, I don't get much of a chance to play football; it's normally all about the boys, and that ain't fair. So gonna give it a go while I've got the chance. What you doing, Shell? You gonna do the running?"

"Yeah, running, of course, but it ain't just running, you know; Miss Ring said it was other stuff as well, like high jump and long jump and even hurdles…but I do want to swim, so I'm going to do the same as Mickey and Lucy, a bit of athletics, a bit of swimming. You know? See how it goes, and if I fancy changing my mind, well, no problems! I just wanna have a good time."

And if Shelley Jelly Belly had known then exactly what this East London summer course, for what is euphemistically called 'underprivileged kids', was going to lead to, then she would have gone down on her hands and knees and worshipped the gods for what they were about to bestow upon her.

JoJo was off to football; Mickey, Shelley and Lucy walked out onto the poolside for the first swimming session, a little self-consciously, perhaps. It was all very well being mates and hanging around together, even being in shorts and T-shirts for running and sports day, but this was the first time that they'd been together in the half-undressed state of swimming, and there was little wonder that some embarrassment might come into play.

Dan Bullet looked over at the dozen or so would-be nieces and nephews of dolphins and wondered what—if anything—he was about to discover. Danny Bullet could tell immediately which of the kids were swimmers, and by that, he meant those who had already attended swimming clubs. They were the ones carrying bottles, stretch bands, goggles, wearing the latest long-legged speedos. And then there were the other ones, the ones brave enough, or maybe naïve enough, to put themselves on the line, for truth to tell, if you weren't a swimmer by the age of eleven, then it was always going to be a game of catch-up from thereon in. And if there was anyone who knew the truth of that, then it was most certainly Dan Bullet.

Lucy was looking at the kids with the best swimming costumes (in her mind the phrase, 'All the gear and no idea' was already floating around…Where had that come from?) and asking herself why she had decided to subject herself to the humbling that she knew she was about to undergo. But she knew exactly why, because Mickey had decided to do swimming, and therefore, according to the laws of the universe according to Lucy, then Lucy would also necessarily choose swimming. And then Lucy looked properly at the real swimmers and saw that they—every single one of them—were staring at Mr Bullet with an almost reverent look in their eyes. What the hell? Lucy had thought that she'd seen Dan Bullet somewhere before; these kids obviously had. And then Lucy noticed something else as well: she was the only black kid there, only black kid at the poolside.

Well, there was one other with the same skin colour as her, and that was Dan Bullet. Lucy felt a little bit more assured. But then…Why the hell was she even thinking about the colour of the kids around her? Lucy was a member of TMRG, and so whatever colour you were, it really didn't matter; it was even a source of pride.

"Anyone need goggles?" Dan Bullet was holding half a dozen pairs of goggles in his hand. Lucy, Shelley and Mickey along with one other put up their hands. A couple of the 'real' swimmers nudged each other and half-smiled. How could you come to a swim session without goggles? Durrh! The Bullet came over to them and smiled. "Here you go, guys, maybe best to keep them until summer school is over." And all the time he was thinking, *So these are three of the kids that Chris was telling me about; we shall see.*

"So here we go, then. I'm sure that we're going to have a lot of different standards of swimming here; let's see how it goes. We'll swim for ten minutes as a warm-up, don't care about the stroke, don't care how fast or slow you are, just want to see where we're starting from, OK?"

And as the club swimmers dove into the water and started their initial swim under the Bullet, the Bullet himself called the four non-goggled novices over to him. "Pretty new stuff for you guys, yeah?" And all four nodded their heads. "OK, that's fine; actually, that's better than fine; clean slate, clean start. We'll all do the best we can and see how it goes, yeah?"

Nods again, then the Bullet said, "This is how to put your goggles on and tighten." The Bullet showed them. "And until you get used to wearing them, probably best not to dive in with them on. I remember the first time I did, they fell right down my face…Oh, the shame of it!" And the Bullet's grin displayed that he felt absolutely no shame at all, and oh boy, did that make Lucy feel better!

Mickey Honey turned to the boy standing next to him.

"Hiya, I'm Mickey, and this is Lucy and Shelley…Shit, I'm nervous!"

"Me too." He grinned. "Sorry, I'm Jacko; this is all new for me too." And that made it all OK.

The Bullet watched them as they did as he'd told them and jumped into the water, pressing their new goggles against their faces rather than diving in. What the Bullet had noticed was that even while he was showing them the goggles, three of the four novices had been watching the experienced swimmers already in the water.

"OK, nice and easy, you guys, nice and easy." And the three of them and Jacko, who was so obviously watching and following what they did, swum their first length and listened while the Bullet made his observations. Every single length, the Bullet stopped them. Every single length, the Bullet made observations, well, rather, he made one single observation after each length was swum. And the Bullet demonstrated on the poolside exactly what he wanted them to do.

One point of technique only each time. And the Bullet could immediately tell by the smiling faces that the points he made were hitting home and each of the newbie swimmers was seeing an immediate improvement, stroke by stroke, length by length.

The session was almost over…almost. The Bullet called all the swimmers together, then said, "What we'll do now is finish off with a fifty-metre timed swim—that's two lengths of the pool for those of us who are just starting out on this swim journey—and I'll get a time for everybody, yeah? Listen, and listen good, because this is important; it's not a competition between you as that wouldn't be fair because it's obvious that a lot of you are already in swimming clubs and some of you are just starting out. I believe that all of you deserve my respect for that; you guys coming away from your club coaches to me—that's a lot of trust. Thank you. And you guys starting out with me, that's a lot of trust as well, and I thank you equally." The Bullet paused, then said, "OK, it's not a competition, but what it will give us is a starting point for the summer; we can see how much, or maybe 'if', you improve, fair call?" And the nodded heads demonstrated that yes, indeed, it was a fair call.

The Bullet lined them up two by two, and by an incredible coincidence, Lucy and Mickey were side by side while Shelley teamed up with Jacko. The club swimmers had already seeded themselves; this was old hat to them, done it a million times, fifty sprints to finish off the session.

The experienced swimmers went off first; the Bullet made sure he took all the times, but he was watching the new guys, the late starters, while they were watching those in the water. *These kids have got something; Chris was right; they're taking everything in, learning from the guys in the water. This is going to be a very interesting summer for them and for me.* Lucy and Mickey went first; they touched almost together, and the Bullet took down the times, and finally Shelley went alongside Jacko. Within five seconds of the push off the wall, Shelley was a full body length ahead; by the end of the two lengths, Shelley had taken almost a half-length out of Jacko.

"Fuckin' hell, Shell, fucking hell! How d'you do that?" Mickey was shaking his head and grinning at the same time. "Oops! Sorry, Mr Bullet, sorry, but wasn't Shell awesome!"

"Apology accepted, Mickey." The Bullet laughed out loud. "And yes, Shelley was indeed, as you so perfectly put it, awesome! The thing is, when you start swimming, you never know how quickly or how slowly you'll improve. Some guys I know just couldn't seem to get started when they began, and you could see them looking at the others and thinking, 'Why aren't I improving like they are?' That's the tough bit; that's when you have to keep going."

"That's exactly what our teacher, Mr Warren, says; he says that it's the people who keep plugging away are the ones who are gonna make it," Mickey said, thinking back on Mr Warren's words.

"Sir, Mr Bullet, I think I remember Mr Warren saying that he knows you, that you used to work together before he was our teacher. Is that right?" Lucy decided that she was going to put herself on the line with what she was going to say next…she hoped that she had the bottle to say it.

"Lucy, you really don't have to call me sir, you know. I'm not a teacher, no way." Dan smiled at her. "I just like coaching kids. I love watching them improve when they try hard, like you guys were doing this morning. You know what? The improvements that all four of you made today, first proper swim session ever, yeah?"

Shelley, Lucy, Mickey and Jacko all looked up at the Bullet. Shelley was smiling, and there were three anxious expressions on the other three faces. "Well, that was brilliant; it really was! The stuff you did, Shelley, was amazing. I'd expect that sort of improvement to normally take around six weeks; honest, I would." And Shelley's smile just got wider and wider. "And you three? Well, again, great improvements all around, honest. I wouldn't say it if I didn't mean it; praise is only real praise when it's the truth." And three more smiles joined Shelley's.

"Mr Bullet…Mr Bullet, it feels funny to me when I say 'Dan', but I'm going to try to remember to say that to you if that's OK?" A smile and nod of the head indicated that it was perfectly OK to say 'Dan'. "Dan…I think I might be being really stupid here…But, but, but have I seen you on the telly?"

"I don't know, Lucy, have you seen me on television?"

"I did, well, I think I did. I saw you on telly last year, Mr Bullet, Dan, I mean. Were you at the Olympics…I think it was in Sydney? Dan, did you do swimming for England at the Olympics?"

Lucy's fists were clenching and unclenching, here it comes: "I saw you; I did see you; you got a medal, didn't you? You got a medal in…was it butterfly, something like that?"

"Oh, Lucy, yes, I was at the Olympics, and yes, I did get a medal in the two hundred metres butterfly. I got a bronze medal for third place. But it wasn't for England, it was for Great Britain. How lovely to be remembered!"

"Mr Bullet, Dan"—and Lucy was on the edge of tears now—"don't get me wrong, please don't get me wrong, but like you were the only black person in that race, I don't think I saw another black person in all the swimming, don't think so anyway. And then I saw you, and you were brilliant. I'd never seen anyone black swimming that good, never thought that you could swim properly if you were black, and then you did that!" And a few tears were now beginning to trickle down Lucy's face—just a few. "And you did, you did!"

And a few more tears now, and Lucy just about managed to stop herself from breaking down, but only just. And the Bullet only just managed to not break down as well, but he knew, and he thanked God that, for this one little girl at least, he'd made a difference.

And Mickey Honey, the Duracell Bunny, walked over to Lucy; he put his arms around her, squeezed her tight and kissed her on the forehead, then kissed her on the cheek and kissed her again. And then Lucy really did lose it, and she burst into tears, and she had never felt so happy in her life.

"Great kids, Chris, really great kids." The three of them, Chris, Gilly and Dan were sitting in the pub just over the road. "Eye-opener, you know?" And Danny Bullet relayed the day's session to them. "All of them, they've got that focus, you know? That ability to concentrate fully, not to be distracted, they've got that from you; they really have."

And Gilly Ring and Chris Warren also knew that, for these kids at least, they'd made a difference.

Chapter Twelve
A Kiss Is Just a Kiss.
Morning-After Thoughts

He kissed me, he kissed me, he really did kiss me! That's not a bad thought to wake up with, is it? He noticed me, he did, he did, and he kissed me, and I never ever thought that Mickey would kiss me. Well, I sort of hoped he would, but, like, he never sort of did anything to make me think he liked me. I mean, like as a girlfriend. And Lucy blushed a little inside as that particular thought went through her head. Like he's always talking to Shelley, and she's always so, I dunno. And Lucy searched for the word. Confident, yeah, confident is what she is. Like she always seems to be able to act like she don't care…I wish that I was like Shelley sometimes. I really do…No, you know what, I don't mean that, I might have used to, but, no, you know what? I'm beginning to like being me; I really am. That Mr Bullet, oh man, he's been to the Olympics, and he's teaching me, and he said that I was good! Oh man, I think I can; I really think I can. And Mickey kissed me, and even if he never does it again, he did; he kissed me. And Lucy's smile welled up from the inside and burst out all over her face.

Oh man, fucking hell! Shit, I kissed Lucy. Bloody hell, what if she never talks to me again? What if she thinks I'm just some tosser like the flash boys down the estate? I dunno; it just happened, felt like the right thing to do. No, don't even mean that; it just was, had to be. She's so shy, Lucy. I like that, honest. But like Shelley's not shy, not shy at all, but sometimes I think she's sort of covering up stuff, you know? My dad is sort of around; he hasn't been around at all this year, though, has he? I don't really care; no really, I don't. It ain't like he was ever doing stuff with me when he was around, not like going down the park and playing football. He never done that, and Mum was always nervous when he was there.

Not scared…Well, maybe. Just like anxious in case anything kicked off, and he started having a go at her. Piss-head as well, fucking nightmare when he'd come home after a Friday night piss-up with all those geezers he called his mates but were just laughing at him. So, no, I can do without him, but at least he was there some of the time. Shell, though, she ain't never had a dad. That's probably why me and her get on so well, innit? We can talk about stuff like she was my sister and I was her brother; that's good, you know. There's lots of real brothers and sisters who don't even do that.

To be honest, Shelley is my real sister. Just 'cause it ain't blood, doesn't matter, does it? You remember that thing I read somewhere? It was in Mr Warren's class, and he was talking about families, you know. Said there were all sorts of different families, and it didn't have to matter. There was something about adopted kids, and one of the dads, well, I think it was a dad, but it might have been a mum, well, the little kid they'd adopted has having a bit of a wobble, said something like, "I dunno who I am, I dunno where I fit in," And you know what this kid's new mum and dad said? Yeah, it was the mum; she said, "You may not have been born in my tummy, but you were born in my heart."

And all of us in Mr Warren's class went a bit quiet; every single one was thinking a bit, you know? Fucking hell, can you imagine? A lot of good people out there, I got lucky, I guess. I got to meet some really nice grown-ups. Anyway, so hope I haven't messed up with Lucy; she's lovely, just took me a little bit of time to realise just how lovely.

How long did it take him? Too bloody long, that's how long. Mickey's lovely; he really is, but he can be a bit thick sometimes, can't he? Now don't get me wrong, I love Mickey; he's always been there for me. But not in that way; no, honest, nothing like that. Just ain't me and him. He's like my brother, honest. No, I mean it; he really is like my brother. He'll always stand up for me, always, always, always. When those pretend bigshots down the estate started pulling on me, all that 'Really fancy you, Shell', Mickey will just stand there and front them, and they sort of know that he ain't gonna back down, and is it worth it to beat up a kid five years younger than they are? That's gonna do a lot for their rep as a gangster, innit? How long's Lucy been loving him up? Dunno, seems like forever to me. All the looks, all the 'can't quite meet his eye' sometimes.

All the staring down at her feet and blushing when she thinks she's shown herself up. She's so shy, Lucy; she really is. I love Lucy; honest, I do. And then Mickey went and kissed her yesterday! Fucking hell, man! Mickey kissed her!

She would have been over-the-top, waiting all her life or something like that! She's a brilliant runner, and she don't even know it really. Like she wouldn't want to finish any race in front of Mickey. Why not? Gotta do it sometime if you can, girl, don't know what she got. Me? Well, I know what I'm like, and I know lots of kids, even some grown-ups think I'm super confident, maybe even a bit flash, but I ain't, you know? A lot of it's a big cover-up. I get scared, get nervous, get worried 'bout stuff. To be honest, it's a lot less now. That Mr Warren, how lucky was I?

Changed my life this year, no really, changed my life. An' it ain't just me thinking that. Talk to all the others, all of us, we'd all say exactly the same; we would, you know. Fucking hell, hope old Eric's okay, never seen him cry. You never really know what's going on in other people's lives, do you? You think you got it bad, and then you find out something's going on and one of your mates is having a rough time. But you wouldn't know 'cause they wouldn't tell you. And then look at yesterday, there's silly old me doing a swim thing, and all of a sudden, I find that I'm good at something. Like if Dan Bullet's telling the truth, maybe I could be really good at swimming. Can you believe that? Never trained or anything for swimming, and then I find out I'm good at it. Dunno, let's see what happens. Ain't doing too bad at all, am I?'

Do I tell them? Do I tell them what he said to me yesterday? Can't believe it. Well, s'pose I can 'cause it happened. Winding me up? Don't think so, no really, why would he do that? Didn't make any promises, just said I had something special, said, "JoJo, I think you got something." Said even when I was playing in the boys' team that he could see it; he wouldn't say that for no reason, would he? Why would he say that? Didn't make any promises, none at all. Just said he'd like to see me play in a proper setup down at his club, a trial like. His club? Fucking Spurs, is all! Fucking Spurs! No, I ain't stupid; like everyone wants to make it big-time and most don't, so I ain't stupid. But if they gave me the chance, if they gave me the chance, you kidding? Said he'd come and watch me again tomorrow if I was gonna be doing football again. You kidding? I'll be waiting for the gates to open this morning, first one on the door. Fucking Spurs, man, fucking Spurs.

Chapter Thirteen
A Tale of Two Sessions

It had been a little bit embarrassing, but only a little. They'd met up to walk down together, of course. And Lucy looked at Mickey as if to say, 'OK? You OK? Me and you OK?' And Mickey's look and his wink back at her said, 'Yes, it was most definitely all OK.'

"Hi, JoJo, Mickey, Lucy, all good?" And Lucy's smile and look of adoration said that, yes, it was all good. Shelley looked and smiled; sometimes it was just good to be alive and to have friends who cared. Before anyone could reply, somehow Lucy and JoJo had linked arms with Mickey, and Shelley smiled even wider. JoJo shouted at them.

"You will never, ever guess what happened to me yesterday!"

"I dunno, score a hattrick? Did some nutmegs on the boys? Embarrass yourself by falling over?"

"No, nothing like that. Oh, I've gotta tell someone. No, gotta tell you guys; you're my best friends. No, better than that; we're TMRG!" And they all did a little waving of the wrists. "I HAVE GOT A TRIAL FOR SPURS! Honest, one of their scouts was there, and he said he liked what I was doing, how I was playing, said he thought I had something. Me! Little JoJo! Can you imagine? Me! He said that he was coming down again today to have another look at me and maybe a couple of the boys, so I won't be able to do the running stuff with you. Is that OK?"

"Is it OK? Are you kidding, JoJo? That is amazing—really amazing—my mate playing for Spurs, wow! Like you'll be famous, my mate famous!" Shelley had spoken for all them, and then it was time for a group hug, and JoJo knew that she had never been happier in her whole eleven years' worth of life.

And then she said, "It's only a trial, and only if I'm any good today, but I'll bust a gut trying; I really will. I know it's girls' football, and some people are still not sure about it, but lots are, and if clubs like Spurs and Arsenal and Chelsea are giving trials and talking about their academies for girls as well as boys, then it's got to be a bit serious, ain't it?"

"Remember what Mr Warren said, JoJo? He said that where you are today doesn't mean you're gonna still be there in six months' time; d'you remember that?" And they all nodded. "He said that anyone can be who they want to be as long as they try hard enough. He said that most people will give up because they're not prepared to be patient, but you have to keep going, yeah?" And they all nodded again, remembering good old Mr Warren and everything he'd taught them. Shelley took a step back and looked at the remaining three.

"Changed my life, didn't he? Changed all our lives, you know that, don't you?"

"Amazing man, amazing teacher, best grown-up I've ever met." Mickey spoke for them all. "He did everything for us, you know, everything. Look at us, like most of the others had already given up on us, and we're fucking going to Stratford Academy!" And then Mickey did a strange thing: he said, "You know what? I'm gonna try and stop swearing. Ain't impressing anyone, am I? Certainly not impressing you lot. Not saying I ain't never gonna swear again, but you know…gonna try, like. Anyway, JoJo, for me, I think you're gonna make it. No, honest, I do; I really do. You've got to be one of the hardest workers I know; seen you bust a gut more than once. You got something a bit special, girl; you've got the bottle to do it."

And JoJo almost, but only almost, burst into tears, and then she hugged Mickey, Shelley and Lucy one by one, really tight. And then they were at the summer school playing field; JoJo signed in and rushed off to the football.

"Lucy, Shell, tell Mr Warren about the football and Spurs, yeah?" And JoJo was off, maybe to seal her future…Just maybe. Gilly Ring and Chris Warren were waiting for the athletes as Mickey and his two soulmates checked in.

"You good, guys?" Gilly put her arm around Lucy's and Shelley's shoulders. "Never thought you'd get your old teacher doing that, did you?" And then she said, "You too, Mickey!" And as Gilly reached over to him, he blushed and, at the same time, felt just so happy.

"Miss, sir, you'll never guess what…" And Shelley waited for a response.

"Go on, Shelley; what's happened?"

"Well, miss, sir, JoJo's been spotted by a Spurs scout, honest! JoJo's gonna get a trial with Tottenham! Can you believe that?" And as they jogged easily over to the large grass field with the track marked out and the various set pieces of the field events and hurdles already in place, Lucy and Shelley talked animatedly over each other to bring their favourite old teachers up to speed with JoJo's possibly newfound fame. "JoJo's always been mad for football, sir; you seen her in the playground, innit? She's better than most of the boys. What d'you reckon, sir?" And Mr Warren reckoned that yes, indeed, he had seen JoJo in the playground, and yes, indeed, JoJo was certainly better than most and maybe all of the boys.

"Can't believe it, you know, sir. JoJo's so nice. No, she really is nice. No front to JoJo, she tells you what she thinks, but she's always, always, always there for you. That's right, innit, Shell?"

"It is, sir. You saw it in the classroom, didn't you? Like she'd always be around to help you out, you know? She's really clever is JoJo, but she'd never throw it in your face, just gets on with it. And like, when we're having a bad time with stuff like, you know, families and that, JoJo would always be there for you, you know, just listening, giving you like a little hug or squeeze your waist and stuff…She really does deserve it, you know? She'll be brilliant!" And Gilly and Chris looked at each other over the three younger heads and smiled—just smiled.

Gilly took the warm-up again; Chris was amazed at how much she knew, surprised at how she made everything fun, astonished at how so many laughs and funny comments were coming from the dozen prospective athletes going through the motions—some woman that Gilly, some coach as well. And Chris Warren knew that the gods had smiled on him.

"Coach Chris is going to take you through the session; he'll explain what we're going to do, and then we'll get underway, OK, you guys?" A dozen nodding heads.

"OK, this is called interval training. Does anyone know what it means?" A pause, then one hand went up. "Mickey, what d'you think?"

"Sir, I mean, Coach Chris, I think it's when you do a run, then you have a bit of a rest and then you do it again and again…s'that right, sir…errhh, Coach Chris?"

"Yaay! Spot on, Mickey, good man!" And Mickey Honey, the Duracell Bunny, glowed with pleasure. "So, this is it, guys; we're going to do a session of six reps of two hundred metres. Coach Gilly is over on the other side of the track; she'll set you off, and you all run around the track to me, then you jog back over nice and easy, and you go through again until you've done six reps. Oh, sorry, reps stands for repetitions; the interval bit that Mickey explained is the recovery jog in between the reps. Word of warning: yeah, don't go off too fast; be good if you can pretty much keep together at least on the first two or three. Don't want any heroes burning up the grass. If you're feeling good, then maybe just turn it on for the last couple of reps. OK, easy jog over to Gilly, guys!" They chatted as they jogged over to the far side, and Gilly explained a little bit more.

"As you do the reps, every one you do, you're going to be a little bit more tired, a little bit more fatigued, so a part of the session is learning how hard you can go, how you manage the effort, how to pace yourselves, yeah?"

Heads nodded. "Biggest mistake is usually going out too fast to begin with." Nodding heads again. "When I first got into running, probably about the same age as you guys are now, maybe year older or so, I was so buzzing to be actually training that my heart just went mad! I was doing a session just like this and was so excited that I pretty much sprinted flat out for the first rep…boy, did I pay the price later on! It's all about pacing it out, guys, you'll see."

Lucy, Shelley and Mickey made a silent promise to themselves that, no, they certainly wouldn't go out too fast.

They were on the grass track now, four hundred metres around, twice as big as their little school track, where they'd had sports day. Oh man, that seemed ages ago, and it was only last week! Gilly herded them together, a loose group of ten would-be athletes, a few metres behind the start line.

"Jog in together, and as you run past me, lift the speed, two, one…" And off they went. That promise they'd made to themselves about not going out too fast? Yeah, right! Kids have two speeds, flat out and stop, and nothing in between until they've found out themselves what pacing really is. The group almost stayed together for those first two hundred; all of them went off too fast because the initial leader, gotta impress Coach Gilly and Coach Chris! But with fifty metres still to run, a couple seemed to drift back from the group, just a couple of metres but a gap opening.

"Nice one, now nice and easy back over to Gilly and into the second rep." And over they went, even this early, two of the group having trouble keeping up on the 'easy' jog. For Mickey, Shelley and Lucy, it didn't feel too bad; they'd done so much running together on their figure eight runs around the flats that they were used to the effort and recoveries each time.

"OK, pace it, pace it, pace it." Gilly's words and smile lifted them, and off they went again; the group splitting much earlier this time through as they came off the bend into the straight, single runners were peeling off backwards from the pack. "Two down, four to go, easy over."

All the group managed to get over to rep number three, a bit of a straggle for a couple, but the main group jogged behind the start line and waited for them. "And go!" Much harder this time, though, that initial effort coming back to be repaid in spades. It was no surprise to Chris Warren, absolutely no surprise at all, that his three pupils led the way over the line for that third repetition and again for numbers four, five and six while he'd persuaded—not that they needed too much persuading—a couple of the runners to miss a rep, one of them two reps.

High fives for everybody after the final repetition, lots of shaking heads, lots of 'boy, that was tough!' Chris Warren watched his three as they moved amongst all the runners, congratulating, commiserating, smiling, 'yeah, me too!', and he was so, so proud of them. Gilly had jogged over to see her charges in on that final rep. "Great stuff, guys, brilliant!" Hugs all around, then she said, "OK, easy warm down, maybe walk to start with and only get into the run when you're ready for it."

Warm down over, the group walked across to the hurdles.

"What we'll do every day is have a bit of an intro to the field events, jumps and throws, when we've done the run training. Some of it will be a bit different, but some events you will have done already, maybe at school or maybe just practising by yourselves. I'm sure you will all have done high jump and long jump?"

Gilly smiled as the group all nodded or mouthed a yes. "But perhaps not pole vault or hammer?" Some shocked expressions but a lot more smiles as they realised that coach Gilly was joking. "So this morning, it's hurdles. Anyone done hurdles before?"

A few hands went up, and a few muttered, "Yes, miss." Gilly took them through the basic needs and skills of clearing the hurdles, while Chris observed once again how easy she was in explaining the techniques, how easily she was able to get the kids, the athletes, on her side.

Gilly walked them through the hurdle technique, literally walked by the side of the row of hurdles with her lead leg not clearing but alongside and the trail leg leading with the knee and lifting over the barrier as her body leant forward and downward to create the necessary angle. And then the young athletes had their chance with varying, very varying, degrees of success as Gilly and Chris watched. A lot of giggles to go along with the intense frowns of the would-be hurdlers as they gradually gained confidence in the walkthrough drill.

"That's great, guys! Really good, well done! Now if you're happy so far and you think you might like to push it a bit, we'll carry on with this trail leg drill but take it up from a walk-through to a jog-through. How do we feel about that?" And once again, Coach Gilly demonstrated. A little more nervous now, the group went into the slightly more advanced practice.

"Chris, Chris! Look at her! Look at Shelley! Oh my God, she's a natural, Chris! She's an absolute natural!" And she was. It was as if Shelley had been working on her hurdle technique for years rather than a couple of minutes. And Shelley truly was stunningly beautiful in her technique, and most of the other kids noticed.

"Bloody hell, Shell! Oops, didn't mean to say 'bloody'." Mickey grinned at himself. "That's brilliant; you done this before, Shell?" Shelley shook her head no.

"Remember what I said about a tortoise and a hedgehog having sex? Well, that's what I reckon me and most of us look like, but you, Shell, you really do look brilliant, honest!" And then he said, "Miss, miss! Miss, how about letting Shelley have a go properly, like properly over the hurdles instead of half over? What d'you reckon?"

"What do you think, Shelley? You do look smooth. Fancy a go? No pressure, then!" Gilly smiled at Shelley, and immediately, Shelley smiled back.

"I will if you think I can, miss, I mean Coach Gilly. Tell me what to do." Shelley walked alongside Gilly as she checked the distances between the rows of hurdles, making sure that the intervals were correct and appropriate for Shelley.

"Normally, I'd say 'take it easy' on the first run-through of anything new, but hurdles are a bit different, Shelley. You need some basic speed to make sure you get over them. Too slow and it's totally different. Look, go for it, and we'll see what happens."

Shelley walked back to the starting line as Lucy and Mickey put their thumbs up to her. 'Go for it, Shell; you can do it!' The words were silent, but Shelley read them perfectly. Lucy and Mickey thought she could do it, so she reckoned she could as well.

"OK, sweetheart?" Well, that was a new one! Miss Ring is calling me 'sweetheart', oh man!

"Yeah, I'm fine, miss, sorry, Coach Gilly."

"How about just 'Gilly', Shelley? You OK with that?"

"Yes, miss. Thanks, miss. I mean 'Gilly'." And both of them laughed out loud.

"Set…Go!" And Shelley went. Boy did she go! *I'm flying, no really, it feels like I'm flying, really does!*

And as Shelley crossed over the eighty metres finish line, breaking the imaginary tape with a forward thrust of her upper body, every single one of the watching newbie hurdlers burst into applause, not sarcastic at all, but a true appreciation of seeing something, seeing someone, who was just a bit special. Actually, more than a bit special.

They.

Were.

Spellbound.

Absolutely spellbound.

"Shelley, I thought you said that you'd never hurdled before?"

"I haven't, miss…Gilly, I mean. Honest, I've never done hurdles before." And then she added, "It just sort of felt good; you know like I could just get over them without really having to think about it. Miss, Gilly, I'm not being flash; honest, I'm not…I could, like, just do it."

"I've seen sixteen, seventeen-year-olds who've been doing hurdles for a few years, Shelley, and most of them couldn't even come close to your technique…you've got something really special there, Shelley. I mean it; that was just so good!"

Mickey and Lucy looked at each other and grinned, and then both together sang to Shelley, "Good times never felt so good. So good! So good! So good!" Just like they did every single time when they heard the old *Sweet Caroline* song by Neil Diamond; it had become a bit of an anthem over the years. And, of course, not unnaturally, Shelley broke into a big smile and danced around Lucy and Mickey with all of them singing, "So good! So good!" Over and over again, and even Gilly and Chris joined in the singing…And then…Shelley burst into tears.

"Oh, Shell, you all right?" And Shelley Jelly Belly, ensconced in the arms of two of her best friends, one of whom who was a 'bruvva by anuvva', shook her head and put the back of her hand up to wipe away the tears.

"Sorry, I'm so sorry. Sorry, miss, sorry, Mr Warren…I ain't never been any good at anything before; I ain't, not like really good. And now everyone's bigging me up; it just sort of got to me. Like Mr Bullet yesterday said I was an alright swimmer, and I jumped over those hurdles, and you're telling me I'm, I dunno, yeah, like I'm a natural. Thank you, miss. Thank you, sir. I'd never have had the bottle to come down here. I wouldn't, honest." And then, thinking, she added, "I ain't never ever had anyone who believed in me, not really…Well, my mum, of course, but you know, that's different…And now someone—no, not someone—you guys, all of you guys, you believe in me, oh man…"

And not for the first time with his kids, his ex-pupils, Chris Warren just narrowly avoided tears, but only just.

Lunchtime was quiet, but a good quiet, well, except for JoJo.

"That scout came back, yeah, the Tottenham one I was telling you about. He came back with—and I know you won't believe this—he came back with bloody Larry McQueen is all. Larry McQueen! I watched him all the time, all the time. I know I was a forward, midfield really, but I loved Larry McQueen, absolutely loved him. You'd like watch the other team coming at him, and he was so cool, just so cool, back off, back off again and again, and then—bang—he'd be in there, taking the ball away and straight away he'd push it up to midfield or forwards, Sherringham usually, and Spurs would be one up, brilliant, totes brill!"

Then, she continued, "And he spoke to me! Larry McQueen fucking talked to me like I was his mate, honest—oops, sorry, I know we're trying to stop swearing. I don't normally swear, though, do I? Just so excited right now—said he liked what he'd seen, said he'd be happy—no, what he actually said was he'd 'love' to show me around Spurs Academy. He said no promises; no one could make any promises, but he reckoned if I worked really hard, if I got stuck in and listened, listened all the time, didn't think I knew it all already, I might have something. Can't believe it; no really, can't believe this one. Me and Larry McQueen!" And then, she asked, "Where's Mr Warren? Gotta tell Mr Warren, gotta tell him right now!" And then JoJo saw him.

"Sir! Sir! You won't believe this, honest!" And JoJo poured out her heart to good old Mr Warren and pretty much told him what Shelley had told him earlier, and then she just couldn't help herself and threw herself around him and, of course, burst into tears. "Won't let you down, sir, promise I won't let you down…Sir, you'll come and see me if I make the team? Sir? Promise, sir, promise, you'll come and watch me play for Spurs?" And good old Mr Warren promised faithfully that, yes, he'd most certainly come and watch JoJo, not if but when she most definitely played for Spurs.

"Looks like it's down to you and me, Lucy." Mickey grinned at his other half. It just felt so right now. He was so happy, so, so happy that he'd kissed her, and it had been the absolute correct thing to do. "Reckon if Shell and JoJo are going to be superstars, then we're not going to miss out, are we?"

"It's what Mr Warren said last year, Mickey, innit? All about keep on going, don't give up when it's not going right, don't let the boredom get you, all that stuff, yeah?"

Lucy looked at Mickey and thought that she'd never been happier in her life—JoJo and Shelley on the way to being stars and Mickey looking at her like she'd never seen before. Lucy knew that she could do anything, anything at all, if she tried, and boy, was she a trier. Why not? Why not? She knew she could run; proved that, hadn't she? Knew there was a bit more as well. And Mr Bullet, Danny Bullet, had opened another door. Dan Bullet had shown that she could swim; why not?

Chapter Fourteen
Place, Press, Pull, Push

The Bullet was waiting for them by the entrance to the pool. Jacko was waiting there too.

"All right, Mickey?"

"Yeah, Jacko; you all right, mate? Recovered from yesterday?"

"Sort of, good though, weren't it? Never knew there was so much in swimming, but like Mr Bullet explained it all so well, really felt I was getting somewhere." And then he asked, "Shelley? Shelley, I got the name right?"

Shelley nodded 'yes'. "I watched you swim away from me at the end, and I thought, you know, if she can do that when we were about the same before the lesson, then I can do it too…So, I guess I'm saying a big thank you." Jacko grinned and had the grin right back at him.

Can't believe it, everyone, everyone is just so nice to me. Jacko's thanks made Shelley Jelly Belly even more determined that she really was going to do something with her life. And if she'd known just one tiny fraction of what would happen, she would probably have opted to die and go straight to heaven, but of course those were only thoughts. Real life was even better.

"Hey, guys, you might like to try these on?" Dan Bullet was holding out four backpacks with 'Speedo' printed in large letters on the flaps and pockets.

Lucy was the first one to pull open the cords and watch the costumes, kickboard, pull-buoy, goggles, drinks bottle and towel tumble to the ground.

"Sir? Sorry, Mr Bullet, no, sorry again! Dan." Lucy smiled at the Bullet and also at herself. "Sorry, Dan, but how come? How come you're giving us all this stuff?"

"OK, Lucy, you sussed me out straight away! It's me being selfish. I reckoned that if I gave you some kit, you'd all stay with me for the summer, and I wouldn't get the sack too early!"

"You can't do that, Mr Bullet, no really, you can't do that!" Mickey said, shaking his head. "I ain't stupid; this stuff costs a fortune; you can't go spending all your money giving us stuff."

"Mickey, it's not like that. Much as I love you all already, I couldn't afford to buy you all swim stuff, much as I'd like to. No, this is a freebie from Speedo. I'm a sort of ambassador for them after the Olympics; they give me stuff if I ask. If I recommend someone, a free kit doesn't cost them a penny, and they rely on my judgement. They trust me, if you like, to see that any kit goes out to people who deserve it, kids who'll use it and maybe one or two will get a bit of recognition, and then, of course, so will Speedo; it's how things work with a bit of sponsorship." The Speeding Bullet grinned at them. "You ain't gonna make me cry by saying 'no', are you?"

"You kidding, sir? Oh, sh...Oops! Dan, I mean. I'd love to wear real swimming stuff, 'course I would. I mean all of us, yeah?"

Shelley, with tears brimming, said, "Mickey, Lucy, Jacko, true, yes? Mr Bullet, I'd be so proud to swim in the cossies you've given me; I mean that, honest, I do. I'll make you proud of me, Dan; I really will. Thank you so much!"

They were pulling on the costumes in the changing rooms, Jacko and Mickey, Lucy and Shelley, shaking their heads. Look at us! Real stuff, real swimmers!

"Best thing I ever done coming on this camp," Mickey said. "What d'you reckon, Jacko?"

"Weren't sure if I wanted to come, to be honest, Mickey, weren't sure at all. Then I thought, 'What else am I gonna do all summer? It ain't like I'm going on holiday or anything.' That Mr Bullet, he's a star, isn't he? Don't treat us like little kids; don't have a go at us because we aren't real swimmers...well, not yet, but I'm gonna work my arse off for him, top man, really top man. Can you believe it? Olympic medal and he's treating us like we're his mates."

"We had this teacher at school, Jacko. Mr Warren's his name; he's on this camp as a coach; he's the reason me, Lucy, Shell and JoJo came; Dan Bullet's just like him, treats you with respect all the time, makes you feel important, like you're worth something, you know. Another top, top man." He nodded to himself. "Yeah, top, top man. C'mon, let's go."

A little self-consciously, Lucy, Shelley, Mickey and Jacko walked out onto the poolside.

"Bloody hell, oops! Sorry, gotta stop the swearing, but 'bloody' ain't too bad...oops! Again. Lucy, Shell, you guys look like swimmer; that Speedo stuff is awesome." And indeed, those two girls did look like swimmers like everyone else on the poolside now; they felt they belonged. And they felt like they belonged for all of two minutes as they struggled to recapture that feeling for the water that they'd gradually got to know the previous day. All four went through the warm-up that Dan Bullet had given them and watched through their new goggles as the old hands swept past them; 'flippin' hell, man, never gonna make it'. All four of them felt the disappointment that yesterday's session and the new costumes hadn't instantly transformed them into would-be dolphins. All the swimmers, new and old, held onto the bar or trod water as the Bullet started talking.

"OK, lots of different thoughts going in your head right now. Some of you are feeling great, really at home in the water. Some of you are thinking, 'What's happened? Got to be all right yesterday, now I feel like I'm slipping, not going anywhere', yeah?" At least four heads nodded. The Bullet grinned. "We've got a secret. Any of you club swimmers going to share it?"

Hands went up, and the Bullet pointed. "It's the feel for the water, Dan, isn't it? You just get that when you're swimming a lot of sessions, then if you have a break at the end of the season or for holidays or something, it just doesn't feel right when you get back in the water." Dan Bullet nodded and smiled. The swimmer continued, "Our club coach says that even when we're resting at the end of a season, we should get in the pool a couple of times a week, just easy swimming like, so we don't lose that feel altogether."

"Good, man, well done. Remind of me your name again. I promise I'll get all your names by the end of this week."

"Michael; it's Michael, Dan."

"Michael? Named after Michael Phelps, are you?" A sideways shake of the head, nod 'no'.

"I know Michael Phelps; what an amazing swimmer! He so nearly beat me at the Sydney Games, and he was only fifteen!" And the club swimmers just looked at him. *He knows Michael Phelps and he's coaching us? OMG!*

And Shelley mouthed at Lucy and Mickey, "Who's Michael Phelps?" And the returned double shoulder shrug indicated that they had no idea—no idea at all, although it had been pretty obvious from the excitement from the 'real' swimmers that Michael Phelps was almost certainly related to God. "I had a chat with Michael; no, actually, I had a couple of chats with him in Sydney. Look at me, I'm a big bloke, yeah?"

And all those nodding heads agreed that, yes, Dan Bullet was a pretty big bloke. "So Michael is fifteen years old, fifteen! A couple of you guys are nearly that already, yeah? So how come a fifteen-year-old kid can take me to a couple of tenths of a second in one of the toughest swim events? Well, I'll tell you how: technique, technique is it, and Michael Phelps is one of the best—no, make it the best technician I've ever seen. Couple of months after Sydney, after the Games, Michael goes and breaks the world record for two hundred metres butterfly. Technique is everything, guys—absolutely everything. There's a little old joke that goes, 'What are the three most important things in swimming?' And the answer, anyone?" Two raised hands. "Go on then."

"Speed, endurance and stroke technique, Dan?"

"Well, I said it was a cliché joke…so the silly answer, but also the true answer, I believe is: it's technique, technique and technique." A pause, then he said, "I honestly believe that if I'd paid more attention to technique when I was younger rather than just busting a gut every time I got in the pool, then maybe I could have taken silver in Sydney, maybe even gold, maybe!"

Another pause, then he said, "So we start here, guys, right here. Don't care how fit you are, don't care about your swim background, where you are now. What I care about is where you're going, so my aim these next five or six weeks is to focus on technique, really focus on that stroke technique, and we'll see how we get on. Now, I'm not saying that I'm not going to push you and push you hard when it needs it, but every session that you choose to do with me, there'll be some technique in it, I promise." Another pause, longer this time, then he continued, "Stick with me, you guys, trust me, and I promise to do everything I can to make every single one of you better swimmers…Sounds good?"

They looked at the Bullet with awe; he cares that much! He really cares that much! He ain't gonna sit on the poolside and write up a session on the board and then just shout out the rep times. All of them, the experienced club swimmers, the newbies, the novices and the inbetweeners, shook their heads and called back, whispered back, shouted back, "You bet! Yes, please, Mr Bullet! Thanks, Dan! Thank you so much!" And the Bullet smiled at them.

"So, let's get started, OK? I want you all to swim just two lengths, any speed that's comfortable to you, OK? And I want you to count the number of strokes that you take for each length...I'm guessing all you club swimmers have done this before?"

A hundred per cent nodded yesses and said, "Yes, we've done this before."

"Shelley, Jacko, Lucy, Mickey, new to you, yeah?" Another hundred per cent nodded yesses. "OK, so no worries, no pressure; just swim how you feel comfortable, and we'll see what happens."

Swimming in the three lanes now, following the swimmer in front, making sure you knew if it was clockwise or anticlockwise so you didn't make an absolute idiot of yourself in front of all the others, Dan Bullet's worshippers swum the allotted two lengths, the fifty metres.

"OK, who's going first?" Not unnaturally, the club swimmers piped up.

"Thirty."

"Thirty."

"Thirty-two."

"Twenty-nine," the numbers rolled.

"Twenty-seven."

"Thirty-one." Then from the Speeding Bullet.

"Shelley, Mickey, you guys?" The reluctance weighed down on them. Mickey was the bravest.

"Dan, I took sixty strokes, sixty!"

"Me too, Dan; sixty strokes, well, maybe fifty-nine...maybe," Lucy and Jacko said together.

"Shelley, what were you on?"

"I did twenty-one on the first length, and then twenty-four coming back so forty-five total."

"Nice one, guys. Nice one, Shelley."

The Bullet smiled at them, smiled at all of them.

"Pretty much what I would have expected...Look, you guys"—he focused his attention on the top two lanes—"I need you to help me out now; actually, I need you to help everyone out, yeah? Listen, when you first started with your clubs, was your stroke count every length, then what it is now?"

The negative shaking of heads was unanimous.

"No way, no way, Dan. It's something that happens as you get fitter and get more swimming in...you just sort of learn not to waste energy." The not-quite-Michael Phelps, Michael, leant on the lane rope and smiled at the four occupants of lane one. "Listen, you guys, it's really tough when you start, you know? I remember when I got into the club and I felt I was just useless, honest, just useless! I said to my mum, 'I ain't going back there; I really ain't, Mum!' But of course, I did, and then it just sorta got better. So, I really do know what you're feeling like right now, yeah? Listen, trust me, you listen to Dan, no really listen to Dan 'cause he's awesome. No, he really is awesome, and you're gonna be right up there by the end of the summer, honest. Trust me, you really will!"

Jacko and TMRG smiled; the Speeding Bullet smiled.

"Michael, thank you, thank you so much. You explained that perfectly, you really did." Then the Bullet said, "Michael's right, you know; it just takes a bit of time, and then all of a sudden, it starts to feel right, so let's get onto the next stage, yeah? OK, everyone check your goggles out, any mist or water in them, get rid of it right now. If you're new to goggles, what you do is lick the inside of the lenses, and they'll be fine—better than fine!" And the swimmers did the Pavlov dog stuff and adjusted, licked and readjusted their goggles.

Goggles were snapped into place; they looked at the Bullet…who was peeling his tracksuit off. "Now, I'm going to swim a couple of lengths. What I want you guys to do is to take a couple of deep breaths and hang onto the lane ropes and watch me underwater. Can you do that for me?" *Yeah! You fucking kidding me? You bet your shiny arse I can watch Dan Bullet swim in my pool…*The thoughts might not have been totally identical, but they were pretty close.

The Bullet jumped into the water, hit the bottom and seemed to lift his entire upper torso almost out as he kicked off of the bottom. As he pushed off the wall, all the goggled faces held onto the lane ropes and forced themselves under the water and watched and watched and watched. You know that old cliché? The one about a picture being worth a thousand words? Yeah, that one, exactly that one. Maybe it wasn't perfection, just maybe. But it was pretty near it for the tadpoles and sharks looking on. It's that effortless amazing moment of moving good as an American sprinter once said, possibly not grammatically correct, but certainly entirely true. The Bullet glided through the water but at a speed that seemed impossible with no perceivable effort. Every arm entry surged him forward. They were spellbound—an old-fashioned word but the appropriate one. Mickey felt his lungs bursting as did Lucy, Shelley and Jacko. As the Bullet touched the wall, Mickey surfaced and took a huge deep breath. It was an awakening—a pure awakening.

"Oh my god, Dan! Oh my god! That was just amazing—no really, it was amazing. That looked beautiful." Mickey glanced at the others to check if they were laughing at him for saying 'beautiful', but the expressions on all their faces—the good and the not so good—told him all he needed to know; he'd chosen exactly the right word. "Can you teach us to swim like that, Dan? Really? Can you?"

"Well, I reckon I can help, help all of you...OK, guys, listen, you buy into this, give it a go, even if it feels really weird to start with, and, yeah, I reckon I can help you all become better swimmers; you never know, Olympics or something, why not? I never thought I'd make the Olympics, but my coaches put so much work into helping me that I want...no, make that 'I need' to give something back."

And to the three members of TMRG treading water in lane one, it was almost as if they were listening to Mr Warren back at the start of that school year. Somebody once said, 'An idea is the most powerful thing in the world', and the Speeding Bullet had most definitely planted an idea in the communal brain cells of TMRG.

"Anyone check my stroke count?" A lot of shaking heads. "I made you seven on the way down and eight coming back," said Michael, of course.

"Nice one, Michael, nice one. So, first thing, an important thing, stroke count is important; it's not the only thing, but it's certainly one of the five or six most important things I want to get across to you this summer. Now, stroke count and reducing the number of strokes over any particular distance is going to depend on a few things; the first one, and the unfair one, is that it will depend on your body; height and length of arms particularly. I'm about six-foot-three, so my stroke count is going to be easier for me to lower than all of you guys. But you know what? You're stuck with your body; it's pretty much the only thing you get given for free and the only thing that's gonna stick with you for life, so whatever your body is, learn to love it."

And that particular idea and thought stuck in Mickey's, Shelley's and Lucy's minds forever. "OK, there's an old rule of thumb in swimming that says you do about one stroke per second. Now that's not exactly true, but it's near enough— I'm talking about freestyle, of course, front crawl, yeah?"

Everyone nodded, waited for the next pearls of wisdom to fall. "So, if you're taking sixty strokes for a fifty-metre swim like we were earlier, then your time for the fifty is going to be around a minute; seventy strokes and it's a minute and ten seconds, make sense? Yeah, 'course it makes sense. So, I checked your times roughly, and you know what? It wasn't far off being accurate. So, we've got a pretty silly situation here…you have to swim slower to swim faster." The Bullet grinned at all of them. "I want to stretch out the reach a bit more, and then at the end of the stroke, make sure you push right the way back. OK, let's give it a go!"

There seemed to be little difference in the strokes and techniques of the club swimmers from the previous stroke count efforts, but in lane one, it was a different animal now. The Bullet grinned to himself, kept taking a sneak look at the Speedo clock on the wall and waited for everyone to finish.

Then he asked, "How'd it go, guys?" And the big, no, make that 'huge', smiles in lane one said that it actually went well, actually went brilliantly. "So how many strokes did you drop?"

"Eight."

"Seven."

"Four each length, so eight again."

Dan looked at Shelley, then she said, "Dan, I dropped eight strokes as well. I'm down to forty-three for the fifty now…Can't believe it, just can't."

"And you guys in lanes two and three?"

"Two."

"Four."

"Three."

And then, finally, Michael said, "Eight."

"That's a big old drop, Michael…that's not that far off of my stroke count, and I'm just a bit taller than you are…What d'you reckon?"

Michael grinned at Dan. "I could probably drop more, Dan, you know that, but if I slowed down my stroke that much, then it wouldn't do any good because I'd be focusing so much on it that I would be loads slower; I wouldn't do that in a race."

"Exactly, nice one, Michael. So, all of you, stroke count is important, but it can't be to the detriment of your speed. You could all drop more strokes, 'course you could; you proved that just now. Michael, what can we do about that? How do we keep the speed along with stroke count?" And Michael knew that Dan knew that he, Michael, knew the answer, and he silently thanked him for putting him in a good light.

"It's a sort of game we play, well, we do at the club; it's called the golf score, like golfers have to take the least number of hits for a round, don't they? Isn't it,

Dan?" A nod of approval and a silent 'go on' invite. "Well, what we do is to take the stroke count and add it to the time for fifty metres—two lengths, and that total is what we have to try to beat next time we do the golf score, so, like if I swim thirty seconds fifty and I take twenty-eight strokes, then my golf score is fifty-eight. That right, Dan?"

Another nod. "So when I started at club, my first golf score was about a hundred, about fifty seconds and fifty strokes, and now it'll average something like today or just a bit more." A pause and a look at lane one, and a second glance at Shelley. "So it really is just time and practice, guys. Honest, that's all it is."

And that was how it started, that's how the timid, tentative tadpoles took their first lesson on the way to becoming dolphins and sharks.

Chapter Fifteen
When the Going Gets Tough

It was the best summer—the best summer ever. Every day for Mickey, JoJo, Lucy and Shelley was an adventure, an exploration, a day of new ideas. For JoJo, working on the drills and skills of football, playing against the boys sometimes, working on the set-pieces and above all being taken seriously as a footballer rather than a girl interloper was heaven, just heaven. JoJo grew as a player, grew in confidence, grew as a person. Larry McQueen and the Spurs scout, whose name was Leftie Winger, which JoJo thought was really funny, took JoJo to the Spurs training ground now and again, but only after they had both visited JoJo's home and talked to her parents, told them what was entailed, what it was all about, permission was given and papers were signed. And again, she was taken seriously; the senior players stopped and watched and chatted, occasionally gave advice, and boy, did she tell the others all about it! You bet she did. "They send a car to collect me and bring me home, honest! A car for me, oh man!" And she was improving, improving all the time, and she knew she was improving. Confidence gained, confidence to try something new, confidence in not worrying if it didn't work out; no worries, try it again. Eleven years old and I'm at Spurs. Bliss was it to be alive.

For Mickey, Lucy and Shelley, each day was a revelation. Each day, they learnt something new. Each day, the skills and techniques of swimming, running and field events—high and long jump, shot put and javelin—were taught, learnt, remembered and inwardly digested. It wasn't easy, wasn't easy at all. Some days they were totally exhausted by the afternoon, but it was a good exhaustion. Gilly, Chris and Dan made it fun with lots of jokes, lots of silly games to make the new skills easier, lots of silly jokes and sayings.

"When the going gets tough, the tough get going!" Or sometimes: "When the going gets tough, we sit down and rest!" And they'd all fall about laughing.

"It's the one you think you can't do that does you good!"

"The only tactics I admire are do or die!"

"No gain without pain!"

"If you're not living on the edge, you're taking up too much space."

"Someone, somewhere is training harder than you!"

And they'd all shout back, "Why!"

"Place, press, pull, push, make my stroke go whoosh, whoosh, whoosh!"

"If you're not training your guts out, you're not cheating me, you're not cheating the others, you're cheating yourself!"

"You're not hurting, it's just the pain leaving the body."

"If you're soft and just so-so, don't go running, no, no, no. Running isn't made for you. Running's for the chosen few!"

And sometimes they'd answer back, "Like you and me, and me and you!"

"Whether you think you can, or you think you can't, you're almost certainly right." And Mickey and the others thought a lot about that one, and they grew to realise that it was true.

For all the kids swimming and running on that summer camp, it was a huge growing-up, maybe even a rite of passage to adulthood? Maybe, just maybe. They loved working with and being coached by Chris, Gilly and Dan; they hung on every word they spoke. The kids adored their coaches. And in return, the coaches adored the kids; for everything they sent out, they had it returned a hundredfold. How is it that some adults have that rapport with kids ten, fifteen, twenty years younger than they are? And the answer, of course, is that they care; they truly care. And that's what makes them different.

They learnt the importance in swimming of the high and wide elbow, the importance of body rotation, of using the legs primarily for balance rather than speed, of not lifting the head to breathe but rather turning the head in line with the body rotation, of bi-lateral breathing and of fitting all these skills together as they were all needed to complement each other. They learnt how to use the pull-buoys and the hand paddles, the kickboards and the fins. They learnt how to tumble turn, with much laughter when they missed the wall or their goggles came off.

They looked at the different rates of improvement in each other; they compared themselves. Some days, they were disappointed, and some days, they were happy. And they learnt that that was the way of the world, stuff happens, good and not so good, and you deal with it. They respected and admired each other. They learnt humility. They became swimmers.

They learnt the importance in running of leg speed, of how and where to plant each step, how not to overstride, a good knee lift, how not to lean back no hips back and bum down, of keeping the body erect and not sitting back when they were tired, of using the arms for speed, balance and propulsion, of pacing correctly for different distances. Keeping the shoulders relaxed and untensed, focusing on breathing out rather than breathing in, no rolling or bobbing heads.

Focusing on looking ahead, perhaps on the ground fifteen or twenty yards ahead with the occasional lift of the head to check surfaces. They learnt the coordination drills, the heel flicks, the kick-through, the sideways crossover and back—lots and lots of drills. And they laughed as they learnt them, and they gradually got better and better and more and more coordinated. They learnt humility. They became runners.

The Bullet was holding some papers as they met up for usual drinks at the end of the day. There were just two weeks of the summer holidays to go, just over a week of the camp, and they were all looking forward to a break; the exhaustion had crept up gradually on them, and the Bullet was wondering how Gilly and Chris would react to what he was about to say to them, about what he was about to propose. But first, they all relaxed into the pub chairs and sighed, a good sigh, and then they sipped their drinks.

"It's been a great summer, Danny, a really good summer. You've put together a brilliant camp. Every kid I've spoken to has said how much they've enjoyed it, how much they'd love to do it again…thanks, Danny, cheers!" And they all lifted their glasses and toasted each other.

Danny Bullet kept his glass raised, and as a smile slowly crept across his face, he said, "Gilly, Chris, I've got a proposition for you…" And the Bullet smiled. "Just had an offer, an offer for the three of us to go abroad for a holiday, all expenses paid, to"—and he paused to heighten the tension—"Amsterdam!" Another longer pause then. "There is a bit of a condition, though…" A much longer pause this time, but Gilly and Chris refused to be goaded.

"OK, here goes: the camp this year, including our wages, was funded by the borough, as you know. Now our borough is twinned with similar boroughs in Amsterdam, Paris and Brussels. The powers that be have decided that—for the benefits of British, French, Dutch and Belgium intercultural togetherness—some of our kids from the camp can be ambassadors through sport. You know, meet

111

up with the French kids and whatever and hopefully make friends and connections.

"I still keep in touch with some of the guys I used to swim against over there; the group camp or competition is going to be arranged by a swim club that I've had some dealings with before in Amsterdam called 'Die WaterFrenden', pretty obvious translation, I think? There'll be a swimming gala, some form of athletics, and a soccer knockout for the teams. Nothing desperately serious, although I reckon our kids will treat it like the Olympics and World Cup combined. It's a long weekend, just one week away from now. Kids go free with obviously permission from their parents; I can get a group passport, arrange a coach up to Harwich, and then we pick up a coach into Amsterdam. What d'you reckon?"

Chris and Gilly stared at each other for about thirty seconds, a slight nod, then they said, "You are a bloody silver-tongued lizard, Danny, you know that? The words just drip through your lips, and we get sucked in and blown out in bubbles! 'Course we'll do it. What do we have to do?"

And just like that, it was arranged. Of course, the Bullet had already prepared everything. Chris knew that Dan Bullet would have been totally prepared; he'd served two tours with the Bullet in Special Services, had faced the terrors with him. Had been in that awful place where time moves differently when you're in the presence of violent death.

Where it stretches.

When a moment can feel like a thousand years.

He remembered the mantra: 'Accept nothing. Believe no one. Check everything.'

For a moment, he was there again. Boobytrapped bodies. Pieces and prisoners. Castration and scalping. Skinning alive.

And then that instant was gone, and Chris Warren thanked God, genuinely thanked God, although he could never rationalise whether he actually believed in God or not…But thanked him all the same for allowing him to live, for allowing him to have chosen this life.

Chapter Sixteen
Amsterdam

When the kids all came together at the end of camp that evening, the Bullet called them together, outlined the scheme, gave out the letters outlining the details of the camp, the permission slips that needed to be signed, the details of the hostel that they would all be staying in; everything was there. There was a buzz about the kids and also an element of fear.

"Never done anything like this before, Mickey, never been abroad on holiday, never even been on a proper boat, ferry like. You think the kids over there will be like us? Not too posh or anything?" Lucy voiced all their fears and apprehensions.

"Can't not do it, though, can you? That Mr Bullet, Dan, I mean, and Gilly and Chris." Shelley was confident enough now to say 'Gilly' and 'Chris' without feeling too embarrassed. "They really are brilliant, aren't they? No, like I mean, really brilliant." And Shelley shook her head. "I mean, going to Holland like, talking to kids in a foreign language…oh God! How'm I gonna do that? I got no idea how to speak French or Dutch. I'll just stand there like some idiot child…no, I'm going, definite like…My mum'll let me, 'course she will…At least I think she will…I hope…"

And of course, Shelley's mum allowed her to go, as did JoJo's, Lucy's and Mickey's mums. All the mums and JoJo's and Lucy's dads marvelled at how much their children had grown up that last year and how much that had seemed to accelerate over the summer holidays. They'd got used to now hearing about Mr Warren, Miss Ring and Mr Bullet, and more recently, Chris, Gilly and Dan, and they also marvelled, and thanked God, at how much easier life had become, how there was no longer that constant conflict in the house. And they certainly weren't stupid, oh no, not stupid at all. They, the mums and dads, knew exactly why their children had matured. And so, it was with faith and trust in their well-being that the forms were signed and handed over.

The three coaches, Dan, Gilly and Chris, were both pleased and surprised at how many of their charges were allowed to go. In total, just under half of the summer camp athletes had done all that was necessary and were waiting with impatience, and not a little apprehension, for the coach to arrive and transport them to Harwich for the cross-channel ferry to the Hook of Holland and a brand-new world awaiting them. TMRG were standing so close to each other that, when they realised it, they giggled and moved away…but only a little. Mickey reached out and squeezed Lucy's hand, and Lucy knew the meaning of seventh heaven. JoJo and Shelley already had their arms loosely over each other's shoulders. The four of them were at ease in their own company and, if truth be told, very happy that the other three were with them.

For kids who had rarely, if ever, been outside the confines, rituals, habits and behaviours of their patch of East London, sailing on the ferry was an entry to another world. They walked (together of course) around the ship, up and down the extended decks and onto the open sections with the still warm summer sea breeze blowing in their faces. It was almost a wonderment in their eyes.

"Look at this, Mickey! Just look at this!" And Lucy would point out the seagulls following the boat and repeatedly diving in the wake, searching for fish, and they would sneak out the bread from their packed lunches and throw the crumbs into the air and watch the swooping and the diving and the arguing and the fighting between the gulls as they sought to maintain their supremacy in their own little world.

"Can't believe we're here." Shelley shook her head for the hundredth time. "Can't believe it."

"Blows my mind," Mickey said. "Blows my tiny mind away…Tell you what, guys? Don't know how, but I'm gonna travel. I want to see everything."

"Sir, sir, miss!" And JoJo was about eight years old again as she spotted her mentors and coaches walking towards them. "Oh, thank you, Danny, thank you miss, sir—I mean Gilly, Chris, for bringing us here. Never known anything like this, never done anything like this! Look at us, we're sailing to Holland!" Bliss was it to be alive.

And it got better. Herded together by the Bullet so he could lead them through passport control on their group papers, they emerged into a brave new world, both physically and metaphorically. The signs were in a foreign language—some of which they could understand because of the similar spelling to English. The Dutch people speaking was totally incomprehensible, and they'd stare at each other, giggle and then pretend to speak in Dutch to each other in a ridiculous self-parody. Laughing at themselves and each other was easy now; their summer maturity had given them that.

"We're driving on the wrong side of the road!" As they pulled away from the ferry terminal, Mickey yelled out and then stopped and giggled. "Yeah, right hand side, of course, remember now." The four of them had sat near to the front while the majority of their fellow campers had dashed for the back seats. TMRG just wanted to see everything and reckoned it would be easier from the front; plus, the fact that Chris, Gilly and Dan were at the front as well.

Fingers were pointed, shoulders were shook, scenes were pointed out. "Look at all the bikes!" Mickey shook his head again as they skirted around the city centre. "Everyone's riding a bike!"

"It's a small country, Mickey; traffic gets silly congested over here, so it just makes sense for these guys to ride a bike," Chris responded as the coach started to pull over and into the entrance of the hostel. "Get your stuff together, guys; check down the sides of the seats and in the top if you put any of your stuff in there; you don't want to be without your clothes or sports kit while you're here." The vehicle stopped, and while the brakes exhaled with a slow 'whoosh', they stood and queued to get off and explore their new world.

Checking in was easy; Gilly and Dan stood by the desk and called out names while Chris mixed in with the kids. Two bunk bedrooms for the girls, same for the boys, a bit of a rush for the best beds (whatever the 'best' beds were) while Gilly, Dan and Chris attempted to keep the peace. The three girls managed to bag bunks next to each other, while Mickey felt almost alone for the first time as it struck him that his three best friends (at least for the time being) were girls. And then he saw Jacko, and it hit him that he hadn't even bothered to pal up with him while they were travelling over. A soft guilt moved over Mickey.

"Sorry, Jacko, that was bloody rude of me. I guess I was so excited just to be doing something different that I forgot to say hello properly. You all right?"

A big grin from Jacko, then he said, "Yeah, I'm fine Mickey, wasn't that brilliant? Never even dreamed of being on a ship before, just wandered around all the time. Like, I love London, love where I live…Well, sort of, but getting away to somewhere like this, totes brill!" And Mickey agreed that, yes, indeed it was totes brill to be in Holland.

"Mickey, all right if I knock around with you? Like just this evening while we get sorted out? Ain't no one from my school in this group; no one was allowed to come."

"'Course it is, coming down to see the girls?" And as they cautiously went downstairs to the meeting room, Jacko and Mickey could hear voices coming from the other bunkrooms. Jeez, what were those Dutch kids and the others gonna be like?

The Bullet was planning ahead with Gilly and Chris.

"It's a bit of a three-day whirlwind fitting in the swimming and athletics. Football isn't so bad; the four teams all play against each other so that'll go on the same time as the swimming and running stuff. I've got the outline programme here, and all the kids have filled in what they'd like to do. It isn't a team competition as such, but you know our kids, well, all the kids, aren't going to see it like that. The swimming's not too bad; we've got all the club swimmers, of course, but I'd like to fit in your three: Shelley, Lucy and Mickey as much for experience as anything else. All OK on that?" And of course, Gilly and Chris concurred.

Mickey and Jacko met the three girls just as they were about to go into the poshly titled lounge. There was a nervousness, of course. Even entering a new territory in their area of London caused nerves so that was to be expected here as well. The five of them went over to the water cooler and helped themselves to orange squash and then lifted their heads and looked around to see a slim, blonde, smiling boy approach them. He held out his hand to Mickey first.

"Hi, welcome to Amsterdam. My name is Kaas Prinz." Almost too formal handshakes followed with Jacko and then Shelley, JoJo and Lucy. "OK, introductions over, what sports are you doing? I'm swimming." Kaas Prinz's English was superb. He smiled again, and Shelley felt a tremble in her stomach that she couldn't quite fathom out. What the hell was that? And she saw Lucy and Mickey looking at her and smiling.

"Cat got your tongue, Shell? Struck by lightning, eh, Shell?" Mickey mouthed, and then he winked at her. And Shelley had the good grace to blush a deep red, while JoJo and Lucy both giggled at her discomfort. But Shelley recovered; of course, she did.

"Hi, Kaas, I'm in the athletics, but our swim coach wants us to do one event in the swimming as well, just for experience 'cause we've only just started swimming this summer. JoJo's doing football; she's really good, you know. She plays for Spurs!" Putting JoJo immediately on the spot.

"I do not play for Spurs!"

"Well, sort of," said Lucy, and Kaas looked on intrigued and lifted his eyebrows quizzically.

"All right, well, one of their scouts came to see me play, and then he and Larry McQueen took me up the training ground to look around, and I sort of went and did a bit of training there as well and met some of the first team." JoJo blushed. "But I don't play for Spurs…But if they take me into their academy, well, you know…"

"That's fantastic, JoJo. Is it JoJo?" A nod, yes. "If it works like over here with Ajax, then I think that maybe you will play for Spurs." Kaas grinned again, and the second female member of TMRG felt that little flutter in her tummy. They chatted; a couple of Kaas's friends came over and joined in the banter. It was a good evening, and it started to feel a little bit more adult, more grown up being able to chat with kids from another country. And once again, they thanked god for Mr Warren…And Gilly and Dan, of course.

Chapter Seventeen
One Scared Little Girl

Lucy hadn't felt one hundred per cent when they had all gone up to their dormitories; just a little bit queasy, bit of a tummy ache; nothing desperate, maybe just from the travelling and the excitement. No big deal. Mickey had even kissed her on the cheek and squeezed her hand as they went their separate ways. Gilly had come into their room, wished them all a 'goodnight, sleep tight', then checked if all of them knew where her room was, 'just in case of emergencies', but they all knew that there wouldn't be any emergencies.

When Lucy woke up, it was pitch black, and she felt like a fist was grinding into her tummy. She lay still, willing the feeling to go away. But it didn't, cramping and re-cramping, on and on and on. She could feel the sweat on her forehead, felt it as it began to run onto her face, into her eyes. No, this wasn't right, really not right. *What do I do? Am I going to be sick? Am I going to die?*

"Shell? Shelley?" Lucy whispered and gently shook Shelley's shoulder. "Shell, I feel really rough, really…Shell, I think I've wet myself…oh God, I'm so embarrassed."

And lovely Shelley was wide awake in less than a second.

"C'mon, Lucy, into the bathroom." And as Shelley switched the light on and locked the door, she saw the pale blood seeping through Lucy's pyjama bottoms and knew immediately of course what was happening. "Lucy, Lucy, you've got your period; it's fine, honestly; Lucy, is it the first time?"

One very scared little girl nodded her head, hugged Shelley and started to cry. "Oh man, Lucy, that's not fair, is it? Come away to Holland and get your first period, oh, fucking hell!" And Shelley swore for the first time in a long, long time.

"Am I gonna be all right, Shell? Tell me the truth, gonna be all right?"

"'Course you are, Lucy; my periods started like six months or so back. I thought I was gonna die to start with…Lucy, is it alright if I go and get Miss Ring, Gilly I mean? She'll understand and know what to do, honest. I'd trust her with anything." And wrapping a towel around Lucy's upper legs and grabbing a sweatshirt for her, the two of them knocked on Gilly's door. "Miss, Gilly, can we come in? Please, miss, Lucy's just got her first period, and it's really got to her, please, miss." Gilly didn't even need to answer; she put both her arms around Lucy and hugged her closely while Lucy sobbed her heart out.

"I'm so sorry, miss, so embarrassed. I just feel like an idiot."

"Oh, Lucy, there's no need to feel like that; we all go through it, and even if you're supposed to know all about it, when it happens it's still such a shock…I thought I was going to die when it started! Honest, I really thought I was bleeding to death. Look, darling, go and have a shower, and we'll get you sorted out, yeah? Are the stomach cramps getting easier yet?" And yes, they were, the sobbing and unburdening herself to Shelley and Gilly had lightened the load on this scared little girl.

"Shell, will you come in the bathroom with me? Is that all right, miss…Gilly?"

"'Course it is," they spoke simultaneously, and then all of them giggled, just a little bit.

Gilly managed to find a pair of knickers and shorts for Lucy while the two girls were in the shower and started to plan ahead. *Poor kid, everyone goes through it, but when it happens on a group trip, you feel like it's the end of the world.* And then, *Shit! Need to tell Danny, can Lucy swim…? Will she want to swim? Oh fuck it!* The two girls came back into the bedroom.

"Oh, miss, I truly am so sorry. I feel really stupid now, like my mum told me, but it was like 'yeah, yeah, Mum', and then that nurse came into school, do you remember? All the boys got taken out for extra PE, and us lot got told all about periods and bodies changing and all that stuff. But, miss, when someone's talking to you like that, like it's a lecture sort of, it's not really real, is it? It's another bit of school that sort of has to happen just 'cause it's always happened, but you never think 'oh, this is for me', so you just sit there and listen a bit and drift away a bit, innit?

"And you know what, miss, as well? Well, I don't think it's right that the boys weren't there as well. Like we're not from another planet, are we? It's periods, is all, and the boys ought to know about that. Like they not going to realise for a million years that girls have periods? They should be there as well; they really should."

Gilly thought, *You're absolutely right; we've got to make it real for these kids. Bloody hell, it's my class next year, and I don't want any one of them to have to go through what Lucy's just had to.* It was a resolve that she swore to stick to.

Then she said, "Lucy, we need to tell Dan; you're supposed to be swimming tomorrow." And this brought a fresh flood of tears.

"No, miss, sorry, Gilly, I can't; no really, I can't. Oh, fucking hell, miss— sorry, miss, Gilly—no, I can't, honestly. Like he's done everything for me, just like you and Mr Warren—Chris, I mean, oh fucking hell, miss, sorry, miss, Gilly, I won't even be able to look at him. I'll just be so embarrassed."

"I'll tell him, Luce, or like I'll come with you and tell him." Shelley wasn't speaking; Shelley was making a statement. "Lucy, Dan's a sweetheart, no really, he is…Miss, do you remember when you called me 'sweetheart'? I'll never forget that, no, never forget that; it was when you got me doing hurdles, remember? Made me believe in myself, honest. No, Dan'll understand. I know he will; he's just one of those blokes you know you can trust like. He ain't never gonna put you down; feel like I've known him forever, and it's only this summer…no, Dan'll understand, I know he will."

A pause which grew longer, then, "Dan's like you and Chris, miss…Gilly; he cares; he really cares about us." And then Gilly Ring, Miss Ring, couldn't stop herself as she started to cry just a little and pulled Shelley and Lucy into her.

"You know what, you two? You're going to be special; I mean that. You have something different; JoJo and Mickey do as well, trust me. Your lives are going to be very special; you have that something inside you, you really do. I reckon that when I'm an old lady, I'm going to wake up one morning and read all about you in the newspapers or maybe when I'm not quite that old!" And if Gilly, Shelley and Lucy had only believed one tiny bit of that statement. But in a very important small way, they did believe it. And in a very small but important way, it was absolutely true.

Gilly walked back to the dormitory with the girls. "Goodnight, sweethearts." And they all giggled again, but it meant something to all three of them.

"Shell, can I snuggle up with you tonight?"

"'Course you can. I was just gonna ask you the same thing!" And the two newly baptised sweethearts snuggled in together and slept better than they would have believed one hour earlier.

Chapter Eighteen
The Swim Meet

Gilly was with Lucy and Shelley as they walked over to the swimming pool after breakfast. Gilly had already filled Dan in on the happenings of the previous night.

"Oh man, poor kid. You know we also used to say going into swim meets or training camps that the girls would always get their periods early, and the boys would always get constipated!" Then he added, "Gilly, I'm not trying to be funny or make light of it, honest, but we saw it so many times. All right with you if I talk to Lucy? She's such a lovely kid; I'm really fond of her…but don't tell her that!"

Dan was waiting, hoping that he'd say the right things.

"Ladies!" He even said it with an exclamation mark. "Ladies, I've got the three of you; this is truly an honour!" *He really is a lovely man*, Shelley thought.

"Dan, gotta tell you something." And Dan looked at Shelley while Lucy had her head hunched into her shoulders, and the Bullet waited, again hoping that he'd say the right things.

"Shelley, this sounds serious." And the Speeding Bullet put on his caring, serious face, and although he'd been prepared for this, he was still hoping that he'd say—and do—the right things.

"Well, Dan, Lucy had her period last night; it was her first one, and it scared her shitless. I know I'm not supposed to swear, and honest, I try really hard not to, but like, this sort of feels like it needs some swearing, you know."

And the Bullet despite all his preparations didn't say a thing. Instead, he went over to Lucy, put his arms around her waist and picked her up and hugged her. "I know I'm not supposed to do that, all the politically correct stuff, you know…but I reckoned that in these circumstances, sometimes people need a hug…I so hope that's OK, Lucy?" And Lucy put her thin, little girl arms around the Bullet's neck and sobbed her heart out for the second time in twenty-four hours.

"And I want to tell you something, all of you, that's you, Gilly, as well as you two. I want to tell you that coming up and telling me is—first of all—very brave, and secondly, that by telling me, you make me feel very humble; you also make me feel very privileged that you can trust me, and I thank you from the bottom of my big, black, unfeeling heart for that." And the Bullet had just lifted the world a little, actually, make that 'a lot'.

"London kids grow up quick, you know, Dan? I see other kids from outside London and it's like they're a couple of years younger than us, you know?" Shelley looked at Gilly, who nodded and then directly at the Bullet said, "So when you say about us trusting you, 'course we do, 'course we do! That's right, innit Luce?" And Lucy, safely secure in Dan's enveloping arms, nodded a yes.

"Thing is, Dan, we know who the pervy blokes are; you just suss it out. All that stuff we had before summer camp, you know 'if you don't feel comfortable…Come and talk…Something feels inappropriate…' Yeah, all that stuff. We ain't stupid, just 'cause we're kids from the estate don't mean we're stupid. Dan, we know; honest, we know. We suss it out pretty damn quick. Look at all those plastic villains down the estate, wouldn't give 'em the time of day. All of us growing up, TMRG, we stuck up for each other all the time; didn't matter if it was the girls or the boys, didn't matter who was black or white or Asian or mixed race; it didn't matter one bit. What mattered was that we trusted each other, knew that someone would come running if anything bad happened; there'd always be someone at your back. Honest, Dan, we just know."

And the Bullet held it together, just about held it together as he looked at Gilly, and she smiled back at him.

"Phew, thought my eyes were gonna leak then." And they all smiled and laughed. "Shelley, thank you so much, truly. Look, can I tell you a story? If that's OK, and then we'll get ourselves sorted out for today, yeah." And Gilly nodded a yes as well. "Well, it's a pretty silly story but…well, let's see what you think."

And the Bullet began, "These three blind men were sent into the jungle to collect some food. See, I told you it was a silly story, who'd send blind men to collect food? Anyway, one by one, they all came in contact with an elephant, but because they couldn't see, each one of them thought it was something different. One of them grabbed the elephant's tail and thought it was a vine of a tree or a plant; the second man touched the elephant's trunk and decided that it was a python; and the third man got hold of the elephant's leg right down by the foot and thought it was the base of a big palm tree…So that's the story." And the Bullet waited…but not for very long.

"So what you're saying, Dan, is that everyone sees the world in different ways, especially if you don't see the whole picture?" Dan smiled.

"Spot on, Shelley, absolutely one hundred per cent spot on! And you guys see the best; you see the positives in every situation, however bad other people might think it is. That is a fantastic attitude; it's what I've always tried to do." And the Bullet paused and decided if he should carry on. "Look, Shelley, Lucy, there's a thing called 'self-fulfilling prophecy', ever heard of it?" And now Lucy pulled her head up from Dan's shoulders and shrugged herself down to the ground.

"Not sure if I've got the right words, Dan, but is it something about you expecting something to happen, you want it to happen, and so you do all the stuff that you reckon is needed, and then it does happen. Is that right?"

"Wow! Two out of two, great stuff, Lucy! So, what happens now is that you've got your period out of the way and you know it's happened and it's going to happen again and again; it's just how it is. But now that first one is done, you dealt with it, and you know that you'll deal with it next time because you'll be prepared. You're very special, you know?" And Lucy and Shelley looked at each other and smiled; twice in a day we're told we're special! "And whatever you say, it is an absolute honour to coach you and, importantly, to be trusted by you!"

Lucy felt that an enormous weight had been lifted from her shoulders, Gilly and Dan totally understanding, Shelley being well, just Shelley, best of the best. They walked into the pool and onto the poolside. "Shelley, you go and get changed, easy this morning, just a warm-up for the gala this afternoon." And as Shelley walked away, "Lucy, on the poolside with me; today, you're my number one assistant coach." And Lucy didn't even think about arguing; the decision was made for her—another relief.

The swimmers were waiting, Shelley and Mickey included.

"Guys, I have a new coach this morning, you all know Lucy, and I need to have another pair of eyes with me today so we can see if there's anything desperate we need to do before the gala." And not one voice was raised in surprise or dissent. Although Mickey did raise his eyebrows and looked over.

"S'all right," Lucy mouthed back. "Tell you later." And Lucy felt far more confident of telling Mickey than she would have believed just a little earlier.

The swimmers went to work. Being on the poolside with the Bullet was an utter revelation to Lucy. As the sharks and tadpoles went through their mystic moves, the Bullet pointed out to Lucy what was good and what was not so good, why this hand entry and not that one, elbows too flat or just perfect, body roll in line or the dreaded zigzag, same with head position, feet flat or pointed, legs balancing or thrashing an over-kick. Lucy might not have been shaking her head in wonder, but inside her mind, she was certainly doing that.

"I never knew, Dan, all that stuff you taught us, but when you see it properly…Well, flipping hell!" And then, "Obs, it wasn't me in the water just now, but it felt like it; it was almost like when you hear your own voice for the first time on a tape recorder or something and you think 'that can't be me!', but 'course it is. You know what, when I get back in the water, I'll be seeing myself when you give me all the stroke corrections…Even if I'm just swimming, I'll be seeing myself."

"It's just the beginning, Lucy, just the beginning. So many new swimmers never get past that first bit. If it's runners like you, then they find it hard to slow down, find it hard when they don't improve immediately, even though they're trying harder than ever. All sports are different. I mean you have to try in every sport, have to put yourself on the line, 'course you do, but they all have different techniques, different stuff you need to focus on to improve, and a lot of times in swimming, you actually go slower the harder you try because that little bit of wrong technique means you're working against yourself. One of my early coaches used to say to us to 'make haste slowly', and we all thought it was being stupid until we realised that's exactly what we needed to do: slow down and learn. You've got that something, Lucy; no really, you do." And those previous twelve hours of shame and embarrassment and 'why me?' had almost disappeared.

The session ended.

"See you at four o'clock sharp for the gala, OK? Everyone know what events they're in? Shelley, Mickey, four hundred metres, yeah? You guys, you're covering all the hundreds and two hundreds between you including the individual medleys." Smiles, thumbs ups, nods, 'thanks, coach', 'thanks, Dan'. A few nervous minds and bodies, and they were off to the changing rooms.

Shelley and Mickey then asked, "You all right, Lucy?"

Lucy smiled a real smile. "Yeah, I'm fine, honest, absolutely fine. See you outside when you're dressed, yeah?" *So, I tell him, don't I? It's a period, is all;*

Shell and Gilly were great. Dan's a bloke, and he totally understood. No embarrassment, no looking away, it's real life. Oh shit, I hope Mickey's all right with it.

Shelley was standing next to Lucy as Mickey with his hair still wet came out of the changing rooms.

"You all right, Lucy?" He came over to her and put both arms around her while Shelley relaxed because she knew, she just knew, that it would be OK. Mickey was like her brother, right? No, Mickey WAS her brother, just because it wasn't blood, didn't make it not so.

"Mickey, I got my period last night, so I couldn't swim this morning. I was so scared, really scared. Shell looked after me; dunno what I would have done if Shell hadn't been there. And Miss Ring, Gilly, as well. Oh, Mickey, I was just so scared; I really was!" And while Mickey kept his arms tight around her; he looked over at his sister Shelley and mouthed, 'thank you so much, Shell. Owe you big time.' And Shelley smiled back and then turned slightly away as she wiped away the tear that she couldn't stop. Mickey knew that he was pretty much out of his depth; big, hard Mickey who'd confront the gangsters five years older than him down the estate, knew that he was out his depth.

"Oh, Lucy, I don't know nothing about periods, well, like I know what they are, but I have no idea of, you know, what it's like to have a period, what it feels like. I'm a boy, never occurred to me to even think about it. But I s'pose now it's real like…yeah, now it's real…'cause it's you. Don't know how you feel, don't know if you're hurting or anything, but what I do know is that it must have taken a whole barrowful of guts to tell me, well, to tell everyone." And Lucy knew, and Shelley knew, and then even Mickey knew that everything was going to be all right.

"We won! We won against Belgium!" JoJo was bouncing up and down outside the canteen waiting for them. "We did, we won! It was two-one, and I got the second goal. Mr Warren came to watch me, and he said I played brilliant; no, he really did; 'brilliant' was what he said! I love it; I absolutely love it. I get out on that field and sometimes I just feel I can do anything!" And then she asked, "So how'd it go for you guys?"

Lucy and Shelley filled JoJo in on the details of last night. "You should have woken me; you should have!" And Shelley explained that it was all so quick and about Miss Ring 'Gilly, I mean' being there and taking control so that there wasn't a need.

"We weren't being nasty or snide, JoJo; honest, we weren't. It was just all about getting Lucy sorted out. Gilly was great; she was just so calm and understanding, made it a lot easier than it could have been. It's all sorted now. Lucy's fine. Ain't you, Lucy?"

"Yeah, can't swim in the gala, though, really wanted to do that, didn't want to let Dan down, but he's so good, and he totes understands. He even let me be with him on the poolside this morning; he's amazing what he knows, made me understand so much about proper swimming."

"Shell, Mickey, Jacko, you all still swimming, though, ain't you? I am so definitely coming to watch you in the gala. You reckon you'll win?"

"I reckon I've got more chance of going to the Olympics than winning!" And that stitched them up completely.

Lunch was relaxed but with an obvious element of nervousness and tension for the novice competitive swimmers. It was a different world for them, and if it hadn't been such an obvious cliché, they would have said that they felt out of their depth. And then Kaas joined them.

"Hey, guys, all good?" He went around shaking hands, smiling always, perfect English, of course, introduced them to a couple of his Dutch swim-mates and then seemed to shoo them away. "OK if I join you?"

Immediately, it seemed, there were gaps made next to Shelley and JoJo; Kaas smiled and took the diplomatic route by sitting in between them. Shelley and JoJo made no sound, but the sigh was almost palpable. Kaas was oblivious, or was he? He looked over at Mickey, and the smile was noticeable, but only just, and only to Mickey. "So, what events we doing today? I'm in four hundred front crawl and then four hundred individual medley; tough call for me! What are you on, Mickey?"

"Four hundred crawl, Kaas. My coach Dan says that I should just use it for experience and try to hold my stroke right through however tired I feel, so that's exactly what I'm going to do."

"Yeah, me the same, Kaas." Shelley's eyes were shining. "Really looking forward to it 'cause Dan said I don't have anything to prove and nothing to lose…really love swimming now. God, it's only five weeks ago we started training properly!"

"I'm gonna be supporting, Kaas; wouldn't want to miss it!" And JoJo's eyes were shining too.

"Lucy? You doing the four hundred as well?" And Lucy was fine; she smiled back at Kaas.

"Naah, gonna miss today, Kaas, but I'll be there, of course, can't not see Shelley and Mickey swim...and you, of course. Me and JoJo are gonna sit together so I can keep her under control."

"We won the football this morning, Kaas," JoJo said. And JoJo was thinking, *Please notice me!*

"Nice one, JoJo! That'll be so good to see you all there...I love galas, all the team bigging each other up. You got a chant or a song for your team?" TMRG all looked at each other, don't know nothing about a chant. Kaas saw the looks, then said, "Yaah, I guess it's different...We have a chant for our team...but today, I think maybe we change it a little for you guys...is OK?" And yes, they all agreed; of course, it was OK. And Kaas just smiled.

Four o'clock: warm up. Dan was on the poolside before any of them. Big smile, big heart, big man. He called Lucy over to him, asked her if she'd help him with the warm-up, and Lucy's glistening, worshipping eyes said yes. And nobody let him down. How could they? He was the Bullet, and they'd never let him down. Mickey and Jacko placed sixth and seventh in the four hundred free and were delighted with that; they'd actually beaten one of the real swimmers, a Belgian guy. Shelley went even better, holding her stroke right the way through, totally disciplined, Shelley moved from eighth and last right through to fourth in the final hundred metres.

"I did it! I fucking did it! Sorry, Dan, sorry, just...oh man...thank you! Thank you so much!" And when the swimmers were allowed out of the pool, Shelley ran over to the Bullet and hugged him and hugged him and hugged him. And the Bullet, hard as nails but really as hard as a soft cushion, didn't even cry...well, not too much. Kaas won the four hundred individual medley and was just touched out in the four hundred free by his Dutch teammate in the race where Mickey and Jacko took sixth and seventh, and waited for both of them after they had climbed out of the pool.

"Nice one, Mickey; nice one, Jacko. Much respect for your first ever race."

But the highlight of the gala for all of them was when Kaas started the team chant just before the final relay events:

"Give us an A!" And the response came back from all the Amsterdam swimmers: "A!"

"Give us an M!"

128

"M!"

"Give us an S!"

"S!"

"Give us a T!"

"T!"

"Give us an E!"

"E!"

"Give us an R!"

"R!" And the British swimmers, including TMRG, could see exactly where this was going and almost started to join in the chant, until, "Give us an F!"

"F!"

"Give us a U!"

"U!"

"Give us a C!"

"C!"

"Give us a K!"

"K!"

"What have we got?"

"Amsterfuck!"

"What have we got?"

"Amsterfuck!"

"What have we got?"

"Amsterfuck!"

And the Dutch and British swimmers were rolling on the poolside, laughing their heads off…and Kaas just grinned. "Said we'd do the chant for you! Hope you enjoyed?" And Shelley, Lucy, JoJo, Mickey and Jacko agreed that, yes, they'd most certainly enjoyed the chant.

"JoJo's got something special, class above the others in the team. She can read a game, seems to know where the ball is going before anyone else, anticipates where to be and she's there. Takes control and the girls all take it from her; she's encouraging but not afraid to tell 'em what to do." Laughingly, they called it the coaches debrief session, an opportunity to wind up the day. Gilly filled Chris in on Lucy's adventures and misadventures, and the Bullet told them about the gala, Shelley and the boys' races and Lucy standing in as assistant coach and then the Amsterdam chant, and that got them chuckling.

"The Dutch kid, Kaas, has got something about him; seems a really nice lad, perfect English, of course, like everyone in Holland; they get a load of English TV programmes over here, including the news, so they just grow up with it." Gilly and the Bullet grinned at each other. "And you should have seen the puppy dog eyes that Shelley and JoJo were making at Kaas; think we might have to rescue him later!"

"We sorted for tomorrow, Dan, Gilly? JoJo's football is in the morning, boys' match is in the afternoon when the athletics is on, so I thought maybe we could all go and support JoJo; pretty sure the kids will go and watch her, and then we've got the athletics in the afternoon. What I was thinking was to put Mickey and Lucy in the fifteen hundred; that's what they want to do—Lucy OK to run?"

"Yeah, she'll be fine," said Gilly with Dan nodding. "I'll have a chat with her early on and help her to get sorted; she so definitely wants to run…actually, I think she needs to run."

"And then with Shelley—Chris, if it's all right with you?—I'd like her to do the two hundred rather than the fifteen…and then hurdles, high and long jump and shot put. Yeah, I know what you're gonna say, 'too much', but I think with Shelley, she'll lap it up; she'll only have to do three jumps in the long and three throws in the shot and then with the high jump, depends what happens, yeah?" And tomorrow's events were sorted, just like that.

"Oh God, he's lush, ain't he, Shell!" They were sitting in the dorm, going through the day's events; JoJo looked at Shelley. "D'you fancy him, Shell? I know I do. What d'you reckon?"

"Oh, yeah, he's a good-looking boy, got something about him as well, that Amsterfuck! Thought I was gonna wet myself!"

"Yeah, that would really have impressed him, wouldn't it? What do you reckon, Lucy?"

"Don't think you need to ask, Lucy, only one bloke in the world for Lucy, innit?"

"No, he's nice. Kaas is nice, made me laugh, cheered me up a lot after all my faffing about; anyway, after all this stuff, we're never going to see him again, so good luck with that one, girls!"

And if only Lucy could have seen into the future and known how wrong she was about seeing Kaas Prinz again.

Chapter Nineteen
Something Special Happens

JoJo was buzzing, absolutely buzzing. Everyone's coming to see me! Everyone's coming to watch me play! Better not mess up then, had I? And JoJo was most certainly not going to mess up if she could help it. Nine-thirty kick-off, JoJo was at the pitch by nine and warming up.

"Good morning," perfect English again. Kaas smiled at Shelley, Lucy and Mickey, and then held out his hand to Gilly, Chris and Dan. "I'm Kaas, and I had the honour of swimming against your team yesterday." Dan smiled back.

"Nice swimming, Kaas, very nice swimming…And even better chanting in your perfect English."

"Thank you, Mr Bullet. Mickey was telling me what a great swim coach you are…I wondered if it might be possible to come with you to watch JoJo play her football? Shelley was telling me when we all met that first evening that JoJo plays for Spurs? I'd really like to see her if that's OK?" And of course, it was OK, intercultural ambassadors or something, wasn't it?

Justification for the trip, and Kaas tagged along with them, and to no one's surprise at all, he walked alongside Shelley.

They'd been rotating the captain, and it was JoJo's turn to be in the centre circle for the coin-tossing ritual and ceremony. Just as she turned away to claim the end, she saw her own little band of supporters arrive…And, oh god, Kaas was with them! No pressure there, then. JoJo waved over to them, and as the whistle blew to start the game, her utter single-mindedness, her professionalism, if you like, pushed itself forward and pushed the watchers (even Kaas) out of her mind. Chris Warren had been right, JoJo was a class apart, a class above.

For the first ten minutes for those watching, it seemed almost as if she was an onlooker, a spectator, but it was JoJo eyeing up the opposing team, looking at the weak and strong points, the players who could be gently bullied and forced into errors, those who could tackle and those who backed off, those who ran always with the ball rather than pass to a teammate in a better position, and particularly those who panicked under pressure. JoJo saw it all and didn't even realise on a conscious level that she was doing it.

Playing as much as a midfielder as a forward, JoJo swept into the tackle and took the ball from the advancing striker; one touch to steady and then a long ground pass to the right-winger, four steps for her, past the defender, who was caught on the wrong foot, and a high ball pulled back from the line into the centre of the goal-mouth for JoJo to race forward and nod home. One-nil in the opening ten minutes.

It could have been all over for the French team, but they rallied. Two big strong centre backs came alive after failing to pick up on JoJo's late run and header, and whenever JoJo touched the ball, she was quickly being closed down. Just one minute before the halftime break, a big throw out from the French keeper and a lack of attention from the wing backs led directly to a three on two situation by the British goal, a pass back to the French striker with all the time and space in the world, and it was one-all. The referee's whistle blew.

The JoJo groupies were half-expecting her to come over and chat during the halftime break but not even a glance over. The animated captain was talking, pointing, a finger wagged, a hand on shoulder, around the waist, a smile, a laugh and then another serious look and gesture as she relayed her instructions. Be here, be there, watch out for this one, for that one; when their goalie has the ball, you should be closing down close on this player and that player. Don't give them room; don't give them any room at all. Make them nervous to even be in possession, make them anxious to pass the ball quickly, that way lies mistakes for them.

That way lies possession and then goals for us. The players nodded, all of them; no one else spoke except to agree with JoJo. Finally, with the teams just starting to take their places for kick-off, JoJo jogged over. "Thanks for coming, appreciate it, really do…hi, Kaas." A smile and a run back to central midfield.

The second touch of the ball sent it to JoJo; she looked up and around and saw no one approaching to tackle. Rather the opposing players were backing off, backing away; they'd seen in the first half what JoJo was capable of and certainly didn't want to be the one to let their team down, the one at whom the finger would be pointed. With no one coming towards her, JoJo ran. And ran. And ran some more. She was a third of the way into their half when at last one brave defender moved to tackle. One step to the side, defender left floundering; JoJo moved the ball to the outside of her left foot, looked up and stroked the ball into the top left-hand corner of the net. The goalie certainly saw it but could do nothing about it—nothing at all. Too fast, too well-placed, too perfect for an eleven-year-old girl. Two-one to England.

JoJo jumped in the air, her team surrounding her, as she urged them back to their positions to defend the expected attack. France's team moved quickly, and well, they'd been taken for mugs; 'sucked in and blown out in bubbles' was the phrase, and that wasn't going to happen again…Except that was precisely what happened. With the English defence now motivated by JoJo, and in truth, just a little scared about what she might say to them if they didn't do what she'd emphatically told them at halftime, they closed down on the ball-carrier, picked up the loose forwards coming into the goal area, hurried and scurried and worried them, and then the keeper scrambled possession from a poorly hit shot.

JoJo screamed at her goalie. "Look! Look up! Who's free? Give it, give it now!" A lobbed throw to left midfield while France were slow in getting back, one direct pass forward, the number ten seeing a huge gap over on the right, an accurate ground pass, the pass returned immediately, and number ten had all the time in the world to pick her spot. One-all to three-one in arrears within two minutes of the restart. French heads went down, a steep hill to climb.

And that particular hill was just too steep; two more goals followed for England, neither scored by JoJo, but both most definitely created by her. The final whistle blew, and not a moment too soon for the French. Handshakes, smiles, hands around shoulders, whispered 'well played', from England, whispered 'bien joué' from the French. And more than a few shakes of both English and French heads as they looked at the English captain who had controlled the game. Truly controlled the game.

Chris Warren looked at Gilly and Dan; Kaas looked at Mickey, Lucy, Jacko and Shelley.

"For sure, JoJo plays for Spurs, for sure." A pause. "I think maybe JoJo is a better player than the boys on our team." Another pause. "Yes, she is, for sure she is." Kaas smiled…and so did Shelley. And Shelley felt envious, felt jealous even, and then felt ashamed for allowing herself to feel that.

"JoJoooooooooo! That was amazing; no really amazing! Oh my god, JoJo!" Shelley and Lucy put their arms around JoJo's sweaty, exhausted frame and hugged and hugged her. "Oh man, you are so good!"

"Oh, thanks, guys, thank you for coming to watch me play, made a difference, made me work my arse off…oops, sorry, Gilly, sorry, Mr Warren, Dan."

"I think in the circumstances you can be forgiven, JoJo. That was so beautiful JoJo. I don't think you're lucky going to Spurs, no, I think that Spurs are lucky having you."

"Sir, really, sir? Couldn't have done it without you, sir." JoJo looked at Lucy, Shelley and Mickey. "Right? Yeah? All of us, yeah?"

"My pleasure, my absolute pleasure."

Kaas stood and thought, thought a lot. He walked over to JoJo, smiled and said, very quietly, "Well done, really well done." It had been quite a morning.

"How come one little girl can go from, well, just being a little girl who enjoys a kickabout to dominating a game? One year, one year ago, JoJo was a kid in the playground with the odd kick at the ball, and now? Really dominating, class apart wasn't even in it."

"Mickey said it for all of them, Chris, you made them believe in themselves," Dan said. "I see it in them in the pool; it's not easy swimming with a group or a squad when you're so far behind to begin with, apart from your guys. Shelley and Mickey, Lucy, even Jacko has come on because he's around Mickey. Those other kids will have been in a club environment since they were four or five years old probably. They will have had all the stroke and technique work drilled into them. I don't mean that in a nasty way at all, but they will have had years of getting it right, and your kids are doing five or six years' work in five or six weeks, quite incredible." A pause then he added, "I'm going to come along to the track meet this afternoon if that's OK with you two?"

"Wouldn't think of going without you, Dan; the kids will be delighted that you're there; they'll expect you to be there; they know you care just as much as we do." And so, it was settled.

Shelley was nervous; she was on first, so that as soon as the hurdles were over, they could be cleared from the track. Mickey and Lucy were jogging around with her, and JoJo—fresh from the morning heroics—was up on the grass verge, watching, still buzzing from the game. Kaas had strolled over to sit with JoJo, and JoJo was a very happy girl. Shelley moved into a few strides and then some lead-leg drills over the hurdles. The marshal's whistle blew.

"Competitors in the girls' seventy-five metres hurdles." Sweatshirts and tracksuit bottoms for those who were wearing them came off. Marshalls directed the athletes to their respective lanes. "Under starter's orders." Moving forward. "Take your marks." Settle and gaze centred forward. "Set." Eight backsides raised into the air. The pistol cracked, and eight Pavlovian-cloned hurdlers pushed and surged.

Shelley leant her body and lifted her lead leg into the first obstacle (*Phew, got that one done!*), and she was into her stride pattern; one, two, three and lift and land and repeat eight times through. She didn't see anyone in the lanes next to her, mainly because she wasn't looking. Absolute focus on her lane, her hurdles, her stride pattern. JoJo watched and recognised the total focus; knew she had been exactly the same during the match earlier. She glanced at Kaas next to her and saw that he too was watching intently. Like Shelley earlier, JoJo felt an instant jealousy and like Shelley earlier, instantly felt ashamed for her feelings.

Shelley leant into the tape, knew that she'd won because the tape was there and not broken by a faster athlete. She looked back and was surprised—make that stunned—to see the second athlete just clearing the final hurdle barrier. There was silence in the watching athletes, coaches, spectators. And then one single hand-clap started, and it was JoJo. She stood up and continued to clap; one by one, the other watchers stood and clapped and clapped and clapped. Dan and Chris looked at Gilly.

"Jeez, Gilly, you've done something a bit special with that one, different class; no one else was in the race."

"Wish I could claim the credit, Dan; the kid's a natural. She'd never been over hurdles before when we introduced them, and yet she looked like she'd been hurdling for a hundred years. Yeah, Shelley's got something; she works her backside off, but she's got that awareness of her body... I reckon she could make a success of just about any sport she tried."

"Yeah, you're right." Dan was nodding. "First time, she got into the pool, well, second time maybe, you could just see that she had that awareness. She was able to take on board in minutes and seconds all the stuff, the stroke work, the technique that would take most new swimmers months and years. By far, the best improver in my little group."

"Excuse me, Mr Bullet, may I?" Kaas was polite as always. Dan grinned.

"Of course."

"So, Mr Bullet, we see your group train because you were scheduled just before the Amsterdam team for the warm-up sessions. Shelley had told me that she'd only been swimming with you for a few weeks, so when we did see your group in the water, we couldn't believe how good they were—all of them. And her hurdle technique just now…So good; really, so good."

Shelley waved at her groupies, all smiles now. And then she did a magical thing. She put her open palm up to her lips, kissed her palm, looked up at Gilly, blew the kiss to her. And Gilly did the same, blew a palm kiss back to Shelley. Shelley smiled again and waved and then followed the tannoy announcement: "Competitors in the high jump." Shelley hadn't felt overconfident for the hurdles, but after Gilly had praised her up in the training, she thought that she could do okay. But winning like that!? Oh man, how good!

The high jump was a different animal; she'd taken part in the training sessions, watched and learnt the techniques, the different styles, how far from the bar to take off, how much speed in the run-up. But now she stood and studied her opposition as they warmed up. In the training and learning sessions during the summer, Shelley had started on the scissors jump and had gradually grown in confidence to use the western roll; she'd even tried the Fosbury flop a couple of times but lacked the confidence to go all in…And now as she watched the high jump specialists approach and soar, it was obvious that the Fosbury flop was the number one style.

Shelley was remembering Gilly telling her the history of the flop; how Dick Fosbury had just come into the Mexico Olympic Games (oh my god, nineteen sixty-eight! Did the world even exist then?) and created this totally different, strange method of clearing the bar that no one had ever seen before. And he'd won Olympic gold and that had changed high jump forever. Dick Fosbury had done something that no one had ever seen or even imagined previously. He'd run up to the bar, turned his back and leapt over backwards! Head clearing first, then shoulders, a huge arch of the back and upper torso and finally legs and feet clear. He'd changed the discipline, and the world followed. Shelley let her memory join with her perusal of her opponents and made a decision. Shelley took a couple of practise run-ups, two take-offs but landing back on the pink all-weather approach and then one effort with a full Fosbury, and she'd cleared.

Why not? Gotta give it a go, and these girls are all right with it, know what they're doing…or looks like it, same age as me. Have a bit of bottle, Shell, what's to lose? Shelley had never heard the phrase 'positive thinking', but she was one hundred per cent carrying it out. She smiled at the officials, acknowledged her name, smiled at the other girls…and cleared the opening height at first attempt.

And as the bar raised, the second and the third and the fourth. All eight remaining, then six, five. At the fifth height, Shelley fluffed and the bar fell. Shelley's second try at that height, over! Only three jumpers remaining. Up again, another failure, then over. Shelley and one other left. London, Amsterdam, Britain, Holland. They eyed each other and grinned.

"Hello, I'm Shelley."

"Nice clearances, Shelley. I'm Marianne, Marianne Deussmann." Smiles again. But even with the smiles, Shelley's fairy tale ran out, and she failed three times, and Marianne cleared easily. They shook hands.

"And you compete again, Shelley?"

"Yeah, got long jump, shot put and two hundred metres sprint!"

"Wow, busy girl! I'll see you in the two hundred metres later." Marianne smiled and winked.

"Yeah, see you later."

There was just time for Shelley to get a quick catch-up with the groupies and a hug with each of them. Strangely, Kaas seemed to have become an honorary groupie and so was included in the hug. Over to the shot put, and for this Shelley had no aspirations other than to try her best, but no inhibitions either. Gilly had told her that it was 'putting the shot' rather than 'throwing the shot', which didn't seem too big a deal to Shelley, but when she took the time to look closely at her opponents after her first effort, she quickly took on board the rudiments of the necessary technique.

An unremarkable initial distance to begin with was followed by a second superior effort, followed by even more intense examinations on the other throwers ('Oops! Putters') as the rounds progressed, and with emphasis now on thumb underneath, elbow out and straighten arm, start body lower and swivel for speed, Shelley improved from stone-cold last to a creditable fifth place. One big happy sigh, another wave to the groupies and a short break before the long jump. Sweatshirt on, sips from the water bottle, happy girl.

"She's good, Shelley, isn't she?" Lucy and Mickey were jogging easily around the outside of the track.

"You're right, Lucy; she really is." A short pause. "I got a lot of time for Shell, you know."

"Errh, yeah, pretty obvious, Mickey, me too…I love her to bits, Mickey; she's always, always, always there for me, sort of big sister but more than that.

Like the other night, she was magic. She's so grown up, knows what to do, takes control. She's always so confident."

"Shell's not always as confident as people think, Luce; it's a bit of a show for the world. Shelley never had it easy growing up—well, I ain't saying any of us lot had it easy, but Shell never knew her dad; he done a runner before she was even born, I think. Shelley's mum's brilliant; my mum says she never went on about it, actually never even talked about him, just got on with her life. Like she wasn't much more than a kid herself when she had Shelley, seventeen or eighteen is all. And Shell's mum didn't even have her own mum and dad around; she did it all by herself. Got a job, got two jobs just so she could bring up Shelley properly. That's where Shell gets the confidence, well, why she seems so confident even when she's not. She gets it from her mum, all the hard work stuff as well."

I gotta ask him! Oh fuck, I'm scared! What if he says…I can't, I can't…I gotta.

"Mickey, why me? Why not Shelley? Shell's really pretty. Oh, I ain't stupid, we all know she's real glam. You see all the hoodies throwing a pose at her, and she's like four or five years younger than all those weed boys down the estate…Mickey?" It was quite possibly the hardest words Lucy had ever asked. "And Mickey, like Shelley's white, and I'm black…Why me, Mickey?"

And Mickey didn't say a word, not one word to start with. He stopped running, turned to Lucy, put his arms tight around her, hugged her tighter and tighter.

"It's you, Lucy, always has been. I just didn't know it properly, too much of a kid. Still a kid, I know, but I think we all grew up last year with Mr Warren. Don't want anyone else, just you. Black? White? You kidding me? Colour don't matter, does it? All us lot, TMRG, we ain't never had that black and white stuff, have we? Not ever. See it around, of course, see it a lot, but it ain't us kids; it's always the grownup or sometimes some kids 'cause their parents are just prejudiced. Not me, Luce, not you, not us lot."

Mickey shook his head, smiled and kissed Lucy on the mouth. "Oh, Lucy, sorry…Is that all right?" And with her eyes brimming with tears but certainly not crying, lovely happy Lucy put her head on Mickey's shoulders, let out the biggest sigh, then pushed herself onto her toes and kissed him back.

"Most definitely all right, Mickey, most definitely, couldn't be better." And with only a few minutes to spare, they half-walked and half-jogged over to where the officials were calling for the competitors in the distance race.

There was an absolute calm and confidence about Lucy as she waited for the marshal's call. There was one other black girl waiting for the start, wearing the orange vest of Holland. Lucy smiled at her, and the girl in the orange vest smiled back. The unsettled tummy had become almost settled now; it was still there but just a part of being the new, slightly more grown-up Lucy. Make that much more grown-up, make that much more mature. Mickey wanted her, always had, no one else. Ever.

And Mickey was all that Lucy had ever wanted. Some people didn't get it, couldn't understand. 'Just kids', they'd say. But Lucy knew different. Nothing could go wrong with the world, her world...Could it? Lucy even looked up at the now-her groupies and even managed a soft smile and a wave as the starter called out, "*Auf die Platzen.*" The gun lifted and exploded...and there was Lucy, running free, as free as she had ever run.

As Lucy danced on an angel's wings coming through the finish line for the first time, three hundred metres run and three more laps totalling twelve hundred metres to go, she was already ten metres clear of her nearest pursuer. She glanced up at the spectators, no Mickey there of course; he was waiting for his race, but she could see and hear her little band of groupies chanting out her name, "Go Lucy, go!"

So, Lucy went. No increase of speed although she felt that she could increase her pace at any time. Behind her, the chasers were waiting and anticipating a fall from grace. No one could start that fast and continue, could they? Maybe if they'd been alive to watch the amazing Filbert Bayi back in the eighties and the single way that he ran all his races, then maybe, just maybe, they might have thrown caution aside and tried to bridge the ever-increasing gap. But no, that little girl couldn't stay ahead, could she? They'd close her down and drag her back in. One full lap completed, and Mickey shouted out to her, "Oh man, Lucy, awesome, just awesome!"

So, I'm awesome now, am I? Maybe I am; that's how I feel. The spectators began taking more and more notice of the lone runner. Another British girl! Like that kid who won the hurdles earlier. What are they feeding them over there? With two laps to go, the gap had doubled. As she had done before, JoJo stood up and began to clap. And as they had all done before, one by one, every watcher stood and clapped along with her. It was stunning, so much more than random applause; this was special; this was very special. Somewhere in her mind, Lucy could hear the clapping, but it was just circling around like windmills, the windmills of her mind. She sensed Mickey shouting again, but it was more of a blur this time.

Focus, focus! Total concentration. What was it Miss Ring had said? Look forward not down, don't let your backside drop, run tall, as soon as your feet touch the ground, bring them up quickly, think like the ground's electric and you'll get an electric shock if your feet are on the ground longer than a tenth of a second. Focus, focus, focus! Just one final lap, the gap now almost fifty metres. And the chasers knew that, barring an appalling accident, no one was going to catch that not-so-long-ago scared little girl. That one-time scared little girl who was now running with all the confidence and majesty of an Olympic champion.

It was hurting now, the body, her body. Lucy wasn't hurting but knew that somewhere there was a hurt and it was connected to her. But she just didn't take it onboard right now. Why should she? Because Mickey had said that it was her, Lucy, always had been, so what was a little hurt compared to that? Nothing; nobody could ever hurt her, not ever.

It was the length of the finish straight when Lucy broke the tape, one hundred metres between her and the rest of the world. She stood and waited while the watchers went wild. Stood and waited and shook hands, patted shoulders, smiled and hugged as every competitor crossed the line. Acknowledged them one by one. Had a special squeeze for the girl in the orange vest; of course, she did. Why not? And the girl in the orange vest smiled and hugged her back; of course, she did. Lucy looked up and waved; JoJo, Gilly, Chris, Dan, Kaas all waved back and shouted and screamed at her. And then Lucy jogged back over to the start and pulled on her sweatshirt as the sweat continued to fall from her face and body. Mickey pulled her close to him; of course, he did.

"Luce, I said 'awesome'. Luce, that really was awesome!" And Lucy felt she was in heaven. Felt she belonged there.

"I think it's your turn now, Mickey. Remember all those figure of eight runs we used to do? Yeah, me too. That's how it started for me; that's how it's gonna continue now…for us." Lucy stood on her tiptoes and kissed Mickey on the mouth, the very first time she'd had the confidence to do that. She sighed. Mickey smiled and then laughed.

"Yeah, down to me, eh, Lucy? Thanks for that!"

The whistle blew, tracksuits off, a shake of the arms, a shake of the hands and wrists. Again, "*Auf die Platzen.*" Crack! Mickey moved to the front, but unlike Lucy's race, everybody stayed together. They'd all seen what that little girl—must have been the smallest in the race, yeah?—had done a few minutes before. This wasn't going to happen again. Like Lucy, Mickey felt a freedom in running. Always had, had been an escape from the ordinariness of life.

As they came through the line for the first time, Mickey was confident but nervous. Running was what he did, wasn't it? But now, probably for the first time ever, he had to prove it. Needed to prove it. There was a little uncertainty; he'd won the figure of eight runs with TMRG, had even won the school sports, although he'd eased and shared the victory with TMRG because—he knew— that was the right thing to do. Actually, the only thing to do. But this one was different, this one was against the best runners in France, Belgium and Holland.

This was like an international! The thoughts were racing through his head, *Look at Lucy, my Lucy; she really was awesome. Blew them away, wasn't scared, just stuck it to them. Love that girl, no, really love her.* And he did; there was a maturity about Mickey Honey, the Duracell Bunny. It had always been there, but that maturity had been honed in the last twelve months. Two laps done, most of the field still together. When to go? Now? Wait? Mickey made a decision, with six hundred metres—a lap and a half—remaining, he started to push. Not a sprint by any means but a gradual surge in pace. Mickey moved to the front and upped his cadence, kept it at the new tempo.

One lap remaining, the bell rang, the Mickey groupies shouted and screamed and cheered. Lucy was jumping up and down, any pretence at her newfound maturity long gone. Three hundred now, Mickey could hear the breathing of the two who had managed to stay with him on the accelerated pace, and he knew that he had a secret weapon, the secret weapon was Lucy because if she could do it, then he had to do it. Absolutely had to because if he didn't, then he'd be letting her down, and Mickey Honey, the Duracell Bunny, certainly wasn't going to do that.

JoJo was already on her feet, but this time, it wasn't just JoJo who started the single clap, the entire crowd were standing and looking at JoJo, waiting, waiting for her to lead them. And so, she did, that single hand-clap was literally that, because after that one bringing of the hands together, it was a coming together of everybody there. It didn't matter whether you were Dutch, Belgian, French or a Brit; everyone wanted to be a part of something special and watching the boys' fifteen hundred, they knew they were. Suddenly, the elastic that had kept them together was broken. Snapped, vanished, disappeared, gone. Free, alone, Mickey moved away; he didn't seem to increase his speed; in truth, he barely did. But that relentless acceleration had done it. He lifted the tape as he crossed the line with a comfortable fifteen metres' gap.

Lucy could hardly stop herself running out to him but held herself back as Mickey replayed the scene that Lucy herself had set just a few minutes earlier, shook hands, arms around shoulders, muttered 'well dones', fist bumps, respect, much respect. Mickey moved up to the group—his group. Kaas was the first to shake his hand. "Nicely done, my friend, very nicely done."

Gilly put her arms around him. "Oh my god, Mickey, superb!" JoJo and Mr Warren swept low in a mock bow.

The Bullet just grinned. "Good job, Mickey. No, great job!" And Lucy snuggled into his still-sweaty arms and loved it.

And now it was Shelley's turn again. Three down, two to go. Shelley had a couple of run-throughs at the long jump; going through her mind was all that Gilly had told her during that summer: get your run-up right; count the paces and stick to them; accelerate to the board; look for speed and height; arms forward and high; rotate forwards, not backwards; and when you land, fall forwards. All basic stuff, of course, but all contributing to the best jump possible. Shelley placed her water bottle where she intended to start her run-up; thirteen strides in all, first five to get sorted and settled and then next eight accelerating and hoping to hit the board spot on.

Kaas, Mickey, Lucy, Jacko and JoJo had all smuggled themselves down the front area to watch and support closely. Shelley waved at her supporters, smiled and waved again. Then on the runway, she picked up her checkmark, steadied herself, let her right elbow fall back followed by her body, hesitated for an instant of a second and launched herself forward. Five strides out, accelerate, hit the board, yes? Throw upwards and forwards, felt as if she was only in the air for a microsecond. Land, lean, forward fall. Look back, white flag! Yes! Legal jump. And the Shelley groupies roared their approval.

Waiting for her turn, acknowledgement from the official, a smile, steady, run, accelerate, launch, and this time, Shelley felt as if she was in the air for ages. A great jump, she knew it was the best she'd ever jumped! Look back, red flag! Shit! Just that little bit too much. Looked at the board, and there it was, scuff marks in the sand by the take-off plasticine. Just one centimetre, maybe less. OK, no worries, already got one legal, one to go.

Waiting, waiting, waiting; watching for the other girls' efforts to be displayed. Shelley was third but had that second jump been legal, an easy first place holding.

Quiet contemplation.

Thoughts.

More thoughts.

A resolve.

Give it everything, of course I will.

Acknowledgement and another smile from the jumps judge. A smile back from Shelley. Walk to the mark. Think. Move back just one and a half centimetres from her holding checkpoint. Yes, a nod to herself. Right thing to do. If not now, when? If not me, then why not? Fists clenched for an instant. Lean back, now go! Drive, drive, drive, accelerate, up, up, up, feet cycling in the air and she didn't even know that she was doing that. Land. Lurch forwards.

Look back, white flag! Yes! The groupies were cheering and dancing, yes! So much better this one, maybe as much as half a metre on her first jump! She waited, scoreboard clicking. Numbers up, distance up, yes, great jump…but quite good enough. A second place for Shelley, but how good was that? So good!

So good! She grinned at the silliness of the song lyrics repeating in her head. Shelley went over to the Dutch girl who had beaten her. "Great jumping, well done, well done!"

And the Dutch girl thanked her, "And a great jump for you; four events already, isn't it?" And Shelley acknowledged that yes, it was indeed four events for her.

Gilly was hugging Chris and Dan up in the stands.

"Honestly, she really does have something, doesn't she?" And it was pretty obvious to the three of them, and indeed everybody else who was lucky enough to be there on that day, that Shelley did indeed have something. Something very special indeed.

"Hi, Marianne."

"Hi, Shelley." And the hug was as natural as it could be. "What a day for you! Four great events, how do you do it?" Shelley shrugged; she hadn't even thought about it.

"Dunno, just feels great doing all this. I so love it, wouldn't want to be anywhere else, wouldn't want to be doing anything else."

"Yes, me also." Marianne smiled again. "Good luck in our race."

"Oh, Marianne, good luck to you too, feel like I've known you for ages and it's about two hours or something?"

"Me too, Shelley, me too."

They, along with the other six runners, prepared themselves for that final two hundred metres. As luck would have it, the lane draw had placed Shelley in lane number four, just one inside Marianne in lane five. Shelley knew that it was to her advantage…it was going to be 'interesting'. As they got down into the marks' position, Marianne looked over her shoulder and smiled at Shelley; Shelley of course smiled back. Once again, "*Auf die Platzen.*"

Crack of the gun. Flat out from the start, immediately into the bend. Gradually gaining on Marianne…But really just the lane stagger unfolding. Into the home straight, level, striving, striving, striving. Not daring to look over, neither one daring. Still level. Lean, throw at the tape, look at each other, laugh, laugh loudly. "Oh man, brilliant!" And neither Shelley or Marianne really knew who had said it because it could—and probably did—come from both of them.

They fell into each other's arms, still smiling and laughing. They waved at all the watchers and then jogged around the track together.

"I can't believe you did five events, Shelley! I did just two, and I'm tired with those…actually, it feels that my mind is more tired than my body; it's all the concentration and building-up before a race or a jump, and then the actual competition is a release; is that the same for you?"

And Marianne's words (in the usual Dutch perfect English) made absolute one hundred per cent sense to Shelley. It was almost as if a door had opened in her brain; of course, it was a release; it was something that she'd discovered she could be good at. Gilly and the Bullet and Mr Warren had all told her so, and while it had been 'just words' before, now she believed them. She allowed herself a mental swear, *Fucking hell, man, I really could be good, no, like really good!* As they eased to a walk, Shelley grinned at Marianne.

"Marianne, would you like to come and meet my friends?"

"But of course, that would be lovely!"

The two of them walked over to Shelley's group, who started to clap, and Shelley leant into a facetious bow, grinned over at Marianne. "Go on, you too!" And so, Marianne took a little bow and curtsy, which made the groupies clap louder. And with the clapping, Shelley and Marianne could barely hear the announcement of their race; a dead heat! They hugged each other once more.

"Everybody, this is my new friend, Marianne; Marianne, this is JoJo, Lucy, Mickey; my coaches and teachers Gilly, Dan and Mr Warren—Mr Warren, let's me call him Chris, but it still feels a bit weird." And they all laughed with her. "And this is Kaas, who we met when we got here."

Marianne looked directly at Kaas first.

"Hello, Kaas, how are you?" And there was a strange look on Marianne's face that Shelley couldn't work out...*Oh God, have I done something wrong?* And then Marianne's face broke into a smile. "Hello, everybody, I am so pleased to meet you." And there was the almost formal shaking of hands. "It is so good that you come to visit our country and to race...and to make friends." And Shelley felt relieved...almost. When you're a London kid, you learn very quickly to trust your gut instinct. Sometimes it turned out to be wrong, but more often than not, that gut instinct was correct. She put the feeling away to be brought out and examined later.

Chapter Twenty
A New Sport

"So, last day tomorrow, guys, then back to lovely London!" Chris Warren was smiling at all of them, the entire group. "We just have the last two football matches, girls and boys, both playing against Holland! Girls in the morning, boys the afternoon. On your feet, you guys! Let's give a big round of applause for our soccer teams." Lots of loud clapping and yelling. "And now all of you on your feet and keep clapping…I want you to clap yourselves because you have been fantastic, every single one of you! Gilly, Dan and I are so proud of you; it's been an absolute pleasure to be with you, and we would Like to thank you as well." And with that, Chris, Gilly and Dan clapped for their athletes, their pupils, and the athletes, of course, clapped for them back.

"OK, one final thing; don't know if anyone will be interested, but the Dutch organisers have asked if any of you would like to take part in a new event; it's something that the swim club have introduced; it's a swim and run event. Doesn't even have its own name yet, it's so new. Anyway, if any of you do want to do it, let me know, preferably this evening. It's a four hundred-metre swim followed by a two thousand-metre run, with no break in the middle; you have to get changed straight out of the pool and then straight into the run. Just a bit of fun, yeah?"

Mickey was the first one to Chris.

"Mr Warren? I'd like to do that swim run thing; is that OK?" And it was most certainly OK, and it was most certainly no surprise at all that Mickey was the first to ask.

"Miss? Gilly, I mean, would I be all right to do the swim run thing tomorrow? Like, you know, my period and all that. It was a couple of days back now. I'd really like to do it, but don't wanna embarrass myself or anything; what d'you think, miss?" And after just a couple of blush-making questions and an explanation of the practical logistics, Gilly assured Lucy that she'd be fine.

"Mr Bullet?"

"It's Dan, Shelley, if that's OK?"

"Sorry, Dan, it's just, you know, like you being a grown-up an' at, but yeah, Dan, I'd sort of like to do the swim run tomorrow, but tell the truth, I'm absolutely knackered, oops, sorry, very tired!"

"Yeah, me too, Shelley. I used to get absolutely knackered when I was swimming heats and final on the same day…but you did five, five events today! No wonder you're knackered! See how you feel in the morning, Shelley, and we'll go from there. I think a Dutch guy I met at the Olympics might be coming along, and I'd like you to meet him; actually, I'd like all of you guys to meet him."

Everyone was at breakfast early; everyone was going to watch JoJo play against Holland because, in all their minds and reasoning, it was Holland and not Amsterdam. JoJo sat with them, of course, but was a much quieter JoJo than usual. It wasn't nerves; it was more the determination and focused concentration on the upcoming match.

Get to the pitch, strip off, warm-up, referee's whistle blew calling the captains together to the centre of the field. The day's designated captain for the day smiled at JoJo. "Your shout, JoJo, you deserve to be captain, not me, honest. You got something special, girl." A hug, a squeeze, a murmured 'thank you, oh my god, thank you so much!'

JoJo shook hands with her opposite number, exchanged pennants, called the coin toss. Brought her team, her players together, talked to them, smiled at them, cuddles, hugs, even a few kisses. Whistle blows, pass forward, then immediately back to JoJo, looked up, no one free, dribble forward, look up, no one free. Keep dribbling, look again, space on the left, one accurate pass; winger took it, defender lunged, winger evaded, more space now, looks over, two strikers waiting in the box, JoJo like a whirling dervish sprinting from behind, central defenders saw JoJo, knew what she can do, seen it before, hesitant, waiting, move away from one of the strikers, picked up JoJo, job done. But no, winger saw now unmarked striker, took time, stroked it forward on the grass, striker has an eternity to pick her spot, goalie rushed out, dived at the feet, one small sideways adjustment and striker smoothed the ball into the unguarded net.

147

"YES!" Successful, happy striker is surrounded by her team. Holland kick off to restart. Holland captain takes control.

"Hold possession! Don't be a sucker! Pass, pass, pass!" Caution won control, match now much more evenly balanced, Holland stop panicking, back in the game, very much back in the game. Halftime, one-nil only. Second half, both captains taking control at halftime, do this, do that.

Watch this player, don't commit early, back off, support. Despite the one goal difference both teams now believing that they could win. Minutes tick by, score remains the same; Holland pressing, pressing, pressing. JoJo now in central defence, seeming somehow taller, stronger, larger than the players around her. "How long, ref?" A three finger reply with a smile, desperate now. "Hold, hold, hold!"

Holland pressing again…And again. Every player from both teams apart from the Dutch keeper in and around the London girls' goal, yet another shot goes in, goalie smothers, Holland start to retreat. "Give me the fucking ball!" Goalkeeper rolls the ball to JoJo, wouldn't dare not to. Holland racing back to defend, not now! Not now after all the pressing, all the attacks! JoJo keeps running, dribbling, looking and looking and looking.

A tiny semblance of order in Holland's defence, still JoJo moves forward, Holland a reluctance to commit, to tackle, a bit more time, marshal defence. Still forwards, one tackle, avoided, a second tackle, avoided. Just JoJo and the keeper, keeper has to come out to try to smother. JoJo sidesteps and avoids, open goal in front of her. JoJo pauses, looks up and back, smiles; the girl who had been generous enough to give JoJo her captaincy is running up to support. JoJo passes back to her; girl can't believe her luck, strokes the ball into the now open goal.

She yelled with happiness, "I scored a goal!" She ran over to JoJo, and both girls ran back to the rest of the team. Referee blew final whistle, eruption of team, mass huddle, mass cuddle. Holland team members approached, handshakes, of course. Dutch captain looked at JoJo. "Girl, you're awesome, best player I've ever seen! Privilege for me to play against you."

JoJo's eyes go moist, starts to cry a little, starts to sob, hugs the Dutch girl. "Thank you, thank you so much!" Looked over at the groupies, saw Mr Warren, started to walk over, then runs, slowed to a walk. *Compose yourself, girl, just nice and steady.* Yeah, right. Dissolved into Mr Warren's arms, sobs and sobs and sobs. Lucy and Shelley are right there with her.

"That was amazing, JoJo, truly amazing!" Mr Warren shook his head in wonder, kept his arms around the little girl whom he'd known and taught for just one year.

Then, "I should be thanking you guys, not the other way around." The kids looked at Mr Warren—like what? Chris Warren hesitated, looked at the Bullet, and the Bullet nodded back. "Dan and I worked together, I told you that, didn't I?"

The four members of TMRG all agreed by nodding their heads 'yes'. "What I didn't tell you because it maybe wouldn't have been appropriate is that we were in the armed forces together, the Marines, Royal Marines, you've heard of them?" Another joint nod of the four heads. Chris Warren hesitated until Dan Bullet nodded 'yes'. "It's not really the sort of job that you can talk about, people who haven't done that sort of job can't understand what goes on—listen, guys, I'm not putting you down or disrespecting you. Truly, I'm not. It's just the way it is, Dan?"

Another nod and a soft smile from the Bullet. "What it is in Dan's and my old job is that you learn to trust, learn to rely, learn to quickly see the phonies and the guys who talk the talk but can't put it into action when it's needed." Shelley, JoJo, Lucy and Mickey were spellbound; they knew this was something special. "You quickly find the people you want to be around, the people you want to spend time with, the people whom you know will never let you down however tough things might get, Dan, yeah?" Another nod, another smile from the Bullet. Chris exhaled one long breath. "When I started teaching you guys, it didn't take very long to understand that you all, all of you had—make that 'have'—something special. I watched how you all supported each other, how you helped each other always. No judgements, no badmouthing, just total support…And you all supported me as well; you know how awful a teacher's job can be if the pupils don't get behind that teacher?" And TMRG had the good grace to first grin and then look a little shamefaced as they looked back and realised that maybe, just maybe, they hadn't always been so supportive to previous teachers. "You touched something in me—and yeah, I know I sound like some silly old fart." They smiled and laughed. "But whatever you think, it's true. So, yes, I do thank you guys; I really do."

Mickey had the good grace and the self-control (just) not to cry, but Shelley and Lucy joined JoJo in the sobs and the hugging, and then, "Me and Dan and Gilly have used the words 'amazing', 'special', 'outstanding', yeah? But they're only words until you put in the words and action to make them real; you guys have done that in spades, so, yes, I do thank you, so very, very much." And Gilly was openly in tears, and even the Bullet's eyes seemed to have become a little moist.

"Can you believe that?" It was Mickey speaking, but it could have been any of the four. "Does everything for us, gives us the whole year, changes our lives, and then trusts us with telling us stuff like being in the Royal Marines. Mind you, I'm not so sure about when he and Dan told us that they got a medal for rescuing the general's pet monkey…! Man, that's special…Yeah, I really do want to be like Mr Warren." And Lucy, JoJo and Shelley all agreed with Mickey.

Lucy and Mickey were approaching the swimming pool; JoJo and Shelley were over at the running track where the new event would finish. There were a last few words of advice from Gilly and Dan, lots about pacing the race out but also and importantly some instructions about how best to change over from the swim to the run; Dan called it 'transition'; stay in your swimming costume no time to change clothes, have your running shoes open and ready with laces nice and wide so you can get your feet into them easily, have your running top spread out ready to pull over your head. Dan even had towels for them to stand on and some talcum powder that he sprinkled into their shoes just before they got on the poolside for the start. "Makes it easier to slide your feet in especially as you won't have time for socks."

It was the boys event first, for which Lucy was grateful as she could watch the—what was the word the Bullet had used? Oh yeah, 'transition'; that was it. She waved and smiled at Mickey as he, along with twenty-three others, lined up in the eight-lane, twenty-five-metre pool. She saw Kaas there as well and managed a small wave to him. The Bullet was on the poolside, of course, standing next to a tall, blonde-haired man who was absorbed by Dan's words. The blonde guy looked over at Lucy and waved and smiled. Lucy smiled back. Who's that guy? The race officials and starter explained the procedure to the boys, and Lucy listened intently while looking at the girls around her; mostly swimmers, she realised, that was going to be a tough one to begin with.

The athletes jumped into the water, three to a lane; lane one go clockwise, lane two anticlockwise, lane three clockwise and so on through the eight lanes. Muted discussion between the swimmers working out who would lead so as to minimise bumping and boring; not surprisingly, Mickey was last to go off in his lane as the starter's whistle blew, but it was maybe half a second down on first and second, and he was quickly on the feet of the swimmer in front. Two lengths done, and Mickey was still hanging on but gradually becoming detached from the two swimmers in front; as he turned, he looked across and saw that he was last with fourteen lengths remaining, a strong resolve now, hold that stroke, hold that stroke! The gaps opened bit by bit, halfway now, and he was almost a length behind. Don't go silly, don't overreact, count the strokes, rotate, stretch, lengthen…Keep it smooth!

As Mickey turned into his final two lengths, he could see the leading swimmer push himself out of the pool and run to his shoes; focus on yourself, nobody else! With just under one length remaining, Mickey was alone in the pool; no panic he told himself, hold that stroke again. Dan Bullet watched his neophyte swimmer and grinned to himself; he'd be fine. This kid, he'd be absolutely fine. The Bullet nudged the man alongside him, pointed Mickey out. Out of the pool now, Mickey Honey thrusting his feet into the talcumed shoes, pulling a vest over his head and chest, he ran out of the door and onto the big playing field. One large lap of sixteen hundred metres and then the final four hundred metres on the running track to the finish tape. Mickey took three runners as he came onto the grass, four more on the first long straight; he could see all his rivals in front of him; was that Kaas up front?

Eight hundred metres done now, and Mickey was up to twelfth, halfway into the run and halfway in the ranking order. He tried to maintain his stride, his form, his feet fast off of the grass. Another four hundred done, four hundred on the grass area and then onto the track, a bunch of five overtaken, getting tough now, getting pretty tough, still a couple of hundred before the track. Two more taken, and another; onto the track in fifth place, four runners scattered within one hundred metres in front of him. Really hurting now, hurting so much; up to fourth, then third, two hundred metres left, two orange vests in front of him…Kaas?

Yeah, Kaas, got to get him, got to! The first orange vest passed, chest screaming at him, barely able to breathe, feeling the sweat in his eyes; hundred metres, into the straight, JoJo and Shelley screaming out loud, no hand-clapping now, eighty metres now, level with Kaas, still level with Kaas, neither daring to look at the other. Mickey could hear Mr Warren's words in his head: "Never let you down, never let you down." Mickey Honey, the Duracell Bunny, dug as deep as he'd ever done, felt the tape snap across his chest but could see Kaas level with him as he did; who'd got it?

As Kaas came over and they first shook hands then hugged, Mickey knew that it actually didn't matter that much who'd won, what mattered was that he, and Kaas, both of them, had given everything possible, then, "I think, Mickey, with your running and my swimming, maybe we win the world championship?" And that stitched them both up. The judges were divided on the winner, so common sense prevailed, and it was a second dead heat of the extravaganza.

And now it was Lucy's turn; it started almost as a rerun of the boys' event. Lucy had gone into automatic mode early; she recognised that she was likely to be outclassed in the pool but vowed to focus and concentrate on what the Bullet had told her about pacing and stroke; she could almost replay the time she had spent with Danny Bullet on the poolside and listening to his words, listening to his wisdom. like Mickey, she was almost fifty metres down coming out of the pool…and then she entered a different world—a different class.

Dan was shouting at her, "Bee-oot-i-ful! Just beautiful!" And that was enough for Lucy; she had overtaken three girls before she had even exited the poolside. Her shoes were on in a flash, a little puff of talcum powder that she could smell; how was that? Out onto the grass, two more passed. Lucy looked up, oh man, they're streets ahead! Back into race mode, fast turnover, fast feet, look forwards and upwards, two more and then another.

Halfway around the grass now, eight hundred to go and then final track four hundred. In twelfth position with over half the distance to go, three more taken, tenth. Lucy's mind was buzzing. *Two days ago, I thought I was dying; I really did. Shelley, Gilly, Dan, even Mickey, I am just so lucky to have these guys, so lucky.* A little sob came from the back of her throat. As Lucy turned into the track, there were three girls ahead of her, but the contest was over already, fifty metres in front was the leading girl, again an orange vest over the swim costume, but the watching crowd saw that fifty metres evaporate within the space of a couple of shouted 'you go, girl!', and then Lucy was free—free from everything—she felt.

She lifted her arms along with her heart and danced down the straight, clapping her hands above her head, waving at Chris, Gilly, Mickey, JoJo and Shelley, even the Bullet who'd sprinted back from the poolside to see his little angel come home. The man she'd seen with Dan at the poolside was with him. Over the line, still clapping the spectators, still smiling with the delight of someone who escaped…escaped from what exactly? It flashed through her brain, but she knew that yes, she had definitely escaped from the life that she once thought she was destined for, and she vowed, maybe without even knowing it, that she would embrace that new life with everything. Smiles, hugs, claps, a mutual respect for all the girls who followed her over the line. JoJo got to her before Mickey, and they danced together back down the home straight, and then they went up to their little group.

"Brilliant, Lucy!" said Dan and Gilly together, and JoJo put her arms around Lucy and pulled her even tighter to her. Kaas waved his fingers and then sent over a kiss from the palm of his hand that Lucy immediately returned.

And then…One of the members of the boys football team came up to Dan Bullet. "Mr Bullet, sir? I think we got a problem." The Bullet listened and thought deeply what to do? He smiled; he knew instinctively what to do.

"JoJo, how you feeling?" JoJo looked back at him.

"Mr Bullet, sir? I'm feeling fine. Why, sir?"

"How're your legs, JoJo?"

"Yeah, they're all right, Mr Bullet."

"JoJo, we've got a tiny problem, probably not a problem at all. Three of the boys have had to drop out of this afternoon's match." They'd actually all come down with a severe case of the 'trots' rather than constipation. "Fancy being a sub for the boys team…? Just in case?" And JoJo couldn't have been more delighted. Another match, hopefully get on the pitch, experience with the boys, brilliant!

"Yes, please. What time's kick-off?" And she ran to get her kit, and she hoped, hoped, hoped that she'd get a few minutes of playtime.

When the boys on the Dutch team saw JoJo kitted up, there were a few grins and quiet laughs, not so from Kaas, who had not unnaturally gone along to watch; he'd seen JoJo play previously as had several members of the Dutch girls' team who had gone along to support. Neither Kaas nor any one of the girl footballers said a thing; why would they? JoJo was itching to play, itching to get on the field but wasn't at all sure that she'd be called; she knew she was an insurance policy in the first instance.

At halftime, the score was still nil-nil. JoJo was desperately hoping that she'd be on for the second half…but if her silent plea was heard, then it certainly wasn't acted upon. JoJo kept warm, kept hoping, kept watching the action, noting what she thought were the weak and strong points in the Dutch setup. There were only fifteen minutes to go when the world changed for her. An anguished cry from the striker, a clutch of the hamstring, a fall to the ground, face tightened in a grimace. Dan Bullet was on the field as the referee beckoned him on.

"Pulled it, Ricky?"

"No, don't think so, Dan, just feels like an awful cramp." Holding tight onto Dan, striker Ricky half limped and half hopped over to where JoJo was peeling off her sweatshirt. "Go, JoJo, you go, girl. Seen you play, know what you can do…and those buggers don't!"

It took five minutes for JoJo to adapt to the pace, passes slightly harder hit, ball moving with more speed, quicker pick-up and closer marking. Possibly, the Dutch opponents were a little more relaxed and complacent than they should have been. The ball came up from defence, JoJo just on centre spot with back to the Dutch goal controlled and pushed it down with her chest, feinted left, then right, left again, turned and went, then pushed the ball under her foot behind the trailing leg and left her marker three paces behind, which is a mile when you're on the attack and the opposing defence are too static, too confident about their ability to close down a weak player, a late substitute.

JoJo looked up, saw no one alongside her and headed for the twelve-yard box. Chasing, chasing behind her, raging at their idiocy, their laziness, the defence started to close, but it was too late, much too late; JoJo stood poised on the penalty spot, the goalkeeper lunged, then committed and dived for JoJo's feet. Too obvious and too late. JoJo stroked the ball backwards with the underside of her foot, watched the goalkeeper spread-eagled in front of her and side-footed the ball into the unguarded net. She turned, raised one hand in the air, grinned, looked over at the Bullet, raised both thumbs and walked back to the centre spot for the kick-off, while the boys on both teams stood and put their hands together in appreciation and, more importantly, respect.

The Dutch rallied, but it seemed that the energy had gone out of their game. The final whistle blew, and it was over. The usual handshakes, hugs and claps. And then the Dutch boys did a remarkable thing: they stood in a single line and clapped that single little girl who had come onto the pitch and beaten them, and everyone there knew that they had seen something special.

Shelley was the first to JoJo. Lucy and Kaas were there as well, Mickey and Jacko, Marianne even. The Bullet, Chris and Gilly all shook their heads, a little bit of respect, a little bit of wonder.

"Kid's got talent, kid's got talent," Chris said.

"Yeah, for sure, but she's got that work ethic; that's what's important," Dan Bullet said.

Kaas bowed and kissed JoJo's hand.

"Much respect, JoJo, much respect." JoJo's heart soared, and Shelley didn't have it in her to be even a tiny bit jealous. "We all have a good day, I think." Kaas smiled, spread his arms out. "A really GOOD day!" And then, poor old Kaas, just like Ricky had done on the pitch, collapsed on the floor clutching his leg. "Aah, cramp, cramp!" And then, "Ooh, stretch my leg, stretch it out!" Marianne was about to put up a warning hand, but it was too late. JoJo and Shelley together ran over to the writhing Kaas, and together, they grabbed hold of Kaas' ankle and attempted to stretch it out…and as they did so, Kaas erupted with a magnificent fart, probably as good and as loud as Bobby Carter the Farter had ever done. JoJo and Shelley looked at each other, stunned. And then they looked at Kaas…He grinned. "Aah, thank you so much, that feels much better. I think the cramp just fell out of my body."

"I wanted to warn you, but it was too late; it's Kaas' party trick," Marianne said, and she smiled wryly. "He's done it to me as well, and I fell for it just like you two. Kaas is so polite, yeah, and all the girls like him because he is so—how you say?—cool? And so, he gets away with murder."

JoJo and Shelley stared at each other; how to react? And then they reacted exactly as they had done a million times with Bobby Carter the Farter; the smile started, turned to a grin, turned to laughter. 'Sucked in and blown out in bubbles', neither said it, but they both knew it. Kaas stood and smiled. "Is OK, ladies? I hope so; it was a joke. I hope to see you both later," and he was gone.

"Lucy, Shelley, JoJo, Mickey, I'd like to introduce you to a friend of mine. I met him at the Olympics last year." Dan Bullet beckoned them. They all walked over. *Who's this guy?*

"So, guys, this is my friend, Rob Barel; he does a sport called triathlon, made the team for Holland for the Olympics because he was so bloody-minded. People told him that he was too old, that he'd been racing for too long, but Rob didn't listen to them; he went around the world doing as many qualifying races as he could, and he made the team for Holland; they couldn't not pick him. Rob is one of the most respected athletes in the world, yes, really…and he said that he'd like to meet you."

"Hi, guys, I used to swim with WaterFrenden swim club here who set all this up. Listen, ladies…And Mickey, yeah?" The four of them nodded back at the

Dutch Olympian, waiting. "OK, here goes: to go to the Olympics is the best thing that can happen to an athlete. You have to be supremely fit, of course, but you have to have something else; you have to be very, very mentally strong." They were intent, listening. "My friend Dan has told me all about you. I've watched all of you these three days: the swimming, running, track, football and the swim-run event, and as I said, my friend Dan has told me about you. He thinks that you all have something special, and so do I. I think you all have something special." A pause. "Use it, guys, use it well. If you choose to, there is nothing in the world that you cannot do, trust me."

The four of them looked at Rob Barel, rather they stared at him while they drank in his words. *This man has been to the Olympics; he knows what it's like! He's talking to us like we're mates almost...Oh my god.* Rob Barel went on, "What I believe you all have, all four of you, is the ability to cross over; what I mean is that you've all shown that it's not just one aspect you can succeed in. Mickey, Lucy, the swim and the run. OK, I know the swim can be better, but that's exactly what it is; it can be better; it will be better because Dan has told me when you started swimming. Your swimming will improve and improve. Shelley, you can swim as well, Dan told me that. But your athletics; run, throw, jump and hurdle so well, that is tremendous! And JoJo, I watched you play all three—no, four—matches. And I see that you can play as a forward and a midfielder and also in defence. Maybe I should see you in goal?" And they all laughed, of course.

"That's a rare ability, JoJo, and you have it; you really have it."

Rob Barel smiled. Then he went around to all of them and shook their hands, very formally. "Good luck, you guys, but you won't need it because you really do have that something special." And he was gone over to the Bullet, and they talked together and laughed, and then Chris and Gilly joined them.

And then Rob Barel, triathlon superstar, turned away from his group and came back to the four stunned youngsters. "Two things, guys, I don't think you'll need them because I believe that you've already decided." He waited a little, and then said, "You're one decision away from a totally different life than most people live; every single day, you make a choice." Rob smiled and walked away for the second time.

"Do you remember what Mr Warren said just before the end of term?" The three girls waited, and then Mickey said, "He said, 'Don't be someone else even if you admire them, just aim to be the best version of yourself.' I think that's what Rob just said as well."

A short silence then from all: "That's it, that really is it. I'm gonna be the best version of myself, starting right now." And not one of the girls spoke because they were already deciding exactly that.

Chapter Twenty-One
The Party

The thoughts were rushing through their heads—all four of them. Sometimes it's hard being just eleven years old and the grown-ups are bigging you up. Sometimes you just want to be left alone like, 'Can't it wait till I'm a bit older?' But then sometimes that realisation comes along, sometimes that realisation that people, really nice people that you respect, admire, like, love a little bit even; they believe in you. They want you to have the best life that you possibly can. And that realisation is so good. But it's also more than a little bit scary because all of a sudden, at eleven years old, you're being given a choice—a huge choice—to take the responsibility for your own future. And many—make that 'most'—kids, grown-ups, don't take that responsibility. For them, life is something that just happens along the way, and any particular circumstances that come along are just accepted; that's the way it is, get on with it. And that life becomes just a living out of, maybe, quiet desperation. How did I get here? What did I do wrong? Why don't good things happen to me?

Lucy

"You make a choice," that's what he said. "You make a choice." That Dutch guy, he was nice like Dan and Chris and Gilly. Do I have to make a choice? Do I? I gotta talk to someone; I really got to. Don't want anyone laughing at me, not that I think they would. They care, those guys, they really do care. Who do I talk to about it? Will anyone think I'm just stupid? Like this is important to me; honest, it is. I think I can do something, you know? I do now. I'm beginning to believe in myself. I gotta talk it out. I just have to. I need to. But there was only one person that Lucy could talk to about this particular decision; she already knew that.

Mickey

Amazing, just amazing. That was really nice of him, you know, the blonde guy, what he said to all of us. Reckon he meant it? Yeah, I do, actually. So, what if Dan Bullet got him to say all that stuff, he didn't have to do it, did he? Sounds good that sport he's talking about, what he went to the Olympics on, 'Tri-flon' or summink? Might have a go at that. Swimming ain't too good yet, but I reckon I can do stuff there; 'course I can.

Shelley

Oh my god! Can't believe it! Naah, yes, I can actually; now I can believe it. Weren't just Gilly or Mr Warren, it was Dan as well as the Dutch geezer, he was really kind, you know, didn't have to be like that, went out his way to help us. 'Fucking Hell!' Shelley allowed herself a little mind-swear 'Fucking Hell!' What a year, what a year. This summer, this trip. My mum ain't never been away, ain't never been out of England, probably not even out of London, really. And I'm in Holland, talking to Dutch people…like real, friends. Marianne is so nice, love that girl. And that Kaas is nice as well, well, you know. And Shelley allowed herself a little blush and a little fantasy. I dunno, what if he did fancy me? Sometimes I think he sort of does, and then he looks at JoJo just the same. Hope he ain't a scammer, don't think so, though. Maybe see if anything happens at the party tonight before we go home tomorrow.

JoJo

I played for the boys team, and I scored the winning goal! Yeah, I did! Me! Fucking me! And then all the boys, like all of them, told me I'd done really good. Even the Dutch kids like, even the Dutch kids said it! I am so lucky. I know I am. Gonna make the best use of it. No, I am this time. I am. 'One decision away from a totally different life', yeah, that's me now. I can, I will, I must. Kaas? I dunno, sometimes I think he fancies me. I really do…and then I see him look at Shell as well, and you know, like what's he thinking, what's he really thinking?

Lucy

"Mr Bullet…Dan, may I speak with you, please?" Lucy was being extremely formal without even realising it.

"'Course you can, Lucy, you all right? This sounds a bit serious."

"Dan, gotta ask you a question." And Lucy asked the question that had been bugging her for forty-eight hours. Dan thought and considered, then said, "No, I don't think so, Lucy, can't recall."

"OK, Dan, so…" And then Lucy asked the second part of the question to go along with part one.

Again, Dan Bullet considered carefully before answering, and then he smiled. "You know what, Lucy?" And then he stopped talking, smiled, nodded his head up and down in a 'yes' motion. "Yes, I think so, why not?" And just as she'd done before, Lucy leapt into his arms, and it was entirely right and proper that she did so.

It wasn't really a party as such; it had been billed as a goodbye get-together by the organisers, but all the kids knew it was a party, really; it was just that the organisers didn't know it.

They were standing around chatting and laughing. The CD player was on in the background, but no one was actually brave enough to get up and dance; you kidding me? Eleven and twelve years old and I'm going to dance in front of a load of other kids, yeah, right! Piss-take or what…but sometimes you just wish that you had the bottle to do it anyway. They were pretty much all wearing the 'party uniform', you know: jeans and a T-shirt and sweater, maybe a few still in tracksuits and sweatshirts; all the athletes were; Brits, Dutch, Belgium, French, and then Kaas arrived, and Kaas was wearing a suit! He was wearing a fucking suit! And because he was Kaas, he got away with it.

Actually, he more than got away with it because he had had the bottle to dare to be different. JoJo and Shelley looked at each other, shrugged shoulders, grinned. Marianne had said it, Kaas is cool, and boy, did he know it. Kaas' suit was light grey; he wore a light blue shirt and a dark blue tie, and he also wore a big smile—and it was the smile much more than the suit (although the suit certainly played a part) that got to JoJo and Shelley.

And Kaas could dance as well, just as cool as a mule, loose as a goose. Very gently, he started to move—by himself—around the floor. Nothing outrageous, very subtle, very absorbed in himself…But actually, watching for any reaction, any reaction at all. And about seventy-five per cent of the boys and around one hundred per cent of the girls there just wished they could dance like Kaas. The current song came to an end, and there was even a smattering of applause from the watchers. Kaas walked over to where TMRG and Jacko were standing. Mickey was the first to question. JoJo and Shelley were still stunned.

"How on earth, like where, like how do you do that? Where d'you learn to dance?"

"My mum, Mickey, my mum said that it was—how do you say?—a social skill, I think, is it? My mum said to me that it's worth a little bit of embarrassment, that as I get older, I'll be happy that I can dance a tiny bit." Then he asked, "Look, I teach you, yes?" Mickey shook his head 'no'. "JoJo, Shelley, you dance with me, yes?"

And how could the Kaas-smitten duo say no? Of course they couldn't. What if JoJo had said no and Shelley yes? Or the other way around? Don't even think about it; don't take the chance. So, very tentatively, JoJo and Shelley allowed themselves to be helped by Kaas, and the necessary placing of his hand to help move their bodies into the correct position was heaven. And then, they actually started to enjoy the dancing for its own sake. Of course, it was Kaas, but they could dance, oh man! And then Jacko joined in and then Marianne. And then because that initial dare had been taken, gradually the others—the Dutch, Brits, Belgium and French all started following Kaas' movements in a semblance of dancing. Even Mickey at Lucy's cajoling made the effort, and it wasn't too bad— not too bad at all.

And then it went bad, very bad indeed.

Lucy needed to go back to the dormitory, and Shelley went with her.

Kaas asked, "JoJo, maybe you like some fresh air?" And of course, JoJo definitely liked some fresh air. They walked outside. Kaas felt for JoJo's hand; he turned her towards him and kissed her, gently, then a little harder. And JoJo had absolutely no idea of what to do—no idea at all. So, she waited…And then she felt Kaas' hand under her T-shirt, like 'what the fuck!' *What do I do? What do I do? This ain't in the script. Yeah, I like him, but no, no, this ain't gonna happen!* JoJo pushed him away hard, and then ran off as the tears started. She couldn't go back into the lounge, not yet, not like this.

Lucy and Shelley got back from the dormitory. Kaas smiled at them. "Hi, Shelley, maybe you like a walk away from the sweaty bodies?" And Shelley most definitely liked a walk with Kaas away from the sweaty bodies; of course she did. This felt so right…But what was she going to say to JoJo?

It was no surprise when Kaas turned to kiss her; Shelley had been in similar situations down the estate, usually with the sixteen-year-old gang-bangers who thought that they could talk her into anything, like she was only a kid, and they were men; dealing drugs, wearing bling, gonna be rich and famous. And Shelley had dealt with them. But Shelley knew that this particular incident wasn't going to turn out like those ones; this was Kaas, and he was really nice. She returned his kiss. Oh god, it felt so right! And then, like JoJo (although she didn't know that), she felt Kaas' hands roving. Oh fuck! No worries, just tell him.

"No, Kaas, don't do that." She pushed his hands away. But Kaas didn't want his hands pushed away, and he persisted. Shelley pushed away from him. "I said not to do that, Kaas, all right?"

He shrugged and smiled. "Sorry." And as they resumed the kiss, Shelley felt his hands crawling down the front of her pants—no, this ain't gonna happen.

"Kaas, stop, stop now."

But Kaas didn't stop. Shelley pushed away from him, looked him in the eyes, and her eyes were dead. "I said 'stop', just stop or you're going to be sorry." And Kaas smiled and didn't stop. "I told you. I tried to be nice." Shelley took half a step back, looked at Kaas once again with her dead eyes, lifted her knee and, with great accuracy, kneed Kaas in the groin, hard. Kaas collapsed on the floor. "I told you, Kaas, I told you."

He lay there, groaning. "Shelley, Shelley, I'm sorry." Shelley, with a tear in her eye and not a backward glance, walked away.

"You all right, Shell? What's the matter? What happened?" Mickey saw the brimming eyes and knew it was bad. If whatever it was had got to Shelley, then it had to be bad.

"Shell?" Lucy said.

"Nothing, nothing really…oh shit, look, I'll tell you, but you promise me you won't do nothing, yeah? Promise?" So, Mickey promised, and Shelley told him, "Kaas tried it on with me, that's all. I told him, but he never listened." Mickey and Lucy just stood there. "You promised me, Mickey, you promised, remember? Please don't do nothing, please!" And then JoJo arrived; she'd managed to stop crying and wanted, needed, to be with her friends. And she saw Shelley and the tears, and she knew, knew immediately what had happened.

"He tried it with me n'all, Shell; he tried it on. I really liked him, like I REALLY liked him…ain't fair, just ain't fair."

Mickey Honey walked out of the door. *I'll fucking kill him; I fucking will!* Kaas was easing himself up from the ground.

"Hi, Mickey, you all right?" And there was that little bit of fear and uncertainty in his voice as he watched Mickey approach. Mickey smiled.

"Hi, Kaas." And then his face went dead. He lifted Kaas up and immediately threw him against the wall. One hand went around Kaas' throat, the other made a fist and lifted behind his head. Those almost forgotten East London estate instincts came flaring back…and then he remembered, he'd promised, promised Shelley.

Mickey dropped his fist. "You know what, Kaas? You know what? You disgust me, you really do. I thought you were a friend—a good friend. I liked you a lot. You were a laugh, a real laugh…and then you go and do that, you total wanker. My sister and her best friend—what! How dare you? I won't waste my time." And Mickey walked away as Kaas, with head drooped low, just stood there.

"He's gone, won't bother you again." Shelley and JoJo both hugged Mickey.

"You never done anything, Mickey? You didn't hurt him?" Shelley said.

"No, never touched him, didn't need to. You won't see him again." But Mickey was wrong. They did see Kaas again. And it was much sooner than they could have expected.

"JoJo, you all right?" They were in the dorm.

"I dunno, Shell, to be honest. I didn't know what to do. No, honest, I just didn't know. I've never done anything, like you know, sex an' 'at." A pause. "Shelley…You ever done it, like for real?"

"No, ain't gonna, not till it feels right, just don't want to. My mum says that I'll know when I want to, when I really want to. My mum gave me the big talk, you know? All like, 'It's your body, and it's your rules.' I thought I was going to be so embarrassed, but it was all right, actually. My mum's all right, really. She was only seventeen when she had me, and she said that I was the only good thing that came out of it. I ain't never seen my dad, don't want to, actually. I could never, never do what he done, basically just ran away 'cause he couldn't take the responsibility of being a dad. How could you do that, JoJo? I just couldn't. Thank god for my mum, so I s'pose that not having sex is a lot down to her. An' you seen the blokes who've tried it on with me? I'm eleven for god's sake, eleven! And they're sixteen and seventeen, and they certainly ain't gonna be someone I'll end up with, no way. I've seen the life I want; this last year has been amazing; Mr Warren, Gilly, Dan Bullet…And all us guys, of course, all good old TMRG."

And then Shelley started to chuckle, and JoJo looked at her. "JoJo, you know what Kaas tried to do? He tried to touch my minnie! Not a chance, I kneed him right in the bollocks!" And then JoJo started to chuckle as well, and all of a sudden, it wasn't too bad.

"Snuggle up?" JoJo nodded yes, and they snuggled up in bed.

They were up early to catch the coach back home to London. Marianne was waiting at the coach as the tired London kids started to make their way over.

"Hi, Shelley. Hi, JoJo."

"Hi, Marianne, that's nice of you to come and say goodbye." They exchanged kisses.

"JoJo, Shelley, Kaas told me what happened. He's a—how you say?—a fucking idiot?" And both JoJo and Shelley burst out laughing at the perfectly accented swear words coming from Marianne's perfect English accent. "Listen, Kaas wants to say sorry; he is sorry, and I believe him. I've known him for a long, long time; he's not all bad, but he's scared to come over in case you have a go at him. Can I tell him that you'll at least listen to him?"

"I dunno, Marianne, think he broke my heart a little bit," JoJo said. "Shell, what d'you reckon?"

"Please, Shelley," Marianne said.

"Oh, OK then, it'd better be good."

Kaas came from behind the coach; he was carrying two bunches of flowers, his face was grey, and he looked like he hadn't slept, which he hadn't.

"JoJo, Shelley, I am truly sorry. I'm ashamed of myself. I promise you that I've never done anything like that before; honestly, I haven't…Marianne?" And Marianne nodded to agree that, as far as she knew, Kaas hadn't done anything like that before. "I don't know how to explain."

A silence, then he said, "I thought I was supposed to do it, to try it. It was as if I was expected to try it. All the older boys say so…I am truly sorry." And Kaas held out the flowers, and it was the first time that JoJo and Shelley had ever been given flowers. And then Kaas started to cry, not loudly but with the tears streaming out of his eyes. "I really…am sorry." I words were coming out between the dry sobs. He turned and started to walk away, shoulders down and body still lurching from the sobs. Shelley and JoJo looked at each other.

Shelley nodded first, then JoJo. They walked after Kaas.

"Kaas?" He turned, not daring to look them in the eye but staring downcast at the ground. "All right, Kaas, but never again, right? Don't ever try it on again with someone who doesn't want to know."

"I won't, I promise you. I promise, I wouldn't." And then both girls did a remarkable thing, and they both knew that the other was thinking the same. They went to Kaas, and they kissed him softly on the cheek. "Bye Kaas. Bye Marianne. Thank you, Marianne." And they both got on the coach.

Part Three
Belief

Chapter Twenty-Two
Carpe Diem

It was different getting back together. Of course, it was. They looked at each other in their starched, slightly too big, slightly uncomfortable Stratford school uniforms, and they grinned. But they didn't laugh; to tell the truth, they were all a little apprehensive, make it a little scared. It wasn't juniors anymore; it was big school. No, it wasn't; it was Stratford Academy, and they all deserved to be there. All eight of them, of TMRG, had had those experiences in the summer, those experiences that make an impression, maybe even change you.

They were spread into different class groups; tutor groups they called them at Stratford. Ms Hajisoteris had explained the system at the first assembly—all those kids in the same year! But it was good nevertheless. All of TMRG barely saw each other during that first week; so much to learn, so much to find out, so many corridors and classrooms. All the lessons in the first year were in their tutor groups, but Ms Hajisoteris explained that as they progressed through the school and the years, there would be various options and that pupils would be helped and advised as to what particular subjects would be best for them: different subjects, different levels, different opportunities to seize life chances for each of them. Ms Hajisoteris had finished that first assembly with a quote.

"Now Year 7, I'm going to ask you a question: did any of you study Latin at junior school?" And not a hand went up, of course not. Latin? What's Latin? "Latin is an ancient language used by the Romans. There are many, many instances of Latin still being used now; it's the mother of many languages, Romance languages, European languages. Now the Romans had a saying, and that saying was, 'Carpe Diem'."

Ms Hajisoteris looked at her year group and smiled. "And Carpe Diem means 'seize the day'. Seize the day, boys and girls, seize every single day, and you will get the very best from your lives." And Ms Hajisoteris walked off the stage.

For Joshi and Alisha, the thought that summer was going to be boring, so boring, was quickly extinguished. Alisha and Joshi were introduced to real life by their mum and dad—the real life of working and earning a living. And they loved it. After moving into the chemists and the accommodation over the shop, their dad showed them the reality of life. The reality of phone calls and emails, when emails and electronic mail were still pretty new, of ordering and checking orders, of deliveries and checking deliveries. The realities of running a business. The whys and the hows and the whens and the 'how much does it cost?' became a day-to-day item. And they took to it like the proverbial duck to water.

Bobby and Eric had kept in touch through that long summer, and for Eric, it was a lifeline to sanity. Thrust into an alien culture where he didn't want to be, those almost daily emails (and how Eric thanked the inventor of emails even though he had no idea who it was) to Bobby had kept him in the loop, and even after he relaxed a little and became more assured about the house and the district and the extended family and the kids in the area, and truth be told, old Epic Eric found it initially difficult to understand and comprehend the voices and the lilts and the lingo, but he gradually acclimatised; he needed that contact with his 'real' home.

And old Epic Eric through that long hot summer was slowly but gradually beginning to make sense of who he could be, where he could go, what he could do. And very slowly, he opened his mind and his heart to Bobby Carter, and Bobby Carter found Eric's ideas extremely interesting. And Epic Eric's mum and dad were back together, and that was good—better than good.

And the summer camp kids, the Holland-bound kids. Well, you know that already. TMRG were ready to move to the next big thing.

And then there was the surprise—the big surprise. Lucy was walking in the corridor on day two, struggling to find the classroom where she should have been when she almost bumped into an adult.

"Oops, sorry, sir, wasn't looking where I was going, can't find my classroom." And then she looked up into the smiling, laughing face of Dan, the Speeding Bullet. "Dan? Dan! What you doing here?"

"Had to get a job, proper job, so the council told me that Stratford were looking for a swimming instructor, a swimming teacher. Take some of the physical education lessons; non-swimmers and some of the older pupils who opt for swimming in PE and games and then run a swimming club after school as well…Fitted in well for me…also meant that I could keep in touch with some of my favourite people, Gilly and Chris, of course…But some of my very favourite young people as well." So, Lucy just put her still little girl arms around Dan Bullet and hugged him—almost to death.

"So, there's going to be a swimming club, Dan?"

Dan very slowly and exaggeratedly winked back to show Lucy that he hadn't forgotten her questions, hadn't forgotten at all, and Lucy smiled her big Lucy smile right back at him. "Thanks, Dan," she whispered.

First week done, Mickey had called them altogether at the end of the day.

"'S'all right, innit? Mr Warren was right; he's always right. He said that Stratford would be good for us, said he believed we deserved to be here if we worked for it, and we did, didn't we?"

Nods of the head and smiles. "So I reckon what we should do is this: I reckon that we should meet up every Friday after school. With all this stuff going on and in different groups, well, we might not see each other too much in school and even after school what with homework and clubs 'n stuff. So, I reckon that, yes, every single Friday, we need to meet up just 'cause we're TMRG, and I will always want to be a part of TMRG." Mickey's voice very nearly cracked. "I had the best time with all you guys at junior school with Mr Warren, but down the estate as well as when we were playing out and doing the figure of eight, you know." Mickey's voice very nearly cracked again. Shelley took control.

"Mickey's dead right, you know. I like it here at Stratford already; I really do. Ain't saying it's easy, ain't saying it's as good as Mr Warren's class, 'course it ain't. but it IS good, and I'm gonna do what Ms Hajisoteris said, you remember? She said 'Seize the Day', and that's what I'm gonna do…OK, all of you put your hands in the middle." And they all obeyed Shelley.

Eight hands outstretched on top of each other. Shelley smiled at all of them. "Might sound a bit silly coming up, but I mean it anyway." They all listened carefully. She started, "I'm in TMRG, and I'll always be in TMRG." Shelley gazed at them until the penny dropped, seven voices together. "I'm in TMRG, and I'll always be in TMRG."

Shelley then said, "And I'll never ever let my mates down." The seven repeated. "And every Friday, we will meet up, every Friday unless something makes it absolutely impossible." The seven repeated again. Then Shelley laughed as the hands dropped away. "And I don't care about having to be a bit grown-up 'cause I'm going to kiss every single one of you." So, Shelley did indeed kiss everyone there, and there may have been a few tears in a few eyes, but who cared?

And of course, Stratford Academy was different from their junior school—very different indeed. It was so much bigger; actually, it was huge. From a two-form entry primary school, with between fifty and sixty pupils in each year group, into an eight form entry of between two hundred and two hundred and forty pupils, their year group was as big as the whole of the four years in junior school. Different lessons, different classrooms. No more staying with one teacher in the same room, oh no. Now it was travelling with your tutor group to different classrooms for different lessons: science laboratories, foreign language labs, a gym and a sports hall. But when you're eleven years old, you very quickly assimilate and acclimatise. And the extra activities and clubs and sports—something for everybody, something for every member of that exclusive club, TMRG. And TMRG took every opportunity. Of course, they did. Mr Warren had taught them that, and for some of them, Dan Bullet and Gilly Ring had also taught them.

Ms Hajisoteris' phrase, 'Carpe Diem', became their own catchphrase. "What you done today, Shell?"

"Oh, just carpe'd that old diem a little bit." And they'd all laugh. There was swimming club, gymnastics, cross-country, dance; there was debating, science, chess, and TMRG threw themselves into it.

That growing up stuff accelerates at secondary school; of course, it does. Eleven-year-olds look at eighteen-year-old sixth formers in the same school and the realisation hits them, 'That's gonna be me soon...Jeez!'

The four of them who'd been to summer school and then Amsterdam had their plans already. Maybe they weren't defined exactly, but they were there, and they were in place.

And the four who hadn't been to summer school, Epic Eric, Bobby Carter, Alisha and Joshi, also had their plans set out. Maybe they weren't defined exactly, but they were there, and they were certainly in place.

That final primary school year with Mr Warren had prepared them all...They had learnt to take responsibility for themselves, to accept that most things would not be easy, that continued hard work plus a fair bit of frustration was required to meet that final destiny. 'My one precious life' may not have been on their lips, the words might not have been spoken or even really thought as in words, but that idea was in their minds—in all of their minds. They were desperate to see

172

Mr Warren again, desperate. "We'll go after school, go back and see him!" And it was Shelley, forever wise, who cautioned against it.

"Wouldn't be right, wouldn't be right at all. Mr Warren taught us to take responsibility, taught us to grow up really, so it wouldn't be right to go back just yet; it would be like saying we still needed him when he's taught us not to." And Shelley was right, of course. And the others knew that. "Mind you, I'm not saying NEVER go back, am I? Maybe half term, yeah? I think that would be appropriate…And you know what? I'm pretty sure Mr Warren would like that; he'd like to see us all again." And once again, Shelley was correct in the decision and also that Mr Warren would like—make that 'love'—to see them all again.

And so that term was a coming to terms with starting to grow up—to grow up properly. They threw themselves into Stratford Academy, took advantage of everything that was there. Chose their clubs and societies, tasted them, sucked some of them in and some they blew out in bubbles and then chose what felt right for them. Swimming and cross-country felt right for Lucy, Mickey and JoJo. The added advantage of the Speeding Bullet gave that little bit of reconnection to Mr Warren and to Gilly and to that magic summer they'd shared. And, of course, Lucy still had that shared secret and ambition with Dan Bullet. But nobody else, not even Mickey, knew that particular secret and ambition.

JoJo went to the trials for football club and the school football team, and JoJo wasn't that surprised at all to find that she was the only girl there. There was a little bit of questioning, a little bit of 'I don't think so' from some of the boys, but that didn't last long, didn't last long at all. Not when the male teacher who was taking responsibility for that Year 7 team and year head Ms Hajisoteris said that team practice was open to all and that if they thought JoJo wasn't good enough for the team, then there wouldn't be any problem at all because if she was good enough, she was in, and if she wasn't good enough, then she wouldn't make it. And the two teachers had a little grin and also a little bit of self-righteousness knowing that they'd done the correct thing for sex equality, even though they knew that JoJo had no chance of making the team, would probably get bored and fed up very quickly and would drop out of practice.

And very quickly, the two teachers found out and the entire boys team members found out just how wrong you can be for judging people by long-held prejudices. At that first practice, JoJo showed, with the various skills and drills that they warmed up with, that she was entirely deserving of being there, of being at practice. And then after the warm-up and the splitting into two teams, JoJo became an instant sensation, almost an instant hero. JoJo scored twice. JoJo could have scored two more but chose to lay the ball off to two teammates. JoJo bossed the team (her team) very quickly, and the team listened to her and learnt from her and admired her, and one or two even started to worship her. And JoJo took it all in her stride because she knew exactly what she was doing.

She knew exactly what she was good at. And she knew exactly where she expected her one precious life to lead her, just as long as she put on the hard hours and the hard miles, and JoJo was more than prepared to do exactly that. And when the football team was put up on the sports noticeboard for their first inter-school match for Saturday, there was no surprise at all when next to JoJo's name was 'V.C.' and no surprise when several of the boys in the team came up to congratulate JoJo on being vice-captain. What JoJo didn't know but eventually found out was that the PE teacher had quietly and individually spoken to the majority of the team and almost half had felt she thoroughly deserved the accolade.

Shelley threw herself into everything. Swimming, of course, because Dan was there but also because she absolutely loved the freedom that she felt in the water. And then there was gymnastics club, and although Shelley was by no means a natural gymnast, she had that body-awareness that she'd gained from the swimming, hurdling, jumping, running and throwing. And Shelley was building that all-round fitness and mobility that would stand her in the best possible stead when her (as yet) unrealised and unspoken ambition would creep into her mind as a possibility.

She relished the cross-country club, ran with the boys and the girls, and at that age, there was still no enormous demarcation between boys' and girls' performances. That would come later when the full blasts of body development, maturity and raging hormones would appear on the scene. And anyway, Mickey and Lucy were in the cross-country club as well (of course they were), and JoJo would turn up whenever she was able, given the training that she was undergoing with the school football team and the demands of the Spurs Academy, and it brought back those lovely memories of only a few months back when their figure of eight runs were at least a weekly occurrence.

And Mickey and Lucy? Well, they pretty much did everything together. To all of them who'd decided that the physical world was for them, it seemed that they didn't have a spare moment, and they loved it. They loved the busyness, the involvement, the need for careful timetabling to fit everything in before school, during lunchtime and immediately after school.

For Joshi and Alisha, Stratford Academy was a paradise. Their natural intelligence and curiosity were on perpetual alert and led them to new discoveries. To join the science club was almost a given; the rapid introduction during that summer into the whys and wherefores of choosing a particular product, a particular chemical or medication had been explained by both their parents, and their understanding was—if not immediate—then very close to that immediacy. As brother and sister, they grew closer, became as much friends as siblings. Alisha's natural sense of humour and her interpretation of the absolute ridiculousness of life generally started to implant on Joshi. His sensible exterior had long masked a sense of humour akin to his sister's, and with Alisha's encouragement, it began to exert itself more and more.

Joshi became more gregarious, more outspoken. His classmates began to grow quiet when he spoke because they knew that often, make that frequently, there would be a sting in the tail of his words. The school debating society beckoned, and after much giggling and discussion, both Alisha and Joshi joined. For a couple of weeks, they listened, drank in the atmosphere and learnt the procedures. Most of the society club members were a little bit older than the twins. Even at secondary school age, it takes a lot of nerve to stand up, talk, debate and make your point in public, and most pupils in their first year are reluctant to make that stand. On the final week of that first half term, it was time. The subject:

'This house believes that natural talent will ensure success naturally.'

The twins listened closely and carefully to the proposer and opposer, made notes, weighed up the arguments, the pros and cons. Joshi and Alisha looked at each other. Joshi nodded, and a tentative hand crept up. "The house recognises the lady." Very proper, very formal. Alisha stood up.

"My name is Alisha Buzdar, and I am a Year 7 pupil at Stratford." Alisha spoke clearly, not too loudly to ensure that everyone there had to concentrate on her words. "Being accepted into Stratford Academy is one of the things I am most proud of in my life. I worked hard, and so you might say that my natural talent and ability has ensured success in my being here. My brother sitting next to me is Joshi." Joshi gave a quietly embarrassed small wave. "And I know that he is as proud as I am of being here—twin natural ability." A small laugh from the listeners as they appreciated the use of 'twin'. "Twin natural success."

Alisha paused for effect. "But you see, it isn't a natural path, not at all; Joshi and I live on the Grange Estate, and if we hadn't been accepted here at Stratford, we would have gone to Grange Secondary. We were at Riverside Junior School, Joshi and I, and so were fifteen other pupils now here at Stratford. Seventeen of us took the entry examinations, and seventeen of us got accepted." Her voice rose now to emphasise the points. "So all seventeen of us had that natural talent, that natural ability to succeed?"

Alisha looked around the room, almost everyone there older than she, and everyone entranced by her words. *Got some bottle, that first year kid, got some bottle, gotta admire her.* "All seventeen of us were in the same class, and no, it wasn't streamed at junior school; so why us? Why seventeen of us, all-natural talent?"

She shook her head. "I think not; I very much think not…So, what did we have, all of us that got us here? What we all had was the same teacher; his name is Mr Warren, and he made us believe in ourselves; he made us go for it, so, yes, natural talent will take you some way, but it's the person or the people who make you utilise that talent that's the difference!"

Alisha sat down, and then one of the senior girls, seventeen or eighteen years old, stood, smiled and started to applaud, and a lot of others joined in. "Well spoken, Alisha, very well spoken…welcome to the debating society." Joshi looked at his twin sister and, without any embarrassment at all, hugged her tight.

Over those first few weeks, old Epic Eric had started to outline his plans and his dreams to Bobby Carter. The ideas were more than a little tangled, jumbled and confused, but they were there nonetheless, and Bobby recognised that. What both of them would have loved would be that there was a business studies group, although the phrase 'business studies' didn't appear in their thinking; it was just that they were seeking guidance, advice, input on where they could see their precious lives leading them. They both joined the chess club; it wasn't a rational decision of planning, more that they felt they needed something to do; they needed to belong. The teacher responsible for the club helped them in all sorts of ways, none more so than the necessity of forward thinking, forward planning.

Both Bobby and Epic bought into that. In those few weeks their strategies, which had largely been taken from playing draughts and knowing the basic chess moves, accelerated enormously. They listened to advice, acted upon it and shared their ideas and the 'whys' and 'what was the point'. Their thinking and planning—not only in the game of chess but in life—became more rational, more an understanding of what was going to be a long haul, but both boys had no doubt now that their ideas and plans were gradually forming and they were going to be successful.

Shelley had other things to deal with along with swimming and running and gymnastics, and, because she was who she was and had dealt with these things before, Shelley dealt with them. "You're so pretty, Shell!" Lucy had said it.

And because it was Lucy and not one of the would-be gangies, Shelley had laughed and replied, "Yeah, thanks Lucy, but there's a lot of pretty girls out there!" But now Shelley was in secondary school, and there were older boys—a lot of older boys—out there. Shelley attracted attention, a lot of attention. *How the fuck do they know my name!*

Shelley, like the others, rarely swore now, but she allowed herself the mind-swearing that only she could hear. *How do they know my name?* And the answer was because they (the boys) noticed Shelley, really noticed her, and so they found out her name and made it their job to say 'hello', 'hi, Shelley' and hoped for a response. And Shelley would give the response, 'oh, hi, there. You OK?', and that individual boy would go away just a little happier and would start dreaming of when—not if, when—he and Shelley would be going out as boyfriend and girlfriend. Shelley had stopped being pretty. Shelley ("We love Shelley with the big fat belly!") had transcended from pretty to beautiful.

Shelley had a presence about her, had always had that presence, which had been nurtured and honed even at junior school and down the estate with hoodies hitting on her all the time. But it had become a bit different now. These older boys—two, three, four, even five years older—were (what her mum would have called) 'nice boys'. They were polite; they were respectful; they didn't make suggestive, double-entendre comments. Well, most of them didn't.

Shelley had entered that period of awkward early puberty as just about everyone—boys and girls—did, with a little bit of fear and a lot of wonderment. Those mornings of dreading waking up because 'how the fuck did that happen?', changes that seemed to have occurred overnight. Shelley had lived through those times and had hated the much-earlier-than-most changes to her body, had wanted desperately to stay the little skinny, flat-chested, no hips, hate the body-hair kid that all her friends still were. But it had happened; of course, it did, and now she was entering that world of being happy in her own body while most of her friends were struggling with the changes that she'd endured. Shelley wasn't aware of it, but she had that golden glow that attracted everyone around her.

177

They wanted to be in Shelley's company because…well, because she was nice and she made them feel good about themselves. Shelley had that oft-mentioned but seldom realised attribute, charisma. And because she had it and wasn't really aware of it, it made it all the stronger and all the more attractive. Of course, all the boys fancied her! They were teenage boys, after all, and their hormones were jangling and buzzing and fizzing around ninety-nine per cent of their waking hours.

But not Mickey Honey; he and Shelley had that connection, and both wondered how that had come about. Or rather they didn't wonder, it had just happened somehow. They'd always been close, always been close before that horrible time when girls and boys start to notice each other as boys and girls, notice each other as the opposite sex. But that hadn't happened somehow with these two. They referred to each other as 'my brother' and 'my sister', and it was true.

They were walking to the swimming club after school now: Shelley, Mickey and Lucy. Shelley and Lucy had become even closer; Lucy knew that Shelley posed no threat at all to her relationship (*What a weird word*, she thought) with Mickey. They were approaching the pool and gym changing area with so many pupils rushing in and out, rushing to get changed for whatever physical activity they were involved in. "Hi, Shelley."

"You all right, Shell?"

"See you later, Shell." There were maybe a dozen greetings to Shelley, maybe one or two to Lucy and Mickey. Mickey and Lucy grinned at her.

"And please welcome Miss Congeniality!" Mickey laughed happily for her, as did Lucy. And then they both stopped laughing because they saw Shelley had tears in her eyes. They stopped walking immediately. If anybody had made a member of TMRG cry, then something needed to be done about it.

"Shelley, what's the matter, baby?" asked Lucy, six inches smaller in height than Shelley (although that height difference wouldn't last), was the big, caring sister straightaway. "Come here, you," and Lucy's arms were around Shelley while Shelley sobbed quietly into her shoulder. For once, Mickey just stood there, no idea of what to do.

"Shell, you all right? Somebody done something to you? What's happened, Shelley? Tell me, tell me and Lucy."

"Oh, Lucy, I don't know where I am. I dunno what I'm doing; everyone's so nice to me here, like everyone, and I ain't done anything for it, not anything. It's like all the boys fancy me. I ain't stupid, 'course I see that. But I just don't care, you know? It sort of feels like I have to live up to who they think I am, and I'm just me. I still feel like I'm that little kid in junior school hanging onto Mr Warren's words, like everything's gonna be all right now 'cause Mr Warren said so…You know what I mean?" Mickey and Lucy smiled; Lucy squeezed Shelley a little tighter.

"Yeah, know exactly what you mean, Shell, really do." Lucy paused and deliberated; she knew that what she said next was pretty much going to be important. "But Shelley, all that stuff we did in the summer, the training and then going to Amsterdam, that was all about the beginning to grow up; it was most definitely what Mr Warren had said all the time; you know about getting what you deserve because you work hard for it and you keep going when it's tough, yeah? Well, we did all that, and I know exactly what you mean. I do, honest.

"I never thought I'd be here in grammar school. I never thought I'd be in another country. I never thought I'd actually be good at running; never thought I'd ever be a swimmer, and I'm not yet, but I'm going to be. I really am going to be." Lucy thought again of that secret and that dream that she and Dan Bullet shared. "So, I really do understand, Shell; honest, I do. You're my best mate; you're like a sister to me. Really, you are. All that stuff in Amsterdam, you looked after me; you done everything for me when I was terrified, like I was really terrified, and you did it. You made me calm down; you made me realise that…well, you know, that it was a part of life…you deal with it, don't you? Everyone deals with it." There was a really long pause from Lucy now, really long.

Mickey and Shelley stayed silent, then Lucy said, "We are so lucky! No, honest, we really are so lucky! Easy to forget where we could be now, what we could be doing now, but we ain't, are we? If Mr Warren hadn't been there when we needed him and we didn't know then that we needed him, did we? Well, if he hadn't turned up, you know we'd be down the comp, just accepting that's what we were meant to do, just go on living a sort of life that we'd all do 'cause that's what we were supposed to…Well, that ain't me anymore, Shell; that ain't any of us—not just us three but all of TMRG. You see what Alisha and Joshi are doing in the debating club? All the big kids listen to them when they get up to speak; honest, they really do.

"Eric and Bobby, they're like the intellectuals in the chess club! Can you imagine, old Epic Eric an intellectual! Shit man, oops, sorry! But you know, and

JoJo! Look at her, just look at her! All the boys in the football team are in love with her already, you know? And she is just so cool about it, so cool. We're that little bit special. We are, mind you; we've always been that little bit special, haven't we?"

Lucy laughed out loud, then said, "Listen to me, just listen to me! But we are, you know, we ARE special. And I know exactly who to thank for that...I am so glad we're going back to see Mr Warren on Friday, so looking forward to it, honest!" And another long pause. "Shell, don't be sad, please don't be sad 'cause it makes me and Mickey sad as well...Remember what Mr Warren and Gilly and Dan were saying to us all summer and then in Amsterdam as well...well, they said a whole load of stuff, but what it all came down to was that they believed in us; they believed that we really were something special, and if Mr Warren and them said that, then I totally believe them. You gotta do it as well, Shell. I look at you and everything: what you do, how you blank off the posers who are trying it on with you...Shell, you're amazing; honest, you're amazing. That athletics stuff in summer and then Amsterdam, how you dealt with Kaas...shit man, awesome!" And they all laughed then, but it was a bit of a ragged laugh as their minds flashed back to that 'awful night'.

"Shelley, we're going to be fine...no, we're going to be special!"

And if Lucy had known just how special they were going to be, she might not have said it out loud in case she put the jinx on it.

Shelley hugged Lucy really tight, didn't say anything, just hugged her. And then Shelley hugged Mickey as well, and they walked into the changing rooms and then onto the poolside. And all three of them hugged Dan Bullet, even Mickey hugged him without really knowing why. But actually, they did know why, and without saying anything, Dan knew why as well. He realised that a bridge had been approached and crossed successfully. And Shelley, Lucy and Mickey had one of their best swimming sessions ever.

Chapter Twenty-Three
Cakes and Cokes

Chris Warren was waiting for them on that Friday. JoJo had called into her old junior school that week and asked if it was OK for them to visit, and Chris Warren had agreed immediately. Jeez, how he'd missed those kids! Of course, he had his new class now, still with Year 6, of course. And the kids in his new class loved him already. They were getting and feeling that full force that TMRG had felt the year before. but Chris missed his first-ever teaching class; they were special.

Gilly was there as well; she'd asked Chris if it would be OK because she missed them as well, especially missed the four that had been with her in the summer and in Amsterdam, couldn't wait to see them again, and she had a few things that she wanted to share with them.

The eight of them walked into their old school and into their old classroom. They were all wearing the Stratford Academy school uniform, with Chris and Gilly thinking, *Oh my god, how grown up they look!* They saw the cakes and glasses of Coca Cola on the teacher's desk and went to their chairs in their old desks and sat down without even realising they had made that unconscious decision. There was a little initial embarrassment, which quickly disappeared, and then they were all talking at once about swimming, running, gymnastics, debating society, science club and chess club.

"How's the football, JoJo?"

"I made the team, sir. I made the boys team!"

"Sir, Mr Warren, JoJo's too modest; she's vice-captain of the team, honest! She was voted as vice-captain! All the boys voted for her! Can you believe that the boys wanted her as their vice-captain! And they've had a really good start to the season. It ain't only the local schools; they play on Saturday mornings as well in the London league, and they're doing really well…But JoJo can't always play on Saturdays."

"Why's that, JoJo?" But Mr Warren knew the answer to that before he asked.

"'Cause JoJo's playing for Spurs, sir. She's playing for the girls academy team; sometimes we get to go and watch her up at Enfield, where Spurs training ground is, Mr Warren. JoJo's one of the best in the team; really, she is."

"How was Jamaica, Eric?" Chris Warren grinned at Eric because he was anticipating the answer.

"Me g'wan hometown, teacher mon, me g'wan good in Kingston!" And they all laughed, but then old Epic Eric stopped. "Sir, I hated it. I really didn't like it. I'm a Londoner, aren't I? All that stuff I was doing last year, all the chat, what a mug I was; didn't know how lucky I was being here, all my mates." Epic Eric spread his arms at all of them. "Didn't realise how lucky I was to have these friends…and you, sir, miss. I really mean that. Found out just being over there how lucky I am to be here where I belong with my friends…but it was good in a way, made me grow up a lot. Made me have a big think about what I want to do with my life, yeah, really got me thinking." Eric looked over at Bobby, smiled, then said, "We got plans, me and Bobby." A pause, then he added, "Thank you, sir. Thank you, miss."

"Everyone treats us with respect, Mr Warren; just because we're the kids from the bad side of town, no one cares. They take us for who we are, for what we do. Mr Warren, Alisha stood up in debating club, like she's only a first year and she had the bottle to get up and talk…and everybody, like everybody, listened to her, listened properly. And one of the sixth form girls clapped and talked to us afterwards. Said how good Alisha was, said she looked forward to hearing us, both of us, talk again. You know what that did to our confidence? Amazing, sir, amazing." Joshi stopped talking, then added, "But it was great, sir. The sixth formers, they're grown-ups, and they treat us like we're the same as them…like everyone says, thank you, Mr Warren, thank you for getting us there!" And that was a big speech from Joshi.

"I had a bit of a meltdown last week, Mr Warren." Shelley smiled, but there were still elements of sadness in that smile. "And you know who got me through it? Lucy and Mickey, that's who. Thing is, Mr Warren, it was Mickey and Lucy, but if they hadn't been right there, then it could have been, naah, not could have been, would have been Eric or Bobby or Joshi or Alisha or JoJo, Mr Warren. D'you remember when you were telling us about you and Dan in the Royal

Marines? About how you knew the people you could rely on? Well, yeah, that's me; I know, I absolutely know I can rely on these guys, all of them, always have, always will. They have never, ever let me down. Maybe take the piss a bit—sorry, sir, sorry, miss—but you know, yeah? It was like, I don't really want to grow up, don't really want to be a proper grown-up, all those responsibilities, have to stop having a laugh, don't want to do that. And then Lucy and Mickey made me see that it don't have to be like that; we can choose what we want to be, choose how we want to live, yeah?"

And the other seven TMRG members all nodded their heads because they all knew exactly what Shelley was talking about because they had all thought it and felt it too. "It was you, sir, and you, miss, you told us that we could be whoever we wanted to be, like we really could. And like nobody, nobody ever had made us feel like that before." Shelley looked at all of them. "That's right, yeah? Right, innit?" And the smiles and the nods and the yeahs made it absolutely one hundred per cent totally true.

"Oh, Shelley, thank you so much, sweetheart—am I allowed to call you 'sweetheart' now?" And they all laughed, of course. "Having you guys in my class last year, my first ever class, remember?"

Of course they remembered. "It made it special—really special. I used to look forward to coming to work, and I bet there's not a lot of people who can say that. You guys gave me so much more than I could ever give you, so much more." He paused for an instant. "You're right, Shelley; it was a bit like me and Dan and the others in the Marines; you know very quickly what people are like…and you treat them the way they deserve. And you guys deserved a lot, probably the word I'm looking for is 'respect'."

Shelley, Lucy, JoJo and Alisha couldn't help themselves, and Mickey, Joshi, Eric and Bobby wished that they couldn't help themselves, but you know…got up and went over to Mr Warren and once again hugged him, and then with Shelley leading them, they went over to Gilly and hugged her just as tightly. And Gilly dissolved into tears as well.

"Cake anyone?" Chris Warren took charge. And while they were eating and drinking, Mr Warren said, "Listen, I knew that you'd all made a successful start, you know why? OK, Ms Hajisoteris has kept in touch, not a lot, just a couple of times. And she's said that our junior school should be very proud of what our pupils have already achieved at Stratford already. You guys, of course, but all the other pupils from our school. That was such a lovely email to get, made my day, honest."

They sat at their old junior school class desks and drank coke and ate cake. And they chatted to each other, and they chatted to Gilly and Chris, and they had never felt closer. And then it was Gilly Ring's turn.

Chapter Twenty-Four
Sisu

"Loved the Amsterdam trip. Sorry, Eric, Bobby, Alisha, Joshi, I know you weren't there, but it was good! Great to hear that Spurs have followed up on you, JoJo, and you three are still swimming and running with the school, yes? It must have been a real surprise when you saw Dan there as well! I'm sure he's looking after you all?" Nods of agreement, then he said, "My club, Vicky Park, are trying to tie in some stuff with Stratford Academy, you know. Any kids that the teachers think are good enough and have potential, they're going to suggest that those pupils come to us for extra training. It's a bit of an 'everyone wins' scenario; it's good for the club to have sort of talent scouts out there, and it's good for the school because if you do well when you're representing the school, then it looks good for them. And guess who got recommended? Yeah, right, first time without even opening your mouths! I know it's a busy time for everyone, getting used to a new school and trying to fit everything in, sort of juggling loads of stuff, but we would really like you to come down to Vicky Park for training if you'd like to."

And just like that, the enthusiasm that had been a little subdued because of all the changes in their lives was rekindled. It had still been there, but it had been bubbling under, and now Gilly had reignited it.

"Love to, miss."

"Thanks, miss, I mean thanks, Gilly."

"Are we good enough, Gilly?" And it was a most emphatic 'yes' as the response.

"Are you doing any foreign languages at Stratford?" They looked at Gilly.

"Yes, miss…Gilly, we do Spanish this year, and then there's an option for next year; not sure, but I think you can do French or Italian; some of the sixth form do Chinese as well! I think it's called 'Mandarin' or something," JoJo answered for all of them.

"So, you don't do Finnish?" They all stared at Gilly, and Gilly smiled at them. "Of course you don't. I'm only joking; there's only one Finnish word that I know; it's 'Sisu'."

They waited. "And it doesn't have an exact translation into English; it sort of means, 'guts', 'determination', 'resilience', 'never giving in', 'keeping going'. I think you see what I'm getting at, yeah?" They were spellbound listening to Gilly, well, it was back to listening to 'Miss Ring' when they felt as they did then. "Now I know that I didn't teach you; Chris did, and I was jealous; no, honestly, I was. He talked about you all the time, about how you were getting on, about how you all supported each other, about how you were taking charge of your own lives, that you'd all made up your own minds about how you were going to live your lives. And you know what? I was doubly jealous; no, that's the wrong word. I was envious, envious because you had that vision of where you were going, that you were all growing in confidence. Now I know that you'd all say that it was Chris who'd put that stuff into place, am I right?"

Nods all around, but not a word spoken. "And I'm sure he did; of course, he did. But the crucial element is that you chose to listen; you chose to take it all on board; you chose to take control. There's a hell of a lot of kids; actually, there's a hell of a lot of adults, who wouldn't have been brave enough to do that…but you were brave enough, and you had the guts and determination and resilience, and you never gave in; you always kept going…always, and I know I shouldn't say this, shouldn't even think about saying it, but I love you all to bits…truly, I do."

And all that got to the boys as well; Mickey and Bobby had tears in their eyes for the first time that they could remember.

And so it began: four sports junkies and four academics, and if you'd ever called Bobby and Eric 'academics', then they would have looked at you blankly…)

"Miss…Gilly…I'd do anything for you; honest, I would. I'll never forget what you did for me out there in Amsterdam, never ever. You never panicked, never told me off, just helped me when I really needed it…Never forget that, miss, not ever." Lucy, of course.

"Lucy's right, miss, don't get me wrong 'cause I'd never be disrespectful, but you were like a big sister, you know? Like you'd been there, done it and got the badge. So yeah, just like a big sister…Or what a big sister should be like…Miss, is that all right? Honest, I don't mean to be rude; it's honestly what I feel," Shelley said.

"You came and watched me, miss, came and watched all my matches when you could. You didn't have to do that, just taking us all out there, you know? That was brilliant, but you came and watched me play, made me feel important, made me feel like it was all worth it, and it was most definitely worth it," said JoJo.

"Gilly…miss, I gotta say something too. That stuff, you know, all the running training? Changed my life, well, I think it's changed my life. Always liked running, always wanted to be a good runner, still want to. Going to do everything to try. And you saying we're good enough to get extra, proper training, well, yeah, say it again…changed my life, miss, can't thank you enough; really, I can't."

Then Mickey did a most unlike-Mickey thing; big hard Micky Honey, who would call out and front out the big kids, the ones who thought they were gangsters, went over to Gilly Ring and hugged her properly for the first time, and it felt so good to him…and to Gilly, like it was absolutely the right thing to do. It was a barrier broken, if Mickey was uncool enough to hug Gilly, then so could Eric, Bobby and Joshi. It was a big step; it was a very big step. For all of them.

The kids had all gone home, hugs all around once again, boys as well as the girls. Chris and Gilly were basking in a self-righteous glow, quite rightly.

"I think we did something good, didn't we, Gilly?" Gilly nodded, not quite trusting herself to speak, still thinking of the words that had been said, the amazing compliments. "So I'd like to say something as well…" Chris Warren got out of his chair, walked over to Gilly Ring, went down on one knee, then said, "Gilly, I love you to bits. I truly do, Gilly. Please will you marry me?"

Chapter Twenty-Five
"You Bought the Ticket"

Fitting everything in was difficult to start with; they became professional jugglers, juggling school work with school clubs and teams with Vicky Park athletics training, as well as keeping up the swim sessions with Dan Bullet. JoJo joined in as well, and it was double tough for JoJo with the travelling up to Spurs Academy for training. But JoJo loved being with her mates, and TMRG were going to be together forever…weren't they?

The running and athletics skills sessions were tough but not so tough that Mickey, Lucy and Shelley didn't enjoy them. Certainly not so tough that they didn't want to go again; the exact opposite, after every session and the initial fatigue, they were looking forward to the next one. And it was great, just great having Gilly there to help and to coach; they created that lovely bond of mutual respect and pure friendship that only athletes and coaches can recognise and understand. And Chris Warren was there as well sometimes, and, of course, they all still adored him. Gradually, session by session, day by day, week by week, month by month, they all improved. Their first term at Stratford Academy came and went. Christmas holidays flashed past in a blur, and then it was cold, cold January and—what is laughingly called—'Spring' term.

It was a given that Mickey, Lucy and Shelley would all be in the school cross-country team; they'd earned their selections very early on during the training sessions and the PE lessons. There was little doubt that Lucy was the best distance runner in the school year. Mickey was right up there, jockeying with another couple of the boys for bragging rights, while Shelley was thereabouts but didn't find the new bumps and curves arriving on her body best-suited for distance running. JoJo had squeezed into the team; perhaps unconsciously, her PE teacher had seen the connection with Lucy and Shelley and given her the go-ahead.

The London Schools Championships in any sport is a big deal; the sheer number of kids in schools and the intensity of the competition in every aspect of life in London makes it so. And it's a stepping-stone to national competition. If you win London, then you're in with a good chance for the English schools. Not that the English schools competition was on the immediate horizon for any of our heroes; first year kids don't go to English schools; second and third years (that's Year 8 and 9) are the first age group of competition, then Years 10 and 11, and finally the sixth form pupils, years twelve and thirteen.

It was the first real competition since that lovely Amsterdam trip that they looked back on and talked about all the time; most conversations started with a "Do you remember when…?" And they'd fall around, laughing as the memories came flooding back. Not all the memories were good, of course. But that final meeting with Kaas had put the bad stuff largely to rest; Kaas had apologised, hadn't he? Was genuinely sorry, wasn't he? But the memory was still there.

Parliament Hill Fields is the venue for so many cross-country races, including the national championships and many, many local races. The bus with the Stratford kids and the kids from the other schools in the borough drew up in the parking area between the open-air swimming pool and the four hundred metre tartan track. A big whoosh as the doors opened and the wannabes disgorged…and looked around. They disappeared into the changing rooms, re-emerged as athletes, flaunting the borough and school colours in most respects, the occasional individual in their own choice of competition wear. Jogging, warming up, staring at the initial hill that they'd been told about. "Don't go too fast, don't go mad!" Teachers' and coaches' voices. A whistle blew, and they gathered for final race instructions.

"Ladies first." Scottie Peters, a grizzled old lifelong PE teacher, who doubled as a coach and loved both aspects of his life, smiled at them. "OK, girls, we don't have too many entries in the under-thirteens and the under-fifteen age groups; that's Year 7 for under-thirteens and then years eight and nine for under-fifteens. It's the same distance, so we're going to run you together, if that's OK? It'll save too much hanging around, and as your race numbers are different colours, you'll still get your finishing position in your own age group. All good with that?" And the girls started to strip off their tracksuits and sweatshirts.

Lucy, Shelley and JoJo huddled close together with the other runners from their borough, Newham. Shelley was as tall as, taller than, most of the under-fifteen girls; Lucy was very nearly the smallest of the under thirteen girls. JoJo was nervous, she was the one now out of her comfort zone; Shelley looked over at her, saw the nerves, moved closer, hugged her.

"You'll be fine, JoJo, you'll be just fine, honest."

Two thousand metres around Parliament Hill Fields is very different to two thousand metres on the road, on flat parkland, on a running track—very different indeed. At Parly Hill—as everyone calls it—you start the race with a steep, long three hundred-metre climb on wet, muddy grass. For the novice runner, the pain is huge; novice runners will start out too fast and almost immediately get into oxygen debt. There will be that feeling of not being able to get enough breath in, that feeling of muscles taking on their own life and not doing as instructed by the brain. It's a feeling never forgotten and quickly learnt from. Lucy had, once upon a time, had those feelings, and Lucy had learnt instantly from them. Now she had that ability, that inner sense of knowing how to balance the hurt and the effort and the pace and the realisation that there was still most of the distance remaining. As she pulled over the summit, she looked at the girls with her…And there were very few, and Lucy was like a little kid amongst seniors, and she cared not one stuff.

Lucy knew her worth now, knew how hard and how often she had trained. Lucy knew that she wasn't going to beat many of the older girls, but she was determined that she was going to finish as close to the front as she could in her own age group. The leading pack eased a little as they ran down the slope— happy payback time for the initial climb—and into and over the first stream— don't try to leap right over, wasted energy, one foot in the middle and keep running—up there with that leading group, Lucy was feeling relaxed and in control.

Slight hill again and around the ponds, was it really true that swimmers were in these ponds the whole year around? Certainly was. Lucy saw a couple of older female swimmers in the water, and she giggled to herself. How crazy is that? Halfway now, Lucy still with that leading group, how many other under-thirteens? Lucy knew, well, she hoped, that there couldn't be many. Turn again, heading over to the west now, the posh part of Parly Hill, cross over a concrete pathway and her spikes slipping and scraping on the surface, slight downhill slope and you can see the finish about six hundred metres away, keep running, stay in control, wait for that final turn and just two hundred metres on the flat. Just two older, bigger girls in front of her in a small pack of runners, how many had slipped away in front? Lucy didn't know, and she couldn't waste the energy to scan the distance; pick up the pace, stay in control, up the pace again, one girl slips behind, Lucy a brave, hard effort to outsprint her nemesis, but no exhausted over the line, Mickey waiting, of course.

"Fucking hell, Luce! Fucking hell!"

One sweaty, muddy little girl body against one warm, tracksuit covered male body.

"Was I all right, Mickey? Did I do all right?"

"Lucy, did you do well, are you kidding me? That girl in front of you, she went to English schools last year and came in the top ten; she's two years older than you and she only just out-dipped you!"

"How many in front of me' n her, Mickey? How many?" And then Mickey grinned.

"You really don't know, do you? You really…Oh, I dunno…Lucy, no one was in front of you two. No one! You've stuffed the Year 7 age group and took second overall. Lucy, you really, really, really were amazing!" And then Lucy burst into tears just as the overall winner, a tall, elegant black girl, came up to her.

"Hello you, you absolutely scared the poo out of me!" Lucy's tears turned to a big grin and a laugh immediately.

"Oh, thank you, thank you so much!"

"You're in a running club, you must be; that was a fabulous performance. I think another hundred metres and you would have got me; honestly, I do! Lucy, is that right that you're Year 7, really?" And Lucy nodded yes. The senior girl held out her hand. "I'll be seeing you again in races; I know I will…Oh, yeah, my name's Sami, Sami Richards…And you're…?"

"Lucy, Lucy Newton."

"Like I said, Lucy, I know I'll be seeing you at events in the future," and then she asked, "Hey, Lucy, do you want to have a jog warm-down with me?" And the winner and runner-up, rather the two winners, jogged off together as the starter's whistle blew for the Year 7 boys. Big enough entries this time for separate races.

Mickey was stripping out of his tracksuit as Shelley and JoJo came past him, wearing huge grins as a result of finishing third and tenth in the Year 7 race, and both top twenty overall. Mickey half-smiled at them, but he was already going into race mode; his mind was narrowing into a single concentration, and there was little or no room for anything else.

"Ready, runners." The gun was held high and then exploded. Mickey was into his stride immediately; he felt good, and he knew (and hoped) that he was running well. In the big lead group up the hill, over and won and stretch out the stride length, look around, check it out, hold the position, look up and ahead, get ready for the stream and run through it with one single stride and push off and up and gain a couple of metres because the practice had been done before and learnt and remembered. Slight incline, course veering slightly to the left, past the ponds on the right, leading group beginning to break up now, Mickey holding position, feeling good, halfway done already. Top of the rise, heading west, still in control, group breaking apart, some just losing gradually, some exploding backwards, payback time.

A left turn, see the track and the pool down below, keep concentrating, time to push? Yes, time to push, gradually upping the pace, then more, still feeling in control, another left and now on final flat; pool and track on the right shoulder; Mickey Honey, the Duracell Bunny, accelerating once more; suddenly, no one beside him, and he knew, now he really knew, that he was going to win. Lucy screaming as he dipped through the finishing tape, and then it was her turn to throw her arms around him.

"And the boy done good!" Both of them laughing, the other runners coming up and congratulating, even Sami Richards smiling and giving the thumbs-up with a grin.

With all the events in all the age groups over, Scottie Peters called the London schools officials over for the selection process for the English schools cross-country championships. Most of it was extremely easy: pick the first eight in each age group to cross the line, but Scottie had an idea and wanted to get that idea across.

"The little kid, you know, the Year 7 girl who finished just behind Sami in the under-fifteens?" All the selectors knew Sami; she had been a mainstay for London. "Yeah, that one, Lucy something, oh, yeah, Lucy Newton." Scottie paused. "I'd like to discuss picking her for the team, the under-fifteens…What d'you all think?" And with a very strange and unusual amount of common sense, it was agreed that Lucy Newton, Year 7, would represent London in the English Schools Championship. There had been some discussion, of course, mainly focusing on whether it would be too much pressure for one so young. But Scottie Peters had his ace card barely hidden up his sleeve; he'd already spoken with

Gilly Ring and the other coaches at Vicky Park, and they had no doubts at all; Lucy would be just fine.

Scottie called Lucy over just before she was getting back on the coach to go back to Newham.

"Lucy? Hey, Lucy, can I have a word? Won't keep you, promise. I know you want to get back home." Scottie Peters smiled his big, big smile. "Lucy, you've been selected to represent London in the English schools cross-country under-fifteens. I know you're out of age group, but your race today was absolutely superb; it really was. We wouldn't have selected you if we didn't think you'd be OK with it. Actually getting so close to Sami, wow, that was brilliant! Lucy, would you like to be on the team? All the selectors think you'll be great!" And for the second time that day, Lucy Newton burst into tears, and for the second time that day, she turned and hugged Mickey to her.

"Yes, please, Mr Peters, yes, please, I would love to be at English schools." And another piece of the jigsaw was put in place.

"Mickey, Mickey! Mickey, I got into the English schools under-fifteens, running against all the older girls, Mickey, I did! I did! Can't believe it, well, you know, can't wait to tell Miss Ring, Gilly…and she'll tell Mr Warren, won't she? Oh, Mickey, English schools, me!" And Mickey smiled and felt not even one modicum of envy.

"'Course you did, Lucy, 'course you did. You bought the ticket when you started it all, didn't you? That's what you did—that's what I did as well, I hope, bought the ticket; gonna be some journey for us, gonna be some journey, really is."

*****

The English schools cross-country in 2002 was held in Washington, Tyne and Wear, up in the north-west of England. The athletes had met in Westminster on Thursday to travel the three hundred miles up by coach. Lucy at twelve years old (just), six years younger than the sixth formers, many of whom had represented London schools for four, five, six years already. Lucy had received her London schools tracksuit and race kit a couple of days earlier and was brimming with excitement wearing the tracksuit as she arrived at Westminster, right by the Houses of Parliament. Lucy was a little nervous—it was the longest trip that she'd been on. "Even further than going to Amsterdam," she told

Mickey. "Can you believe that? It's further in our country than going to Europe with a ferry and all that?"

Mickey had gone up to Westminster with Lucy; of course, he had; he just grinned at her and then said, "Told you, Lucy, you bought the ticket. I didn't manage to get the ticket for this trip, but I will next time. I will next time, I promise." Mickey wasn't jealous, but he was indeed envious.

The coach was already there, and Lucy's nerves were beginning to play up...and then she saw Sami. Sami waved at her and immediately came over.

"Hey, Lucy, hi, Mickey, first one, eh, Lucy?" Lucy nodded and was in a millisecond close to tears, this was all so new to her. Sami picked up on it instantly. "Lucy, you sit with me on the coach, yeah? Is that all right?" And the relaxation vibes coming off of Sami were in a further millisecond transported to Lucy and Mickey.

"Lucy, getting outside London is a bit different, you know? Ain't meaning to be rude, Lucy, but you ever been outside London? Properly, I mean?" Lucy shook her head 'no'.

"Been to Amsterdam last summer, me'n Mickey and a couple of others, my mates Shelley and JoJo, went on a sports trip, brilliant, really totes brill! But in England, no, never, not really. Went down to the seaside with my mum and dad when I was little, Southend and Clacton, but that was all. And Southend and Clacton, they're really just an extension of London, aren't they?"

"OK, look, we'll have a chat on the coach, yeah? Sometimes getting out of London can be a bit...oh, I dunno, different." And Sami left it at that.

Lucy kissed Mickey goodbye as Sami watched and smiled.

"He's really special to you, isn't he, Lucy? Like really special?"

"Sami, can I tell you something? Sami, feel like I've known you forever; honest, I do, you were so nice to me at London schools and now...Sami, he's my world; no really, I know I'm like a little kid. Jeez I've only just turned twelve for God's sake, but I can't imagine my life without Mickey...I really can't...don't laugh at me, Sami. I couldn't bear that, just couldn't. So, I'm telling you the truth, the absolute truth. I adore him; he's my world. I would honestly do anything for him...Yeah, really."

And Sami felt her eyes watering just a little, and she hoped and prayed that Lucy would be all right, really all right. One side of her knew it would be OK, and the other side knew that things and expectations and life didn't always go as people planned and expected them to.

And that was called real life.

Scottie Peters was ticking their names off a register as they boarded the coach. "Sami, Lucy, you good, guys?"

"Hi, Mr Peters. Yeah, we're all good. Me and Lucy are going to sit together, if that's OK? Lucy said that she'd look after me!" And all three of them laughed, and Scottie Peters knew he'd been correct in putting Lucy forward for selection, and he also knew that he had an absolute diamond in Sami Richards, a true-blue, seven carat, absolute diamond.

"So, Sami, you're the most experienced girl on the under-fifteens; you've already been to cross-country and track for London at English schools. Congratulations, Captain!"

They sat and chatted together for the whole journey. Lucy felt instantly relaxed and secure, Sami was immediately her adopted big sister, and Sami felt just the same with her new little sister. A couple of Motorway stops for drinks, snacks and toilet breaks; Sami introducing (very casually) Lucy to the other girls; making contact with both girls and boys in the older age groups—and they all knew Sami, and now they knew Lucy as well. And they treated her with the utmost respect; if Lucy was friends with Sami, then Lucy was friends with all of them.

It was the final few miles of the journey now. Sami squeezed Lucy's arm and said, "Lucy, look, in London, we're all different, but we're all the same. Look at you and Mickey; he's white and you're black, and that's totally all right, innit? Like all of us growing up, that's just the way it is, yeah? Anyone ever say anything about you and Mickey going out? The two of you together?" A negative shake of the head. "So, things ain't the same outside London, you know? I've been really lucky, been to English schools a couple of times already, hopefully again this summer…if I qualify, hopefully. Well, so, it can be different…Some places in England, they ain't really seen black kids, well, they've maybe seen them but not ever really got to talk to them or know them, so what I'm trying to say is that it might feel a bit weird, yeah? If people, grown-ups like, look at you a bit different, they ain't being rude, well, actually, they are being rude, but they don't realise it. Now look, I'm certainly not saying that people—grown-ups—aren't prejudiced because some of them are, but what I'm saying is give them a chance and let them see that being a good person is a hundred times more important than what colour you happen to be…without being flash, Luce, you could change people's lives."

Sami sat back and thought, then she smiled. "Mean that, Lucy; you have the power to change people's lives just by being nice…by being you. Don't let other people's unconscious prejudices affect who you are as a person." It was a big speech, a huge speech from a fourteen-year-old kid. Lucy sat back, shook her head and inside her head the thoughts, *Fucking hell, I so want to be like Sami…No, what I mean is I want to be like her; I just want to be a good person. I hope I am; I truly hope I am.*

A huge 'whoosh' was heard as the coach drew up, footbrake and handbrake on, engine shut down. The athletes sat and waited; Mr Peters stood up.

"Here we are, guys, here we are. My first ever English Schools Championships when I was your age; absolutely loved it. It was called County Durham when I was racing back in the seventies, and now it's Tyne and Wear…*Plus ça change, plus ca reste!*"

Scottie smiled. "Yeah, I know, pretensions of adequacy with me speaking French; it means 'the more things change, the more they stay the same'." He carried on, "Everyone's billeted, of course, some singles, some in pairs, but I'll check you all out before anyone disappears. Tonight is free time, but I guess some of you will get together later for a coffee or something like that?"

Shakes of heads, nervous laughter. "Not going to set a curfew, that would be pointless, how could I check on everybody anyway? Just remember that this is the start of a journey for a lot of you, and it's a journey continuation for some of you. Make the best of it, you know, and I know that your friends, the guys you train with, would give anything to be in your shoes; don't let them down." Scottie smiled. "You won't let them down, and you won't let yourselves down; I know that. Course recce tomorrow, be in your kit and tracksuits and bring spikes, meet here for eleven.

"OK? Good luck, everybody, be nice to the families you're with; they have to be nice people by definition to have you lot staying with them!" Lots of nervous laughs. "Truly, be nice, having you guys stay with them is one their lives' highlights as well; otherwise, why would they do it?" And the athletes reflected on that statement; it made total sense.

Lucy hadn't thought about the billeting properly until then, and it was with a sense of relief when her and Sami's names were called out together. Sami just smiled. "Ain't gonna leave my new little sister and future world champion alone in this mad scary world, am I?" And once again, Lucy knew how lucky she was.

As they were both introduced to the couple who were looking after them, Sami put out her hand, and Lucy quickly followed. "Thank you so much for putting us up; that is so kind of you!"

It was only a short walk to the house, and Lucy listened in awe and learnt quickly as Sami kept up a conversation all the way there. Their hosts' house was as welcoming as their hosts, Mr and Mrs Harris by name, and of course involved in athletics and made it totally obvious that it really was a pleasure to be hosting two athletes from London. As soon as they walked through the front door, twin girls wearing tracksuits, maybe nine or ten years old, came over to Sami and Lucy to shyly introduce themselves while their parents looked on.

"Hello, welcome to our house; my name's Tammy."

"And I'm Trudy." Both little girls held out their hands to shake as their parents had prepared them to do, but Sami smiled.

"I've got a better idea." She looked at the Harrises, and whatever she saw there, she knew it was going to be OK. She bent down, hugged them and kissed them on the cheek, and Tammy and Trudy put their hands around their faces and giggled while their parents smiled at all of them. Sami nodded at Lucy, and Lucy kissed the twins while Sami was delving into her kit bag. "Tammy, Trudy, I'm guessing by your tracksuits that you run for your junior school or you're in an athletics club, yes?" Identical nods of heads. "Well, I wonder if you'd like these?"

And Sami held out two small T-shirts with the logo 'LONDON SCHOOLS ATHLETICS' printed boldly on the front. "These are from me and Lucy if you'd like them and if it's all right with your mum and dad?" And it would have been a very brave mum and dad to say no. Identical gasps from identical girls.

"Oh, thank you, thank you so much." Tammy and Trudy gasped, and together, they hugged Sami and Lucy. "Really, thank you so much." Mrs Harris wiped away a tear, while Mr Harris suddenly found his shoes very interesting to look at.

"Tammy, Trudy, why don't you show Sami and Lucy to their room? You're in together, girls; hope that's OK?" And that was another relief for Lucy.

"Are you two going to come and watch me and Lucy in the cross-country on Saturday? We'd really like that, wouldn't we, Lucy?" Two nods of two heads from two little girls still in a state of awe. *They gave us proper running T-shirts! Gave them to us!* "Aah, bless you! Well, now I'd like to ask you a favour, a huge favour, but Lucy and I need to ask your mum and dad first, shall we go downstairs?"

Lucy was wondering now as well. "Mrs Harris, Mr Harris, I'm being a bit cheeky here, but I'm going to ask anyway…" Mr and Mrs Harris would possibly have agreed to any request from the visitors, what with their two little girls being made so happy. "Well, Lucy and I need to go out for a jog, just a bit of a loosener after all the time travelling up here, so we were wondering if Tammy and Trudy could show us where to run, come out with us; we'd look after them, of course, but I know it's a big ask…"

"Mum, Mum! Dad, pleeese, Dad, please, Mum, let us go running, please let us go running with Lucy and Sami!" And there was no answer to that one, well, there was, but it had to be yes, of course!

They ran easily, very easily, for less than ten minutes, and all the while, Tammy and Trudy were desperately hoping that someone from school or their running club would see them with these London runners—real runners who were going to be in the English schools cross-country, and they had chosen to run with them! And they got lucky; they were spied by two school friends and two girls from the running club who were nearer in age to Sami. And Sami smiled inside because she knew how much it meant to them—how much it had meant to her when she had been that age. Be nice, make a difference. Lucy was spellbound with Sami; how did she know how to act like that? Everything Sami did and said was good, and Lucy was perhaps getting a huge girl crush on Sami.

Lucy and Sami spent the evening after dinner watching television with Mr and Mrs Harris and, of course, Tammy and Trudy, who just sat there looking at their brand-new heroes with barely a word spoken, just those looks of adoration.

And then it was Friday, the day before the English schools cross-country championships. The London team met altogether—eighteen-year-olds down to twelve-year-old Lucy—with Sami always by her side, not protecting but rather reassuring. The course was—in the epic words of Sami—whom Lucy hadn't heard swear before, 'An absolute bastard!' Two laps with a total distance of two thousand four hundred metres and an extra twenty per cent might not sound much…unless you were running for that extra time when you were already in amazing oxygen debt. And then there was the hill—that ridiculously steep hill to be covered each time, each lap. Sami had looked over at Lucy while they were running easily up it.

"Naah, not a hill really, more a slope!" And again, they both laughed. A few of the older boys came over after the recce run. "Looking good, Sami. You too, Lucy, looking good!" And Lucy could see in their eyes and hear in their words that the words were meant because she was looking good; she was indeed looking good. Sami and Lucy cruised around the rest of the day, had a chat with Mr Peters, who also told them that they were looking good. They sat with Tammy and Trudy that night, and Tammy and Trudy assured them that they would be there to watch them run and to win. And both Sami and Lucy laughed at their words, but hidden deep in the secrets of their minds was the thought: would they? Could they win?

At three-thirty precisely, as the final bell of the day rung at Stratford Academy, Danny Bullet ran out to the hired minibus, waited at least thirty seconds for TMRG: Joshi and Alisha, Eric and Bobby, Shelley, JoJo and finally Mickey (less Lucy) to join him, drove over to Riverside Primary School, where Chris Warren and Gilly Ring were waiting for them, picked up the North Circular road, then the link road onto the M25 and, eventually, the M1. Sitting in the back of the minibus, Shelley and the girls, Mickey and the boys, were struggling out of their school uniforms. "Close your eyes, you guys; you're not supposed to see me in my knickers," said Shelley, of course, and they all roared and struggled into the jeans, T-shirts and sweaters that were the absolute essential things to wear when you were eleven and twelve years old in East London and you were required to be cool; 'cool as a mule', 'loose as a goose'.

And TMRG very much needed to be cool because they were going up to watch the English schools cross-country, to watch their friend race, to support Lucy, who, they all knew, was racing above her age group because she deserved it. And Mr Warren, Miss Ring and Dan Bullet all felt very proud, indeed.

Dan Bullet looked over at Gilly and grinned.

"D'you get that stuff I ordered from Speedo, Gilly?" And the seven members of TMRG were immediately alert...

"Yes, all sorted, Dan, all sorted." And the three adults waited...and waited...finally, Mickey broke first.

"Dan? Sir? Miss Ring? I know I shouldn't be asking but..."

"Mickey, wasn't sure who was going to crack first...OK, we got some T-shirts printed up, you know, to support Lucy." And when they all saw what and how they had been printed, they howled, really howled, and it was a howl of laughter but also, importantly, respect.

Chapter Twenty-Six
What Is Your Greatest Fear?

"You nervous, Lucy?"

"Yeah, 'course I am, aren't you?" Sami smiled and stretched out, still snuggling in her warm bed. There was a knock at their door. Trudy poked her head through shyly.

"Mum said would you like a cup of tea before breakfast? Mum said she didn't really know how you prepared for a big race, didn't want to bother you, said whatever you wanted, just to let her know."

"Trudy, that would be lovely, thank you so much…and thank your mum. A cup of tea would be lovely, and we'll shower and come down." And Trudy skipped away, smiling.

They both showered and were, as ever, comfortable in each other's company.

"Your house like this, Lucy?" And Sami laughed. "No, me neither!" And then she said, "Lucy, need to tell you something, no big deal, honest, but something I need to say before, you know, we go over to the race." And Sami started with the words that she'd been rehearsing on and off since she'd met Lucy. And then she stopped. "You know what, Lucy? I think I'm going to show you what I was going to say to you…Someone said it before me, and she said it a lot better."

Sami delved into her kit backpack and pulled out a sheet of A4 paper that had been laminated. "Lucy, come over and sit next to me, yeah?" And, of course, Lucy did exactly that. Sami ran her hand over the paper and put it on both their laps. And Lucy read through the words printed there.

What Is Your Greatest Fear?

'Our deepest fear is not that we are inadequate, our deepest fear is that we are powerful beyond measure. It is our light, not our darkness, that most frightens us. We ask ourselves, who am I to be brilliant, gorgeous, handsome, talented and fabulous? Actually, who are you not to be? You are a child of God. Your playing small does not serve the world. There is nothing enlightened about shrinking so that other people won't feel insecure around you. We were born to manifest the glory of God within us. It is not just in some; it is in everyone. And as we let our own light shine, we consciously give other people permission to do the same. As we are liberated from our fear, our presence automatically liberates others.'

–   Marianne Williamson.

And then Lucy read those words again, more slowly this time, savouring the words, as she digested them. Sami waited patiently, then she smiled.

"We were doing this in English, poetry actually, when I was in Year 8, last year, and it just made sense to me, I printed it out, and I carry it pretty much everywhere with me, especially when I'm racing or training...I thought you'd like it, Lucy."

Lucy interrupted, "Sami, I love it. I absolutely love it! Thank you so much...again!"

"So?" Sami smiled, and then Lucy smiled back.

"There's some stuff there that I don't really get yet, but I will when I keep reading it, and I will keep reading it. I will...it means that no one should be scared of being good, yeah? That's it, Sami?" Sami nodded a yes.

"Spot on, Lucy, you got it. Lucy, when they told us that Year 7 would be in our race at London schools, it was a 'yeah, all right' because all my age group knew that the race would split really quickly, you guys in Year 7 wouldn't be able to stay with us, and you proved us totally wrong, you and a couple of other girls—one was your friend, Shelley, right?" And Lucy nodded another yes.

"So today is English schools, not London schools, 'big time, shoot a dime'." And Sami's awful American accent for the phrase made Lucy choke on her cup of tea. "But it's not that different, Lucy; honest, it's not. So, what I'm saying is don't be scared, put yourself on the line because you have Absolutely. Nothing. To. Lose—absolutely nothing."

A pause, then Sami said, "You ran me so close, Lucy, I honestly didn't know if it was going to be me or you, so maybe I got lucky, or maybe, being a bit older, I've been there before, you know, close finishes, sprint finishes. Age matters, 'course it does, but it's not the only thing, not by any means; what matters is having some talent and using it, doing the training and putting yourself on the line when it matters…And I see someone sitting next to me who's got all that…in spades…and I ain't sure if anyone's allowed to say 'in spades' any more…even if it's two black girls!"

And Lucy screamed with laughter, put her arms around Sami, really tightly and murmured 'thank you', and they managed to get down the stairs to breakfast without releasing their arms were around each other's waists.

Everything was on offer for breakfast, but both Sami and Lucy opted for cereal and toast; Sami explained why they couldn't eat too much and why it was the cereal and toast rather than a cooked breakfast. Mr and Mrs Harris smiled and filed the new knowledge away for when Tammy and Trudy would be at English schools because the twins had told them the previous night that they were definitely going to race at English schools when they were in big school.

TMRG and their teacher minders were up early at the hotel; truth be told, none of them had slept too much; even the fatigue of a long journey couldn't compete with the excitement of going to watch Lucy race, and Lucy not knowing, not having the faintest clue, made it even better. And then there were the T-shirts as well. They ate breakfast together, and it was subdued until Dan Bullet started to tell them the most ridiculous stories about his time competing internationally, and even if the kids knew that ninety per cent of the stories weren't true, they lapped them up anyway. They left the hotel in plenty of time for the first race, which, as usual, was the under-fifteen girls event. They needed to be there in good time because they had decided exactly where they were going to stand and cheer from and exactly when they would reveal their T-shirts.

Mr Peters called the London athletes together, went through a few specific areas of the course, wished them all luck, told them all that he was really proud of them and knew that they would all race their hearts out. And then the whistle blew, and it was time, time for the first event. Over two hundred girls stripped off their tracksuits and stood at the top of the hill; it would be downhill to begin with, not too steep, but the payback time was that, as they went through lap one and at the finish of the race on lap two, the athletes would be faced with that steep, steep hill. In Lucy's head, she could hear Sami say, "No, not a hill, just a slope," and she grinned.

At the bottom of the hill, TMRG stayed hidden…and checked their covered-up T-shirts.

The start line: massed ranks with teams individualised by the county-coloured vests. Lucy and Sami were together, and just seconds before the gun cracked, Lucy saw that Sami had become like Shelley: always there, always helping, always supporting. Why the hell hadn't she seen it before…but she had, of course, just hadn't put it into words or rational thoughts. She grinned, then laughed out loud. Sami looked at her, eyes wide, with an unspoken 'you all right?' not even mouthed, 'I'm fine', a squeeze of the hand, and they were away. Lots of bumping, barging and boring on that initial two hundred metres downhill; Lucy saw runners getting away in front of her but was determined to stay with the pace that she had set herself—no first-minute heroics from her! Lucy knew that she didn't have a magic turn of speed, but what she did have was superb endurance and superb mental strength.

What she also had, or rather didn't have, was much bodyweight in her tiny frame, and that would be a big advantage on the two hill climbs, the second leading directly to the finish line. Lucy could see Sami in the distinctive London vest just ten metres ahead of her; another runner who knew all about pace control and Sami had finished in the top ten last year. Lucy was using her new big sister as pacemaker, why not? The course veered to the right, and Lucy used the panorama to check her race position, wow! Certainly, top thirty, probably better than that. On that first lap, Lucy was picking off runners; one here, another one, a couple pacing each other, one by one they came back to her. Sami still that elusive ten metres in front. First lap almost done. Lucy lifted her eyes and focused on the hill…And then she heard, "Lucy! Go, Lucy, go, Lucy!"

They were bouncing up and down like crazy people! It was her mates, her boyfriend, her best friends in the world; it was TMRG! And there was Mr Warren and Gilly and Dan Bullet! They'd all come to watch her run, oh my God! Lucy felt the sob in her throat and attacked the hill, the slope. More runners taken as she danced over the soggy surface, most certainly in the top ten now, and she could sense rather than see some of her rivals beginning to slow. Over the crest now, other runners being caught as they paid the price for too much effort on that bastard of a hill as Sami had called it. One further runner passed, then another, and then no one for what seemed like an eternity and might have been as much as thirty seconds. Seventh now, seventh in the English schools.

Eight hundred metres to go, into sixth; five hundred metres, fifth with Sami in fourth and both of them slowly catching, catching, catching. Time and distance running out, final turn on the flat, seeing that bastard of a hill just ahead, Sami ahead of Lucy. And then as Lucy started to prime herself for the climb (maybe I'll get one of them?), TMRG emerged from the crowd, wearing identical T-shirts. They turned their backs towards the runners, towards Lucy. And each one of TMRG had a capital letter printed large on the backs of the T-shirts. They had arranged themselves into a single line-up and that was important because each of them had a single letter on the back of their T-shirt spelling out a message, and as they turned and shouted, the message was G.O. L.U.C.Y.! and Lucy saw the message and responded; sprinting up the hill/slope/bastard now, half laughing at herself and half so very proud that TMRG and her teachers had taken the time and trouble to do that.

Both Lucy and Sami gaining, gaining, gaining and then passing! Sami third, Lucy fourth; one hundred metres; Sami past another and then the final pass into first place, Lucy past a desperate runner into third; sprint, sprint, dig deep, now deeper…And Sami Richards became English Schools Champion while Lucy Newton took the bronze medal against girls two years her senior.

And Scottie Peters, London Schools' team manager went wild.

And Chris Warren, Gilly Ring and Dan Bullet went wild.

And seven members of TMRG went absolutely wild.

And Tammy and Trudy Harris went wild and burst into tears.

And Mr and Mrs Harris went wild; both had tears in their eyes.

Sami and Lucy fell into each other's arms, not forgetting to congratulate the Yorkshire athlete who had split them by placing second. The older age group London runners, girls and boys, came up to hug and congratulate, and there was just a little bit of awe in many eyes as they looked again at the diminutive figure of Lucy; how the hell was so much strength and power and guts in someone who looked as if she could still have been in primary school?

And then it was more controlled bedlam as both girls went over to TMRG, and the teacher trio and were followed by Tammy and Trudy and their parents. A hug for Mickey first, of course, and then it seemed like everyone was hugging everyone else; Joshi and Alisha, Eric and Bobby, Shelley and JoJo, Gilly, Dan, Chris, and then Lucy and Sami turned to their youngest supporters and picked them up and hugged and kissed them, and Tammy and Trudy knew, they just knew, that they had died and gone to heaven.

And then it was prize-giving and awards, the under-fifteen girls first not unnaturally as they had raced first.

"In third place representing London, Lucy Newton."

"In second place representing Yorkshire, Sarah Ramsbottom."

"And in first place and the winner of the English schools cross-country championship, representing London, Sami Richards." And as the crowd either politely clapped or impolitely cheered, Sami and Lucy took Tammy and Trudy by the hand and insisted they stand on the podium with them. "Because we couldn't have done it without you, could we, Lucy?" And Lucy nodded her agreement while the spectators acknowledged the gesture, and Tammy and Trudy now knew beyond doubt that they were the two luckiest girls in the world.

The meal that evening was a riot; Lucy couldn't believe what they had all done for her, travel up from London and the T-shirts. Sami was invited, of course, as were Mr and Mrs Harris and the twins. And for once, Mickey and Lucy weren't able to sit together because Tammy and Trudy monopolised their two heroes. Scottie Peters had been invited but had declined in case it looked like he was favouring some athletes above others, and that was a shame.

A few of the older athletes were in the restaurant; London athletes and from the other counties, and almost all of them came across and congratulated Sami and Lucy. Sami was recognised and known to many of them; they'd seen her run last year at both cross-country and also the English schools Track and Field Championships in the fifteen hundred metres, but Lucy was the new kid on the block, and she'd run the two in front of her so, so close.

Mr Harris was quiet, smiling and nodding to himself and then smiling at everyone around him. He looked over at his two girls…Actually, make that his four girls: Tammy and Trudy of course, but also his new almost-adopted London girls, Lucy and Sami. He shook his head, shook his head in wonder. There had been so many stories, as usual Dan Bullet had the floor, all that travelling, all those important races and qualifications and all those laughs. And of course, those Olympic Games in Sydney. Mickey and Lucy and Shelley and JoJo drunk it all in, and Tammy and Trudy really did have their mouths open. Mr Harris kept on shaking his head and smiling at everybody and nobody. The meal finally finished; there were handshakes, hugs and kisses and two carry-homes for the exhausted Tammy and Trudy. There were promises from everyone to see everyone else off tomorrow, the London coach and the TMRG minibus; more handshakes, hugs and kisses and then it was home and hotel.

Chapter Twenty-Seven
The Journey, a Dream

It felt like thousands, but in reality, there were only around a hundred or so people, athletes and their retinue massed around the London schools coach. Scottie Peters was holding order, always smiling, always relaxed, always (although he didn't always feel it) in control. A clipboard, a whistle, a quiet word, a smile and, occasionally, a hug. TMRG along with Dan, Gilly and Chris were already there, waiting, when Lucy and Sami arrived holding hands with Tammy and Trudy who still looked at them in wonder; if they had been offered the chance of getting on the coach and going to London...Well, you know the answer.

Mr Harris walked up to Scottie Peters.

"Mr Peters? Mr Peters, may I talk with you?" *Oh shit!* Thoughts were racing through his head. *What had happened? Sami and Lucy get drunk and spewed up everywhere? Nice kids, no, lovely kids but sometimes stuff happens...*

"Mr Peters, I don't know how to say this, but I have to say it anyway..." It seemed as if a silence was falling. "You see, Mr Peters, we don't have too many people around here who aren't white; we just don't; it's not wrong or right, we just don't...and so, we don't have the opportunity of mixing and talking and getting to know who they are." The silence intensified.

Their little group was listening hard. "So, I don't know if I'm prejudiced, how would I? But I've done all the stuff, you know, laughed at the racist jokes, 'cause it never meant anything, why would it?" And a huge sigh and a pushing out of breath. "And then...and then...you gave us Sami and Lucy to stay with us—and to be honest, it was a bit of a shock; first black kids I'd ever spoken to or got to know, you know...sorry, Mr Peters, I'm just trying to be honest here...Well, Sami and Lucy, they are the nicest, the absolute nicest kids I've ever had the privilege of meeting. The way they looked after Tammy and Trudy—look at them now, just look at them; they adore them."

The group listening was tighter and even quieter. "And then last night at the meal—I am so sorry that you weren't able to be there, I really wanted to thank you then—I can honestly say that I enjoyed it so much; everyone made me feel a part of it. I was so happy, felt so privileged to even be there…I was just watching and listening; there was black and white, the Asian brother and sister, Alisha and Joshi, Bobby—do you say mixed race or something else now? Everyone was getting on, didn't seem to matter kids and grown-ups, teachers and pupils, and I would never have had that opportunity of meeting them all if Sami and Lucy hadn't invited us. I said it was a privilege…I was wrong; it was an honour, an absolute honour." There was absolute silence for as long as five seconds, and that is a long time in a conversation. Mr Peters broke the silence.

"Mr Harris, sir, it is my privilege to meet you, thank you so much, sir, thank you so much for sharing. I'll take a bet that it wasn't easy?" Mr Harris shook his head. Mrs Harris squeezed his hand. Tammy and Trudy disengaged themselves from Lucy and Sami's waists and flung their arms around their dad.

"No, not easy, Mr Peters, but it needed to be said; wouldn't have forgiven myself if I hadn't said it. Funny old thing, running, isn't it? Well, all sports a bit funny, really; try and rationalise it, and it doesn't make sense. All those cliches that you hear, I could spout about fifty by myself, all the stuff you hear athletes and coaches saying…But I'll tell you one cliché that is absolutely true." Even tighter and quieter now, the whole group were mentally leaning forward to hear Mr Harris's next words.

"That stuff about bringing people together, you know? Well, that is so true. You know what? I'd probably still have those old-fashioned ideas, those old barriers if Lucy and Sami hadn't stayed with us, and I'll tell you something else…This has been one of the highlights of my life; no really, it has." Mr Harris shook his head one more time as if in disbelief of himself. "Yeah, highlight of my life, and of my girls…right, girls?" And Tammy and Trudy nodded their heads 'yes' almost as if they didn't trust themselves to speak…and they didn't, and then it was Sami's turn.

"Mr Harris, Mrs Harris, me and Lucy can't thank you enough for looking after us, inviting strangers into your home—and your home is beautiful—is kindness itself." Sami paused for an instant. "Saying what you just said, oh man, that is SO brave; I dunno if I'd ever have the guts to make that sort of statement.

Me'n Lucy loved staying with you, and we loved having Tammy and Trudy looking after us and coming to support us…May I please have a hug?" And Sami hugged Mr Harris, while Lucy hugged Mrs Harris, and they all managed—just—not to burst into tears.

"One last thing, girls, and then I'll let you get on the coach and talk to your friends instead of a silly old sentimental bloke like me…what you did for my girls, for Trudy and Tammy, was amazing. I don't think they've taken their T-shirts off yet. Have you girls?" And Trudy and Tammy grinned and shook their heads 'no'. "And then you took them onto the podium with you; they will never forget that; that sort of memory lasts a lifetime."

Final hugs, a solid handshake from Mr Warren and Dan to Mr Harris. Whispered 'thank-yous' seemed to come from everybody to everybody, and then they were on the coach and in the minibus, and the great adventure was finishing.

There was absolute silence in the TMRG minibus for almost half an hour; everyone was reliving and absorbing that final scene: Mr Harris' words. Mickey broke the silence.

"Got some bottle, that Mr Harris, some bottle. Guts to say all that, man, that takes something else…Hope that I'd have the same guts if I ever had to do something like that, no, mean that. So much easier to just ignore stuff, take the easy way out and hope it'll go away. Respect, much respect."

And in the London coach.

"We got lucky, didn't we, Sami? We got really lucky. Just overhearing some of the other kids, they didn't get looked after anything like we did…yeah, we got lucky." Sami smiled.

"Oh, Lucy, 'course we got lucky…but you make a little bit of luck for yourself, you know. Were we polite? Yes. Did we offer to help? Yes. Did we make friends with Tammy and Trudy? Yes. So, we tried hard, and we got lucky back." They smiled at each other. "I read something once, oh, yeah, I'm a real bookworm, me! It was one of those self-help books, you know? And it was something like, 'The Smile You Send Out Returns Three Times'. I liked that, made sense to me." And it most certainly made sense to Lucy.

"Sami…Sami, when we get back, would it be all right if we kept in touch? Like, I know you're older than me and all that…But I'd really like to, well, you know, be your friend…" And Lucy blushed. Gone too far? Maybe, maybe not.

"Lucy, my little angel, get this, me'n you are gonna see a lot of each other, trust me. Some people you want to keep in your life forever…Me'n you, definitely!" And a very happy Lucy sighed, leant her head on the older girl's shoulder and fell asleep.

And in the minibus.

"She done good, Lucy, didn't she? Like, REALLY good!" Shelley said the words, but it could have been any of them—kids and adults. "Can't believe it, well, I can 'cause she did it; she's our age and stuffed nearly everyone in the race, not far off winning, up close to Sami, and Sami's been around, done a couple of English schools already…and Lucy was pretty much up with her…amazing."

And then it was JoJo, but she hesitated first, then said, "You know me, I want to be a footballer, always have, always will…But there's always that thought, you know, like 'naah, not me, ain't gonna be me, don't deserve it, ain't nothing special'."

Another pause, longer this time. "I'm dead lucky, me, going up to Spurs, in the academy, like, loads of kids jealous, I know that, ain't stupid, no, not stupid at all…Sir, miss, you know how many actually make it? Like really make it to play pro? Well, I'll tell you, not even one in twenty, one in twenty! And that's in the academy players. And for girls, it's even less, like maybe one in fifty. And everyone up the academy thinks they're gonna be the one, the one who does make it, but there's always those doubts, always…You know what? Not me, not me anymore. I really am going to make it; really am."

JoJo shook her head as if to get any negative thoughts out of her brain. "I see Lucy, she's like me; she's like all of us, and she's got a medal at English schools through pure hard work. Never gives in, does she? Ain't never seen Lucy give in. Pure hard work, that's Lucy, and that's me from now on, just gonna work my arse off—oops, sorry, miss. Sorry, sir. Sorry, Dan." Dan, Gilly and Chris all grinned, said nothing and carried on listening.

"And that's the difference, innit?" Shelley asked. "You believe in yourself, like you really believe in yourself, and that's the biggest difference between those who do and those who don't make it. Mr Warren, I know I've said it before and I'm gonna say it again, and I'm not even embarrassed about it; it's you that made the difference—Sorry, miss. Sorry, Dan—I mean you as well; honest, I do, but it was Mr Warren who did it first, first proper teacher we had."

Alisha, Joshi, Eric, Bobby, Mickey and JoJo all said, "Yeah, right, absolutely. Look at us lot, still together…And all of you took us up to watch Lucy."

A huge shake of the head. "Can't believe it, can't believe how lucky we are, all of us…Lucy's done it already. JoJo's told us what she's gonna do, so now it's my turn…miss, Gilly, I mean. Gilly, will you help me? Will you coach me? I'll work my arse off, miss; honest, I will. I want to go to English schools as well like Lucy."

Then Shelley started quietly crying and buried her face in Mickey's shoulder while Mickey silently put his arm around her—brother and sister, in fact, if not in blood. Gilly leant back and squeezed Shelley's hand.

"Of course, I will; you know I will."

"Shelley's right, Mr Warren." It was Joshi's turn now. "My mum and dad were always telling me I was going to be a doctor, and I was like, 'Yeah, Indian kid, parents are gonna tell me that, aren't they? And then you came along, Mr Warren; you came along out of nowhere, and suddenly, I believe it; I can be a doctor, not just for my mum and dad but because I want to…Yeah, why not? I believe in myself, yeah, I do; different innit, Alisha?"

"And I, of course, am by far the more serious and, indeed, better looking of this twindom; is that a word? Twindom? Well, it is now!" They all laughed. "My brother's being intelligent for once; cut a long story short, you did make us believe, Mr Warren; you really did. When you told us where you grew up and everything, all of a sudden, it's like, 'He IS like us! He does know our lives!'. And me? Well, without being funny, it was usually about Joshi at home; that's just the way it was. I was supposed to be quiet and docile, do what I was told, know my place, but I was never going to do that."

"I remember you lots of times starting something in class, whispering under your breath, making someone laugh and get into trouble and then them getting sent out and not you…You were brilliant!" Epic Eric interjected. "Not with you, Mr Warren, before you." And they all laughed.

"So, I was always going to have a go, honest. It's just you made it easier for me, sir, like everyone's said, 'believe in myself'. I decided that I was going to be a teacher, was gonna do something for kids just like you did for us…And now? Well, still want to do something, help others. I've found out that I'm quite good at talking, debating—no laughing, you guys!—trying to persuade people…I still want to be a teacher…sort of…But I'm thinking about doing social work with kids…Or…don't have a go at me, don't laugh now 'cause I'm trusting you all with this"—there was absolute silence in the minibus—"I'm seriously thinking about politics, no really, then you can get things done, change people's lives. Can you imagine me on Newham Borough Council?"

"I can, I really can," and those words came from the other nine mouths in the group. Joshi slid over the seat nearer to his sister, put his arm around her and hugged her tight. There was silence now while the words were taken in and inwardly digested. Then Bobby looked at Eric and nodded 'yes'.

"S'pose it's me an' Bobby's turn now, innit? Seeing as you lot have shown you got no shame, no shame at all!" And they all laughed again. "That summer I had in Jamaica, you know? Well, I hated it, totally hated it. All my West Indian chat, all the 'me gwanna do' stuff, all an act, all a façade. I'm a Londoner, don't matter if you're black or white or whatever, not in London; well, not in my London, in our London. My mates are in this minibus, innit? Apart from Lucy, of course; couldn't care a stuff about colour, race, any of it. Know it's around, 'course it is, but not in my world, never in my world. See Old Mickey over there? White, isn't he? 'course he is; you can tell just by looking at him…"

They all erupted with laughter. "Well, Mickey's a bit special. Mickey's the glue that holds us together, always has been. He's got a—what's the word?— presence; yeah, presence is the word. I'm right, aren't I, guys?" And TMRG nodded and 'yessed'.

"Must have been about a million times down the estate when Mickey stepped in, stood up to the bullies, the so-called hard men who were bullying, trying to take our money, trying it on with the girls—right, aren't I, ladies?"

"Yeah, he did, always." Shelley squeezed Mickey's hand, squeezed it tight.

"And do you think Mickey cared one stuff who was white or black or whatever? Naah, 'course, he didn't. You remember, Alisha, when those kids who were stoned out of their brains were giving you a real hard time? Remember?"

Alisha nodded 'yes'. "White kids and black kids, yeah, having a go because you were Indian? Mickey went right up to the biggest one, happened to be white, could have been black, didn't matter to Mickey; that stonehead was about four or five years older, and Mickey smashed him in the nose, blood everywhere. Mickey didn't say a thing, just stood there fronting all of them…and they walked away; they fucking walked away! Sorry, miss, sir, didn't mean to swear, just slipped out. Anyway, like I said, didn't like it in Jamaica, didn't want to be there, but I was, so I decided to do something; had a look around, saw what was similar to London, saw what was different, what was good and bad, what I liked and didn't like…

"And I got this idea, well, me'n Bobby got this idea 'cause I was keeping in touch with Bobby most of the time, kept me sane, and you wouldn't believe Bobby could keep anyone sane...Not for long! So, this idea, some of the stuff I did like was the paintings and the embroidery, some of the clothes that were different. And I thought, well, if I like that stuff, I bet there's other kids and grown-ups in London who'd like them too. Talked to some of the shop owners, talked to my uncle about it; he was all right. Got back home—thank God!—and me'n Bobby had a proper talk, asked Bobby's mum and dad about it, and they said they'd help...long story down to very short story, me'n Bobby are starting a business—a real business. We're going to get stuff sent to us from Jamaica, import stuff like, and then sell it in Bobby's mum and dad's shop and do a bit of advertising, maybe in school, if we can...Phew, that's it! I'm exhausted just talking about it!"

Then, "Sir, miss, Mr Bullet, what d'you reckon?"

A short silence, then, "I, no, we, we all think that is absolutely amazing! Well done, Eric. Great stuff, Bobby!" Chris Warren spoke for the three grown-ups. "Looks like we've got a couple of businessmen millionaires, a doctor, a future prime minister, one professional footballer and a superstar athlete in the bus, along with three very old, very tired, but actually very, very inspired teachers and coaches."

And they were all waiting for Mickey, for the glue, to speak. And he did, a huge sigh, a grin, then, "My life is in this minibus, my whole life. Everyone I care about, well, obs Lucy and my mum, of course!"

They laughed, just a little. "You've been like a dad to me, Mr Warren. If I'm honest, my dad's a waste of space; you know, I ain't seen him now for over a year, a year! He don't even know I'm at Stratford Academy, that ain't a dad, not a real dad. Tell the truth, I'm glad he ain't around anymore, so's my mum. My mum's so relaxed pretty much all the time now. You know what? If he did come back, I don't think I'd let him; that ain't just words. I wouldn't let him spoil what me and my mum have now. We've never got on so good; my mum's not on edge any more, not at all."

TMRG and the grown-ups all stayed silent, thinking, because they all related to what Mickey was saying. They'd all been there to a lesser or greater extent. Shelley squeezed his hand a little tighter. "So yeah, I wanna do what Shelley and JoJo were saying, what Lucy's already proved you can do if you want it enough, and it's just the same as Joshi and Alisha and Bobby and Eric; it's about being a success, about being the very best you can be, don't matter if it's sport or business or anything. It's about deciding what you want to do and giving it absolutely everything you've got…So yeah, I want to be a runner—a real runner—not just pretty good, really good. I want to be the best."

"Miss, Gilly? I know Shelley's already asked you, but would you help me as well? I'll do anything, anything at all, if you will."

They stopped at a service station, coffee for the grown-ups, coke for the kids, pizza for all of them.

"Can't leave it there, Chris. Can't leave it there, Gilly. You've got something special with these kids. Not just saying that; I've been around these guys 'big-time, shoot a dime' forever. These kids are the real deal—once in a lifetime. Seen it a million times before, those who can and those who think they can and those who know they can. Is it all right if I say some stuff when we're back in the bus?" And there was no answer to that—no answer at all. In truth, Chris and Gilly were waiting to hear what Dan was going to say.

"You ever hear about a runner called Dave Bedford?" They were back in the minibus.

"Yeah, I read about him; it was ages ago, wasn't it, back in the seventies or something?" Mickey said. "Distance runner? Did he run marathons?"

"He was a great distance runner, Mickey, had the world record for ten thousand metres. British Championships one year; he won the five thousand and the ten thousand metres on consecutive days. And in cross-country, he won two championships on the same day! The junior and senior championships for the Southern Counties, and that was at Parliament Hill, where you did the London schools. Dave was pretty famous, very outspoken, always good value for the newspapers. He did run the London Marathon one year, but he wasn't that fit then. He's been involved in organising the London Marathon for a few years now,"

Dan Bullet paused, then said, "Somebody asked Dave once what they'd need to do to be a great runner, an international runner, and Dave replied, 'Don't even think about it!' Then he said, 'If the idea comes into your head, put it straight out, and only if that idea keeps on coming into your head and won't go away, then maybe go for it.'" The seven members of TMRG were listening intently, as were Chris and Gilly.

"Not being funny, Dan, but I don't really get it, why'd you want to put it out of your head?" Mickey said.

"What Dave Bedford was saying, Mickey, was that to be the absolute best at anything takes an incredible amount of hard work and a lot of suffering be it in sport or business or a career. You have to put a lot of things on hold, and it's not for everybody. Look, I'm going to be a bit flash now, so apologies first, OK?" And now they were enthralled, Gilly and Chris as much as the kids. "I was a good swimmer, went to the Olympic Games, got a medal; for a little while I was one of the best swimmers in the world, and I'm very proud of that. I trained really hard all the time. Sometimes I was so tired that I couldn't lift myself out of the pool. Once I even fell asleep on the poolside between repetitions." They gasped and laughed. "And my coach kicked me back in the pool to wake me up!" And they laughed again.

"Really, Dan? Really?"

"Yeah, really, I promise." And they all knew it was true. "OK, what I'm trying to say, guys, is this. If you're sure, if you're really sure, then go for it; not just sport but business and career as well, yeah?"

Nodding heads again. "There are three stages, and these are important to understand. Stage one: know exactly what you're aiming for, not just a 'oh, I wanna be good'. That won't do, decide exactly what you want. Stage two: know what you have to do to get there, and for sport, it's the training. Alisha, you guys, I can't tell you what it is in business because I don't know. I'm not clever enough." They laughed, but just a little. "And stage three—and this is important—is knowing what you have to give up to get there, and that can be the toughest one to take on board. Your mates are all going out to a party and you want to go, but you can't because you have to be at training early the next morning, and later on, they're all going off on summer holiday, and you can't go because you've been selected for an international meeting."

They were still spell-bound. "I'd do anything to run for my country," Shelley whispered almost to herself, and Mickey squeezed her hand again.

"And there's other stuff as well; some of it you can't control and some of it's not fair, but it's what it is." *I wish I could write this down*, Mickey thought, but he didn't have to worry because neither Mickey nor anyone else were ever going to forget Dan's words. "For a start, there's body changes, all this growing up, boys as well as girls, all of a sudden, you feel like your body's just doing what it wants to, and you can't control it."

"Story of my life, Dan!" said Shelley.

They laughed again, but again softly. "You're training harder than ever, but you're getting slower, and that's a toughie; that's a real toughie. You have to grit your teeth and get through it. And there'll be injuries, and you have to get through them as well; it's tough, and it's not fair…So that's why Dave Bedford said to put it out of your mind, still want to go for it?" And all seven of them knew that was exactly, exactly, what they wanted.

They were back at Westminster to collect Lucy just a few minutes before the London coach arrived, and they all stood and clapped as the London athletes got off the coach. Lucy and Sami thanked Scottie Peters, and then Lucy threw herself into Mickey's arms, and Sami just grinned.

"Can we give you a lift, Sami?"

"No thanks, Mr Bullet, but thanks for asking. It's all arranged; I've got a lift home sorted out." Sami shouted over at Lucy, "Oi! Leave him alone, put him down, come here, you, come here right now!" Lucy giggled and went over. "Look after yourself, little one, and promise to give me a ring in a few days, yeah?" And Lucy hugged her and promised, and Sami was gone.

The minibus arrived at the estate, and the eight descended—hugs and emotional thanks all around, of course. Dan drove away with Gilly and Chris waving out of the window. The eight looked around at their home territory, and suddenly, it was dispiriting; it felt like the magic weekend was over.

Over to the east, the city lights and Canary Wharf lights were mocking them, contrasting their grey surroundings. TMRG looked around, recognised it all. London can be beautiful. London can be ugly. London can be cruel. Sometimes London can only be beautiful from a distance, and this was one of those times. TMRG had seen something different; already, it seemed a different world, a hundred years ago and a thousand miles away. Already in their area, there were broken-down cars cruising, looking for far-too-young kids willing to sell themselves, little girls desperate to be older, grown-up in their immature minds; their minders only a few years older, already on that fast downward spiral. Kids already broken by their environment. 'Live fast, die young; who cares?', it was a mantra they had all heard.

The bling boys half-hidden in the shadows, in the corners, under the stairways and by the usually broken lifts, waiting to sell the first score of the evening. 'Not me, I ain't getting into drugs, not me', the cry of the loser, already lost, already using the profits to score for themselves, 'stop when I want, no worries'. The wannabes in their cheap copies, using cool American slang, which was so uncool outside America. The smell, always the smell, a smell of dirt, of rubbish, of sewers, of overcooked fat, the smell of the estate. Vomit on the ground and on the stairs, stink and stain of urine in the lifts; needles discarded everywhere. Mickey pulled Lucy close to him, and Lucy felt him shiver.

"I'm not living here all my life, Lucy…Listen, you guys, we are not going to live here forever. I promise you, and I promise myself. There's another world out there, and we can get that world. This weekend changed everything again; it was like when Mr Warren started and we understood what we could do…You've started it this time, Lucy, at the cross-country." Mickey pulled Lucy closer. "You showed everyone what could be done. And then Dan Bullet in the minibus, what he was saying, explaining—I'll tell you later, Lucy—he's showed me, showed all of us what can be done, what it takes. Those three—Dan, Gilly, Mr Warren—they've shown us the way…and I'm going for it." And Eric and Bobby and Shelley and JoJo and Alisha and Joshi and Lucy and Mickey held each other tight, so tight, and dreamed of the future, of their future.

Chapter Twenty-Eight
Assembly

"That's some commitment!" Dan was bringing the drinks over.

"Well, yes, I'd do anything for those kids; really, I'd do anything," Gilly said.

"Me too!" Chris and Dan both said together, and they laughed.

"Dan, what d'you think? Really, what d'you think? What you said in the bus, jeez, Dan, you got me going. The kids took it all in, all of it; they listened to you, every single word. You got that magic voice, you silver-tongued lizard." They all laughed. "You've been there, done it, got the badge; of course, they listened."

"Cheers." Dan lifted his glass of wine. Gilly and Chris reciprocated. "I told the truth; those kids accept the truth; they appreciate being spoken to like adults…In a lot of ways, they're pretty grown-up already…And without being funny in any way at all, I honestly believe that they've created a magic bond, which is not too far off what we had in the services, Chris, yeah?"

A nod of agreement. "They stick up for each other; they respect each other; they rib each other, of course, but listen to the words, listen to the words they use; it's just as Mickey said, those kids' lives are totally entwined with each other, in the nicest way. Mickey was right, their lives were in that minibus. They have a buzz when they're together, don't they? I listened to Alisha speak, first time this weekend that I've had the opportunity to get to know her a little, and you know what? She blew my mind away, blew it away. How can anyone that young be so mature? Depth of understanding, not scared of anything.

"Talking about going into politics! I don't think I even knew what politics was at her age. Same for all of them; Bobby and Eric starting an import business, my god! All I was worried about was getting my sweets and comics on a Saturday when I was twelve years old. Those kids said it, Chris, but I'll repeat a million times, you showed them the way—you really did. That old cliché, 'role model', that's you, mate, you—and you, Gilly—should be very proud."

"Thank you, my friend." Chris punched Dan lightly on the shoulder. Gilly leant over and kissed him.

"So, what do I really think? OK, here we go. Back when I started swimming, I managed to get to nationals when I was twelve years old, you know, age group stuff. Did front crawl and butterfly, even qualified on backstroke once. That first year I went, I reckon there were about sixty to seventy of us in that age group spread across all strokes, and each year I qualified, there were fewer and fewer of us. By the time I got to seniors, like real national champs, you know how many of us there were from my age group?" Shakes of the heads.

"There were eight of us, eight! And in butterfly, there was just me and one other; that's the reality of top-class swimming, of top-class sport; it sorts you out early. Now there's no guarantee that a good junior is going to make it as a senior, and it's not always the good juniors who make the top seniors. The difference between those who do and those who don't is pretty much belief and determination. Sounds pretty cliched, doesn't it? But I believe it's true. There were quite a few kids my age who were better than me, but it's one of the things I said in the minibus; it's making that choice, 'How much do I want it? How much am I prepared to give up to get it?' And I wanted it; oh man, I wanted it, wanted it so much.

"It was a way, a real way of getting respect. First time I put a Great Britain tracksuit, you know, it was in the front room with my mum—my dad wasn't around too much—and my mum cried, sobbed her heart out, so I did too, and I knew that I'd done something right, done something right by my mum. So, these kids, Mickey and Lucy, Shelley, JoJo, they're doing something right; they have my respect already, honestly. Look at little Lucy, heart of gold but the heart of iron, cliché again…yet look at her, sometimes I forget and think she's about ten! And then I see what she does in training, what she puts in during the race, kid's magic, kid is bloody magic! They all are, every single one!"

A long pause then, "One big strength they have, these four, is that they feed off each other. OK, I know JoJo is into football rather than running, but that doesn't really matter. What they get from each other is that knowledge that others close to them, very close, are putting in the same physical effort, the same training hours as they are, and it makes them so much stronger. I'm talking mental strength now, listening to JoJo speak, no option other than success, dedicated to making it, all negative thoughts dismissed, not allowed in her thinking. You can see the effect it had on the others, all of them; it was like 'Well, if JoJo can, I can!'"

Another pause. "Bottom line? Don't know, life can be cruel, and for athletes, it can be very cruel. One injury, one bad illness, different physical development—no one can tell for sure...And the chances of all four of them hitting the big-time? Four kids from the same estate, the same class in junior school? Odds on that one? Million to one? You wouldn't get any takers, nearer a billion to one. They're not from some eastern European-sponsored hothouse, not a sports specialist school like they have in the States, not even one of our public schools like Millfield or Rugby, or some of the sixth form feeder colleges by the universities, so the chances?"

Dan Bullet shook his head. "My head says no...but my heart, my big old black, cynical, uncaring heart, says, 'Yes, why not?' These kids...Anything might, just might, be possible." Another long pause. "Gilly, Chris, I'd love to stay and drink wine with you and talk more, but I need to get home, need to be in school even earlier tomorrow before swim training...have a drink for me!" And Dan Bullet, Olympic medallist and mentor to those young wannabes, was gone.

"Love that guy, love him. Some of the stuff he did for me when we were active, out there in the badlands..." Chris shook his head.

"Me too, Chris, one of the world's good guys...He loves those kids like we do, and I do mean 'love', for all of us...I'm right, aren't I?"

"You're always right, Gilly...that's why you chose me!" And they both grinned, but they both knew that everything that had been said was correct.

Danny Bullet had already spoken to Dr Fisher and Maria Hajisoteris (it was no surprise to him that teachers were in school just after seven o'clock) before he stood on the poolside for the early swim session, and he was not one tiny bit surprised that Mickey, Lucy, Shelley and even JoJo were there already. They looked at him in something akin to adoration, and for a moment, he felt embarrassed, and then it was gone. The swim session was fine, lots of emphasis on technique. Dan was aware that maybe, just maybe, he was adjusting the sessions to his (and he was embarrassed to admit it, but knew it was true) favourites.

"Lucy, do you have your English schools' medal with you?" Lucy was embarrassed.

219

"I do, Dan. How did you know?"

"Lucy, when I first went to English schools, I wore that medal around my neck for six months; of course, I know! Lucy, will you trust me? May I borrow it for a couple of hours? I promise I won't lose it, just want to show it around, big you up, tell people that I know a champ!" Lucy blushed but felt so, so proud that Dan Bullet was proud of her, me, little Lucy Lastic!

"Have a good day, you guys," Dan Bullet was talking to all of them. "It's Monday; don't be late for year assembly!" And with hair still damp, and that clinging smell of chlorine however much you shampooed and showered, the four of them joined up with Eric, Bobby, Alisha and Joshi for assembly. As they filed into the assembly hall, the Speeding Bullet rushed to the school gates to await his guest.

Sami pulled up in a minicab just as Dan showed his security pass, wearing her own school uniform; she was a little flushed but very excited.

"Thanks, Sami, really appreciate this. Any issues with school?"

"No, they thought it was great! They were very proud of me and said that what I was doing was exemplary, no problems and not to rush back."

Dan and Sami were waiting behind the curtains by the hall stage, hidden from the two hundred and fifty Year 7 pupils. There was silence as Ms Hajisoteris stood in front of them; she smiled, smiled broadly and proudly.

"Boys and girls, we have a very special assembly this morning." She looked directly at Lucy and the group around her...And Lucy felt her tiny heart tremble. Ms Hajisoteris smiled again. "I, Dr Fisher and the entire staff are extremely proud that Stratford Academy had a Year 7 pupil representing London schools in the English schools cross-country championship on Saturday, and she was competing against girls in Years 8 and 9. Year 7, I want you to put your hands together for Lucy Newton who came third and was just two seconds behind the winner! Lucy, will you come up onto the stage, please?"

Lucy blushed and didn't move until Mickey nudged her. She climbed the stairs onto the stage while two hundred and forty-nine pupils and ten group tutors clapped and cheered. And, as she shook Ms Hajisoteris' hand, Dan and Sami came out from behind the curtain...and Lucy just held it together. The whole year group stood and stared. What the hell? Who the hell was this kid in a different school uniform?

"I know what you're thinking...? Who's this girl? What's she doing here in our school? Well, my name is Sami Richards, and I was captain for our team at the English schools; I won the event, and this young lady"—Sami put her arms around Lucy—"has ran me the closest in two races now…and she's two years younger than me. So that's why I was invited here this morning by Mr Bullet, Ms Hajisoteris and Dr Fisher, to present Lucy." Sami put her hand in her pocket.

"With the first of the many, many medals she's going to win. This girl is awesome, and I'm extremely proud that she is my friend!" And Year 7 clapped and clapped and clapped…and Lucy blushed as Sami put the medal around her neck.

"Lucy, would you like to say something?" Ms Hajisoteris encouraged her.

"I'm not any good at this, miss, not any good at speaking out loud…but I want to thank everyone, truly I do." Lucy waved at her year group in the hall. "And I want to thank Mr Bullet and the other teachers and coaches and grown-ups who helped me to get this medal." She picked it up and waved it gently. "You see, they trained me, and more importantly, they believed in me. And Sami did as well." Lucy smiled at Sami, who smiled back directly.

Encouragingly, she said, "That's all I can say, miss; thank you for letting me do this." And the whole year group erupted again as Lucy picked her way off of the stage and re-joined her little group…and she smiled inside and out as Mickey squeezed her hand.

Everyone wanted to talk with Lucy that Monday: the kids in her tutor group, all the teachers for each lesson, seemed like every kid in the school during breaktime and lunchtime. Even the big kids, even the sixth formers, came up and congratulated her, and they even wanted their photo taken with Lucy. And Mickey was by her side the whole time, and Lucy was so happy that he was there. He deflected gently those who stayed too long, steered her away when he knew she was getting anxious, put his arm around her, whispered to her, took the pressure away. Shelley and JoJo and Alisha; Bobby and Eric and Joshi, all of them were there when she needed them.

TMRG all met together directly after the bell went for the end of last lesson; they hadn't planned or arranged it; they all just felt they needed to be together. Mickey had already given Lucy the entire content of the journey back, the encouragement from Chris and Gilly, the advice and motivation from Dan…

"Need to say something, just have to." Lucy was in the middle of the group; unconsciously, they were still protecting her. "I don't know if that weekend was the best in my life, I've had some lovely times; honest, I have…going to Amsterdam in summer was brilliant, changed my life I think, but when you lot

221

turned up with Dan, Gilly and Mr Warren and I saw you all while I was racing…It was amazing; really, it was amazing…I just felt special, very special; honest, I did. Can you believe that all of us are still together in big school?"

Lucy grinned. "I mean secondary school, of course."

They all grinned as well. "Those T-shirts! Amazing as well! Sometimes we don't say thank you enough; we just sort of think that our friends don't need it…Well, I do need to say thank you. I honestly love you all to bits. I feel safe with you, not saying that I'm not safe by myself, but I get a sort of a—I dunno—a sort of a warm glow in my tummy when we're all together…I know how stupid that sounds, but I don't care. Mind you, don't you ever dare tell anyone else I said that!"

"Luce, you said it for all of us." Shelley, still towering over Lucy, put her arms around her and hugged her tight. "I couldn't imagine being without all of us together; you're right, it feels safe. We're meant to be together. It's always just been just me and my mum…But you guys are my family; honest, you're my family, so I wanna say thank you as well, to everybody here, just for being here and being you. Lucy said it but I've got to say it as well, love you all to bits." And it was another group hug for TMRG, and somehow it felt like an extra strength was born.

"You know what?" Mickey said. "We're stronger for being together; probably no one would ever believe us, but I reckon we'll be together forever." Lucy looked at Mickey with her adoring eyes and desperately hoped that it was true, and Shelley loved him once again as her big brother, and they all knew that he really was the glue that held them together. And they were stronger together, much stronger. There was a feeling in each one that if they didn't try to do their absolute best in everything, then they'd be letting the others down, and they would never do that, never.

With the cross-countries done and the competitive schools football coming to an end, suddenly it was summer. Mickey repeated the half-joking mantra to them all on their Friday after-school meet-up.

"Us athletes are like flowers; we grow and develop underground in the winter; we ripen in the spring, and we blossom in the summer!" It always cracked them up when the mantra was heard; they all joined because they knew it off by heart…And they all believed it. JoJo was training a little more with them now; she was fully accepted at the Spurs Academy, but that schedule was now just three sessions each week for her age group, and she wanted to give herself a little edge on the other footballers, so the running, mobility, conditioning and the swimming all contributed to that depth of fitness.

"Do you remember what Dan told us that time about Michael Phelps?" They'd finished the swim session, and Dan was very much on their minds and their thoughts. "Dan said that Michael told him that he trained every day while nearly everyone else had one day off a week, and when Dan asked him why, Michael said, 'To be the best, you have to do things that other people aren't willing to do, and I reckoned that because all my rivals did six days a week training, then I would get an extra fifty-two training sessions a year.' And that gave him the edge."

They were all quiet, thinking of where they had come from, thinking of where they were now. "It's not just sport, though, is it, guys? What you're doing is amazing." Mickey smiled at them, and they all looked back at him smiling and with the utmost respect.

"I always loved just listening to Mr Warren when we were back in junior school," Bobby said. "He just made sense with everything he said. And then Gilly as well, amazing. So, this weekend, first time, me'n Eric and Alisha and Joshi have ever met Mr Bullet, Dan, well, properly like apart from seeing him around sometimes at school, and he's amazing as well. I felt like I was a little kid being tucked up in bed and read a story; it was that good. I was wishing that journey back could've gone on forever."

And, in many, many ways, that journey did go on forever.

Chapter Twenty-Nine
Growing Up, Catching Up

It was a good summer term for all of them in 2002. Alisha and Joshi received a headteacher's commendation certificate for their contribution to the debating society. Bobby and Eric received their first three orders for their import business, due in no small way to Bobby's mum twisting the arms of friends to buy and made a magnificent profit of five pounds, which they swiftly blew by treating all of TMRG to pizzas. JoJo received a letter from Tottenham Hotspur football club, inviting her to re-sign with the club and the academy for the next season with the added bonus that all her kit would be provided and all travel expenses reimbursed. Shelley, Lucy and Mickey excelled themselves in the London Schools Athletics Championships held at Crystal Palace. Lucy won the Year 7 girls eight-hundred metres by the proverbial mile; she simply went from the gun and ran away from the rest of the competitors.

Mickey did similar but sat slightly back from the early leaders as they set off at a suicidal pace before paying the price and blowing up. Shelley starred; she won the hurdles by the same distance that Lucy had won the eight-hundred metres, the proverbial mile, finishing before the second placer had cleared the last barrier. Shelley also won the long jump and was the third runner in the four by hundred relay, taking over in fourth place and handing over to the final leg in equal first. Shelley was noticed by the other athletes and by the staff from other schools. She was noticed by several coaches from the athletics clubs who were there watching, maybe talent-spotting.

After the final event, the relay, which was won in great part due to Shelley's bend running, Shelley was noticed by Lucy and Mickey; they stood with her while she put her tracksuit on, jogged around with her for the cooldown, and then Mickey put up the imaginary microphone to his mouth. "Well, ladies and gentlemen, boys and girls, with us today in the studio is the new Golden Girl of

British Athletics, three-time gold medallist—please put your hands together and welcome...Shelley Jelly Belly!" And, as it was meant to, it cracked them up. With their input, Newham won the inter-boroughs trophy, and Stratford Academy's final assembly featured the three-star athletes.

Despite their exertions and training commitments to athletics, they continued their progression in swimming. Sometimes the other members of TMRG would come and watch the sessions. Dan always welcomed them and their support. He too knew how their strength grew from each other, and he welcomed it and encouraged it. And the Speeding Bullet had ideas—big ideas, huge ideas. He did a lot of planning, a lot of research, and even more working out the costs, the implications, the very necessary paperwork before he could even approach the school management committee. He made an appointment to speak to Dr Fisher and outlined his proposed plans, and Dan knew that ninety-nine per cent of whether or not his ideas got the go-ahead would depend on what Dr Fisher thought before they even went to the management committee.

Dr Fisher listened intently, asked several questions on how the programme would start and progress, then said, "Mr Bullet, Dan, if I may?" Dan nodded 'yes, of course'. "I have been very impressed with the work that you've put in this year, your commitment to the pupils and how they have responded to you. It has been noted and remarked upon by the teaching staff, so, yes, I like your ideas, and I agree with your plans. You will need to present everything to the committee, of course, but you have my backing; let's see if we can get it cleared. Dan, one more thing, as you know, your initial contract was for one year and that year is up. We would like to offer you a permanent contract as of now...Would you be able to accept it, or do you need some time to think on it?" And there was absolutely no need for an answer to that.

"Dr Fisher, ladies and gentlemen, I would like to start a competitive swimming club at Stratford Academy. Since I started just one year ago, I have thoroughly enjoyed my time here. I hope that I have added something to the content of physical education lessons by ensuring that non-swimmers have the opportunity to become swimmers and are also given a further option to the extra-curricular activities. I believe that swimming can be as much a social skill as part of a well-balanced health and fitness regime.

"But now I would like to move further by setting up a competitive swimming club, based in and around the academy, of course, but also capable of holding our own against pure swimming clubs, competing against them in local, district and national competition. From what I have seen in our pupils this year, I believe there is the determination and the will to succeed. If I may use one of our pupils as an example?"

Dr Fisher nodded 'yes'. "Year 7 pupil, Lucy Newton, showed what can be done with hard work and the mindset to go along with it. To even make it to English schools is a superb achievement, to medal at that level is even better, and to medal against girls two years older and with a lot more experience is outstanding. I believe that the ethos in our Stratford Academy was a major factor in Lucy achieving what she did. The ethos, ladies and gentlemen, that you have put into the academy. The very nature of our academy is a pursuit of excellence, and I would like to help our pupils to achieve that excellence in one more area."

Dan went on to explain the structure of the club, the necessary funding that could be accessed through the national governing body and the local authorities, the coaching and administration. There was little argument in the meeting; there were even several offers to help administrate and support the welfare and coaching, all of which Dan welcomed and gratefully thanked. Dr Fisher brought the meeting to a close, and then he looked over at Dan and gave one long exaggerated wink.

Announcements and bulletins were placed on the noticeboards: timetables, schedules, trials, squads, commitments and requirements. Lucy Newton still carried that secret thought in her mind, and the Speeding Bullet did as well, and although neither discussed it (not just yet...) perhaps it was the final building block in the necessary structure.

That summer was different from the previous one, of course. But that previous summer had laid down the ground rules, had shown them the way. They still had Gilly and Mr Warren over at Vicky Park; they still had Dan now at their academy with a full swim-training structure, and there was no thought from them that they wouldn't take advantage of what was offered. Without actually planning it (or had they?) Chris, Gilly and Dan had formed their own structure, a coaching and support structure for TMRG, all eight of them.

For although Bobby and Eric, Alisha and Joshi hadn't made that decision of the other four to pursue a sporting career, they still enjoyed and looked forward to going for a run; they even still revisited their own figure of eight run where they had all started. And there were other things to deal with as well: physical growth, maturity and the dreaded puberty onslaught.

Although it was a crowded summer break, there weren't any lessons to deal with; there wasn't the hurry to fit everything in. There was time, time for friends, time for relationships. If anything, TMRG grew even closer to each other. There was huge respect from each of them for each other for what they were doing, what they were achieving. Sometimes they'd sit outside the flats and just talk, laugh, share their thoughts, dreams, ambitions, talk of what might be…and then laugh at themselves because they were still the kids from the estate; how dare they have those dreams and ambitions! Mickey reminded them.

"You guys remember when we got back from watching Lucy at English schools?"

They nodded 'yes, of course' they remembered. "I said it then, and I'll say it again now because I meant it, I am most definitely NOT going to spend the rest of my life living here…I love it with you guys; no, honest, I truly love it; we have something special, all of us…Other people don't understand what we've got; they don't see it; they don't have the…"

Mickey paused, searching, then said, "They don't have the imagination…and we do; we most certainly do!" Mickey stopped talking and went into thinking mode; nobody spoke or interrupted, then he said, "D'you ever think what it's like being a grown-up? Like properly think? I try to, and, to be honest, I find it difficult to imagine…to me, being thirty or something is really old, but then I look at Dan, Gilly and Chris and they've got to be somewhere around there, yeah? But what I can't imagine is ME being thirty…I can sort of see me there, but it's always a bit fuzzy, like it's just going to happen and I'll be there; am I stupid or something?"

"Feel like that all the time, Mickey," Shelley said.

"Yeah, me too," all of them said with shy smiles, slightly embarrassed grins, shoulders shrugging, elbows into each other's ribs.

"It is so weird being twelve years old!" JoJo shook her head, laughing at herself. "So weird! Can you believe it was less than two years ago when Mr Warren started as our teacher? Two years! Seems like forever in one way…And seems like yesterday as well. Can't believe how quick the time's gone…But then sometimes it seems to go on forever…I s'pose it's when you look back that you see how quickly it's gone."

"It's not that I'm scared or anything…" Mickey was still pondering on getting older, as were they all. "Well, sort of, I guess, like I wonder who I'm gonna be, where I'm gonna be…and then I think about how good it is with all of us still together, and I suppose I'm a bit scared that might just stop one day, someone moves away, or something happens—something you can't control. But we'll all move sometime; 'course we will…like I said before. Ain't going to live around here all my life, no way…Maybe we'll all get a mansion when we're rich and famous and live together; what d'you reckon?"

And they all laughed because that was never going to happen, but secretly, they all thought it was a brilliant idea.

Part Four
The Dream

Chapter Thirty
"I Just Cannot Believe That!"

And now they weren't twelve years old anymore; now TMRG had achieved that ripe old age of fifteen. And if the two years between Mr Warren and finishing the first year at Stratford had gone quickly, then the three years into 2005 seemed to have raced by. The years had been good—very good in many ways. Incredible to others but absolutely normal to the eight TMRG members; they still met up every Friday after school; they still hung out together, and sometimes they even jogged around their old figure of eight course, giggling and laughing and remembering.

Alisha had put herself forward to be a member of the Stratford Academy pupil and teachers school council. In many school situations, the school council can be an 'in name only' occurrence; pay lip service to it, but what happens is what the senior members of staff want to happen. And of course, there were elements of that at Stratford. But not all, by any means. It needed strong pupil members, strong pupil voices to be heard. And Alisha would listen to proposals, plans and developments, consider them and then speak out. And Alisha would speak out strongly and forcibly.

The confidence that she had honed and developed in the school debating society, the ability to make a case and to hold by it, gave her an authority that was remarked on by other students and also by the teachers. And Alisha loved it, loved it all. Alisha felt and knew that she was making a difference, and that was what she intended to do with her one precious life.

Bobby Carter grew in confidence. Bobby Carter had found success, found success in playing chess, found success in his fledgling business plans. And that double success in different fields gave Bobby more confidence and, therefore, more success. Bobby had joined the business studies club at the academy; he and Eric were the two youngest members; nearly everyone else was in either Year

231

11, just about to take their initial exams, or in Years 12 and 13, looking at final school exams and then university or the big bad world of work.

Bobby, along with Eric, was already looking at the big bad world of work, or rather, they were both already ensconced in it. Those tiny seeds planted in Jamaica had started to develop into flowers, and the blooming flowers were beginning to bring rewards. Rewards in money and also rewards in the pride of a job well done.

There was something different about old Epic Eric now. That summer in Jamaica—how many years ago?—well, it seemed a lifetime had taught him many things. And one of those things was that everything can be turned around, everything. You just have to want it enough and you just have to put that into practice. And that was exactly what Eric had done; he'd wanted it, and he'd turned it. For a start, his mum and dad were back together, and that was good; that was very good. Eric appreciated that so much. Having been so near to losing it for no fault of his own, he was so happy that he had it, and he was determined to keep it.

Old Epic Eric went out of his way to be nice to his mum and dad; of course, he did. 'You don't know what you've got 'til it's gone' was a constant vibration in his mind. Old Epic Eric knew what he'd got, and there was no way that it was going—no way at all.

JoJo had signed the contract on her fifteenth birthday, the one she'd been waiting for all her precious life. Spurs had outlined her possible future, had asked that she make a 'declaration of intent'. JoJo had signed that if Tottenham Hotspur football club offered her a professional contract on her sixteenth birthday, she would accept it. Sign it? Of course, she did. It was her life, always had been, always would be. JoJo wasn't playing in the Stratford boys football team any more. At the age of fourteen, the rules had struck, and the various health and safety aspects and the professional guidance had said 'no'.

In her final match, the London Schools Cup Final, played at West Ham's ground, JoJo had scored a hat-trick and been voted 'man of the match', which she and all her idolising teammates roared at. JoJo was sitting in her changing room when the knock at the door came. JoJo was invited into the boys changing room; her captain went out of his way to assure her that nothing was inappropriate; there was far too much respect there.

The opposing team was already there; their captain presented JoJo with a bottle of champagne that he'd smuggled in, expecting that his team would triumph. Their captain shook JoJo's hand, kissed her on the cheek, and boy, was JoJo shocked at that! Then he said, "Much respect, JoJo. I'd heard about you; 'course I had; we all had, but it was a bit of 'yeah, right!', but I have to say this, you are the absolute best footballer I have ever seen, played against, ever, really mean that. You'll play for England one day, really mean that as well."

All the team members from both sides lined up, shook hands with JoJo, kissed JoJo on the cheek and then presented her with the card, signed by all of them (the opposing team in a hurry). And JoJo cried softly and knew that her life had maybe, just maybe, changed forever.

Joshi was an enigma; he was an enigma to himself, let alone to the others. He said little, but when he did say something, everybody listened because everybody knew that it would be worth listening to. Joshi had, in some weird way, become a comedian. He saw—absolutely saw—the ridiculous side of everything. And Joshi the Doc would bite his tongue (to start with), and then— when the time was right—he would comment on whatever ridiculous statement, whatever ridiculous pronouncement, had been said. Joshi had developed this habit; if he was talking and someone interrupted, Joshi would just stop talking, completely.

And because everyone knew that what Joshi said would be worth listening to, gradually no one ever interrupted him. And when Joshi was about to speak, everyone on TMRG would grow quiet because they knew that Joshi's words would have them in hysterics. Joshi loved all of them, and they all loved Joshi right back.

Shelley had bought the ticket. Shelley had bought the very same ticket that Lucy had bought, the ticket to the English Schools Athletics Championships. Shelley's ticket had 'Hurdles' written as the destination. She had qualified for the final while she was still in Year 8, and the following year, Year 9, Shelley won the under-fifteen age group hurdles as well as being part of the winning London schools relay team. And the following year, moving up an age group, Shelley won English Schools again, against the girls one year older. Shelley was competing for her athletics club as well now, a regular in the Young Athletes League, taking the opportunity to compete in the sprints and the jumps as well as hurdles and, occasionally, the throws.

Shelley would even volunteer for the eight hundred metres sometimes. When asked why, she'd reply, "Because it hurts…and I love it!" And now and then Shelley would be asked if she'd race in senior southern league races, and once even in the Women's National league, which meant moving up to the one hundred metres hurdles and the higher barriers. And Shelley raced well, enjoyed it and learnt and learnt and learnt. The senior women athletes took to Shelley, not only in her club but the women she competed against. She made a point of thanking everyone: athletes and officials. People notice that; people really notice that, especially when it is a teenager doing the thanking.

Mickey bought the same ticket—that same ticket that Lucy and Shelley had bought—the ticket to the English Schools Championships. In his second school year, Mickey had qualified for the cross-country and then the fifteen hundred metres on the track. Neither went brilliantly, outside the top ten on the country and failing to make the final at fifteen hundred metres. Mickey took it all in, absorbed it, thought about it a lot. Talked to Gilly, talked to Chris, talked to Dan. Went away and thought, thought hard. Learnt from defeat, learnt a lot.

Trained as hard as he could, listened to Gilly, listened to Chris and Dan. Came back the next year and did the double, won the English Schools cross-country and also the fifteen hundred metres on the track. Won them both by running intelligently and using the experience of the previous defeats to ensure those victories. Moving up the age group, Mickey also moved up a distance to three thousand metres on the track, and Mickey won that English Schools three thousand metres along with a top ten position in the cross-country. It was another marker, another marker to that destination that Mickey wasn't yet quite sure of, but he knew that there was something waiting, something that he could achieve because of hard work; make that 'ridiculously' hard work.

Lucy had the season ticket now—that season ticket to English Schools. She'd earned that ticket, earned it as a twelve-year-old and kept renewing it. But she still needed to pay the price of that ticket, had to keep working hard to find the money. And Lucy did exactly that; she worked hard because she'd already seen the rewards, as that little girl racing with and against Sami.

Whenever Lucy thought about Sami, she smiled. *How lucky am I to have someone like that! And then Mickey, Shelley, JoJo and the others—how lucky am I? So lucky that I am never going to let it go away.* And that is a very good place to be in. And Lucy was in that exact place. She was known now, Lucy. She was pointed out by the athletic fraternity. "That kid over there? Yeah, the little one; she's the one that medalled at English school when she was still in the first year, yeah, I know, awesome!" Winning the cross-country wasn't easy,

Nothing that bites into your body like that is ever easy. But Lucy won, and then won again in the junior age group. Lucy doubled with the fifteen hundred metres on the track as a final year junior. Moving up to the intermediates, she thought that she'd be up against Sami again, and Sami was the defending champion.

"Hello, little one!" Sami had grinned at her before enveloping Lucy in a massive bear-hug.

"So, am I racing against you again, Sami?"

"Not this time, Lucy. I'm in the sixth form now; can't really believe that; we miss each other again…and to be honest, I'm glad, you're class, girl; you're really class, and age doesn't come into it…so wouldn't it be great if we both won?" And in fairy tales, they both WOULD have won, and as this is a modern-day fairy tale, they did both win. Lucy also won the three thousand metres on the track, and suddenly, suddenly, she and Mickey were the golden couple.

Gilly Ring and Chris Warren were married in the early summer of that year. Dan Bullet was best man; of course, he was. Dan Bullet also gave Gilly Ring away in the absence of her recently bereaved father, and nobody there thought it strange in any way at all. There were a lot of uniformed guests at the wedding. There were also eight young people who were extremely proud to have been invited, extraordinarily proud.

That pride was reflected by Gilly and Chris, and Dan, of course. At the reception, Shelley stood up and made the most eloquent speech to the bride and groom. TMRG had decided and voted on Shelley to do it. Those eight young knew how much they owed to the three adults who had and continued to change their lives, and it was demonstrated in Shelley's words.

And then came the announcement that was to change (once again) all their lives. It was just before the summer holidays were about to start, on July sixth, one final week of school and then release. The tannoy system in each of the Stratford Academy classrooms hiccupped into life; it was Dr Fisher.

"Staff and pupils are invited into the main hall for a special presentation. Any staff and pupils who would prefer to remain in their lessons are welcome to do so." And there were very few who chose to do so. All the curious and excited gathering sprinkled into the assembly hall; they saw that all the television screens had been switched on, and the massive backdrop screen on-stage was also broadcasting—the BBC news announcer.

"We're live from Singapore; it has just been announced that Moscow, New York and Madrid have been eliminated from the bidding process to host the 2012 Olympic Games. We now go directly to IOC President Jacques Rogge." The cameras zoomed in on the president.

"Our final two bids for the Olympic Games of 2012 are from Paris and London. In the final vote, Paris received fifty votes…London has received fifty-four votes…I therefore award the Olympic Games of 2012 to London!"

And while the entire bidding group for London, including Sebastian Coe, Denise Lewis and Steve Cram, went quietly mad. JoJo, Shelley, Lucy and Mickey all stared at each other, and just one thought, just one thought, went through each of their minds.

Chapter Thirty-One
Council of War

"It's not fair. It's not fucking fair!" JoJo never swore now, never. But this was different, and she was allowed. "We don't have a women's football team in the Olympics; what the fuck is wrong with people! Got a chance of going to the Olympics, really would have a chance, and now it ain't allowed!"

But JoJo was wrong, and JoJo found out that her chance, her one precious life's chance, would be allowed. And all she needed to do was to be good enough. And that isn't easy, isn't easy at all. The British Olympic Committee decided in its wisdom that although Great Britain had never entered a women's football team from 1996, when women's football was first on the Olympic programme, they would now take the choice as the host nation to do so. The history was that traditionally England, Scotland, Wales and northern Ireland had separate teams in the major football championships, and the Olympic Games was Great Britain. Fortunately, common sense prevailed. And all JoJo had to do at the ripe old age of fifteen was to prove that she would be good enough in seven short years' time. The Olympic Charter designated that football teams—both men and women—would be under twenty-three years old with the option of two overage players. And JoJo would be twenty-two years of age in 2012. And so she was squeezing it…squeezing it hard.

For Shelley, Lucy and Mickey, the age factor was almost reversed. At twenty-two, would they be experienced enough? Would they have had enough years of training and competing at top level? Bottom line, would they be good enough? The Speeding Bullet was expecting them; they were on the poolside the next morning, and he grinned as they went through the tough training session, somehow holding themselves back from the questions. He didn't mention the Olympics, not once. And at the end of the session.

"Nice one, guys, see you this evening for those on double sessions, tomorrow for ordinary mortals!"

"Speak to you, Mr Bullet, speak to you, Dan…please, please!"

"Been in touch with Chris and Gilly already, how about coffee and cake this evening? Reasonable? Sound good?" And it sounded very good, very reasonable indeed.

But before that meeting could take place, the world changed, the world changed forever. Dr Fisher's voice came over the mass tannoy, and every single pupil noticed that somehow his voice was different.

"Boys and girls, members of staff, there is something that you all need to be aware of. Please make your way to the assembly hall immediately." And this was to be a very different assembly to that of yesterday. There was an absolute silence as the pupils filed into the hall. They knew; they just knew that something serious had happened or was about to happen.

Dr Fisher was pale, very pale. "I have just been informed that there have been a number of explosions, possibly bombings on the London underground system; it seems that there have been a number of deaths. I know that many of you have your parents working in London and using the underground for their commute. I beg you not to panic, but there is no easy way for me to share this information. Those of you who have mobiles are welcome to use them; anybody who doesn't, can use the academy's phone lines.

"We will ensure that the academy is open all day; we see our academy as a place of safety. Similarly, if anyone feels they need to be at home, there is no problem, ask your group tutor for an exit pass. Lessons will remain, but we understand that there may well be disruptions during the day. I know that your teachers will do everything that they can do to help you. My door is open, if you want or need to see me, to speak to me, I promise that I will be available and listen. Your year heads have been taken off teaching duties today and will also be available in their offices. We will now take an extra recess for half an hour."

The eight of them were together immediately, dazed and close to tears, how dare someone do this to our London! Joshi spoke first.

"Me'n Alisha's mum and dad are OK; they're in the chemists all day, not going out to collect any meds or prescriptions at all. Bobby, your mum and dad at the shop?" A quick nod from Bobby.

"Yeah, usual day for them, at the shop all day."

"My mum's fine, usual work stuff but around here," Mickey said.

"Same with my mum and dad, working but not going Central." They said 'Central' when talking about going right into London.

Eric looked relieved, then said, "Shelley, Shell, you all right?" And Shelley was most definitely not all right, deathly pale; the light had gone out of her eyes.

"My mum started a new job today; you know all that cleaning stuff she did just to make sure that I was OK growing up? Well, she's been made a supervisor; it's some big-deal solicitors offices in Holborn. I think it's in Lincoln Inns Fields or something like that…she had to go in early, on the tube, left before I got up for school and training…oh fucking hell, I keep ringing her, and I can't get through!"

Instantly, they were all around her; Lucy directly in front, arms around Shelley's neck, face buried into her, Alisha and JoJo on either side, the boys stood there feeling useless. What else could they feel?

"Your mum'll be all right, Shell. If she went in early, it would have been before all that stuff started; we would have heard it before." But Mickey wasn't sure, wasn't sure at all.

On their mobiles now, all of them; Shelley had made them realise how quickly their wonderful world could change.

"Mum? Dad? You all right? No, I'm fine, just checking, you know, those explosions on the tube." And gradually, the picture became a little clearer, and then they heard that there was another explosion, almost certainly a bomb, this time on a bus…and still, still, Shelley couldn't contact her mum.

"My mum, my mum! What am I gonna do? What's gonna happen to me? Oh, Mum, please pick up, please, Mum!"

And then the miracle happened.

"Hello, Shelley, hello darling, you've been trying to ring me, looks like a lot of calls I've missed; everything all right?" And Shelley burst into a fresh outbreak of tears, couldn't speak and handed her mobile phone to Mickey.

"Mrs Steele, it's Mickey Honey here; Shelley's just given me her phone." And Mickey went on to outline the details of the newscasts of that morning to Shelley's mum.

"Not a thing, haven't heard a thing, Mickey. Listen, I'm fine. I've been in a meeting since I've been here; quite intense, Mickey. Is Shelley OK to talk now?" Shelley nodded.

"Oh, Mum! I was so worried, didn't know what to think, didn't know what to do. Mum, when you home? Mum, please, please, please don't get the tube or a bus, please. Get a taxi or walk if you have to…Mum, I love you so much!" And Shelley burst into tears again, and the other seven members of TMRG all had those same tears in their eyes.

No one had actually said, 'I'm going to see Dan, going to see Mr Bullet', but it seemed they just gravitated to the swimming pool. A knock on the office door, and it was opened while the final knock was still echoing around the changing rooms. Dan Bullet's face was grey, his face was etched with lines that they hadn't noticed before, and now they couldn't help but notice.

"I am so glad to see you guys." He kept thinking, *Do not cry in front of them, do not cry.*

"We had to come, Dan, we just had to; we got all shook up. Shelley got seriously worried about her mum. Her mum had to go Central London this morning, Holborn, and Shell couldn't get in touch with her…But she's all right; yeah, she's all right." Dan took Shelley in a huge bear-hug, and Shelley relaxed a tiny bit more, feeling safe in the arms of a grown-up whom she trusted and would trust forever.

"Mr Bullet, Dan, you OK?" Mickey said.

"Well, Mickey…You know I was telling you bits and pieces about when Chris and I were in the services?" All of them nodded 'yes'.

"OK, bottom line, we were dealing with stuff like this quite a lot of the time, bombings, explosions, boobytraps, people who didn't care about life like we do…And I guess this morning just brought it all back. Not good times, not good times at all." And then he said, "This changes the world, you know? It really does…Makes you think what's important, makes you think about what you have and how easy it can go wrong. Those people on the tube this morning, why them? Just going about an ordinary day, probably thinking about what they'd be doing this evening, who they're seeing, go for a meal or a drink, stay in and watch the old telly, play with their kids…and now that's gone, taken away in a second. Wrong place, wrong time, not their fault."

They were all totally silent now, just listening. "Makes you realise how lucky we are, can be taken away in an instant. Listen guys, I know we said about meeting up this evening with Chris and Gilly, yeah? Well, I'm guessing you want to be with your parents, but if you can, I think it would be good to meet. Gilly said we can go to their place, their new flat. Would that be OK? Check with your mums and dads, and if it's no good, we can rearrange." And they loved the Speeding Bullet like a second dad.

There had never been such well-behaved, attentive kids. Cups of tea and coffee were made and delivered to mum and dad, the washing up was done, even fifteen-year-olds cuddling up to mum and dad, so 'not cool' but so essential.

'You don't know what you've got 'til it's gone,' was ever-present in their minds and thoughts. Mickey realised that now, Shelley even more so. Every single one of TMRG knew it. And then, "Mum, is it all right if I go out with my mates? Mr Warren has asked us around for tea and cakes, is that all right, Mum?" And all the mums (and dads) still worshipped Mr Warren, and so TMRG met together outside the estate and went to their destiny. Very quiet going over to start with, walking with this one, then that one, twos and threes, positions changing and changing again, so comfortable in their own company; gradually the spirit lifting a little, gradually a few more giggles and laughter.

They arrived at the new address, felt a little nervous, knocked on the door, but in truth, Gilly and Chris had been watching and had seen them arrive, and they went in. Life was about to change again.

Chapter Thirty-Two
The World Stood Still

For the first time in a long, long time with Mr Warren and Gilly, the atmosphere felt strained, nervous. Two days ago, life had been ordinary, ordinary but good. Then came the London Olympic Games announcement, and life had become fantastic, awesome for them. And then the tragedies of today, and it seemed that their new awesome life had been snatched away from them. The world truly had changed. And then, after the sandwiches, cakes, tea and coffee had been handed around, Chris spoke…Chris, Gilly and Dan had already discussed what he was about to say; to Chris, it was almost as if he was preparing for a job interview.

"I cannot believe how grown up you are! Thank you so much for coming tonight, the stuff that happened today, I was going to say, 'I can't believe it', but sadly, I can. Shelley, that must have been so tough for you today, not knowing if your mum was OK. She's all right, yes?"

Shelley nodded a yes. "For all of you, awful times, just awful, sometimes the world is not a very nice place, but it's our only place. We can't control what the idiots do; 'course, we can't, but what we can control is what we want to do…What we're going to do." The eight 15-year-old almost adults nodded a yes again.

"I know that you want to talk about the London Olympics, not just the four who are into sport but you guys who are so good at supporting; I've said it before, and I'm very happy to say it again, you can be whoever you want to be; you really can. I believe it, and I know that you believe it. Seven years, seven years to our Olympics, London, here, just down the road. Everyone is thinking of Crystal Palace, but if you look at London's bid, Seb Coe's speech, they're looking to build a new stadium right here in Newham, Stratford…wouldn't that be awesome? London kids in the London Olympics, better than that, kids growing up in Newham doing the Olympics in Newham, wow, that would be amazing!"

Spellbound, speechless, stunned, shocked, all eight of TMRG drank in every single word. "Gilly, Dan and I have talked about this a lot…And, if you're OK with this, we will do everything, absolutely everything, to try to help you qualify. Every single one of you is the best in the country in your age group; you've already proved that. And that is fantastic, but this is the Olympic Games! The absolute best that you can be! The best in the world!" And they drank it all in—every single word. Then he said, "Dan?" And the Speeding Bullet smiled, a little of the day's horrors had lifted from him.

"When we were all coming back from watching Lucy in those first English schools, in the minibus…remember?" Of course, they remembered; it had been a life-changing talk. "We spoke about what was needed; we said about three things…anyone remember them?"

"I remember every single word, Dan; honest, I do, every single word. It was knowing what you wanted to be, to do, exactly, not just 'oh, yeah, I wanna be good', then there was the training you needed to do to get there and then it was what you had to give up, the things you couldn't do, sort of sacrifices you had to make, right Dan?" And they all stared at Mickey, kids and adults alike, just about word-perfect.

"Bloody hell, Mickey, you need to go on *Mastermind* or something, or some memory programme, you'd make a fortune…Come and work with me and Eric!" And they giggled at Bobby's words.

"Look, don't laugh at me…When I got home that night, Lucy came around my place, and I told her everything you'd said, Dan…And then…And I said 'don't laugh', I actually did write it down, as much as I could remember…I've still got it; it's on a piece of paper in my bedroom, and when things are getting tough, when I ain't sure about going training, I pick it up and check it out. Sometimes I read it out loud, honest, me! Reading to myself in my bedroom." And then he said, "Sir? Mr Warren? It's called something like a mantra, isn't it? Like you live your life by it?"

"That's exactly what it is, Mickey, exactly."

"Sir, Mr Warren, you know how many training sessions I've missed with Gilly and Dan since that journey back? Listen, I'm not being flash, I promise…I haven't missed one single session, not one. I told you that night I wanted to be good, to be good at running, and I reckon I've proved it a little bit, English schools and all that; even my swimming's got a lot better, hasn't it, Dan? And something else I need to say. Lucy, Shell, JoJo, is it all right if I say?"

Of course, it was all right. "None of us has missed a session, not one. JoJo is amazing, all the stuff up with Spurs and she still comes training with us whenever she can, that's how much it means," and that was a long old speech from Mickey Honey.

"And that, ladies and gentlemen, is one part of the equation, nice one, Mickey." The Speeding Bullet reached out and shook Mickey's hand in a genuine show of admiration. "Not sure if I ever had the guts to say anything like that, Mickey; that's brave; really, that is so brave, much respect."

Lucy's eyes were shining, shining with a few tears and a whole lot of love as she looked at the boy—the boy who was now a man—whom she'd loved forever. "And so to part two, exactly what do you have do to get to your Olympic Games?" Your Olympic Games! Dan had said 'your' Olympic Games!

"Well, I guess you have to qualify…and that isn't easy, not easy at all. So, let's have a look…Exactly."

He turned to Gilly, and it was her turn to turn dreams into harsh realities. She took out the notebook that she'd carried to almost every session over the last four years. *A history of a life*, she thought to herself.

"Working with you guys, coaching you has been an absolute pleasure. Down at Vicky Park or when I've come into Stratford for some of those sessions has been superb. I honestly couldn't have asked for anyone better, and what you've all achieved, all of you, has been so well-deserved. I talk to other coaches, to teachers at other secondary schools, and they cannot believe that you've all stuck together all this time."

Gilly smiled at JoJo. "And they can't believe you, JoJo, playing for Spurs, pro-contract next year, I'm guessing?" An embarrassed smile and a nodded 'hope so, yes' from JoJo. "And you still come down to my training sessions, that's pure class, girl, pure class!"

JoJo blushed, blushed happily. "And you know what's really classy, JoJo? You never talk about it, never. Some of the guys at the Football Academies, some of them never stop telling everyone how good they are, how they're going to make it big-time, and they don't hold a candle to you, nowhere near."

Gilly smiled at JoJo again. "JoJo, have you told these guys, your mates, what's going to happen this summer?" JoJo shook her head 'no'. "May I tell them, JoJo? Or maybe, why don't you tell them?"

"Miss, Gilly, I was going to tell everyone, but I was, like, a bit embarrassed, didn't want to be flash, you know, waiting for the right time."

"You ain't never been flash, JoJo, never!" Shelley held the floor. "Since that first few weeks at Spurs when you couldn't stop talking about it, and that's totes understandable, you never say a word, you're the least 'flashest person' I know…Well, apart from me, of course!" And they all laughed. Shelley was like the big sister again. "So I would REALLY like to know what you're doing this summer, JoJo, and if you or Gilly don't tell us right now, I may have to forget that I'm a lady"—Shelley swished her hips, put her head on her shoulder, pouted her lips and flickered her eyelids and had no idea of the effect—"and tickle you to death! JoJo, can you tell us? Listen, you don't have to…" But of course, JoJo had to now.

"Well, all right." JoJo took a deep breath, a very deep breath. "I got in the schools' team…I've been selected to play for England Schoolgirls against Scotland, Wales and Ireland." Shelley got to her first, just as the tears started to roll down JoJo's cheeks.

"I am, no, we are SO proud of you! So, so proud, aren't we, miss, sir, Dan?"

"JoJo, anything else to say?"

"Miss, it sounds so flash…Oh, all right then. OK they've made me captain, captain of the English schools' football team." And now it was Alisha's turn to hug JoJo, followed by Lucy and then all the boys.

"And the girl done good!" Mickey, of course, squeezed JoJo tight and kissed her on the cheek.

"Oi, JoJo! Put him down, girl, he's mine!" Lucy burst into laughter, and then they all did.

"JoJo?" Gilly asked. "Anything else?"

"Miss, should I? Really?"

"These guys love you more than anything in the world, JoJo, you should let them share your happiness, your amazingly good news."

"All right, miss, if you say so." And now there was absolute silence until JoJo broke it. "Well, Spurs have asked me if I'd like to go on the pre-season tour with them…Like the first team, the proper team, the senior women, adults, the pros, they asked me! Me! Said it would be good experience for me at fifteen, be around the pros, wouldn't play like, well, maybe come on, as a sub a bit." And then JoJo really did burst out sobbing, and this time, it was Mr Warren who got to her first.

"Oh, JoJo! That is just brilliant for you…and you didn't tell anyone, wow!"

"Well, I did tell Gilly just after I heard but asked her not to say anything…you know. I really didn't want to come over all flash, like 'look at me! Aren't I great!' That's honestly not me, Mr Warren…"

"No, that's most definitely not you, JoJo; there's a lot of that little girl that I taught five years ago still in there. Much respect, young lady, so much respect to you."

JoJo sighed happily. "Sir, will you come and watch me next season at Spurs? They told me that I've been put up to the under nineteens for next year…I'm a little bit nervous, but it's exactly what I want to do, always wanted to do…Got to thank you again, Mr Warren, believing in me, that's everything, honest."

Then JoJo said, "Gilly, Dan, everyone, I think that's about enough of me for now, don't you?"

"Yes, enough already! You're just so flash, JoJo!" Shelley smiled and released the tight hug.

"Thanks, Shell, thanks all of you, don't know what I'd do without all you lot." And all of TMRG looked at each other and had exactly the same thoughts, all still together, quite amazing.

"Probably the hardest thing to get to the Olympics is going to be qualifying," Dan said. "When I went to the Sydney Games, it was hard enough to make the GB team, but all the Aussie guys that I got to know out there, and you see everyone in the training pools, said that it was so much harder trying to make the team when it was your Games, and London, you young ladies and gentlemen, is most definitely going to be your Olympic Games. The Aussie guys were saying that it was every Aussie swimmer and their Joey kangaroos going out for the team, and that's going to be the same for you guys. JoJo, just before we start talking about the athletics, I need to tell you that if you keep doing what you're doing, it is going to be your Olympics as well; I've been around professional sport for long enough to know that if Spurs are taking you away pre-season, then they absolutely believe in you. It's big business, and it's big money, and if they're investing in you, which they obviously are, then they believe in you. Don't you be afraid, go for it with everything you've got, and you will be there! And…So will everyone in this room to cheer you on, right guys? Now Mickey said that it was all about knowing exactly what was needed, and that's what we need to examine, Gilly?"

Gilly turned over the first page of her well-thumbed notebook.

"If we're serious about this…"

"Miss, sorry, Gilly, I dunno if Lucy, Shelley and Mickey are serious about the Olympics, but I am, I most certainly am!"

Alisha was on her feet, impassioned. "Can you imagine, the Olympics here, my backyard! Newham, Stratford and my mates, my absolute best friends in the world are going to be in it, no pressure there, then! I'll tell you what, miss? I am going to be involved; no, I am. Don't know how yet, but I will. I promise I will. I'll be in that stadium—if it is going to be a new stadium—and I'll be supporting my mates, yes, I will. Look, I gotta say something else as well, all right? JoJo, Lucy, Shelley, even you Mickey"—they all laughed just a bit—"if I can do anything, anything at all, I promise you I will do it; no really, I promise. I'll even get my pompoms and my raa-raa skirt!" And that did crack them up.

"Think that might take a little bit of time getting that particular image out of my mind, Alisha, mind you…" Eric snatched a wink at her.

"Thanks, Eric." Alisha smiled back.

"A little bit of order here, please, ladies and gentlemen." Gilly brought them back to reality. "You want to go to the Games? OK, here's what you have to do. First of all, which events you going for? JoJo, you're easy, twenty-two-year-old captain of Great Britain football, yeah, you're easy." And they all realised this was serious now, and it wouldn't be easy at all. "Mickey, put you on the line, what do you think?"

"First of all, I would absolutely love to go to the Olympic Games; 'course, I do. Everyone dreams about it, don't they? And then for most people that dream dies a little bit, and then a little bit more, real life takes over, and it goes away, don't seem that important any more. Well, for me, that dream hasn't died. I wouldn't let it." Mickey Honey stopped and then said, "I'm not stupid, well, you might think so when I open my mouth—"

"No, never, Mickey, never, not when you open your mouth, only when the words come out!" Joshi said with a big smile. "Actually, my friend, sometimes I find it difficult to work out how much sense you talk…Not all the time though…" The atmosphere was lighter now.

"But this might sound just a little bit stupid…" They waited. "I know I'm quite good at running, but what I'm really good at is hurting, you know, suffering, pain."

Mickey looked around at them. "Don't know why, just am. Some of the guys I've run against are miles better than me, but if and when I beat them, it's because

I can go on hurting for longer than they can; there comes a point, and I know, I just know that they're going to drop off because the hurt is too much for them…Does that make sense?" Lucy smiled at him, knowing exactly what he meant because that was in her make-up as well.

Mickey went on, "So it would make sense to go for distance; it's what I'm good at, could never be a sprinter like you, Shelley, don't have all that fast-twitch stuff they talk about down Vicky Park. So, the longer the better…But then there's the catch, isn't there?"

They waited again, getting into Mickey's words and thoughts now. "It's a lot of what you said, Dan, way back, about when you started swimming and gradually over the years so many of your age group dropped out and what's left is the best of the best and age doesn't come into it. So that's the thing, isn't it? There's runners out there already in the British team, already been to the Olympics or Europeans or Commonwealths, and they're going to be looking for London; of course, they are. So can I hurt longer than all those guys out there who've already competed for Great Britain? I dunno, but I'll try. And then I think, 'Jeez, man, you're still only a kid, you haven't even raced for GB yet, and now you're talking about the Olympics. What kind of fool am I?' But then I also think, 'But it's seven years' time, seven years from now.'

"Look how much I've improved since you started coaching me, Gilly. And I start doing the sums, year to year, distance by distance, event by event, and so I think 'why not?' Why not me? Why not Lucy? Why not Shelley? JoJo's proved what can be done, and that's amazing, one of us, really one of us! So, I'm going to keep on training, keep on hurting, keep on dropping the times. I'm going to make a chart, well, I sort of have already…it sort of makes sense to me to go for the longest event that I can, so that's obviously the marathon, but I'm also very realistic, and if the guys that I'm likely to be up against are already, say, twenty or twenty-five years old, then they've had all those extra years of training, so maybe I should think more about five thousand or ten thousand metres."

Mickey paused, looked up, smiled at Gilly, then said, "I guess I need to talk to my coach and take advice. What do you think, Gilly?"

"I think you've set it out pretty well, Mickey, and there's one thing that came across really well, but you never stated it; it was just there." And they were all waiting now. "And that unstated thing was not having a fear of failure, and that is so important. There are a lot of people out there who never give it a real go because they have that fear of failure and that stops them even trying, so what I think, Mickey, is that you keep your options open, why not? There are a lot of similarities in training for those three events, so keep it open, and then if we have to, we'll make a decision down the line…Mickey, does that sound about right? Done deal?"

Gilly Ring adored Mickey Honey, just adored him. Saw through that oh-so-tough exterior to the still-sometimes-little-boy who had refused to accept his so-called destiny and had somehow managed to persuade and carry his friends along with him. Yes, Gilly had a lot of time for Mickey Honey. In many ways, he reminded her of herself, that vulnerability hidden. And Gilly also adored the way that Mickey protected Lucy, loved Lucy. If there was one love story that she desperately wanted to arrive at the fairy-tale ending, it was this one. She yearned for them, both of them. "So, with your charts and stuff, Mickey, do you have an idea of what sort of times you're going to need even to make the team?"

"What I did, Gilly, was to focus on the ten thousand. I thought I'd—well, we'd—go for the one in the middle and see how it pans out, and I reckon I'd probably need around, I dunno, maybe twenty-seven thirty? Does that sound about right?"

Gilly nodded and waited, then said, "And what do you think you could do now, Mickey? Any idea?"

"You know the Vicky Park 10K race, Gilly?" Gilly nodded 'of course'.

"Well, I went over to watch it. Some of the older guys at club were running, and I thought I should go and support, like they always encourage me, don't they? Anyway, it sort of got me going, so I went back in the afternoon, me'n Lucy went back, and I ran it by myself, sort of like a time trial, yeah? I ran a thirty forty-five, and I was working hard for that. So"—and now they were enthralled, listening hard, doing the sums, over three minutes adrift, not a chance—"so if I was running that sort of time on the track, then I reckon I'd get lapped three times by the top guys, three times! But then the stupid part of me started thinking, got to drop over three minutes just to make the team, impossible! So, I kept my stupid thinking, and I thought, well, seven years, that's only thirty seconds a year, and that's only three seconds for each kilometre every year, so basically, it's a doddle!"

They smiled and laughed cautiously because now it was getting more and more real, and there was more of an insight into just how hard it would be. "Gilly, what d'you reckon, honestly, me and you, yeah, can we? I reckon there's a chance. I honestly do…Remember, I'm good at hurting!" And Gilly Warren's heart went out that little bit more to him, the boy who had become a man, an athlete, a warrior.

"Yes, I believe you can, a bit of hurt and no fear of failure, yes, I believe you can…Look, I have to take a break!" And Gilly Warren went into the toilet and thought very deeply.

Two days before, that magic news of a London Olympic Games and then, immediately after, that tragic news that no one is really one hundred per cent safe, not ever. And their small group felt just that little bit safer being in that group. Chris and Dan had seen the other side, the bad side, up close. Gilly knew it also through their words and conversations, and now it had been thrust upon the eight members of TMRG, and their group became even closer. And that was good.

"Lucy?"

"Oh, miss, sorry, I still can't get used to calling you Gilly…Well, I can, but then I forget!"

"I think you're forgiven, Lucy, you can call me whatever's comfortable."

"It's pretty much the same as what Mickey said, Gilly, I have to go long; it's what I'm good at…you know what? I hate saying 'what I'm good at!' It does sound flash, doesn't it? But I s'pose I am." Lucy was thinking hard now, mulling it over in her mind. Should I tell them? Should I? She looked over at Dan and knew immediately that Dan was reading her mind, and she also knew immediately that Dan would let her decide…

"I did the Vicky Park 10K at the same time as Mickey, not with him, though, just me…And yeah, I know that I'm not supposed to run that far, but I just had to. I went a thirty-three long, and I know before you ask me that Paula Radcliffe went just outside thirty a couple of years ago, but she's miles ahead of the other British girls, so I think I'd need a, what, maybe a mid-thirty-one to make the team, possibly lower than that, so I have to drop two minutes, maybe a bit more…I can do that, yes, I can do that." Lucy decided that her and Dan's secret would live a little while longer; she needed to tell Mickey before anyone else; of course, she did.

"And that's looking at the ten thousand. I haven't ruled out the 5K or the marathon…Or could I do two of them? That hurting thing Mickey talks about, that's pretty much me as well…Wow, we're both pretty weird, aren't we?"

"I don't think you're weird at all," Gilly, Chris and Dan had all spoken exactly the same words at exactly the same time, and they laughed out loud.

"Yeah, we planned that!" Dan said.

"Shelley, thoughts?" *Oh my god, just look at her! She has no idea what she looks like, well, maybe she does, but I don't think she cares a stuff! She makes it big time on the track; they're gonna come begging her. Shelley looks like a model right now, and she's what, fifteen years old. Shelley makes it and Nike, Adidas, Asics, they're all going to be throwing themselves at her.* The unspoken thoughts spun through Gilly's head; she was miles away.

"Miss? Gilly? You all right, miss?" Shelley said.

"Oops! Sorry, Shelley, I think I was having a brainstorm…That's what old age does to you! Sorry, Shelley, tell me again."

"It's got to be the hurdles, hasn't it? That first ever time you got me hurdling, do you remember, miss?" And it always seemed back to 'Miss' rather than Gilly when Shelley was going over those lovely past memories. "Never forget that, never; it just came easy…no, I don't mean that…But you know what I mean, just felt like something I could do, so yes, hurdles for me."

And then Gilly smiled because she knew that the bomb she was about to throw was going to cause some huge thinking about. "Of course, which hurdles, Shelley?"

"Errh? What d'you mean, miss, sorry, Gilly. I will get used to it! There's only one hurdles—" Shelley stopped midway through, and she gasped, gasped out loud. "Gilly? The four hundred? You think I could do the four hundred hurdles, really?"

"Well, there are a couple of Brits who moved up to the four hundred from sprint hurdles, and they didn't do too badly; David Hemery, Olympic gold way back in 1968 in Mexico City, and Sally Gunnel in Barcelona in 1992, and her time there is still a British record…it's worth thinking about, Shelley. I'm certainly not saying you have to choose now; of course, you don't, but isn't it nice to keep your options open? You run the eight hundred occasionally for Vicky Park in the club meets, don't you? OK, so think about that coming together of stamina from the eight hundred and sprint speed and hurdling technique from the hundred hurdles when you move up to a senior, that is, although you've done a couple of hundreds in senior club meets, I think?"

"Yes, I did a couple of the 'B' races in Southern league; they were all right, didn't mind the extra distance or the higher hurdles, Gilly. You think the four hundred is a possibility, really?"

"Yes, I definitely think so. Look, Shelley, it's seven years' time, seven years! So much can happen in that time, so the same as Lucy and Mickey, keep those options open." Then with a smile she said, "There's always that third option of hurdles though, isn't there?" And now Shelley was puzzled; she hadn't even considered the four hundred hurdles, and now Gilly was telling her there was a third option, Shelley was racking her brains, and then there was glimmer of a thought that grew stronger and stronger and stronger.

Shelley looked at Gilly, stared at her rather; the idea grew and grew, smiled now, then she said, "Do you really think I could do that, Gilly, do you?" And Gilly smiled right back at Shelley because she knew that Shelley was right there with her. "You mean the heptathlon, don't you, miss...Gilly?" And Gilly Warren lifted her eyebrows and smiled right back.

"Got it in one, Shelley, got it in one...What d'you reckon?"

"Oh...my...God! Hadn't thought about that one, not ever. I dunno, miss. I really don't know..." But the more Shelley considered it, the more appealing it became. *Loved doing those five events in Amsterdam all that time ago, really did enjoy that, and then doing the odd event for Vicky Park, yeah, that's good...Maybe I could, just maybe I could.*

"God, Gilly, do you think so? Gilly, I don't even know all the events, not properly, tell me again?" And TMRG were listening intently, total focus on this one. Lucy, Mickey and JoJo knew a little, but for Eric and Bobbly, Alisha and Joshi, this was a different country. What even was heptathlon?

"OK, three events on the track: hurdles, two hundred metres and eight hundred metres, then the two jumps high and long, and two throws shot and javelin. It's over two days, so it takes a total focus, total concentration along from the physical effort. Shelley, track and jumps are pretty good already; shot put you know; javelin would be new, but you have seven years, seven years to your Olympic Games...You wouldn't want to get bored, would you?" And now Shelley was starting to focus already.

"We had a great heptathlete in the Sydney Games, didn't we? Her name was Lewis, something Lewis?"

"Denise Lewis, Shelley, Denise Lewis, one of the greatest British athletes ever; met her while we were on team holding camp up in Brisbane coming into the Games." Dan spoke for the first time in a little while. "Yes, really one of the all-time greats, absolute total commitment." More thinking now from Shelley.

"Gilly, Dan, to be honest, I just don't know, like it would be great obviously, but hurdles, well, I think I might have a proper chance of making the team on hurdles, but heptathlon...I just don't know. I wouldn't want to throw away any hurdles chance." Reality was forcing its way through now.

"Ever hear of an athlete called Mary Rand, Shelley?" A shake 'no' of the head. "Anyone? Any of you?" All negative. "Of course not. Mary Rand was in the Tokyo Olympics back in 1964, different world, totally different world. When I was growing up and just starting to get into athletics, Mary was my hero. She could do anything. In Tokyo, she won the long jump, took second in the pentathlon as it was then just five events, and she even got a bronze medal in the relay for Great Britain! Three medals! Can you imagine, three! Remember what we said, 'no fear of failure'? That was Mary." Then, she softly added, "You actually look a little bit like her, Shelley...when she was young. Mary Rand was the first one that the press called 'Golden Girl'."

And that was a lot, a hell of a lot, for Shelley to take in. Mickey looked over at Shelley, then stole a glance at Lucy, who knew immediately what Mickey was thinking and nodded a 'yes' to the other part of her being, the other part of her soul. Mickey took the four steps over to where Shelley was sitting, reached out and put his arms around her, and Shelley responded straightaway.

"Thanks, Mickey, you're always there for me, for all of us..."

"No fear of failure, Shelley, not ever, not for us, not any of us." And just about everybody found it necessary to stare down and examine their shoes and the floor very closely.

"Time for a break, I think! Tea, coffee, soft drink, anyone?" Dan instinctively knew it was time to lighten the mood. "Chris, Gilly, all right if I put the kettle on? Lucy, want to give me a hand?" And Lucy's heart reached out to him, and Dan's heart rose as he took it. "Come on then, little one! That's what Sami Richards called you, wasn't it?"

"Yes, still does." And then, thinking out loud, Lucy said, "Look, I might be out of order here...But like, if we're going to go for this, like serious 'cause I think it is, and I'm totally, totally buying into it, would it be all right to maybe get Sami involved? She's training most of the time with us now, isn't she, Gilly? She's so nice, totally looked after me at those first English schools, and she is class, pure class! And I don't only mean the running stuff, she's got no side, no side at all, just a lovely person...What d'you reckon?"

"Can I come in here for a minute, Lucy? Maybe this will help. When I was swimming properly, there were always swimmers who wanted to change coaches, always looking for the easy way, the quick way, the shortcuts, and when you get someone new in a squad, it can change the mood, change the dynamics. What our coach did—and he was brilliant!—was to put it to us, he'd say, 'OK guys, we've got someone who wants to join us, what do you reckon?' And we'd actually do a secret vote on it, and it pretty much needed everyone to say 'yes'. Without being funny, and I'll tell you that I think Sami Richards is an awesome lady, my thoughts would be to do something like that…just my thinking…"

"Not being funny, Mr Bullet, I'm not sure we need a secret vote, all these guys here"—and Mickey threw his hands out sideways—"we've known each other since pretty much we were born, certainly since we were allowed to play outside without our parents down the estate. We have, and I hope this is OK to say it?" And he smiled at everyone again. "A trust, an absolute trust in each other. Anyone can say anything, and it'll be respected. We might take the total poo out of each other, but the trust is always there…and I'd like to give the first vote…I'm one hundred per cent for Sami coming along to the party. Sami's one of the world's good guys." And Mickey Honey raised his hand, and seven other hands rose immediately. And Gilly Warren adored Mickey Honey even more.

"Dan?" They were waiting for the kettle to boil and washing the cups.

"Yes, little one?"

"C'mon, Dan, 'give me a hand, Lucy', who you kidding? Well, is it still on? That stuff we talked about a long time ago now, still doable, you reckon?"

"Mind-reader as well now, Lucy…yes, still can do I reckon, like to talk about it a bit more obviously, but not now, maybe after the next swim session?" And so, it was agreed.

"It has been the most fantastic evening, particularly after everything that has happened, and I know we all want to thank Gilly and Chris for having us here"— a myriad of cheers, hand-claps and thank-yous—followed by a 'no, thanks to all of you for coming on such a difficult day'.

"I've got my Olympic hat on again, apologies for the boasting; it is absolutely so important to do what we all did tonight, including what Mickey started to talk about, making a graph, a chart, a plan to follow, breaking it all down into smaller, manageable bits and ticking them off when they get done. So many athletes, athletes in all sports, never even get that far. It's a hell of a lot of work, probably even more than you can imagine at the moment. So, a word of caution, I guess;

don't try to do it all right away, don't go mad and overtrain. That way lies injury, disappointment and disillusionment, increasing training both in volume, the amount you do and the quality of the sessions has to be done so gradually, maybe five per cent a month at most, and you need downtime as well; every few weeks you take a recovery week or low-key week, yes?"

The heads nodded. "And this might sound a bit over-the-top, but I think that, if you can, you should keep the swimming in your schedules, lots of reasons. Aerobically, it will do you good; you can't be knocking your legs out all the time, and the volume that we can do in swimming, the pure endurance work, will really help that. Then there's the water massage. Every time you get in the pool, just getting the water flowing over you will help. Swimming will most definitely stop you getting bored; trust me, I'll make sure the sessions don't allow you to get bored! And, importantly, you're all good swimmers now; seriously, I mean that…you never know…we'll talk a bit more in-depth later, yeah?"

Chapter Thirty-Three
Conversations and Confessions

Lucy

"Mickey, I got to tell you something." They were in Mickey's bedroom after walking back from Mr Warren's. "Mickey, look, I should have told you this; please don't hate me…"

"Could never hate you, Lucy, not in a million years."

Mickey looked at her and smiled, and her heart turned over. Lucy told him about the thoughts and the secret she'd shared with Dan, and Mickey smiled at her again and nodded his head 'yes', "That would be fantastic, unbelievable… well, not unbelievable because I think you can, no, I know you can, and you know what? I totes understand why you kept it to yourself…tell you what, Luce, isn't Dan just the best, the absolute best?" And Lucy sighed just once, threw herself into Mickey's warm embrace and sighed just once again.

Joshi, Alisha, Bobby and Eric said, "Mr Warren, can we talk to you, like properly? No, don't go, miss, you too if that's all right?"

Gilly smiled a big smile. "Mr Warren, Gilly, we want to do something, all of us." Joshi moved his head from left to right and back again to include Alisha, Bobby and Eric.

"Sir, miss, we want to do something like properly for Shell, JoJo, Lucy and Mickey; dunno what it is exactly, but like we want to help, you know, properly help. Thing is, we are so proud of what those guys are doing, honest. We're the kids from the estate, aren't we? The kids who aren't going to make it, the ones who are going to drop out, disappear when it gets a bit tough, but we ain't done that—not one of us," Eric said.

"It was you who made us that way, sir, and you, miss, and we'll remember that for the rest of our lives; we would never have got into Stratford without you, wouldn't even have thought of it…"

"So, what Eric's trying to say in his usual erudite way is that if—and we know it's a big IF—they do go to the Olympics, then we're going as well 'cause we know where we all came from, and now, we know where we're going, and if they get there, well, in a way, so do we…does that make even a little bit of sense?" Bobby said.

"We actually see the world in a different way now, sir; we see all the good stuff that can happen if you believe, if you think you can, and we believe now…the business that me and Eric started when he got back from Jamaica?" Bobby looked over at Eric, who nodded back. "Well, we're doing all right, making a bit of money now, saving most of it, and some of it we're putting back into the business, but we're doing it slowly, taking it bit by bit. We were only kids when we started, and we learnt so much. Did loads of things wrong, but we did learn, and now, yeah, we're doing all right, aren't we, Eric?"

"Yeah, even got a bit of money in the bank; can't believe it sometimes."

"Enough already! God, I'm the one who's supposed to never stop talking." Alisha had taken the floor. "So we had a talk, us four, and we want to support in every way we can. If it's money, like if any of them need to see someone or need massage or, you know, stuff to keep them healthy, then we're gonna do it. No really, it's not just words, it's for real, and we mean it. Look what Bobby and Eric have done! Well, that means all of us in TMRG can do it as well…

"Sir, do you remember when we asked you if you knew what TMRG meant? And you came straight back to us? We couldn't believe it! Like it was our secret, and grown-ups would never know, and right away you did. That was a big thing with us. I think we knew it was going to be different with you…oh poo, I'm talking too much as usual."

"No, you're talking absolute sense, Alisha, all of you; you're stars, I mean that," Chris said. "I'm right, Gilly?" And Gilly quietly nodded a 'yes'.

Chris and Gilly

"Can they? Can they, Gilly? Can they? Can they, Gilly?"

"Yes, of course, they can, Chris…and I have to say something a bit crass as well, the reason that they can do it—and can do doesn't mean they will do—is because you put that belief there; you put that belief in them when they were ten

257

and eleven years old. No, don't shake your head; you did. I saw it, from outside to start with, but then, well, you know, me and you, they adored you then, and they still adore you now. Of course, they do; why wouldn't they? You changed their lives, you listen to any one of them, and it's so obvious, 'obs' as they'd say, and it is obs.

"You changed their lives, and they will never, ever forget you. They talk about you all the time, Chris, when we're doing a session down the track or over Vicky Park; it's 'Mr Warren said this' or 'Mr Warren said that' or 'do you remember when…' And it's always such good memories that they have…I will do everything in my power, everything; I mean it. I really do. Did you hear what Alisha was saying? They're willing to give them money! Those kids don't have any spare money and what they do have they're going to give to their mates. Bobby and Eric, all they've worked for and it's their friends who come first. That is just unbelievable, but no, it's not because we know these kids, and we know what they're capable of.

"So yes, they can do it; they can go to the Games. It's not just the talent, lots of people have talent but don't use it or can't see the long journey, but these kids can; these kids really can. They have that belief, your belief. Bloody hell, Chris, that was a long old speech, even for me! Change lives? You've changed those kids' lives, and you know what? Those kids will change other kids' lives because they can, and now, get me a glass of wine! We deserve it!"

JoJo

"Is that right, Mr McQueen? Is that right that you're coming on tour with us?"

"It's Larry, JoJo; it's Larry for you, that all right?"

"Sorry, Larry, I just don't want to be disrespectful, wouldn't do that…but you're on tour with us, yeah?" And Larry McQueen, Spurs icon, looked back at JoJo and grinned.

"Couldn't keep me away; I live for it, always have, always will."

"Oh man, that's me, that's me as well; it's everything to me, football, everything!"

"Saw that from the first time I saw you play, JoJo, was so obvious; you live the game; it's part of you. I know that. Look, let me tell you something, JoJo, yeah?"

"Of course, yes, please."

"OK, most of the time I was playing, I had trouble with my knee, big trouble. Couldn't even train properly a lot of the time, knee wouldn't take it, spent a lot of time on the bloody—oh, sorry—exercise bike when all I wanted to do was to be out on the pitch with the squad, but I couldn't. But when Saturday came, or mid-week, the knee pain went away, disappeared in the heat of the game. I just loved the intensity and the concentration; no room for anything else. But when the match was over, boy, did I pay for it! Spurs were great to me, all the medical team, the physios, absolutely superb. I had that hunger, JoJo. I needed to play whatever…and I see that in you, JoJo; you have that hunger, the intensity, the focus. Saw it first time I came to watch you at that summer camp."

"Really, Mr McQueen, sorry, Larry?"

"Really, JoJo, absolutely one hundred per cent, and now you're captaining English schools; you're still a year under age as well? And on tour with us, with Spurs. They're serious about you, JoJo, and I mean that as well. Look at you, 'big time, shoot a dime!'"

Sami

"So, what you saying, Lucy, what you telling me? You telling me that you're going to the Olympics? Really? You sure, girl?"

"No, not sure 'girl'." Lucy and Sami both grinned. "But what I am sure about is that I'm going to try, and I'll die trying, and what I'm saying as well is that if I can go to the Olympics, the London Olympics, then you can—'girl'—you can. You're a brilliant runner, you know that. You're winning southern league senior races already, and you're in national league most of the time, so yes, the Olympics, in spades!" And they both roared, remembering that time back in Washington at Lucy's first English schools and Sami had said 'in spades' and that long-lasting link had been instantly forged.

"Bloody hell, Lucy, you know what? I hadn't even thought about it, not properly like, but now…Yeah, give it a go, real go, like you said before. Seven-odd years, yeah, why not? Better get myself a proper coach now as well."

"Well, thing is, Sami, me'n Mickey and actually all our lot including Gilly…Well, we wondered if you'd like to string along with us, like train with Gilly's group all the time, would you, Sami? Would you? Please, Sami, please say yes, please."

"You think that much of me? Bloody hell, Lucy—and now that's twice I've said 'bloody'—well, three times now—and I never swear… Well, you know…Yes! Yes! Yes! I would love to be a part of your group, a real part, now I feel like the little kid saying thank you." Sami squeezed Lucy's hand and then kissed her on the forehead. "Thank you, little one, thank you so much." And then Sami said, "Be good if we both got to go, wouldn't it? Be good if we both got to make a final, wouldn't it? Be good if we both medalled, wouldn't it? That couldn't happen, could it? I mean, me and you medalling in the same race? Never happen…oh, actually, I think it did once, so fame, glory, all that stuff, beckons!" And the dream had started.

The Speeding Bullet

"It'll be tough, Lucy, so tough. I know why you want to do it, and I think it's brilliant, but you have absolutely nothing to prove, nothing at all. You have every chance of making the Olympics on the track, maybe even the marathon if what Gilly tells me is to be believed, and I believe Gilly one hundred per cent. But what you're setting yourself is awesome. And then I say to myself, 'Why not be awesome?' Why not? Fear of failure doesn't exist with you four, does it? You feed off of each other; you build each other up so much, you four together, you're stronger than four individuals, much stronger. You said anything to Mickey yet?" Lucy nodded 'yes'. "It's got to be a team thing, you know; maybe just maybe you should tell all of them? It's not being flash, it's being honest, and I've never seen more honest kids, well, you're not kids any more, are you? Most definitely not kids. Olympic prospects is what you are, Olympic prospects."

"Dan, Dan, this dream of mine, and I know it's a dream; it doesn't have to be the Olympics; really, it doesn't. I just want to make the team, even once would do…Jeez, listen to me! Make the team, just once! Fat chance, girl, big fat chance." Lucy stopped, and Dan waited patiently. "It's like…oh poo, I know what this is going to sound like, but it's you I'm talking to, so I will say it, anyway…it's making a statement, that's what it is, making a statement. Could you imagine, the first one, ever? Wouldn't that be opening the doors wide to a whole bunch of little girls like me?" And the dream had become even more real.

Lucy

"Thanks for coming, everybody. I know this is a big ask because everyone's got loads of stuff to do. Big thanks to Gilly and Chris again—I can even say Gilly and Chris now without getting embarrassed, well, not too much—for letting us come to their home again, would never have believed that a few years back. And big thanks to Dan, the one and only Speeding Bullet, because without him here, I wouldn't be doing this. OK, I'm going to be silly embarrassed here; Mickey and Dan know why, and I want—I need—to share something with you." Dan was sitting on Lucy's right. Mickey was holding her hand, sitting on her left. She looked at both of them. Dan nodded yes. Mickey squeezed her hand.

Everybody was waiting, and now Sami was as well. "Here goes…about a million years ago, well, feels like that anyway. Some of us met this big smiling bloke sitting next to me, and in so many ways, he changed my life; no really, he did."

And there really was absolute silence now; no one would have dared to break it. "You see, Dan taught me—us—how to swim, and I knew I'd seen him, well, I thought I had, and it was true, I had seen him. I saw him on telly at the Sydney Olympics, and that was only five years ago, and you know what? Dan was the only black swimmer there, the only one. And it was like, I'd never seen a black person swim properly before, not ever. It wasn't something you did if you were black, and all of a sudden, it was. You could be black and swim, like, swim properly, like Dan. And it got me, got me right there." Lucy put her hand, the one that wasn't holding Mickey's hand, on her heart.

"So, I talked to Dan, talked a lot, probably too much, if I'm honest, and I reckon I was totes boring. But you know what? Dan listened, listened to me every single time. And I told him that I had a dream, a big dream, actually. I told him that I wanted to swim like him, wanted to swim for Great Britain or England, wanted to be a black girl swimming for the country, and Dan never laughed at me, not once. Totally took it all on board and believed, yes, believed in me. Told me that if I trained hard, if I believed, if I gave everything, then I could, said there was nothing about being black or white, said I could swim for Britain. Now I ain't stupid, and I know it ain't gonna be roses and honey all the way, but I gotta give it a go. I just have to! Do you know how many black girls have swum for Great Britain?"

Lucy looked around at them all. "Not one, not ever, and that ain't right, ain't right at all. And it's not just Great Britain, listen, even America, USA, didn't have a black girl in their swim team 'til the last Olympics in Athens just last year. That's unbelievable. USA! How many black people in America?"

Lucy shook her head. "S'not right, not right at all. But that black girl, her name's Maritza McClendon; she actually got a silver in the relay. Fantastic! She changed things; she changed the way black kids thought about themselves—

same way Dan made me change the way I thought—and now there's a load more black kids, especially girls, swimming properly, like in clubs and everything, in America. You wait and see, few years' time there'll be loads of black Americans in their swim team. Only takes one, and the gates are opened. So, it's something I gotta do; I just have to. Would be like letting myself down if I didn't give it a go. And I know it's going to be tough, so tough, but so what? I'd rather die trying than not go for it. So that's it, needed to tell you all. Don't get me wrong, I want to go to the Olympics; 'course, I do, and I know swimming probs isn't on the cards, but running is. Me'n Sami, well, we're going to get a double medal, aren't we, Sami?"

Sami grinned back and didn't dare say anything because she still felt new in the group, but, boy, was she so glad to be there. "But so I've got this other little thing going for me. I am truly, truly, truly going to try to swim for England or maybe Great Britain…all right, have to say something else as well, and if anyone laughs at me, I'm going to punch them in the face…Well, I'll ask Mickey too. I sort of want to be a—how d'you say it?—a role model. Yeah, that's it, a role model. I want to be a role model for little black girls." And with that, all the energy drained out of Lucy, and she turned her face to Mickey while Alisha, JoJo, Shelley and Sami rushed over to her and tangled themselves up trying to hug her at the same time. Gilly looked over at Chris and Dan, shook her head and rushed out to the kitchen just before she embarrassed herself.

Chapter Thirty-Four
Welcome to the Club

They were at the track. JoJo had asked to come along, so there were five of them, warm-up completed.

"It's called a parlaaf, just a variation on the normal interval stuff we do, Sami. You done anything like this before?"

"Think so, Gilly; it's like a continuous relay, yeah? You do the rep and then just hand over to whoever's in your team and goes on like that!"

"Got it in one, Sami. Welcome to the club! OK, we're going to put a little sting into it, make it a tiny bit more interesting…"

"Any time you say 'interesting', Gilly, I start to worry." Mickey grinned. "Me and the chicks, isn't it? Reckon they're all going to gang up on me."

"White boy in his place!" Lucy leered over at her soul mate. "Gonna rip you apart and stitch you up big time, white boy!"

"You leave my big brother alone! He can't help being white!" Shelley put her head on Mickey's shoulder and sighed loudly, very loudly. And it was the nature of their group with new member Sami that this was totally normal and totally accepted. Sami shook her head and thanked god that she'd met Lucy and through her had been accepted into a new group who just immediately welcomed her…And as she had discovered, it was because Mickey had said the big yes and everyone had agreed.

"Actually, I think me and Mickey look like each other, could be twins, I reckon, the heavenly twins, who could tell us apart?" Sami smiled at Mickey, who smiled back.

"Oh my god! This is sick-making! Enough! We gonna do a session or what, Gilly, or we gonna go and get our photos taken and sign autographs?" Mickey said.

"Think the session might just take priority; we ready, guys? OK, the session is twenty by two hundred metres; we're looking at race pace for fifteen hundred, maybe three thousand. Shelley, honey, it's going to be a toughie for you; you good with that?" Shelley nodded 'of course'.

"The one that rips everybody apart in the heptathlon is that final eight-hundred metres; I've seen athletes in a strong gold medal position going from first to outside the medals just because they didn't focus enough in training on that final gut-wrenching run, decided that they could tough it out and get around, take the pain, take the strain...And then they found out they couldn't; iron-man to iron-filings, we're not going to do that, no way. OK, this tiny, tiny little sting for this parlaaf...Shelley, I want you and Mickey to team up, and Sami you go with Lucy, yes?"

"What about me, Gilly?" JoJo asked.

"I need you to run with Shelley; you both go off together, but JoJo, you do every other rep, OK, first, third and so on, yes?" And JoJo nodded a 'yes'. "Now this little sting, we start the reps midway down the straight and hand over midway on the back-straight, and then you jog back across the middle to be ready to take over from your partner, easy-peasy, lemon-squeezy!"

They all grinned at Gilly, who had been debating with herself over the partners, the teams, then she said, "Lucy, you start off with Sami and handover to Shelley and JoJo. Sami, you hand over to Mickey, and as soon as you make that hand touch, get yourselves back to start again; twenty reps, guys, just twenty..."

"Yeah, right, just twenty. Cheers, Gilly; reckon I should start calling you miss again with sessions like this." But Mickey knew that every session with Gilly was worthwhile, had been hard thought out and had a purpose.

"Sami, Lucy, you ready? Two, one..." and Sami and Lucy hit their stride immediately, around the bend, hand touches and start jogging back on the grass. Mickey on the outside of Shelley, JoJo on their heels, hand touches, Sami and Lucy back to it, and again and again and again, fourth rep done, fifth, Shelley beginning to blow. *C'mon Shell, hang tough, girl!* Sami and Lucy duking it out on every rep, the ninth and tenth, Shelley hurting, Shelley hurting bad, the doubts beginning. *Am I good enough? Will I ever be good enough?*

Dropping off Mickey's pace, hurting, hurting, hurting, huge effort to get across the grass on recovery to be ready for handover, then Gilly said, "Shelley, miss the next rep." Shelley burst into tears.

"Oh, Gilly, I am so sorry; I've let you down!" And the sobs continued.

"You've never let me down, Shelley, never. You don't have it in you to let anyone down. You've done brilliantly; you're training with probably—and I do mean this—the best distance runners for their age in the country; you know they are. You're training for a different event, so of course you're feeling it; you've been superb, truly. Now, I want you do get back in and run every other rep, so that you're alternating with JoJo and Mickey has someone to run with every rep. You can do that?" Shelley nodded her head 'yes' and jogged back over.

"Sorry, Mickey. Sorry JoJo, had a bit of a wobbly. I'm all right now. Gilly says me and you to alternate, JoJo, yeah?"

"Shell, don't get me wrong here, but I think you did brilliant staying up with me for so long; ain't being flash, honest, you're brilliant!" There was just time for Mickey to get the words out before his takeover from Sami, and he and JoJo were off again. Shelley was back in for her next rep, and she had to dig deep but got through to the end.

Five steaming bodies were spread on the grass in various inelegant displays and poses. Shelley was laying on her front. Mickey and the girls were quiet, not sure how to react, what to say. Gilly did it for them; she spoke very softly but loud enough so that all of them could hear.

"There's a couple of enemies you have to beat when you're trying to be the best, the very best…" And they all waited. "And they're the times that you need and yourself; I think you went beyond both of them just now, Shelley. Well done, Shell; I mean that; you found yourself there."

"Honest, miss, there I go again. Gilly, I mean, was I all right?"

"What d'you reckon, Lucy? Was Shelley all right?"

"Shell, you were great; honest, you were! Mickey's won English schools; he's a boy, and you kept with him first five, and then you still gutted it out when you were suffering; listen, none of us could get anywhere near you on sprints or hurdles, but you stuck in there…JoJo?"

"Shell, I'm doing this stuff for my football, you know that, hoping it's going to give me a bit of an advantage as I get up the ages to the pro girls. I was only doing every other rep, so I had much more recovery, and I was hurting like hell…you aced it, Shelley, aced it!"

"Respect, Shelley, pure respect. I had no idea that you were that good on distance stuff," Sami said. "Listen, guys, shall we warm down? Is that all right Gilly, or have we got any more to do?"

"Do NOT put any ideas in her head!" Mickey said. "C'mon you lot; let's get jogging."

"Easy session that." Sami smiled as they were jogging. "Probably the easiest track session I've done since I was about eleven or twelve…"

"Sami, you for real? Session was wicked, wicked," Lucy said.

"Yeah, all right, it WAS wicked! Listen, you guys always train that hard?" They looked at each other and nodded.

"Pretty much, I guess. We haven't always, but Gilly's been gradually increasing the load, just little by little. It started properly when we got back from watching you and Lucy at English schools up in Washington—that's three odd years ago now, bloody hell, seems like a different world—so you've got yourself to blame, Sami, for that session just now." Mickey started to laugh, then said, "You know what? I love doing sessions like that; honest, I do. I love the hurt, but I also love knowing that the hurt will be over when we stop. Shelley, you reckon?"

"Truth? I hate it and I love it at the same time; it got me this one, really got me. Not in my comfort zone with you guys, am I? Totes different from most of the stuff I'm doing usually, but you know what, Mickey? You're dead right. I do love it…Like even now when I showed myself up, it's pushing yourself beyond, isn't it? It's something you have to do, have to go where you haven't been before; it's a cross between a dream and a nightmare; nightmare because of the hurt, dream because, well, if you can't dream, you won't know when you've got that dream come true. Anyway, I trust Gilly absolutely, one hundred per cent. She wouldn't get me to do something if she didn't think it was needed…If I do go up to the four hundred hurdles and if I do get properly serious about heptathlon, then stuff like that hurt just now will be well worthwhile…I think…"

"IF you go four hundred hurdles and heptathlon, IF you go? My reckoning says you're a lot more than halfway there already, Shell." Lucy smiled more to herself than to Shelley, and Shelley smiled back, but she was thinking, thinking, thinking hard. Could I? Could I really? Naah, stick to the sprint hurdles…But then, well, maybe…

And Gilly was thinking as well, analysing what she'd just seen happen. *Shelley's got it; she has. They all have it, all of them. That session, just feeding off of each other, so glad Sami's in the squad; she adds that extra bit. Lucy works even better when Sami's there. Big sister figure? Maybe, maybe…and JoJo, she doesn't need to be here, but she wants to, wants to for Spurs, but you know what?*

266

She wants to be with her mates as well. JoJo adds a lot, and Mickey—love that boy—Mickey and the Chicks!

They adore him, and Lucy loves him; she really does love him. She still has that little-girl look in her eyes, looking at him when she thinks he doesn't know. Don't break that one up, Mickey; don't you hurt that little girl...She'd die without you. No, Mickey wouldn't do that, would he? No, don't think so. Lifetime together already it seems, love story for the ages...wouldn't it be great if...well, you know...If... Gilly ran after them.

"Hey, wait up, you guys! Your old-age coach wants to warm-down with you." And they laughed as she caught up with them, and Shelley mouthed 'thanks, Gilly' and reached over and squeezed her shoulder. The grand design was coming together. Each bit of the jigsaw was fitting in now. Seven years to go, seven years. Can we? Can we really?

Dare to dream, just dare to dream.

Chapter Thirty-Five
Dare to Dream

"Do you remember that very gentle guy I introduced you all to back when we were in Amsterdam, the triathlete, went to the Sydney Games?" Dan said on the poolside.

"Ray, Richard, Robin something, Burrel? Barrel?" Lucy said.

"Getting close, Lucy, very close; Barel, Rob Barel, one of the nicest gentlemen I've ever met. Always had time for everyone, always willing to talk about training and racing. I learnt a lot. Rob had this thing that doing more than one sport, well, more than one discipline was how he put it, was actually good for training in just one sport. Rob felt that the chance of getting injured was so much less. Running particularly is always a big injury worry, too many miles and you get inured, too much speedwork and you get injured, try to do more and more too soon and you get injured...get the picture?

"Well, Rob's thinking is that endurance sport is a mixture of building up that aerobic capacity, heart and lungs, working on the specific muscle groups for whatever particular sport—so that would be very different for swimming and running—and maximising the skill level that you need in each particular activity—and that would be very different between swimming and running and even cycling—which is what Rob did of course, the triathlon. And he said that the other important thing—actually, the word he used was 'crucial'—was mental attitude—have a strong mind to get you through the tough times.

"So, the two things that you need in any endurance sport are aerobic strength, stamina aspect and mental attitude. Mental attitude and aerobic capacity are transferable; they will apply to any single discipline, which is a pretty long-winded way for me to say that I think swimming training will help your running. Stamina is obvious, but even swimming the sessions, the hours in the pool when all you're looking at is that think black line on the bottom is going to help that strong mind, look at a black line for an hour and your mind's got to be strong!"

They were spellbound, looking at Dan and drinking in every word. "There's a young Kenyan guy, name of Eliud Kopchoge, won World five thousand metres when he was just nineteen, and I tell you that he is going to be around forever; well, Eliud has this saying, this mantra, 'I don't just run with my legs, I run with my heart and mind,' and that's what it's all about you three; you give it everything, everything. Now I'm certainly not saying that every training session has to be one hundred per cent flat-out, of course not; that would be a disaster. But for every session, you must know what you're trying to do, what the aim is, yeah? OK, in the pool, four hundred metres warm-up on front crawl, every fourth length kicking on your side." And Dan, like Gilly and Chris, like Shelley, Lucy, JoJo and Mickey, dared to dream.

*****

JoJo wasn't able to be at the pool for the swim session, much as she loved being around, being part of that group. Spurs were taking up a lot of her time now, and she adored that she was able to follow her own particular dream.

JoJo was waiting at Heathrow Airport with her mum and dad.

JoJo was the only Spurs player with her parents there for the very simple reason that she was so much younger than the other players: mostly first-teamers, a few apprentices and just one other academy girl.

JoJo was wearing full leisurewear emblazoned with the Tottenham Hotspurs motif.

JoJo was carrying two travel bags, also emblazoned with the Spurs logos.

JoJo was feeling more than a little nervous.

JoJo was feeling more than a little self-conscious as passing passengers were looking over at her and the group wearing the Spurs clothing, whispering and pointing.

JoJo was feeling more than a little excited. JoJo had never flown before, never been on an aeroplane, and now she was about to. She was glad that her mum and dad (her very, very proud mum and dad) were there with her, but now she was hoping that they'd go away. *Don't embarrass me; please don't embarrass me!*

"Mrs Jackson? Mr Jackson?" Larry McQueen was there shaking hands with her mum and dad now. "We are so pleased that you've allowed JoJo to travel with us. You must be extremely proud of her. We believe that she has a great future if she continues to apply herself. You're happy with all the chaperoning and care details that we sent you through? Yes? That's good.

"May I introduce you to our team manager for this trip? Well, team manager for women's first team at Spurs, of course, Alice Smith, played for Spurs for five seasons, captained us and played for England as well. I promise you that JoJo will be in safe hands." Goodbyes were said; handshakes were exchanged. JoJo suddenly realised that she was leaving her comfort zone and hugged her parents, just managing to avoid tears.

"Thanks, Mum. Thanks, Dad…for everything." And they headed for the underground just about hiding their own tears. *Our girl, our little girl, playing for Spurs!*

The British Airways cabin crew welcomed them on board. To her surprise, she, along with the other players and coaching staff, were directed left into the business cabin. JoJo was stunned. "Oh my god!" she said under her breath. She sat with the only other academy player on the tour, but as soon as the plane took off and the seatbelt signs were extinguished, the players were circulating, moving around, chatting to each other. Every one of them came up to say hello to JoJo, congratulating her on her seasons at Spurs and how she'd risen through the ranks, while many, many others had fallen by the wayside. Alice Smith came over to her.

"You nervous, JoJo?" JoJo nodded a hesitant 'yes'. "When I started to get involved, to think that maybe, just maybe I could make it, I was so nervous. I wasn't quite as young as you when I got selected for my first tour, but even so, all these grown-up players were there, and me, little me…pretty much like you right now, I reckon, JoJo? Right?"

JoJo nodded 'yes' again. "No need to be, no need at all; you wouldn't be here if you didn't deserve it; big time sport…lots of money involved, and the guys up top here wouldn't have you along just for show. You deserve to be here, JoJo; you absolutely deserve to be here. You'll get playing time, I promise you. Maybe not loads, but you'll be on the pitch, and it won't be a token two or three minutes when the game's dead; no, you'll be in the middle of it because you deserve it; you deserve to be there." And JoJo's confidence, slightly shaken by being around the first team, started to rise again.

"You know the schedule, JoJo?" Larry McQueen was smiling at her.

"Well, sort of. We're in Madrid, play Atletico day after tomorrow, two days after that. Real, then off to Barcelona for the final match of the tour. Is that right?"

"Got it in one, JoJo, got it in one. JoJo, do you know how many pro men players would die to play at the Bernabea, Metropolitano or Camp Nou?"

JoJo shook her head 'no'. "Maybe a million. No, make that maybe ten million, maybe more...of course, more. Every single footballer dreams of playing at the big stadiums, the big teams, and it's there for you, JoJo; it's there for you right now. Take it, girl, just take it!"

And JoJo, little JoJo from the sink estate, the wrong side of the tracks, given the losing lottery ticket at the start of her life, dared to dream the very big dream. And she leant back in her very luxurious business class seat on British Airways and thanked God, thanked him many, many times, that she had had the absolute luck to be in Mr Warren's class.

*****

The four letters had all arrived on the same day. The UKA logo on the envelopes had already given them an insight into what was inside. With some trepidation and more than a little fear and anxiety, the four of them opened the letters. Lucy went screaming down the stairs of the flats towards Mickey. Mickey was already on his way up the stairs to Lucy. Shelley bumped into both of them just as Sami arrived—hot, sweaty, breathless—and screaming with her letter in her hands.

"I have fucking made the team! I've fucking made the British team! Me! Me! Sami fucking Richards! Oh man, can't believe it! Truly can't believe it! Thank you, Lucy, Mickey, Shelley, thank you so much for getting me into Gilly's training group. Hang on a minute, what you all doing here together this time in the morning?"

"We made the team, made the British team! Under eighteens, Europeans, all of us! We done it! We really done it! You know what? Think I just died and went to heaven!" And Mickey felt the tears in his eyes and then felt Lucy (of course), Shelley and Sami hugging him, and the tears really did flow.

"Errh, 'scuse me!" Gilly was standing at the bottom of the stairs with Chris and another man. Gilly was flourishing an envelope, and it was a minor miracle that nobody broke a leg as they rushed down to embrace their coach.

"Gilly? Will you come and watch us? Please will you come and watch us? Want you to be there; really want you to be there. It was you, miss, sorry, Gilly, it was you who got us there, please, miss, please."

"Oh, yes, I'll be there. I'll certainly be there…thing is, guys, I sort of got selected as well, got my letter this morning same as you lot, asked me if I wanted to be an accredited coach, get the GB trackie same as you, get to travel with the team, get to be with you guys, made the big-time. Can't believe it. Well, I can absolutely believe it. Thank you, thank you so much." And then it was time for a celebratory coffee and fried breakfast in the local café.

"Guys, I'd like to introduce you to a journalist, Mr Caxton here; he writes for the Sunday Times, lots and lots about sport, totally respected." The athletes looked at the journalist. He smiled. "Mr Caxton, I'd like to introduce you to my athletes; no, actually, I'd like to introduce you to four of my best friends who happen to be athletes." Gilly smiled, and they all smiled back. And that was probably when the deal was finally sealed.

David Caxton Writes in the Sunday Times

The Great Britain team for the under-18 European Championships gave a few surprises. Gilly Warren, coaching out of Victoria Park Athletics Club, has no less than four athletes selected for the British team, all for the first time: three middle-distance/endurance athletes: Mickey Honey (3,000 metres), Lucy Newton (3,000 metres), Sami Richards (also 3,000 metres) and Shelley Steele in the sprint hurdles. Mickey, Lucy and Shelley are just fifteen years old, while Sami has just turned seventeen. Remarkably, the three youngest athletes all live on the same estate and attend the same school, Stratford Academy; even more remarkably, the three were not only at the same junior school but in the same class! And for a ragged old journalist to mention the word 'remarkable' twice in the same piece, either means that he has finally lost his marbles or he has truly witnessed something that is remarkable.

Their class teacher at primary school was a certain Mr Chris Warren. Yes, Gilly Warren's husband; a shared love of running and doing the absolute best for the children in their charge brought them together. Perhaps not so remarkable was that our three young athletes, along with five of their friends (also in Mr

Warren's class, of course), attended Chris and Gilly's wedding. The fourth member of this elite training group, Sami Richards, ran into Lucy Newton—quite literally—at the London schools cross-country, three years ago, Sami winning and going on to win the English schools that year, while Lucy, out of her age group, finished third at English schools. There is a remarkable (that word again!) atmosphere in this group, their ethos is geared around supporting each other.

Two remarkable (What? Again!) quotes from young Mickey Honey almost, but only almost, brought this cynical old journo to tears. My question to all of them was, "How come you're so successful as a group?" They all looked at Mickey, who took so much time before replying that I wondered if I'd said the words or just thought them. Mickey's words were powerful.

"Mr Caxton, that man over there, Mr Warren, he was our class teacher at junior school. Well, he changed our lives, Mr Caxton. Mr Warren changed our lives. He taught us that we could be whatever we wanted to be, that it didn't matter where we came from; all that mattered was where we were going. Mr Warren said that we shouldn't want to be like someone else. What we had to be were the best versions of ourselves, and we've tried to do that, owe him everything, owe that man everything. And the other thing, Mr Caxton, is this, we're stronger together; really, we are; we feed off of each other."

Shelley came in on this.

"Mr Caxton, what Mickey says is one hundred per cent true; he's like my brother...Actually, he is my brother in everything but blood, and that's the truth, and these two, Lucy and Sami, they're like my sisters, truth again."

This journalist is not ashamed to say that he learnt a great deal from these young athletes and their mentors. This journalist will most certainly be attending the European Under-18 Athletic Championships in Barcelona next week. And this tired, cynical, old journalist is quietly placing bets on athlete selection for the 2012 Olympic Games in London, perhaps even medals.

David Caxton, The Sunday Times

Footnote: Having a coffee with these quite lovely and personable young athletes, one of them happened to mention that yet another of their classmates—same estate, same junior school and same Mr Warren as their teacher—will also be in Barcelona. Fifteen-year-old Joanna (JoJo) Jackson is currently an academy player at Spurs and, on the edge of an apprentice contract, is a member of the

Spurs touring team—that's the Spurs senior team. And you do not get there on good looks and wheatgerm. Spurs ladies are playing Atletico Madrid, Real Madrid and Barcelona on their tour. Interesting times for these kids from the bad side of town, although I sincerely doubt that they would see it like that. My impression is that they would see themselves as extremely lucky to have been guided in the right direction. This raddled old journo wonders if the Great Britain and Commonwealth Honours system will allow itself to reward true inspiration.

Part Five
On Tour

Chapter Thirty-Six
Madrid

There were twenty thousand spectators at the Metropolitano Stadium on the occasion that JoJo made her senior debut. One or two might have forgotten that they were there, but they were made up of the thousands who weren't there but chose to tell everyone that they were. JoJo sat on the bench. She'd been promised that she would get game time, but how much would depend on how the game unfurled. And the game unfurled badly for the Spurs ladies. Nil-nil at halftime, game very even, none of the substitutes used so far. Whistle blows for halftime, Larry McQueen and Alice Smith giving the team talk, a quiet confidence for the second half. Whistle blows for restart, Atletico score directly from kick-off; the old ploy, play the ball back from kick-off, forwards and attacking midfielders rush on opposing goalkeeper, ball-holder holds as long as possible, sends it high into the goal area, and nine times out of ten, the goalkeeper takes control, but not this time.

Keira Jacques in the Spurs goal, maybe unsettled by the noise of the biggest crowd she had ever played in front of (the biggest crowd any of the Spurs players had appeared in front of), fluffs her lines, and the net is already bulging. No matter, one goal in a pre-season friendly can be taken back. And then the second goal followed immediately—but once again, it was for Atletico. Juanita Faldez playing number ten for Atletico steals the ball and goes on one of those mazy runs, which always ends in failure and usually disaster.

Not this time, brimming with a confidence of being awarded a new contract with her hometown club, Juanita simply ran and ran while defender after defender backed off until it was too late. Juanita sweeps the ball wide to the left and is waiting on the six-yard line as it is returned, and she turns it into the net. Two-nil.

And suddenly, it was serious. Losing a pre-season friendly isn't disastrous by any means, but the manner in which you lose can be. Juanita was on a roll, confidence high as a kite, world beckoning. She repeated her offensive line, took the ball as far as she could while the Spurs defence backed away, reluctant to commit. Three midfielders backing up, choice of pass, make it the safe one because there's always someone waiting for the return. Bing, bang, bosh, three-nil to Atletico. And the twenty thousand crowd went wild.

Larry and Alice were in warzone confrontation. Pads were out, diagrams drawn, tactics discussed. The game was lost now but better to score at least one goal to hold onto that respect.

"Lizzie, Nicola, JoJo, two minutes only to warm-up, need you three on the pitch." Two experienced pros and fifteen-year-old (young) JoJo Jackson. "JoJo, they don't know you, don't know you at all; free rein in midfield. Nothing to lose at all, JoJo. Be brave. Take this opportunity."

And with just twenty-two minutes remaining, little JoJo Jackson ran out onto the pitch and thought for one tiny instant of time just how far she'd travelled and how hard she'd worked just to be here. And she resolved—because Larry McQueen had said so and because she had a whole bunch of people to thank—to be brave, to be very brave, indeed.

On the halfway line, facing back, ball stroked to her. Atletico determined to show this little kid no mercy, no mercy at all. 'How dare they put on a kid against us!'. They went in hard. Had the slide tackle connected, JoJo may well have had to leave the pitch, certainly it would have been a yellow card, but no. Seeing the slide come in, JoJo fixed the ball between her feet and timed the jump in the air to perfection; the defender was clutching thin air, grass stubs on her boots. JoJo had space and went for it. 'Be brave' Larry had said, and JoJo was brave.

One defender out of space gave room to move, room to run, room to look up and distribute, which was what every Spurs player expected from JoJo. But JoJo didn't fulfil those expectations. She ran and ran and ran while Atletico backed off and backed off and backed off, and suddenly, there was more space and three Spurs attackers against two Atletico defenders. Desperation set in, Atletico keeper rushes out of the goal area, two footed sliding tackle into JoJo. JoJo goes down, clutches her right leg, ref's whistle blows, yellow card brandished; crowd is silent. JoJo gets up, rubs bruised leg, grins at keeper, looks over at Alice and Larry, grins again, looks down at the ball waiting for the freekick, looks over at Larry again, thinks she sees his lips move, 'be brave'. Larry nods.

Defensive wall forms, JoJo walks back from the ball, sees the Spurs players all ready, all waiting, makes a decision, 'be brave', hesitates, picks the tight angle, the right angle, edge of the players' wall, three steps back, run-up, hits hard and low, leather shaves and scorches the grass, dips just inside the goalpost with keeper tangled trying to keep it out, net erupts, crowd erupts, Spurs players erupt, Larry McQueen and Alice Smith both erupt. Fifteen-year-old Joanna Jackson on her Spurs debut is lifted high by every white-shirted player on the pitch, and Keira Jacques rushing up from goal to add her congratulations. Three-one down, eighteen minutes to play.

"Bit special, that little girl, bit special, eh, Larry?" Alice Smith stared at Larry McQueen.

"You know what, Larry? When you persuaded me, talked me into it really, bring a fifteen-year-old on tour…Well, wasn't sure, wasn't sure at all. Just proves how wrong a cynical old pro can be, doesn't it? Glad you talked me into it. Very glad. Jeez, that kid's confidence! Only been on the pitch a minute, takes the piss out of one of their players by that double foot possession jump, takes a big tackle that would have shaken a lot of players to bits…and then totally gets her own back by outthinking their keeper…confidence, or maybe luck?"

"Not luck, Alice, certainly not luck. JoJo's determination is what does it. She's seen the dark side; she comes from the bad side of the tracks, and she won't be going back there. We need to sign her, Alice. Spurs need to sign her now. One more year and there won't be a club in the Premiership who won't be chasing her with all sorts of promises, and you think clubs like Atletico aren't taking notice already?"

And the players and officials of Atletico Madrid were about to take a little more notice. On the pitch, Atletico were pushing, pushing, pushing; silly goal given away. That's not going to happen again, no way. JoJo was back helping in defence, and she was enjoying it, relishing it, loving it. It was one of those golden moments when everything seemed to move in slow motion, where she could see the ball's onward direction before it was even kicked, anticipation giving her that extra few milliseconds to get in the right place, and she was in the right place all of the time. The unspoken worries of the Spurs senior players were long gone now. The kid's good! Kid deserves to be here! And there was also that unspoken thought, unspoken but very real indeed, of 'she gonna take my place in the team'? But that was for another time; right now, it was keep them out! Do NOT let Atletico score again!

Keira Jacques plucks the ball off the head of Juanita Faldez, looks up, rolls the ball out to the right, wing-defender controls, right-side striker is running down the touchline, perfect pass. Lizzie Casper, on as a sub, determines that she will be in the starting line-up against Real Madrid, keeps her calm, moves forward stroking the ball. Atletico hesitates. Lizzie carries on forward, hesitates, sees JoJo running inside her, ground pass to JoJo and then Lizzie streaks again along the touchline, screams for the ball, inch-perfect pass from JoJo, who runs into open space—one defender and the keeper in front of her, Lizzie returns the pass, JoJo straight back to Lizzie, movement and pass repeated. JoJo with just the keeper to beat, keeper hesitant now; she's seen what JoJo did just a few minutes before, won't commit and then has to, too late. JoJo stops, foot on the ball, takes it sideways as the keeper tries to cover, and with the goal open, strokes the ball into the net.

Atletico three, Spurs and JoJo Jackson two. The celebration from the first goal is repeated, and this time the crowd stand and applaud knowing that they're seeing something—someone—special. Keeper looks at JoJo and smiles at her. "OK, bene, bene!" Eight minutes remaining, far too late for Spurs to do anything about it now. Atletico go into full defence mode, hold possession, play the ball out the corner flags, turn your back, shield, shield, shield. Six minutes, four minutes, total frustration, then the ball is kicked despairingly into touch by Spurs. Atletico take their time to retrieve the ball, saunter over, the ball-girls slowly, oh so slowly, throw the ball back eventually. Two minutes remaining, and a second of carelessness betrays Atletico, just one split second. JoJo picks up the glance from the thrower, again anticipates the direction…and intercepts. Atletico in disarray; this isn't supposed to happen! We're in control; we're in control here! But no more, no more.

Sprinting back to defend their goal, watching, waiting for the pass or the run, which will it be? JoJo looks up, no one free, dribble forward, defence backs off, dribble again, no committing from Atletico, who wants to be the one to give it away? All eleven Atletico players in their goal area, shouting, screaming, pointing. JoJo still in possession; no one will commit to challenge and perhaps be exposed. Referee is staring at his watch, glances up, whistle starts to rise up the ref's mouth, JoJo sees a top corner of the goal, goes for it, goalie sees it, punches out, Spurs goalie, Keira Jacques shouldn't be there, but she is, throws herself forward as if she's going to save the ball, at the last instant, Keira folds her arms back and heads the ball towards and into the Atletico goal!

Keira screams out loud, goes running back to her own goal with arms flailing, sees no one there, turns around, Spurs players all celebrating, surround Keira, JoJo looks on, Spurs go mad, Atletico totally deflated. And then the usual congratulations, commiserations, shirt exchange (JoJo was too embarrassed to do that, far too embarrassed). Atletico keeper approaches JoJo and puts out her hand.

"I think your first game for Spurs?" JoJo nods a 'yes'. "But not your last game. No, not your last game; we see you in Europe, I think." Another smile, another handshake, then a hug and a ruffle of the fifteen-year-old's hair, one arm around shoulders and leads the new kid on the block through her Atletico teammates who have the good grace, humility and awareness to hug the newcomer. Murmured words of congratulations, of encouragement. JoJo looks up searching for Larry, searching for Alice. And they're there, smiles, hugs again.

"Some debut, JoJo, some debut," Larry said. Alice smiles at her then steps up and hugs JoJo.

"Never seen a kid play like that, not ever." Then she asked, "We got you signed up yet?" JoJo almost sobbed out loud, almost, then shook her head 'no'. "When are you sixteen, JoJo?"

"Next month, miss…Sorry, sorry, Alice, I mean, Alice; September, I'm one of the oldest in my year group at school." Alice Smith shook her head in disbelief, murmured to herself.

"Still at school, still at school. Jeez…" JoJo walked into the dressing room and was greeted with shrieks and hugs and smiles and cuddles by her teammates, all of whom were that much older than her and a couple of them twice her age. And then, not unnaturally, JoJo burst into tears, and ten new Spurs adoptive mums surrounded her and took care of her.

Post-match reception and Alice Smith is talking with Larry McQueen.

"Hold my hands up, Larry, you were so right, that kid is something very special. What are we going to do?"

"What we're going to do is talk to the powers that be and impress upon them just how good she is…although when they read the match reports and they see all the social media stuff that'll circulate, I don't think it'll take too much, not too much at all." Larry McQueen stopped, considering his next words.

"You know Wayne Rooney was just sixteen years old when he scored his first goal for Everton, sixteen, and that was three years ago. Went to Man U at the grand old age of eighteen, a very cool twenty-three million pounds. Now I know the women's game doesn't have that sort of profile yet, but it's coming; it's coming…And JoJo's fifteen, fifteen, Alice! You saw her just now, ever seen anyone better at that age?"

Alice Smith shook her head. "You know the difference between good and great, Alice?" A smile and another nod. "Yeah, you do; you really do. The difference between good and great is executing in the biggest games. That kid's on the pitch for twenty minutes, scores two and makes the third, against Atletico no less, with all the odds against her. Fifteen and best player on the pitch; the other players know it already; 'course, they do!"

Wearing her Spurs leisure clothing, JoJo is standing alone at the reception, looks at the older players, thinking, All that confidence! Will I ever get that? Yeah, I will, I will, sort of wish I was older, be like them, didn't even dare to put a dress on…I'll learn, I'll listen and learn. It ain't just the playing, is it? It's everything that goes along with it, I know that. I will make it; I will make it! Me, me, scored against Atletico, me', and of course the doubts start, 'was it a fluke? Did I just get lucky? Don't think so, all the girls said I was good, like properly good, they wouldn't lie, would they? Still…'

"Hello, is JoJo?" Juanita Faldez is standing there smiling at JoJo. JoJo gasps out loud. Juanita holds out her hand. "I'm Juanita Faldez…"

"Oh my God! I know who you are, watched you at the women's world cup, you were brilliant for Spain! Hat-trick in the semis and two in the final, you were brilliant, just brilliant! That stuff you did with the ball, those back-flicks, the double-dummy, tried to do all that in training, oh my God!" Juanita laughed, dropped her hand and hugged JoJo instead.

"And you, you Spurs player, you were brilliant out there tonight; first time, I've seen you on the team. Where've they been hiding you?"

"Oh, I'm not on the team, not yet. Hope I will be. I'm at the academy. This is my first trip for Spurs, first trip ever."

"So, you're not a professional yet?" A shake of head, 'no'. "But they pay you, of course?" Another 'no'.

"But they're really good to me. Spurs have been so good to me, always get looked after; they make me feel special." Juanita shook her head now.

"JoJo, you are special. Trust me, you are very special." Then Juanita asked, "How old are you?"

"Fifteen, still at school." Juanita shook her head and sighed.

"In Spain, you can sign professional at fifteen." A pause, then she said, "JoJo, maybe you should sign for Atletico, I think!" And it took almost three seconds before JoJo realised that Juanita, one of her idols, wasn't joking, wasn't joking at all, was absolutely serious. And one last question from Juanita: "JoJo, I see you didn't exchange shirts on the pitch. Me neither. I don't usually do that now…JoJo, would you swap shirts with me…please?" And JoJo thought she'd died and gone to heaven.

*****

There were double the crowd number at the Bernabeu Stadium two nights later. All mega-football fanatics, they had read the Spanish Sports newspaper, 'Marca', had read all about the fifteen-year-old who had dared to score twice against Atletico, and being Real Madrid fans, they had allowed themselves a long luxurious chuckle at Atletico's misfortune. It wouldn't happen, couldn't happen to their team, not to Real Madrid, not in a million years. One little girl was about to grow up and see the realities of professional football.

But nobody told JoJo.

Even the warm-up was cheered and dissected by the fans; the Spurs players were given applause. The atmosphere was warm, electric, intense. Sitting on the subs bench when the whistle blew for kick-off, JoJo thought she could hear a rhythmic chanting from the crowd, turned around to look and was greeted by a roar, "JOJO! JOJO!" She was stunned. Larry McQueen smiled at her.

"Give them what they want, JoJo, stand up and wave to them." JoJo stood and waved and managed to blush at the same time and was given an even bigger cheer. She sat down, still blushing. "Welcome to the club, JoJo, welcome to the star-truckers." Larry McQueen had just, only just remembered to say truckers rather than the original word.

Real and Spurs were both hesitant, playing safely and defensively, almost a skills display; room was given, complicated individual manoeuvres rehearsed in training were shown, and for the first half, the Bernabeu crowd loved it. Fifteen minutes break, and the second half began; four subs for each team, and JoJo was on for the full forty-five minutes. After the intro, the crowd started to become impatient. We're Real Madrid, for god's sake! C'mon, show them! After her magical introduction at Metropolitano, JoJo found it difficult to settle.

The Real players seemed faster, quicker to close her down, more assertive, more aggressive on the tackle confrontation. The bruises were mounting, and the doubts beginning to arise; *Am I good enough? Was it a fluke?* The reality was that the Madrid players were aware of her, they'd seen what she could do two days before, had gone through it again on the video, and the closer attention was a mark of respect to her. Frustrations began, more and more frustrations as neither team could break down the defences. Rehearsed patterns of passing broke down; individual moves and attacks were quickly smothered, as the minutes ticked by; it was beginning to look like a lockout. Final minute and Sabrina Ribera in the Real Madrid goal safely collects the ball, sees the referee bringing the whistle to his mouth and kicks the ball long, turns her back and raises her arms to the crowd behind her goal; the game's over—but it's not, not quite.

Just inside the Madrid half, forty-five yards out, JoJo Jackson unmarked, sees a ridiculous chance, takes the long ball on the volley, and with the crowd screaming at Ribera, watches the spinning leather go over the keeper's head into the net. Spurs one, Real Madrid nil. The referee's whistle blows into a stunned silence as both Ribera and her supporters realise what's happened—that kid again! The one who stuffed Atletico, she's done it again, to us, to the best team in the world. Sucked us in and blown us out in bubbles! Eleven white shirts dropped, deflated; Spurs in their away strip of the purple were silent and unmoving for almost one second, then realised what had occurred and ran towards JoJo, who lifted her hands sideways and then dropped them when she was lifted and held in the air.

"Larry told me to be brave, said to go for it, take a chance…That's what I did…that's all I did."

"But no one else did, JoJo, no one else dared…that's what makes you different," Keira Jacques said. "Please, JoJo, may I have your autograph." And that was entirely the right thing to say as JoJo and all the players laughed. But Keira was less than half-joking.

Alice Smith looked over at Larry and lifted her eyebrows in pretend astonishment.

"Guess I might need to get on the phone, maybe right now." Larry McQueen nodded 'yes' straight back to her.

Chapter Thirty-Seven
Barcelona

"You see what JoJo did?" Lucy looked at Shelley, Sami and Mickey. "You see what she actually did, really? Scored against both of them: Atletico and then Real. JoJo, our mate, our mate since junior school, well, since forever actually. Gilly, you seen it? Like I can't read Spanish, but you see her name and the pictures and it's pretty obvious that she's gonna be a star, isn't she? Like a real star!"

"I think JoJo is a star already, and I think that she totally deserves it; she's done exactly what you guys have done, worked her backside off and kept working her backside off…same as you lot."

Gilly considered for a minute. "It's down to choice really, isn't it? Totally down to choice. Forget all about the other stuff, the reasons why people give themselves excuses for not being successful, not making it, if you like; you know, like, 'school was no good', 'no one cared about me', 'we didn't have any money', 'grew up in a nasty area', and a million more so-called reasons. Doesn't matter; just take a look at yourselves right now, guys; you're in the British team, all of you, and don't think for one minute that you don't deserve to be here. You've earned that right to wear a British tracksuit. You made that choice to train, to train harder than I've seen most do. You made that choice, you."

They were sitting at the holding camp—a posh name for the hotel where the GB team were staying—literally outside the Olimpic Lluis Companys Stadium, where the 1992 Olympics had been hosted.

"Be great to see her play, wouldn't it? Can you imagine, us four all in the same city in different sports?" Shelley looked over at Gilly as they enjoyed their secret. "Go on, Gilly, tell them; let them in on the secret." Gilly smiled back. *Oh god, I love these girls, and I love Mickey. Anything for each other, they'd do anything for each other.*

"We're going, all of us; we're going. Spurs match against Barca is the day after we finish. We have a day off, supposedly for sightseeing and stuff, then flying back the day after so we can go and watch JoJo and Spurs…if you want to?"

"You kidding me? Gilly, you're not kidding? Don't break my heart and say it's a joke, no." Gilly's heart went out one more time to Mickey.

"No, this is for real, Mickey, for real. I had a call from their manager, lady called Alice Smith."

"Yeah, JoJo's talked about her," Mickey interjected. "Anyway, sounds like JoJo is golden girl right now, and she asked if she could buy tickets for all of us. Bottom line is we're going as VIPs! Barca—the football club that is—have asked us if we'd be OK to wear the GB tracksuits, reckon that's OK?"

"Gilly, I've been sleeping in mine!" Sami said, and they all laughed.

"Me too, reckon we all have!" And it could have been any one of them who'd said it.

"Nou Camp is only ten minutes down the road, and listen to this, guys, they're sending a limo for us, a limo! And just one more thing, hope this is all right; no, I know it's all right. Chris and Dan are flying out for your events and JoJo's match."

Mickey Honey quickly stood up and walked away from them so that they wouldn't see him cry. *Mr Warren and Mr Bullet—Chris and Dan—are coming over to Spain to watch me run; no pressure there, then.* Gilly had put a restraining hand on Lucy's and Shelley's shoulders as they got up to follow Mickey, and as they looked at her, she smiled softly and shook her head 'no', and they understood immediately.

"You think he's all right, Gilly?" Lucy and Shelley both asked together. Sami was listening.

"Mickey's fine, ladies; he's fine. Look, I know how much you all loved Chris; 'course, I do, but without being funny, Mickey's a boy. Chris really was…actually, 'is' a father figure to him, so it's got to Mickey, that's all. Let's get organised; let's get practical." Just then, Mickey walked back in.

"Sorry, guys. Sorry, Gilly, you know…" Lucy, Shelley and Sami were immediately at his side. "If you guys start that fast in the race, then no one else has got a chance!" And that broke the atmosphere and was exactly the thing to say.

Shelley had heats for her hurdles, then a semi if she got through, and then the final, again if she survived the semi. Straight finals for the others; in a two-day meet, there was no chance of two runs over three thousand metres. For all of them, there was a nervousness, first time in a GB tracksuit? Of course, there was! But it was a controlled nervousness, all the rituals and protocols explained by the team manager and then again by Gilly, and then by Gilly again. Correct kit, warm-up area, signing in, what to do if selected for a drugs test, who to speak to, everything was taken care of.

Gilly was as nervous as her charges, but she hid it well, and her apparent calmness and coolness transferred to all of them. She had already given strict instructions to both Chris and Dan before they arrived, and the atmosphere lent itself to good performances. All of the athletes had hugged Chris and Dan when they'd checked into the hotel, and it was Mickey who was closest to tears, although the three girls were not far behind.

The athletes were ready, as ready as they could be.

Shelley was first on, sign in, get heat number, get competition number, get minute-by-minute timetable, go to warm-up area, talk briefly to the two other British hurdlers and then prepare. Gilly leading the warm-up, a quiet confidence because Gilly was there. Done it a million times before, same routine: jog, stretches, strides, single legs over the top, work the trail leg snap-down, starting blocks, approach, then three hurdles at eighty, ninety, ninety-nine per cent.

Done, get the mind straight, ready, then, "Shelley? Shelley? It is my friend Shelley?"

"What the f...? Marianne? Oh my god, Marianne!" They fell into each other's arms. "How long? Oh my god, just how long, and we're here, you and me, oh my god!"

And together they said, "You haven't changed a bit!" They laughed at themselves and each other.

"Shelley, you go; you must be hurdles, yes? I go straight after you for two hundred metres heats, then we meet up, yes?" Shelley kissed her nemesis, kissed her again, then kissed Gilly, who smiled 'good luck, you'll be fine, I promise'.

"Of course, I'll wait for you after your heat, I'm coming straight back here to warm down, then semi this afternoon...if...if I get through!"

Lane one, not seeded. Youngest competitor, there for experience? Not for Shelley, certainly not there for the experience was Shelley. Most of the athletes two years older, maybe not taller but more experienced, national and international competition, been through the mill, done the apprenticeship, been there, done that, got the badge.

But not one of them was Shelley, not even close. She was a class apart; no, she was two classes apart. From the gun, she was in front, as her spikes hit the pink track they seemed to catapult back up and then down, the barriers came automatically, didn't even seem as if they were there, didn't even feel as if she was breaking stride to lift and snap and hit and three strides and over again and again for those ten times in all. Broke the tape, three metres the nearest to her, point four of a second difference, and that was huge. Hugs, handshakes, some kisses. The athletes who had raced at this level before knew that they'd raced against someone a little bit special. There was a new kid on the block, and she was dangerous—dangerous to their world.

"Shelley, that was brilliant! Superb!"

"Oh, Gilly, was I all right, really? Felt good, felt—and I know this might sound stupid—as if I wasn't really there, as if it was me looking at some hurdler who happened to be me...told you it was stupid." Shelley moved over to Gilly and hugged her tight. "Thanks, Gilly, you taught me how; you taught me everything." And then Shelley cried, just a little bit.

"Shelley, you ran a thirteen-nine, thirteen-nine for god's sake! As a fifteen-year-old, under fourteen seconds. Shelley, you know what qualifying time is for Worlds under twenty?" And Shelley shook her head 'no'. "Thirteen-seven-five, Shelley, you're just fifteen hundredths off of Worlds!"

Marianne passed the two of them as she was heading out onto the track for her two hundred metres heat; she blew Shelley a kiss, which Shelley caught and then returned it as both smiled.

And then it was Mickey's turn. Gilly waved at him as he came out of the holding room with the other twenty-three athletes; he smiled back at her and then looked over at Chris and Dan sitting right in the front seats at the two hundred metre mark, smiled, half a wave, two hands held palms out back to him, and then it was total focus. The marksman and starter separating the field into two sections, so many runners that the start line was split. Mickey found himself in the outer group, so their three metres advantage would be negated after the bend, but no cutting in until halfway down the home straight. Mickey liked calling the home straight 'the stretch' after he'd heard one of the USA Olympic distance runners calling it that in a post-race interview. He'd decided that he'd call it 'the stretch' when he was interviewed...eventually).

A quick look at his opponents, *Christ, they look like men; they're all bloody men!* The whistle blew, toes on the line. "To your marks," and the gun cracked. Elbows and shoulders, tightly packed, too tightly packed. Avoid, avoid, avoid, watch the spikes, watch the cutting in, and as the field squeezed together after the one-fifty mark, there was an almost audible sigh of relief.

No one had gone down. Past the four-hundredth mark, one lap done, six and a half to go. "Sixty-six, sixty-seven, sixty…" middle of the pack, working it but comfortable, still bunching, two, three wide, overtaking, and it was four abreast. Two laps done, then three, a couple of the rabbits dropping back, not Mickey though, definitely not Mickey Honey, the Duracell Bunny.

"Go, Mickey! Go, Mickey!" It was Lucy, of course, her heart beating almost as fast as Mickey's; of course, it was. Lucy was running it with him in her mind and in her heart; of course, she was. Four laps, up the field a little, holding seventh or eighth. "Four twenty-six, twenty-seven." Field splitting a little now, gaps widening. Mickey into sixth, breathing hard but in control, another lap done, another position gained. The German and the Russian vests leading the front pack started to squeeze the pace, not desperate, just squeezing and tightening, two fell away, Mickey into fourth, covering, covering, covering.

Last six hundred. "Six fifty-five, fifty-six, fifty-seven…" Germany and Russia moving away, Mickey losing ground, 'get it back, get it back!' and the other vest, an orange one, fell back. Mickey slowly, oh so slowly, managed to get past. Final two hundred, seven fifty-seven fifty-eight. *Shit! No wonder they're away!* Into the stretch, desperately, so desperately trying to lift the pace, and lifting it more than enough to take third. *Fucking hell, man! Fucking hell! Third! Me! Me! Me third!* And Mickey did a little dance to himself, looked over, jogged back down the stretch and the bend, and as Chris and Dan put their arms down and around him, he could no longer hold it in and burst into tears.

"Eight-thirty, Mickey, eight-thirty! Personal best by, what? Twelve, fifteen seconds?" And Mickey turned and embraced Gilly to him, as Chris, Dan and Lucy clapped and screamed.

And now it was Shelley again; same preparation, same routine. Warm-up, prepare, tick the necessary boxes. Three semi-finals, first two in each semi goes through by right and then two fastest losers. Shelley had been third fastest in the heats and was allocated lane four in the first of the three semis. Gilly smiled and hugged her. "Go on, you go girl!" And now it was a little bit different. Shelley had been seeded, of course, fastest qualifier in her semi, and the girls were aware of her now. Not too many smiles this time; the new kid on the block may just have come of age. Whistle blows, lane checkers and officials make sure that no stray fingers have drifted over the start lane.

Shelley knows no one in her semi, both other British girls eliminated in the heats. "Set…" Starting pistol is raised, fires and away! *Keep low, focus, lift into first and snap and away.* Much tighter this time, no blowing away the oppo this time; fifth hurdle cleared, technique so good, so good and on automatic for Shelley; she senses a slight, oh so slight gap opening; focus, focus, focus…ninth cleared then the tenth, desperate sprint in, chest lowers and pushes, tape breaks…*Was it me? Was it me?* The eight athletes shake hands, some hugs, even a couple of hugs for Shelley that she gladly accepted. *Maybe I'm getting good enough?* Looks up at the big screen for the action replay…*Yes! Yes! Yes!* Name and time flashes up: '1st Shelley Steele, GB, 13.87; 2nd Grete Hautt, GER, 13.91…' Pretty damn close…But I won! I'm in the final!'

"Gilly, I made the final! I made the final!"

"Never doubted, Shelley, never doubted." Shelley looked at her coach, saw the seriousness there and knew the truth…she was good enough. "Go and warm down, stretch, maybe see if you can get a gentle massage, final's tomorrow… And you're ready, one hundred per cent ready." And the confidence, so hard to gain, rose that little bit higher.

*****

They ate together that evening; Chris and Dan managed to get themselves into the team hotel, and if anyone official had seriously tried to stop them, there would have been four very angry athletes to deal with and one even angrier coach. The seven of them were sitting around the table, reflecting on the day's races. Shelley and Mickey were feeling pretty pleased with themselves.

Shelley was holding onto a little nervousness with tomorrow's final to come. Sami and Lucy took it in confidence, having seen what their training group had already achieved. The GB manager came over to add his congratulations and recognised Dan from the Sydney Olympics. A few jokes, and the atmosphere lightened a little more.

"Did you get pulled for the drug test, Mickey?" Mickey nodded back at Dan.

"I had a whole bunch of them when I was swimming, didn't like them, always felt a bit embarrassed even when I'd done loads…but I guess it has to be done; keep sport clean…maybe…"

"They tested the first four of us, wasn't too bad, but you're right, a bit embarrassing when someone's watching you have a wee, and you can't squeeze it out!" The three girls erupted.

"Really? Really? Someone watches you have a wee?"

"Yeah, you have to wee in a bottle, and then they take it away and test it. That's why they can't do the awards ceremonies straightaway, gotta be proven clean. You can have someone come in with you, though, team manager or coach, you know." And the girls all looked directly at Gilly, no question needed asking…

"Of course, I will if you're selected for the dope test! 'Course I will. I'll be there; that's exactly what I signed up for." And Lucy and Shelley thought back to that time in Amsterdam when Gilly had been there for them, and they knew that they'd be able to handle the scenario if it arose.

As early as it was, Chris and Dan bid their farewells and went to their hotel, decided to stay up for a glass of wine or two, and Dan filled Chris in on the very necessary aspects and nuances of drug testing. Chris was shaking his head, 'why do they do that, why?', and Dan was rubbing his thumb against his forefinger. "Money, Chris; it's all about money."

The three girls were sharing a bedroom while Mickey was with one of the fifteen hundred metres runners, close enough, but not too close, and Mickey slept soundly; he knew that he was clean, knew that he'd be on the podium tomorrow. And even better, he knew that he'd be watching Lucy run…and win…maybe win.

*****

Shelley was the first one on programme, final of the hurdles just before mid-day. Sami and Lucy very soon after, just thirty minutes on the schedule. They started their warm-up together then needed to separate as their necessary race skills took precedence over their friendship. And very soon, it was time—time for Shelley. Lucy and Sami kissed her as she left the warm-up track for the holding room. "Good luck, Shelley, good luck." Shelley, Lucy and Sami knew that luck had very little to do with it. Walking out onto the track, Shelley took in all that was going on around her: men's discus over at one end, women's long jump in front of the home straight, men's pole vault close to the long jump. Shelley took it all in, but nothing really registered; she was beginning to realise what other athletes meant when they said that they were 'in the zone'.

Third fastest qualifier for the final, lane three. Russia and Norway in four and five. They all exchanged nervous grins. Perhaps Russia a little less nervous? Perhaps. 13.87 for Shelley, 13.84 for Norway, 13.61 for Russia. Two tenths is a big gap. No, it's not; it's a huge gap. But what do you do? You know exactly what to do. You go for it. *This is what I do. This is who I am.* Settling in the blocks, almost second nature now. Lick the fingers, brush the hair back, stretch the neck. Listen, listen, wait, no, anticipate, don't wait, anticipate. Gun raised…crack!

A great start! Shelley knew; she just knew. *I can do this! I can do this!* One, two, three, flowing, flowing, flowing, flowing, dare to try to accelerate, yes! Still smooth! Tenth cleared, dip and sprint, over the line. But no feeling of snapping the tape. Not this time. The Russian athlete was already prancing down the track, hands up, waving, waving, waving. A huge disappointment for Shelley. *I gave it everything, absolutely everything, couldn't do any more.* She goes over and hugs the Russian winner. Then she looks up at the scoreboard: '1st, Irena Klatchlikova, RUS, 13.59. 2nd Shelley Steele, GB, 13.64.' Shelley ran and ran and ran around the track, smiling and waving at everyone, until she came to Chris and Dan and fell into both their embraces. An athlete comes of age. Cliché…but true. Shelley Steele, girl from the estate, had come of age. And she deserved it, deserved it totally.

But there was still more to come. A lot more to come. If any one of them could have taken back what was about to happen, they would happily have done so. More than happily.

Lucy and Sami were coming out onto the track at the same time as Shelley, along with Irena and Lina; they were being escorted to the dope-testing room.

"You done this before?" Shelley asked.

Irena nodded 'yes'. Lina shook her head 'no'. Shelley just shrugged. Gilly was with her, female officials with Russia and Norway. Single clinical room, female tester along with the subjects and their minders. Shelley blushing…but actually not as bad as she had thought it might be. "Thanks, Gilly; thank you for being with me."

"Get used to me being there, Shelley; the way you're performing right now, there'll be a lot of championships, and unfortunately, the dope testing goes along with that."

Lucy was as calm as she had ever been before a race. She'd seen what Mickey had done; she knew what she'd done in training. She knew that she had nothing—absolutely nothing—to lose. *I'm still a kid with these guys, another two years at this level. You know what? I'm gonna see exactly what I can do...yeah, I am*, she thought, looking over at Sami, nervous.

Lucy got closer and squeezed her hand. "Me'n you, Sami, me'n you, yeah?"

Sami whispered back, "Me and you, little one, me and you." But Lucy could hear the nervousness in her voice. Blow of the whistle. Take your places, split start again, Sami and Lucy both on inside curve, tight and dangerous, be aware, be very aware at the start. Crack! And away. A cautiousness from the athletes (who wanted to get taken out at the start?), and that very caution created problems, much too slow, girls stuttering on the heels of those in front while praying that no one flicked their shoes and heels. The two halves coming together at the one-fifty mark, no fallers! And you could almost hear the sighs of relief.

Through the four hundred, "Eighty, eighty-one," 'too slow, far too slow!' Lucy following Sami halfway down the large pack, edges out, starts to move up the group, Sami instantly following. Lucy picks up the pace, her thoughts, *I don't have a real sprint, have to stretch this out.* Eight hundred mark, two thirty-nine, *That's better, a little better.* Lucy stretches more now; the increased pace is being felt by the still-close pack. Lucy stretched again, still in control. And now the pack stretches out; four athletes immediately off the pace, but twenty are still very much there...But for how long?

A glance behind from Lucy as they go through the twelve hundred mark. "Three fifty-five, fifty-six." *That's better! Split a seventy-five there.* And now the field was stretching, stretching, stretching out. And suddenly, the elastic snapped, and the twenty in contention had become just ten. Lucy's pace was taking them apart. Sixteen hundred, "Five o-nine, five ten," *Jeez, a seventy-four, pick the bones out of that!* Sami still holding tight, but Lucy could hear Sami's breathing loud. Over halfway now, through eighteen hundred, just three laps to go. Gilly, Dan, Chris, all clenched fists, not daring to shout out...but Mickey dared. Oh, yes, Mickey dared.

"C'mon, Lucy! Go, Sami! You can do this!" And Lucy dared as well; if Mickey said that she could do this, well...you know. She held the pace, felt rather than saw the others cracking, only Sami—good old Sami—staying on her shoulder. Two thousand metres, "Six thirteen, fourteen…"

Another seventy-four, hold, hold, hold! Lucy and Sami now away from the chasers, Sami dying several deaths but hold, hold, hold onto Lucy. Six laps now, two thousand four hundred, "Seven thirty…" 'Dropped a couple of seconds but so will everyone else.' Final six hundred, through the bell, four hundred remaining, and Lucy lifted the pace again…and Sami matched her. Ten, twelve, fifteen metres between the two Brits and the rest of Europe. Hard now, hardest ever, really? Really harder than anything? *I don't think so, I really don't think so.*

And with two hundred, the final two hundred, "Eight forty-four," to go, Lucy lifted her head, looked into the stands, smiled somehow and lengthened her stride, holding form, around the bend, into the stretch; the crowd stood and applauded. Sami saw the open space between them and knew she couldn't snatch it back, not this time, but still went for it, closed just a little, five metres back as Lucy crossed the line, a huge smile on Sami's face as well. *Lucy deserves that one, yeah, deserves it. Girl's class, real class.* Into each other's arms, hugging, crying, laughing. Looked up at the scoreboard, saw the times, 9.25.09, 9.27.28, both girls' hands to lips, mouths open in surprise. That fast! Really?

"Well, look at you, little one; just look at you!"

"Sami, you all right? All right?"

"You kidding me, little one? Of course, I'm all right. I just got second to the girl who's going to win the Olympics and break the world record, and she's just pushed me to my best time, ever. Personal best by over ten seconds, yeah, you could say that I'm all right."

Crossing the line, the other athletes in the race congratulated them, looked up at the times displayed and congratulated them again. And the winner and runner-up in that remarkable three thousand metres managed to keep holding hands as they jogged around the track together, wrapping themselves in the applause, the shouts, the whoops, and they were getting closer to Gilly, to Dan and Chris, to Shelley and, for Lucy, especially, to Mickey.

The warning horn blared out from the discus throwing circle; whether Sami and Lucy heard it, it wouldn't have mattered anyway. It was just another one of those sounds that you heard in a meet, didn't mean anything—anything at all. Gilly was running towards them with Mickey and Shelley. Chris and Dan were contemplating climbing over the barrier. Geoff Scarpers, representing Great

Britain, released the discus after his three rotations, watched it hit the restraining net. 'Shit!' Turned away, didn't see the net push the discus out and away rather than cushion it as was supposed, and didn't see the discus skip away from the restraints, bounce just once on the track before it cannoned into the three thousand metres winner's knee. Didn't hear the awful crack, didn't see Lucy Newton collapse on the pink track and certainly didn't hear the screams of agony coming from Lucy's mouth. Didn't see Mickey Honey wrap his arms around her. Didn't hear the sobs coming from Gilly's, Shelley's, Mickey's, Chris's and Dan's mouths. Didn't hear or see any of it.

Chapter Thirty-Eight
Nou Camp

It was quiet in the hospital; nobody knew what to say. Gilly had gone into surgery with Lucy along with the GB team manager. Geoff Scarpers had come running over to Lucy as soon as he'd heard what had happened, with tears in his eyes as well. Nobody blamed him. What's to blame? Blame more on the equipment that had failed, maybe blame whoever of the officials, the technical officers who hadn't checked the discus net properly. But blame didn't matter. What mattered was how was Lucy? Gilly came out of the operating theatre.

"The doctor thinks it's the cruciate ligament…it's not good, not good at all." And Gilly buried her head into Chris's shoulder. Mickey couldn't move; he felt that his life was over; it wasn't, of course, but that was the feeling. *Why? Why? Why Lucy? It's not fair. Why God? Why would you do that? Why not me? It should have been me.* Shelley put her arms around Mickey, said nothing because there was nothing to say. Sami went over, felt that she didn't want to intrude until Shelley embraced her as well, the three of them standing together in stunned grief.

"What they're going to do is strap Lucy's leg and knee, put it in a brace so she can't move it, fill her with painkillers so that she can fly home with us day after tomorrow. If they go into the leg and have to operate, then she'll be in plaster and wouldn't be able to fly for a week or so. I said that would be OK…Chris, think so?"

Chris nodded 'yes'. "Mickey, you happy with that?" Mickey had nothing to say.

"Can I go and see her, please, please?" The Spanish doctor looked at his tear-stained face and quickly acquiesced.

"Lucy? Lucy you all right?" Mickey immediately realised what a stupid thing to say, but what do you say when the other half of your being is laying there, hurting?

"Oh, Mickey, it hurts; it does hurt, but they've given me painkillers—a lot of painkillers. They're keeping me tonight, but maybe tomorrow I can come out...maybe, Mickey. I know I shouldn't feel sorry for myself, but I can't help it. I just keep thinking, why me?" And Lucy cried a little then, while Mickey held her hand.

Lucy's voice was slurring a little now, and her eyes were beginning to shut. The drugs were acting as they should; the pain was a little less, then she said, "Mickey, I still want to go and watch JoJo play tomorrow; honestly, I do. I have to...Mickey; you must make them let me go, you must. Mickey, please?" And then Lucy mercifully fell asleep, and Mickey re-joined the real world, that horrible, nasty, unfeeling, cruel real world.

Mickey didn't sleep too much that night. Truth is that none of the group slept too well that evening. It was grey eyes for everybody at breakfast; they were all just waiting to go back to the hospital. Mickey had a question, a request, a plea for the doctor who was treating Lucy. Dr Ismeldos asked just one question, "Why?" And Mickey explained, tried to explain how important it was not only to Lucy but to all of them. The growing-up, the friendships, the bonding and, importantly, how all of them felt stronger together. And that was what stole it. Dr Ismeldos rationalised that if it made Lucy feel that little bit better, then it was a first step to healing, a first step back to the reality of life, but what he didn't say because he couldn't was how similar or how different that life would be now.

Dr Ismeldos had treated a lot of athletes, a lot. And he knew more than most how chance could serve two masters, two mistresses. Strict instructions were given, promises made. Dr Ismeldos trusted this young man, something about him, something special. He had no doubt, absolutely no doubt at all, that the young man standing in front of him would happily sacrifice his life for the young lady in the hospital bed.

It took a long time preparing Lucy to leave the hospital. Eventually, in the wheelchair, with her leg thrusting out in front, bandaged and braced, Lucy left. Dr Ismeldos watched her go, watched the young man pushing her wheelchair and still didn't know, couldn't know what her life would be like now. Chance, pure chance...but sometimes you can try to manipulate the dice to make the odds better. Sometimes.

Lucy turned to the doctor.

"Dr Ismeldos, *muchas gracias por todo lo que has hecho por mi.*" Cynical old Dr Ismeldos, who'd seen it all many times, bent down and kissed his patient.

"*Buena suerte, pequena.*" Sami translated the 'pequena' into 'little one', and Lucy smiled, then laughed for the first time. Back in the hotel and resting before the match, JoJo's match, Mickey went with Lucy into the girls' bedroom, and not one of the GB team officials even thought of denying him that. Lucy slept while Mickey watched over her.

*****

"You're starting, JoJo." Alice Smith smiled at the fifteen-year-old. "You deserve it; you've proved it. Go out and enjoy it; you deserve that as well. I never played here, never, so I envy you. I'm not jealous, not at all, but I'm most definitely envious!" Alice smiled again, keeping the secret of what was going to happen, what was going to be offered after the final whistle blew, to herself. Well, to herself and Larry.

"Alice, is it all right if I go and see my friends before the match starts? I can't tell you how much it means to me you getting it all sorted for them to come and see me play, and I need to ask how they got on at the Europeans; they're a bit special, my mates, more than a bit special." Alice Smith smiled; she would have given anything to JoJo right now.

"Of course, you can. I'll get someone to take you to the VIP area. Ten minutes, OK? Don't be late back, JoJo; you're starting tonight, remember." *As if I'd forget.* To the lounge…and then JoJo saw Lucy sitting in the wheelchair with her leg raised and bandaged. Mickey, Shelley, Sami, Chris, Gilly and Dan, all were quiet and subdued. Her heart stopped, almost.

"Lucy, what happened? Lucy, you all right?" And Lucy had rehearsed what she was going to say, but it fell apart pretty quickly. The events of yesterday ('Yesterday? Was it only yesterday?') were recounted, the others adding in their words.

"But you're gonna be OK, Lucy; you're gonna be OK?" And with what she saw in Lucy's eyes despite the protestations, JoJo knew immediately that nothing was certain; nothing could be taken for granted.

JoJo kissed Lucy on the cheek and then whispered to her, "This one's for you Lucy; this one's most definitely for you."

Then she stood in front of Chris, in front of Mr Warren, and it took almost a tenth of a second before she couldn't stop herself and hugged him tight. "Thank you, sir; thank you for everything. I wouldn't be here without you." She looked at all of them. "Without all of you guys, I wouldn't be here, I know that…I'm going to try to make you proud of me."

The capacity of Barcelona's Nou Camp Stadium is just around one hundred thousand, and that capacity is filled for every home match. For the men that is, not for the women. But tonight was different; every Barcelona supporter had read in the sports pages about the new wonderkid on the Spurs team, and they knew that it couldn't be true. Against Atletico and Real, maybe. But this was Barcelona, and the kid was going to be blown away. Almost seventy thousand (a new crowd record for a women's football match anywhere) spectators were in the stadium to watch Barcelona show once again that they were the best football team in the world for both men and women.

Sunday Times sports correspondent David Caxton sat in the Press area, thought back on what he'd just received in the telephone call, shook his head and started composing what he would write for the next edition. Sometimes he hated his job.

But this evening, he was about to rediscover how much he loved it.

The Barca crowd were generous; they could afford to be; their team were about to annihilate the Spurs team, and they were there to watch it happen. Whistle blows, kick-off, ball passed back to JoJo, give her the ball early, help her to settle into the game. But no one had told JoJo that she needed to settle. JoJo had something to prove and a lot of people to prove it to. She'd discovered a new hardness in the previous thirty minutes. No, hardness wasn't the correct word, a new steeliness, a new resolve. JoJo looks up. Who's free? No one. Everyone marked loosely but no real freedom, so she goes forward with the ball, dribble and wait for a half-chance.

Despite all the confidence, the Barca players backed off; they'd read about the new kid, didn't really believe all the hype, but you know…Maybe, just maybe. And the new kid kept pushing the ball forward, push and run, push and run, push and run. Bill Nicholson, the Spurs manager in those magic double years, had used the expression first, and it had worked those forty years ago, so why not now? Push and push again, crowd anxious and every right to be. Get her! Cut her down! Show her where she is! Who she's playing against! Almost on the edge of the penalty area, still no Barca commitment. JoJo stops, puts her foot on top of the ball. Waits. Challenge.

JoJo sidesteps, defender goes down, sidesteps again, second defender. Tiny space, left foot, strikes, strikes hard. Net bulges, goalkeeper stricken. Defenders stricken. Barcelona nil, Spurs one. JoJo turned to the VIP boxes, sought out Lucy and the others, held her arm and hand high and pointed, then dropped her arm, both hands on her chest, dropped her head, put the palm of her hand to her lips and blew a kiss in their direction.

Lucy didn't cry, but she was the only one who didn't. Lucy knew exactly why JoJo had scored and who she had done it for. Her heart swelled—swelled for JoJo and for herself. The three adults were looking down at their feet until Dan looked up and saw that Chris and Gilly were quietly sobbing as well and as were Mickey, Sami and Shelley.

Barcelona were serious now. That's ridiculous! She's a kid for god's sake. A kid! C'mon now, we're Barca. And Barca were spraying it around the park, total possession now. JoJo was back in defence, every Spurs player was back in defence, and Barca were dominating every facet of the game; pass after pass with the crowd shouting out, "Ole!"

For every touch. JoJo was loving it, totally loving it. No fear now, no embarrassment of being on the pitch with some of the absolute best footballers in the world. *I deserve to be here. I deserve it!* JoJo had a very good idea of what was going to be offered after this match, and JoJo had decided that she was going to be brave enough to make a few demands (well, let's make that 'requests' to be polite) of her own. On the six-yard line, JoJo intercepts, keeps calm, pushes the ball out to the touchline to Cerise Jones, the only player free for Spurs, runs towards Cerise and screams for the return. Barca a little out of position, all that pressing, pressing, pressing but now running back to cover. Ball back to JoJo, immediate return to Cerise, and suddenly, the counter-attack is on. Ball back to JoJo in the centre, looks up, sprays out to Teresa Medwin (didn't her dad used to play for Spurs?), on the left wing now who's cleared from defence.

Three-pronged attack against a retreating four-person defence, keep it wide, keep it wide, force them to make a choice. Nearer and nearer now, JoJo in the middle dropping back, ball swinging from wing to wing, to JoJo with her back to the goal, just inside the box, two central defenders move in on her, close her down, don't let her turn! So, JoJo didn't turn, as the two Barca players converged on her, she stroked the ball onto the outside of her left foot, lifted the ball into the air, dropped her shoulder and turned inside the trap and, as the ball descended, right foot volleyed into the net.

Three things happened: first, JoJo turned again to the VIP box, smiled and waved to Lucy. Lucy smiled and waved back and could see JoJo's lips moving and knew exactly what she was saying, "For you, Lucy, that one's for you." And then Lucy did cry. Second, the Spurs players didn't run to JoJo, not this time; they stood where they were and clapped. Third, the seventy thousand Barcelona spectators followed the Spurs players; they rose from their seats and applauded; they knew they had seen something—someone—very special, indeed. Less than thirty minutes gone and Barcelona two-nil down at home. When had that last happened?

On the touchline, Alice Smith had her mobile phone clasped to her ear and was almost shouting to be heard above the crowd noise. Larry McQueen just smiled and then laughed out loud. In the Press box, David Caxton was scribbling away and smiling to himself while shaking his head.

"You gonna do the big three, JoJo?" Keira Jacques was grinning. "You know, you've done the left and the right foot, going for the header now?" JoJo grinned back.

"Don't think that's too likely, do you?" And Keira thought, *With you, girl, anything's likely, anything at all.*

Two defenders on JoJo, and any time the ball came anywhere near her, she was closed down immediately. No way of getting away from two of them, but it did give that little bit of extra space for Spurs, and they began to play as if they were enjoying it, which they were. Three match tour, won two and two up against Barca, not too dusty. Much more space on the ball now, ball pinging from side to side, end to end, very little action at either end, grouped in the middle of the pitch, possession switching from one team to the other, Barca gradually getting on top, gradually getting the better of Tottenham.

Long shot in by Barca, Keira Jacques grabs the ball, sees Teresa in the centre circle, long punt up to her, JoJo screaming up the left wing evading the chasers, Teresa takes a chance, long ball into the left side of the goal area, but it's not to be, JoJo is just too far away, but JoJo doesn't think so, too far to get the ball under control, even to get the ball on either foot, but not too far for an extended low dive, throws herself just a few inches above the grass, connects with her head and with the goalie stranded, trickles over the line. The big three!

The whistle blew for halftime. Alice and Larry applauded their players off of the pitch, and Larry hugged JoJo.

"Unbelievable, JoJo, unbelievable!"

A hesitation, then JoJo said, "But you're taking me off for the second half...No, that's OK, Larry. To be honest, I'm shattered...but a good shattered. Look, can me and you and Alice have a chat as soon as I'm showered and changed, please? I'm not stupid, I know what's coming up. My mum and dad have been on the phone. No, they didn't say exactly what was going to happen, but my dad said that he'd given written permission to Spurs for whatever was needed. He said that he trusted you, and he said that Mr Warren would be there if I needed him. Do I need him, Larry, do I? Are Spurs going to offer me a contract, are they?" And Larry nodded a big 'yes'. "That's brilliant; it's all I've ever wanted...But I've got to ask you something—something really important."

"JoJo, don't you want to know what money Spurs are going to offer you?" And Larry whispered a huge number to JoJo.

"That's really nice, Larry. I could probably help my mum and dad get a house, move out of the estate...but actually, there's something more important. Yeah, I know what you're thinking. 'What's more important than money'? But this is, this really is."

JoJo showered and changed in the quiet dressing room and hoped, desperately hoped, that it would be all right. Larry and Alice were waiting for her in the lounge; JoJo took a deep breath and told them what she would like. She didn't make it a condition of signing, but...then, "I need to phone Daniel Levy and probably Martin Jol right now!"

The Spurs manager was contacted first. "Martin, that girl we spoke about, yeah, that one, the special one, well..." And Larry explained the request. Martin Jol chuckled.

"She seems a very determined young lady, Larry. Is she really as good as everyone's saying? Really?" And Larry told him what JoJo had done in the first half against Barca. "That good, eh...OK, I'll contact Mr Levy. Stay by your phone."

It was less than ten minutes. "Larry, short answer is yes, a big yes! My Levy was amused, said, 'so a fifteen-year-old kid is holding us to ransom now!' Actually, he thought it was a great idea, brilliant for working with the local community, all that stuff. Tell JoJo we're good to go! And Larry, soon as you're back, I want to meet this one; truly, I do." Larry put down the phone, sighed loudly, looked directly at JoJo and then gave an exaggerated long, slow wink.

"Spurs nil, JoJo Jackson one!" And JoJo hugged him and then excused herself to go be with her friends and to ask them to come along to the post-match celebration. There wasn't a lot of time, and JoJo spent most of it talking to Lucy and then to Chris Warren. She seemed three, five, ten years older, a genuine maturity. The final whistle blew, Barca had almost, almost come back; the final score was Spurs three, Barcelona two. Lucy sat with her friends and mentors, waiting for all the players to change from the sweaty kit into something acceptable for the reception.

The escorts arrived, and the group was ushered ('pushed' in Lucy's case) to the reception. JoJo introduced her group to Larry and Alice and then to her fellow players, emphasising how important Chris, Gilly and Dan had been to her growing-up and to her friends' growing-up. JoJo was mingling with everyone now, far more confident, still a little shy, but proud of what she'd achieved. The senior players treated her, spoke to her as an equal, spoke to Chris and the others as equals and asked Mickey, Lucy and Shelley about the Europeans.

They treated them with the utmost respect as athletes and as people. They talked with Gilly about their training, about her coaching. They listened, listened carefully, to what she said, asked about JoJo's running training. They listened even more carefully, talked about it between themselves.

"May I have your attention, please." Barcelona FC manager, Frank Rijkaard, was speaking perfect Spanish but still with that Dutch lilt after three seasons with the club, three very successful seasons. "We wish to welcome our good friends, honoured guests and exemplary footballers, Spurs ladies!"

Loud applause all around. "And we wish to welcome especially a footballer who dared to score three goals against the best team in the world, Barcelona, just fifteen years old, put your hands together for Joanna Jackson!"

JoJo stood up, smiling, embarrassed, waved to everybody. "And now I'm going to hand you over to one of the world's best defenders ever, for Spurs and England, here this evening as Spurs coach, Larry McQueen!" Larry rose to his feet.

"I don't speak very good Spanish, ladies and gentlemen, I hope you'll forgive me. I had some of my best experiences playing against Barcelona and against Spain, some of my toughest experiences, believe me. I played against the best players in the world, and tonight I want to introduce properly someone whom I truly believe is going to be one of the best players in the world, and she's going to do that with Spurs! I'm extremely proud and extremely happy—and not to say a little relieved—that JoJo is going to sign her first professional contract with us this evening; ladies and gentlemen, JoJo Jackson!"

Everyone (except Lucy) stood. Then JoJo stood up, silence everywhere, JoJo, a little pale, breathed out heavily, then said, "Thank you, everybody. Thank you, Larry and Alice. Thank you, Spurs…it was an easy decision to sign with Spurs; they've looked after me since I was eleven years old, and that's four years ago, a long, long time! Larry came and watched me play. Larry has looked after me, mentored me, encouraged me; he's been great. But there's other people I want, no, not want, need to thank: my old teacher, Mr Warren."

And there was a hush as everyone there looked around for—what was his name?—Mr Warren. Chris Warren, a little embarrassed, stood and waved. JoJo continued, "You see, people don't realise how important it is to have grown-ups believe in you. I'm fifteen years old, nearly sixteen, so watch out!"

They all laughed. "Mr Warren believed in me; he believed in me and my friends here; they're more than my friends, really; they're my family (Shelley and Lucy had tears in their eyes), and he, along with two other grown-ups who believed in us, Gilly and Dan, got us here. Shelley, Sami, Lucy and Mickey all got medals this week at the European Athletic Championships…If it hadn't been for Mr Warren, we wouldn't have been here; truly, we wouldn't."

There was absolute silence now; people were taking it in; people were empathising with JoJo because they knew it was from the heart. Some of the Spurs senior players were quietly placing their hands over their eyes and faces, just in case, you know. "So I've signed for Spurs; they've offered me the most amazing contract, but they've also done something far more important." Everyone waited. "Spurs are going to make available their medical, physio, massage and rehab facilities to promising local athletes who get injured…one of those athletes is Lucy, Lucy over there, yes, the one in the wheelchair, who's just won gold at Europeans. Lucy, who I've known and loved since we were, oh, I dunno, maybe three years old."

There was a little laughter but only a little. "Lucy is going to be the first one on the Spurs programme, the programme that's going to get her to a medal at the Olympics in seven years' time, seven years' time in London." And now people did stand and applaud for a long time. Frank Rijkaard came over to JoJo. "If you ever want to leave Spurs, we will give you a million pounds to sign for us…but

I don't think you will ever leave Spurs. Much respect, young lady. You are one of the world's special people." And Frank Rijkaard, legendary player and manager, bent and kissed JoJo's hand. And then JoJo did cry, just a little.

David Caxton Writes in the Times

On a day when it was revealed that there were three positive drug tests at the European Under-18 Athletic Championships here in Barcelona, all Russian, in the men's three thousand metres, the women's hurdles and the women's two hundred metres, this raddled old journalist was very near to calling it a day, very near but not quite because my faith in humanity has just been rekindled by a young lady, a young lady by the name of JoJo Jackson, who, at the ripe old age of fifteen, has just signed her first professional contract with Spurs ladies. Some of you may remember I wrote a few weeks ago about Lucy Newton, Shelley Steele, Mickey Honey and Sami Johnson, four young athletes all coached by Gilly Warren, all apart from Sami from the same junior school and same class as JoJo Jackson, taught by Gilly's husband, Chris Warren. I used the word 'remarkable', and remarkable is the correct word.

With the Russian doping disqualifications, Shelley Steele has been upgraded to gold; Mickey Honey has been upgraded to silver; and Dutch athlete Marianne Deussmann has been upgraded to bronze in the women's two hundred metres, these to go with Lucy's gold and Sami's silver in the three thousand metres. Sami is seventeen, and the others are fifteen years old, the same age as JoJo Jackson. Sami joined Gilly Warren's training group because the younger athletes wanted her there. How good is that? I used the word remarkable because that is what it is. Same teacher, same school, same coach. How does this happen? Tell me, and I'll write it. One more thing, Spurs football club has instigated a programme to help young athletes with rehab and treatment after injuries. Fifteen-year-old JoJo Jackson signed her contract just now. Her friend and gold medallist, Lucy Newton, after her freak accident, is the first on the programme. What a coincidence—quite remarkable, some might say…this journo certainly does. Come on, the British Honours System, do something honourable.

Part Six
Ambition

Chapter Thirty-Nine
Yesterday's Child, Golden Girl

It was different now. With Lucy missing from their training group, it had been different. They all felt it, Mickey more than most, hadn't felt right, being there when Lucy couldn't be, hadn't felt right at all, and sometimes Mickey hadn't wanted to train, just didn't like it anymore, and that wasn't good. Mickey dug in; he dug in because, well, because he was Mickey, and that was part of him. *This is what I am; this is what I do.* And he, like Lucy and like Shelley, Sami, JoJo and even Gilly dreamed of the day that all their group would be back together, properly back together.

Eric, Bobby, Alisha and Joshi were brilliant. Once they had been filled in on all the happenings, they set up an informal visitors group so that Lucy wouldn't be by herself, wouldn't be lonely. A visit every day by one of them at least, it was agreed until Lucy needed to say it.

"Listen, guys, I know what you're doing, and I'm very grateful...but look, sometimes I'm good just to be by myself, not being horrible, but sometimes I'm happy being in my own company." And they understood; understood because they'd grown up together, and they pretty much knew how each of the others thought.

But Lucy was finally on the way back, and that was good. It had been hard, very hard. Times when she'd wanted to give up, times when Lucy had wanted to scream. Times when she had screamed, and then she'd felt a mixture of embarrassment and pleasure that she'd done it, the screaming. Her life had seemed to shrink to just two dimensions: the medical centre at the Spurs training ground and the swimming pool.

"Sometimes it's best when I'm asleep, Mickey, because in my dreams, I'm running again...and in my dreams, it feels real...and then I wake up, and it all starts again, you know, the bad stuff." And Mickey had squeezed her hand, kissed Lucy and walked quietly away in case she read his mind.

School had been a godsend during the hard times, and those hard times had gone on for over two years, almost three years! Finishing off GCSEs and then the two years of 'A' level work. Always supportive: teachers, fellow students, and—of course—TMRG. Dan was a brick; the Speeding Bullet was Lucy's biggest supporter. When she was having trouble getting to school or to the swimming pool or in the early days up to Spurs treatment centre, the Speeding Bullet was there, always there. He never questioned why. *This is what I am, this is what I do.*

None of them were surprised by their excellent GCSE results. All eight of them passed all their subjects in almost all A+'s, A's and B's. They expected it now. Their experiences from primary school (good old Mr Warren!) had taught them that you got back what you put in, you got back what you deserved, and they deserved it—all of it. 'A' level choices were easy for most of them; Joshi and Alisha going for the sciences, Bobby and Eric for economics and business studies and even maths. Shelley, Lucy and Mickey for physical education, business studies and then different choices for their third option.

One of the conditions for JoJo at Spurs was that she continued in some form of education for two years, and with much pleading and negotiating with Stratford Academy (thank you Ms Hajisoteris, Dr Fisher and Dan Bullet), JoJo was accepted to take just two 'A' levels and attended Stratford Academy on four afternoon sessions each week. For JoJo, it felt like a bonus, being at Spurs and still being allowed to see her friends almost every day.

And being able to support Lucy. For all of them, it was about being able to support Lucy.

Six months of treatment at Spurs before Lucy was allowed to keep the leg and knee support off for more than treatment time, six months that went on forever. And forever. And then the magic day arrived. "Next step, Lucy, now we move on." Lucy had become a real favourite at Spurs; she thanked God for JoJo, thanked God for her friends and their support. Thanked God for Gilly and Chris, had already thanked God for Dan. She'd hobbled out onto the poolside. All of them had been there; they started clapping and cheering; Lucy hesitated. She was scared, so scared. What if, well, you know, what if it was all over, really all over? But it wasn't. Lucy wouldn't allow that. TMRG wouldn't allow that. She got in the pool. How strange it felt—a different world now.

A few tentative strokes with the pull-buoy between her legs, Dan walking along the poolside, just watching and smiling. One length done, two lengths, a hundred metres, four hundred metres.

"Enough, Lucy, you were brilliant." He put his big old arms around her. But it got better; of course, it did. Four hundred metres became six hundred, became eight hundred, a mile, two thousand metres, and the feeling came back—that magical feeling of getting hold of the water, of moving good. Dan was in touch with the Spurs physios all the time. Of course, he was. Gradually, he moved Lucy away from always using the pull-buoy. Gradually, Dan moved her to full-body swimming, with little movement in the knees and legs, just for balance, and gradually, the feeling of that balance came back as well. Gradually, Lucy started to feel like a swimmer again. But a runner? That took a little more time, but Dan was patient. He had to be because he knew that if the procedure was rushed, then the likelihood of Lucy ever running properly again was non-existent.

So, Dan took the next step: phone calls to Spurs, who were used to him calling and welcomed his calls. Lucy was their favourite as well as Dan's. With her leg left immobile most of the time, the rehab steps were to get the mobility back, from that straight leg into a tiny knee bend, into a five-degree bend, then a ten-degree and slowly, slowly onwards. He got the OK, 'proceed with caution', so he did.

"Pop this on, little one." Dan held out what looked like a lifejacket to Lucy as she arrived on the poolside.

"What? We going sailing, Dan?" Lucy grinned at him; she knew exactly what the flotation support was for. She slipped the covering over her head and zipped up the front. "So what do I do, Dan?"

"You run, Lucy, you run; that's what you're going to do." And in a semi-parody of running, that's what Lucy did. It felt weird—very weird indeed. But only at the start. For Lucy, it was a substitute for what she called 'real running', but it was that initial start back to real running, and that made it more than worthwhile. In the water, going through the motions of running, looking forward, pumping arms, legs and knee still restricted but most definitely bending now. First session back after the initial try-out. "We'll go six by two hundred, Lucy, OK? So, we'll make it 30 seconds of effort and then a jog of twenty seconds."

Almost 'real' running, almost but not quite. "Dan, could we join in?" Mickey, Shelley and Sami on the poolside. "It's always easier when there's a group of you rather than doing the session by yourself...what d'you reckon,

Dan?" Dan reckoned it was pretty damn good. Talks and discussions with Gilly now, throwing around ideas, adapting interval sessions to the water environment.

"Yes, it could work, Dan; it could work well. There's always that possibility of overuse injury when good middle-distance runners are putting themselves on the line, all those miles can knock out your legs…If we're going to be serious about these guys, and we are, aren't we? Then maybe some aqua-running could be the thing, get the mileage in without killing the legs, then the heart will still be right up there." And so, the outline programme was set: a mixture of track, long running on the roads and parks and aqua-running.

"Can't get my heart rate up, Dan; what can I do, Gilly?"

"Arms up in the air, overextend the arm action, hold your breath, there's always a way." And there always was a way. Back to the Spurs physio every week, often accompanied by JoJo, often Dan, often Gilly, and gradually, the mobility began to return.

"You're pretty amazing, Lucy," said Mike Vargan, the head physio. "That mobility is coming back so much more quickly than we'd expected…you're not over-pushing it, are you, Lucy?" A shake of the head, then a smile.

"No, everything's loose as a goose, cool as a mule; we're getting there slowly." And Lucy was indeed getting there. Bend mobility up to fifteen per cent, then twenty. Thirty-degree bend was a big deal.

"If we were dealing with ordinary people, Lucy, that would probably be it; most people don't bend up to thirty degrees…but you're different; you're an athlete, a world-class athlete, you we keep pushing and bending." And another session of intense physiotherapy would begin.

The fitness and the stamina were coming back. God, it had been a long time! But now Lucy could see an end to it, still a long way away, but down that tunnel a faint glow, a quiet glow that was matched on her face and in her soul. And in Mickey's.

It was eighteen months since the accident when Gilly spoke.

"How d'you feel about jogging on the grass tomorrow, Lucy?" And Lucy felt pretty damn good about that! Nervous but still damn good. Everyone was there, of course. Joshi, Alisha, Bobby and Eric were wearing their running kit and tracksuits; the occasion merited it. Sami, Shelley, Mickey and JoJo wouldn't have dreamed of not being kitted out. Even Dan and Chris had tracksuits and training shoes on. Gilly breathed out hard. "OK, let's see how it goes." Running on the grass on the inside of the track, the group of thirteen (Gilly didn't run; she didn't dare in case…well, you know) started off. The entire group were so close around Lucy that she started to laugh.

"Oi! Move over! What you trying to do, trip me up?" She was moving. Lucy was moving! Felt rusty, felt a little bit weird, a bit like when she'd started the aqua-running, but boy, did she feel good! Mickey was about two inches away from her, looked over and saw the tears in Lucy's eyes, but he knew immediately that they were good tears. They were the tears of a comeback starting. The journey was restarting. One lap done, Lucy looked at Gilly as they jogged to a stop. Gilly's smile was too big for her face, much too big, and she replied to the question that hadn't even been asked.

"Yes, one more lap, and that's enough for today." As the group wheeled away, Gilly burst into tears and rushed to pick up her tissues and wipe away the evidence.

Sixteenth birthdays came and went, similarly seventeenths, and it seemed all of a sudden that they were in the final year at Stratford Academy. All except for Sami, of course, or Joshi, who wasn't there either. Joshi had been fast-tracked. "Bit like you're running then, Josh," Eric had quipped, and Joshi had just grinned. Joshi had been called in by Dr Fisher and Ms Hajisoteris on the first school day back in the sixth form. He had been congratulated on his clean sweep of 'A' stars and asked if he'd like to try to cover the two year 'A' level syllabus in a year and apply to university one year early.

Joshi had sat and thought and then answered, "Can I tell you tomorrow morning, miss, sir?" They had agreed immediately knowing that Joshi would be talking to his parents about the possibility. But they were wrong, Joshi did indeed discuss his options with two people and these two people were Alisha and Lucy. Joshi explained to Alisha why he needed Lucy's opinion as well. Alisha listened to him and then hugged him tight.

"All that stuff, Lucy, getting injured, not being able to train after you were European Champion…That must have been so hard! How did you make yourself do it?"

"Because I wanted to, because I needed to, because I'd found something that I was good at, and I wasn't going to let it go away just like that. All those people who've helped me, Mr Warren, Gilly, Dan, all of you guys, if I hadn't kept going, I would have been letting a lot of people down. I couldn't do that." Lucy shook her head. "Naah, couldn't have done that."

And then Lucy looked at Joshi and grinned, looked over at Alisha and grinned. "Go on…" And so Joshi explained what had been offered to him, needed help to make a big decision, wanted advice from someone who'd also had to make that big decision. Lucy, still getting up gingerly so as to avoid any further setbacks, went over and hugged him, hugged him tight. "Go for it, Joshi; there's seven kids your age plus Sami who believe in you, believes in you totally." And so, Joshi went for it, all the catching up, all the extra tutorials, lessons, homework.

Joshi went for it and thrived. 'A' levels were sat and passed, passed again with straight 'A' stars. From all the offers, he accepted the one from Imperial College, London University to study medicine. Full scholarship, many thousands of pounds saved. But even more important to Joshi was that he could live at home, and the cruncher, still be with everyone in TMRG, that was the deal cruncher.

Sami had been offered a place at Bath University to study sports science. Sami was under no illusions that she had been offered the place because of her running ability. Who wouldn't want a GB international runner and European medal-winner on campus? She had accepted the offer but had asked for it to be deferred for two years. Sami had this dream of being at university and training with her friends, her running mates, her soulmates, her little sister Lucy, and Sami was quite prepared to put her university career on hold for that. And there was that big, make that 'huge', advantage: by staying at home and deferring the offer, she'd still be able to train with Gilly's squad, and she adored being part of that group.

Sami's mum and dad were not too pleased, of course, but accepted the reasoning behind it and the promised commitment when she did go to uni. So, Sami did all the usual jobs that students do in their gap year; worked at McDonalds and loved it, did some office and house cleaning jobs, delivered leaflets and, most of all, carried through those two commitments: training hard with Gilly's squad and acting as mentor and head nurse for little sister Lucy.

Final year of sixth form, final year of secondary school. Jeez, man, it only seemed yesterday that they were starting out as first years, where did that time go?

TMRG were spending more and more time together, those in school. There was a freedom in the sixth form that they appreciated. Ms Hajisoteris had gone right the way through with them, right into the sixth form rather than starting again with Year 7, when her protégés had finished Year 11. Dr Fisher had sensed something special and had asked her to continue with her year group and Ms Hajisoteris had happily agreed.

The Christmas holidays came and went. All of a sudden, it was January 2008. They were grown-ups now, still at school but grown-ups nevertheless. Alisha had dropped one of her science subjects in favour of social studies.

"Because I think I'll need it," was Alisha's reply to the teachers who questioned and attempted to dissuade her. "Because I'm going to need it."

"Can I ask your advice, miss?" Ms Hajisoteris smiled and nodded a 'yes'. She listened carefully as Alisha set out her plans, aims, ambitions, listened carefully and quietly. Ms Hajisoteris asked a few questions but only a few. She'd seen Alisha's resolve and strengths of character many times in the preceding six years.

"Why not? Why not, indeed, young lady?" And they started to put the bones of the plan into operation.

"We're halfway there, Lucy, halfway," said Mike Vargan. "Listen, Lucy, if you don't go mad, and it's a big 'if', you can get it back; you can get it ALL back."

"Really, Mike, really?" Mike Vargan nodded. "Keep doing what you're doing, don't rush it, listen to Gilly and Dan, get back here every two weeks so I can have a look at you…can you do that?" And Lucy with eyes shining agreed that, yes, she could most definitely do exactly that.

*****

JoJo was getting more and more game time for Spurs' first team. As soon as she turned sixteen, the appearances for youth and under-nineteens got less and less. The subs bench starts gradually became match-starting; JoJo grew in confidence; age became less important. Getting called up for the England team was a highlight. JoJo didn't get on the pitch that first time, but she met with all the regular England players; then on the pitch as a sub. Then her sub appearances got longer, and within a year, JoJo was starting for England. At seventeen years of age with one year of school still to go, JoJo was a regular. But she was still very much a member of TMRG, and that was so important to her. With the others preparing for university and working towards their 'A' levels, JoJo knew that she would not be going onto university. Her professional football career was very much number one, but JoJo resolved that she would work her backside off to pass her two 'A' levels and pass them with good grades. JoJo was in TMRG, and so it was important. If she didn't work hard, she'd be letting TMRG and herself down, so it was a no-brainer…actually, it was very much a 'brainer'.

*****

"Mickey, we're gonna go to uni if we pass our 'A' levels, OK, yeah?"

"'Course we are, Lucy; 'course we are…and I bet I know exactly where you want to go…Bath, is it?"

"Well, they've offered us both a place already, even though the running's dropped off a bit the last year. When I had the interview, they said that they could see my potential, something about 'strength of character' to get back training after the accident. God, Mickey, it's seems like a different life now! Two and a half years back. Time's weird, isn't it? Sometimes it goes so slowly, and then it just whizzes past, mad." Lucy paused. "Anyway, Sami's going to be there as well, so it'll be a bit of TMRG with us three there."

"Might be a couple more than three of us, Lucy. Shelley's said that she ain't going anywhere without us, and Eric and Bobby reckon the business management and finance courses there are near on best in the country—they've got to get a couple of A's, though; reckon they'll do that?" Lucy nodded a 'yes'.

"Mickey, listen, I still go back to Mr Warren, you know. We've been out of junior school near on seven years now, and I can STILL hear all his words in my head; we're all here because of him, and we'll be at university because of him…and Gilly and Dan, of course. So yeah, Bobby and Eric'll get the grades. I know they will. What about Shelley, Mickey, reckon?"

"Shelley'll walk into Bath, Lucy; she's got an outside chance of the Olympics, hasn't she? Can you imagine? The Olympic Games! Every university in the country will be after Shelley if she does go." Both Lucy and Mickey went silent, thinking of what could have been.

"Could we have gone, Mickey, truly? Gone this year to Beijing?"

"Honestly? Dunno. Really don't know…well, actually, I do think that you would've been selected if, you know, the accident and all that…me? Probably not. I've let it go a bit, if I'm honest. Without being funny, it wasn't the same without you at the track with Gilly and all of us; no excuses, my fault, totes my fault." A big pause, make that a 'huge' pause, then he said, "But I'm going to make London. I really am, and if I don't? It'll be because I didn't try hard enough, bottom line."

"If we do get into Bath, we won't have Gilly and Dan there; we'll have the university coaches; not sure if it'll be the same."

*****

Shelley had progressed in those thirty months; junior GB team and a couple of times in the seniors. And now it was time, British Championships doubling as Olympic Games selection. Alexander Stadium, Birmingham, 11 to 13 July. And there was no way, no way at all that her coaches and her mates weren't going to be there with Shelley.

There were other eighteen-year-olds on the team now. Shelley was still one of the youngest but not the little girl running against the big girls. The apprenticeship had been done: national leagues, predominantly the hundred hurdles but also the occasional four hundred hurdles and sometimes the long jump and high jump, the two hundred and eight hundred metres ("Yeah, I still love that hurt.") and, occasionally, the shot and even the javelin.

Shelley stood out. Not only on the track and in the arena, Shelley stood out wherever she was. She was truly beautiful, stunning. Shelley had that special look, and she carried it well. She'd already been approached to do modelling but had laughed it off; school and athletics was too important, and she hadn't, couldn't, take it seriously. She'd told the others, of course, but had quickly laughed it off with them as well.

"*Jenny from the Block* was the film, wasn't it? So how about 'Shelley from the Slums'?"

"Thing is, Shell, we're all from the bad part of town…but that don't mean we're gonna stay there. You're not, I'm not, none of us are…thank you, Mr Warren, thank you for one hell of a lot. Thank you for making us see what's possible." And there was a bit of a silence after Bobby had spoken, and every single one of them was thinking the same.

Alexander Stadium, Birmingham. Three heats in the hundred hurdles, first two in each heat and two fastest losers qualify for the final. Shelley had nothing to lose; her Olympics were going to be in London in four years' time, so she could afford to give the trials everything, and she did. Qualifying behind Angie Thorpe in heat one, Shelley then struck silver behind Angie in the final with a

317

personal best time of 12.91 seconds, half a second under the Beijing qualifying time for GB athletes; she'd made the team!

"I've fucking made the team! I've fucking made the Olympics." Shelley danced down the track; she was looking for her group, TMRG, Mr Warren, Gilly, Dan. Ninety per cent of the males in the stadium were looking at Shelley. Other people were looking at Shelley. Olympics, good-looking, articulate, young, personable, Shelley ticked all the boxes, and the agents and the sportswear firms were looking hard at her as well. That something special was there, and they were going to use it. But first, there were the Olympics.

Shelley was totally surrounded by the group, adults now. Where had those ten-year-olds gone? Well, they'd gone nowhere, just grown up a little. *'Tout ça change, tout ça reste'*, Shelley remembered hearing the phrase early on in the French lessons at school, and she'd remembered it because it sounded so good and made sense. And that was it for TMRG, wasn't it? Everything had changed, but bottom line, pretty much everything had stayed the same, even though they'd gained four more members: Sami, of course, and the three slightly older honorary members: Chris, Gilly, Dan. And not one of them would have had it any other way.

"Gilly, Dan, Chris." Shelley was just beginning to get easier saying 'Chris' rather than Mr Warren, but only just, only just. "I'm going to the Olympics, me, me, Beijing, and it was you who got me there, you guys!" And not unnaturally, there were quite a few tears of happiness. The minds of JoJo, Sami, Lucy and Mickey were all spinning, all with one thought and one resolve, "Shell can do it. We can do it! London. Yes, London!"

Four weeks between the GB trials and the Games in China, four weeks taken up with kit-fitting, team meetings, protocol, travel, passport and safety, checking out the other team members, fitting in, feeling good about fitting in. And there was a bonus, one huge bonus, Gilly was going to the Games.

"My turn to thank you now, Shelley; they're taking me because of you. Personal accredited coach. I never made it as an athlete, never got near…and now I'm going because of you, so most definitely my turn to say thank you, Shelley."

In those four weeks between Birmingham and Beijing, another significant occurrence occurred; the 'A' level results arrived through the post, and the good times seemed to continue. Eric and Bobby in at Bath University to study economics and business studies; Shelley, Mickey, Lucy along with Sami to study sports science again at Bath. Alisha (straight 'A' stars) accepted at the London School of Economics. JoJo passed her two subjects with 'A' stars as well; she grinned because she'd proved that she was capable, capable of anything.

And in those summer months with the world changing, Gilly, Chris and Dan also had some heart-searching to do.

Chapter Forty
Beijing

It was a different world. A world that Shelley would never have imagined existed, and yet she was now in this new world. Still doubted herself but only a little now. As she talked, groupie-spotted, listened, drank in the atmosphere, Shelley began to realise that she did deserve to be there. Was treated with respect by the other members of the GB team and their coaches, saw the way that athletes and coaches talked and listened to Gilly, and her eighteen-year-old heart was bursting with pride and love for Gilly and for Chris, and she thanked god once again for that time eight years ago now when Mr Warren, sir, had walked into their classroom and changed hers and everybody else's lives.

In the village, it really was a different world now. Brits by French by Americans by Aussies by Kiwis by Jamaicans by Kenyans; black, white, every hue in between; seven-foot-tall basketball players by four-foot-six gymnasts; huge wrestlers by blow-away in the breeze distance runners. Go into one of the many cafes or restaurants, fish and chips, curry and rice, steaks, pork, lamb, salads of every colour, Chinese food, of course, Chinese food that Shelley couldn't recognise, other food that Shelley didn't even recognise, cakes that would stop you walking, let alone running. While she was at the Games, she had a job—just one job—to prepare for her race. And her job consisted of training, resting, eating. The training was the easiest; it was there to do.

Physical activity. Resting and eating? Where's the excitement in that? But the training and the mental preparation, that was the real deal, going through every possible scenario that could—or couldn't—be imagined. Shelley talked with Angie Thorpe, her teammate in the hurdles. Angie had so much experience of representing Great Britain, so much experience of the major Games. Shelley listened, absorbed, inwardly digested and learnt. Shelley talked to Tasha Danville, who was racing in the four hundred hurdles, discovered that Tasha had started at the sprint hurdles, made Shelley think even more. She talked to Kelly Sotherton who was competing in the heptathlon…even more thinking.

And there was the groupie-spotting, the star-trucking (and Shelley grinned to herself remembering what JoJo had said the phrase should really have been). And what Shelley very gradually came to realise in the village day after day was that she was being groupie-spotted; she was the one being star-trucked. And why not? Shelley Steele was eighteen years old, five-foot-ten inches of sheer beauty, physical perfection, a smile either on her lips or lurking just below. In a world where physical perfection was expected, Shelley Jelly Belly Steele went beyond that; Shelley was one in a million. Athletes approached her; many athletes approached her, and not one of them did Shelley dismiss rudely, and so more and more athletes approached her.

Her growing up on the bad side of town had unknowingly prepared her for this; dealing with the druggies and the would-be's and the pretend gangsters and the dealers and the drop-outs and the no-hopers and the losers since the age of just ten years meant that facing off anyone now was easy-peasy, lemon-squeezy for Shelley. Always with a smile, always leaving the would-be wannabe boyfriends with the hope that maybe, just maybe she might be approachable in some distant future added to her magic.

But Shelley wasn't interested, not one bit. Not yet anyway. There was too much else to do. Shelley spent time at the training track even after she'd finished her own work. Spent the time looking and learning, sometimes questioning the athletes' why and how? Considering her options. It was decided now, now that she'd seen this new world and very much wanted to stay a part of it. And Shelley was more than prepared to pay the price in sweat and blood and hurt and tears.

This is what I am. This is what I do.

Every athlete in the Games, every nation, had been given a phone card. Shelley spent time phoning back to Britain, to England, to London, talking to Lucy, to Mickey, to Joo and Sami, they were her family. And Shelley wanted and needed to share her experience with them.

This is what I am. This is what I do.

And then it was time, her time, Shelley's time. First round of the heats. In the holding room. Everything rehearsed. Ready now. Ready for her race, her job, her life. A quick kiss and hug with Gilly (and Shelley even whispered, "Thanks, miss," without thinking, and they both laughed out loud. Led out into the arena, onto the track. Tracksuits already stripped off. Thousands in the stadium, millions in front of TV screens, and those millions included her family: her mum, Bobby and Eric, Mickey and Lucy and Sami, JoJo and Alisha and Joshi, Chris and Dan. The stadium announcer started to call out the names; the BBC sports commentary team did the same for their audience. Shelley waved as her name was called and blew a kiss to the world, wiggled her backside without realising and broke another thousand hearts or so.

The whistle blew. Into the blocks, "Take your marks," settle, "Set," lift that butt one more time, lean in and forward, anticipate, anticipate, anticipate. "Crack!" Total focus, lift, lean, snap down, and again and again and again ten times, off the final hurdle, no memory of how the hurdles were cleared, sprint and lean and dive and over the line. And all eight of them looking up at the scoreboard, that magic storyline that might be about to change one or all of their lives.

The lights and bulbs flashing, and then: '2nd Shelley Steele GB 13.20'. She was through! Through to the semi-final! And Shelley's family in London were all dancing, dancing through their tears. Kisses exchanged, hugs exchanged, some handshakes, and the eight hurdlers returned to the real world, some good, some not so good. Gilly hugging and congratulating, back to the warm-down area, jogging, stretching, light massage. Then eat. Talk about the race. Two points from Gilly, 'trail leg needs to come up quicker after snap-down, more emphasis on speed of elbow to maintain balance'. Shelley listened, inwardly digested, resolved to make herself even better. Rang one number, her mum. Because every single one of TMRG were sitting with Shelley's mum. Of course, they were.

Lucy, Mickey, Sami and JoJo had watched Shelley's race on TV and were waiting for the call. Shelley's mum was on the verge of tears, and then she wasn't on the verge any longer, because the happy tears started to run down her cheeks. And Lucy, Sami and JoJo joined in with the tears. More importantly, in four hearts, that dream to make the London Olympics became stronger, changed from a dream to a need to an absolute resolve.

"She was great, Mrs Steele, your Shelley was absolutely brilliant." JoJo had spoken for all of them.

"I've never said this before properly." Mrs Steele smiled at them. "All you guys have made it come true for Shelley, every single one of you, and that Mr Warren, of course. He really did get you lot going, didn't he?" And the eight heads nodding a 'yes' didn't require any words.

Dreamless sleep. Happy wake-up. *Oh God, I'm in the semi today, semi-final of the Olympic hurdles.* Same preparation, same run-through, same drills and strides. And Shelley wasn't in the least bit nervous. Why should she be? Semi-final at the Olympic Games at the ripe old age of eighteen. Nothing to fear. 'Nothing to fear but fear itself.' Why had she remembered that phrase? And she grinned to herself. Mr Warren had said that in that final week of junior school. He'd explained what it meant, "Don't make things worse than they are by worrying about what you can't control." Shelley knew he was right then and knew that he was right now. Led out to the track. First two in each semi and two fastest losers to make the final. Shelley in the first of the three semis, lane seven.

Shelley knew by the lane allocation that she wasn't expected to get through to the final, the qualifiers were expected to come from the four inside lanes, three through six. Better prove them wrong then. Maybe. Just maybe. Introduction to the crowd, "Lane seven, Great Britain, Shelley Steele." Shelley waved and blew the kiss.

Then one single voice, "Give us a twirl, Shelley, give us a twirl!" So, Shelley gave the seventy thousand spectators a wiggle and a twirl and another thousand or so fell in love with her. "You get over those hurdles like a scared bunny rabbit on heat!" And another crowd roar and another thousand or so hearts lost.

And in the VIP seats above the finish line, a certain executive of a certain sports clothing company made a note of Shelley's name, took a photo and made a mental note to email head office later.

"Set." Silence. Bang!

Just me. Me. Focus. Just focus.

My lane. My world. My race.

Focus. Focus. Focus.

Dip for the tape. Don't look up. Then, sigh, big sigh. Kisses and hugs and congratulations and a few tears. Check the scoreboard. Good news or bad? '3rd Shelley Steele, GB, 12.89.' Personal Best! *Have I made the final? Don't know. It's a good time. Maybe. Maybe.*

The third placer on the second semi timed a 12.81. The third girl in the final semi-final timed a 12.95...*I'm in the fucking Olympic final!* Shelley allowed herself a little mind-swear. Hugged Gilly who was already in tears and ran off to phone her mum and all of her family, all of TMRG who were at her mum's house again. Of course, they were. And even Mickey cried this time.

And the email came back from head office. A lot of questions. But a hesitant 'yes'.

There was a day's rest between the hurdles' semis and the final. And that day's rest can be a very frustrating experience for athletes, especially athletes new to the major games: Olympics, Worlds, Commonwealths. And so, it was frustrating for Shelley; a comfortable training session with Gilly, analysis of the opposition: *It's that Russian girl again!* Stretch and light massage. *I really could get used to this!* Lunch with Gilly and then a very wise Coach Gilly gave Shelley some space and time to herself. "Maybe go and have a nap? Do NOT go the stadium to watch, promise me?" And of course, Shelley promised. Back to her room in the village, Gilly had made herself absent.

Shelley turned the key in the lock, and on her bed were literally hundreds of cards, good luck mementos, little teddy bears seemed to be the favourite, and more than a few bunches of flowers. Messages from all of TMRG, from Dan and Chris as well, of course. A few cards that Shelley immediately dumped as 'tacky'. A couple of marriage proposals, which earned a lot of giggles. *Like some dude's seen me on the track wiggling my bum and that's persuaded him that he wants to spend the rest of his life with me? Yeah, right!* And one particular bunch of roses with an unsigned message that intrigued Shelley, "Have never forgotten you, never will." Some dude off the estate? One of the kids from the academy? Maybe even junior school?

Evening approached, Shelley had even managed a short sleep, dinner with Gilly in the village, literally hundreds of teammates, athletes from all over the world, officials, and so many love-struck admirers all coming over to wish good luck for tomorrow. It could have been exhausting, but not for Shelley. Shelley loved it, every moment. The phone calls home, then with a head full of happiness, Shelley went to bed and slept the sleep of the pure and innocent.

Two Brits in the final, Shelley and Sarah Claxton, two Americans, one Canadian, one Russian, Irena Klatchlikova, who had served her drugs ban and was back competing, and one each from Jamaica and Australia. And despite all the 'no fear but fear itself', Shelley was nervous, not afraid—certainly not afraid because she knew that she deserved to be there. She'd served her apprenticeship, got the badge and was ready for the next step. But nervous, nevertheless. Dawn Harper (USA) and Sally McLellan (AUS) in the middle lanes, Shelley in lane eight, next to Irena Klatchlikova in seven.

Shelley had learnt the system now, introduced last because of her lane position. She smiled, waved, blew out a kiss, then Shelley winked and finally jiggled her backside…and once again, the crowd went wild. There was no doubt who was the crowd's and the BBC's favourite.

"Quiet please." An almost instant hush this time. "To your marks." Absolute silence. "Set." Crack! And seventy thousand throats in the stadium in Beijing exploded, and eleven throats gathered around the television set at Shelley's mum's did the same.

Flying, flying, flying now, just Shelley alone in her lane; over and over and over again. Staying level, maybe the middle lanes inches ahead? Still flying, flying, flying; eight cleared, nine cleared, into the tenth and last, Irena Klatchlikova's spiked right shoe barely touched Shelley's spiked left shoe as they both cleared level, but it was enough to make Shelley and Irena stumble, stumble just that tiny bit but enough to make the difference between Shelley's possible (probable) bronze medal and not. Barely upright across the line and then the indignity of the genuine flat-out fall. Shelley was crying; Irena was crying; all the athletes coming together, the usual hugs and kisses plus the sympathy for Shelley. Eight sets of eyes plus seventy thousand sets of eyes glued to the scoreboard. The lights flash, then: 1st USA Dawn Harper 12.54, 2nd AUS Sally McLellan 12.64, 3rd CAN Priscilla Lopes-Schliep 12.64, 4th GB Shelley Steele 12.65, 5th RUS Irena Klatchlikova 12.65…and Shelley cried her heart out.

Irena came over to her.

"My fault, Shelley, my fault." And then she said, "Shelley, I don't know you. I cheated against you three years ago in the juniors, you remember?" Shelley nodded a yes. "Shelley, you are so lucky; really, I mean that. Your country is a real country, your country is"—Irena searched for the correct word—"moral, yes, moral. We have no choice; we do as we are told, and it's only when we compete like this that we find out there is a choice. Drugs are normal where I am, athletes and drugs, normal. Before…before we have no choices, no choices at all. I see you with your friends celebrating after a race whether you win or lose. I see you hugging your coach, and I am jealous. We are told, 'Do not speak to any athlete from another country, ignore them!' And I would never be allowed to embrace my coach. I don't want to be Russian anymore. I want to live in another country. I would like to run for another country."

Then Irena started crying; Shelley took her in her arms, and as the world watched, kissed her on the cheek.

"D'you think I would have got it, Gilly? Would I have got a medal? One hundredth between me and both silver and bronze, would I have got it if we hadn't touched spikes?"

"Don't know, Shelley, don't know…what I do know is that I am so proud of you; I mean that. You're only eighteen, and you're a superstar. Listen, I need to tell you something…" And Gilly told Shelley exactly what she, Dan and Chris had been discussing. Shelley stood there spellbound.

"You'd do that for me, really? Oh, Gilly!"

"You just made that decision for me, Shelley. I see where you're going, and I want to be a part of it. Deal?" Shelley smiled and cried at the same time; Gilly would do that for her! "Shelley, don't tell the others, OK? I need to sort some things out, you know…"

And then the officials arrived to take Shelley and the others to the dope-testing unit. Clean, every one of them clean on the A samples, so they were properly clean. Irena smiled at Shelley.

"I am so ashamed of what I was made to do; now I'm so proud of being a clean athlete, and I can run as fast as when I was dirty." And Shelley realised that however bad she might have had it as a kid, there was another world out there that was worse than she could have imagined if she hadn't made that jump to where she was now.

But there were still more surprises for Shelley, and both of them were big ones.

He was very smartly dressed, light grey slacks, open-neck polo shirt with a double overlapping Z printed on the left side of the chest, expensive shoes. He looked just a little too old to be a competing athlete at the Games, but he looked as if he belonged there, as if he had experience. Shelley was sitting with Gilly at the restaurant in the village, the initial disappointment—make that heartbreak—had largely gone, and Shelley was buzzing at just how close she had been. Gilly had made her laugh.

"Well, you did get a medal anyway, Shelley." Shelley waited. "The chocolate medal for 4th; it just melts away!" And Shelley knew that Gilly was working on relaxing her. "If you can't make it, fake it!" And this time, Shelley laughed, and the many, many star-truckers looked enviously at her, and a few more hearts were broken.

"Excuse me, may I speak with you?" The smartly dressed man put out his hand, and both shook. "Shelley, Gilly, is it OK to call you that rather than surnames?" Two nods of heads. "I guess everyone in the stadium the last couple of days would love to be here with you, Shelley. Wasn't she just great, Gilly?" He was charismatic, this guy, had that certain air, poise, elan, whatever you wanted to call it…an inner confidence, maybe? "My name's John Smith; unusual name, isn't it?"

The three of them smiled. "So what am I doing here? How have I dared to enter the inner sanctum of the athletes' village? Well, I do have a pass." He showed them the card. "Cut to the chase, I think?" Two more nods of heads. "I ran in the Sydney Games, seems an age ago now, did OK, made the semi-final of the eight hundred, but that was it. Knew then that was my high spot, wasn't going to get a medal four years later so had to make a decision." He paused and smiled. "Couldn't get away from what I was doing, how I was living my life, so…applied for a few jobs in marketing, all sports clothing and shoes firms, you know; Nike, Asics, Adi, Puma, got great experience and just a year ago, decided to set up our own company. We've called it 'Zig-Zag'—a bit like the way I used to run down the home straight—and we would very much like to invite you to be our first client…What d'you think?" And Shelley's mouth literally dropped open.

"Me? Me? I don't believe it!" She was about eleven years old again. Gilly smiled, and John Smith knew that he really did have a golden girl here.

"You'd better believe it, Shelley; you wouldn't believe the interest back in the UK. BBC have had more calls about you than anyone else. People like you, no, they 'love' you; you have that something special. Look, may I leave the details and possible contract with you?" John Smith looked at Gilly then said, "Maybe with you, Gilly?" Gilly smiled back at him. *I knew! I knew! From the moment I saw her run, I knew!* "Not expecting an answer right now, 'course not, take some time, tell me what you think." John Smith, Mr Zig-Zag, just about stopped himself from kissing both Shelley and Gilly and walked out with fingers on both hands crossed.

"Fucking hell, Gilly! Fucking hell!" Shelley wasn't really swearing, she was in a state of disbelief, and Gilly understood—understood totally.

"Tell you what, Shelley, never said this before to you…I fancy a glass of wine to celebrate what you did today. Come and have a glass of wine with me or a coke or whatever?" Shelley nodded her head. *A fucking sponsorship contract!* They walked to one of the village bars; it was buzzing at one end, quietly subdued at the other. They sat at the quiet end, Shelley nursing her first ever glass of wine, never even thought about it before. *Look at me, starting to be a grown-up!* Relaxed now, relaxing more, chatting about the race, but chatting about the growing-up years, the getting started, summer camp, Amsterdam, Barcelona, all those training sessions, races, all of it. It had been a long journey but it had also been a short one.

Eight years to change a life, actually eight years to change eight lives. So many athletes came over, so many congratulations, so many 'that was tough!' commiserations. And the resolve for Shelley for London in four short years' time grew and grew and grew. And with what Gilly had revealed to her, Shelley knew that she had an ace hidden, maybe not up her sleeve but definitely in her running spikes.

"Shelley, I'm off to bed. I've got a coach's debrief tomorrow morning, all about you. You coming up or staying here?"

"Staying here, Gilly. I'm fine, still buzzing actually. Fourth in the Olympics isn't too dusty, is it?" And Gilly agreed that, no, indeed, fourth at the Olympic Games wasn't too dusty at all.

Shelley was looking through the info that Mr Zig-Zag John Smith had left with her. *Look at that clothing! The trackies, the running gear, the leisure gear! They're going to pay me to wear that? Pay me! Talk to Gilly, maybe talk to Dan as soon as we get back. Yeah, Dan'll know; he's been there; he's done it.* Happy and content in her solitude, a smile, a hello and then a shake of the head to everyone who came over to her. And then, "Shelley? Shelley, maybe you remember me? Maybe you can forgive me?" And Shelley knew immediately who he was. Despite everything her heart was fluttering, and her heart rate was more similar to that of pre-race nerves than sitting quietly in a bar.

"What are you doing here, Kaas? You sent me the flowers, you?"

"The easy one to answer, Shelley, is what am I doing here. Same as you, I guess, representing my country in the Olympic Games. The swimming finishes just as track is starting, but I didn't dare contact you before your race, didn't want to take any chances of putting you off, Shelley. Please can I talk to you, please?" And those seven years rushed away, but not yet the hurt and betrayal.

"You hurt me, Kaas; you really hurt me and JoJo. We both really, really liked you. It was weird because JoJo and me, we're like sisters…you shouldn't have done that, Kaas. That was unforgivable." Kaas looked down at his feet.

"I know, I know, it was unforgivable. I can't forgive myself, so I understand why you won't be able to, too." Was that a tear that Shelley saw? A tear? "I meant what I said, what I wrote. I've never forgotten you, and I've never forgiven myself…Look, I'm sorry to bother you, should have known better, won't bother you again, I promise." Kaas turned away, and Shelley saw his shoulders and his head drop, and Shelley was in turmoil.

"Wait! Kaas, come back and sit down. We need to talk!" Kaas realised that he'd been given that one chance in a million, that some people on this earth are big enough, kind enough and—importantly—strong enough, to give—to give a sinner another chance. "Let's start again, OK? Hello, my name is Shelley, and I'm at the Olympic Games representing my country, Great Britain, in the hurdles." Shelley stared at him, a grin just beneath the surface. "And you are…?" Kaas went along with it.

"Hi, Shelley, nice to meet you. I'm Kaas Prinz. I'm from Holland, and I've been swimming the four hundred metres freestyle and four hundred metres individual medley for Holland, but I didn't do as well as you, though. I made the finals but finished sixth in both events." And the ice started to break.

Her heart was in turmoil, absolute turmoil; making the team, making the final, that fourth place, and now this! 'He broke my heart in a million ways; he took all my happy days', the song that Shelley's mum had sung to her so many years ago came drifting back…'and left me lonely nights…' And what about JoJo? Shelley would deal with that one later. All those star-truckers, not interested, not one bit. But Kaas, oh, yeah, need to talk it through.

"Shelley, thank you. You have a phrase I think, 'Cut to the chase'? So now I cut to the chase. Shelley, I am so sorry. I thought I was a cool kid; actually, I thought I was the coolest kid in town." Shelley remembered thinking, 'yes, he's the coolest kid in town'. "I have no excuse; it was like I thought I was supposed to—how you say?—try it on?" Shelley nodded. "I was stupid, stupid, stupid. I was trying to impress you, and I—how you say?—fucked up, fucked up big-time!" And this time, Shelley laughed and replied.

"Yes, Kaas, you fucked up big-time!" She laughed again, and it was getting better.

"You remember Marianne? Marianne Duessmann?" A nodded yes. "OK, Marianne is like a sister to me. I think maybe like it is with you and Mickey?" A nodded yes again. "So Marianne gave me the biggest bollocking—is right word, yeh?" And this time, Shelley couldn't help laughing out loud.

"Yes, Kaas, exactly the right word!"

"So, Marianne gives me the big talk, I felt like a little kid! All about respect, never let people down, treat people like you want to be treated…I felt like a slug! Worse than that. I felt like a bit of poo on your shoe!" Shelley laughed so much that she started hiccupping, which made her laugh even more, and Kaas felt able to smile. *Please, please, please God! Let me make this one right!*

"So please, Shelley, if you can forgive me, I would very much like to be your friend. Is that OK?" Another nodded yes. "You are here for a few more days? Closing ceremony? Maybe we can have breakfast or dinner or a drink or…you know, anything…I would just like very much to spend some time with you. Maybe I teach you to speak Dutch?" Another laugh out loud. Kaas laughed as well. "So, yes, I teach you to speak Dutch to show I am truly sorry."

"I'd like that, Kaas, to spend some time with, maybe not to learn Dutch though. Some people think I can barely speak English!"

"So, Shelley, maybe breakfast tomorrow? Is possible?"

"I'm doing a light training session with Gilly, my coach, first think…how about brunch? You know that word in Dutch?" A smile 'yes'. "OK, I meet you here at eleven tomorrow, yes?" And then as Kaas got up to go and went to shake Shelley's hand, not daring to do anything else, Shelley leant towards him, kissed him on the cheek, put her arms lightly around his waist and whispered, "I've never forgotten you, either."

And two very happy young Olympians went off to their respective beds, maybe to dream a little.

They talked of everything the next day, all the growing up, everything that had happened in those passing years. Shelley asked about Marianne, told Kaas that she had seen her at the European under eighteens; Kaas asked about Lucy, JoJo and Mickey, and Shelley gave Kaas JoJo's story, now a full-time professional at Spurs and a regular in the England team, and Kaas shook his head.

"I think maybe Mickey and JoJo don't like me too much." Shelley had an instant reply, which made things even better.

"They didn't like what you did then, but I think and I hope that they'd like you very much now." *Kaas was quietly praying, Shelley said hope; she said hope!* They talked about their future plans, about universities.

"I think maybe I go overseas to study; in Holland it is difficult to mix studying with sport." They talked about what they hoped for in their sports.

"It's London, Kaas, London! My home, my everything. London for me is the dream. Anything, I'll do anything to catch that dream." Kaas had that same dream, two finals at eighteen years old, and now four years to prepare for the next one. Shelley explained how she, Lucy, Mickey and three others in their group were all going to attend Bath University, and the one big reason was because it had such a good sporting reputation, bit like Loughborough and Leeds. And an idea began to stir and then to grow in Kaas' thoughts, and it grew and grew. But he didn't dare say anything, not just yet. But he did dare to dream, just a little.

They spent a lot of time together in those few days before the closing ceremony, a lot of time. For Shelley, this was a different Kaas, the same Kaas from seven years ago, but a different Kaas all the same. And she kept asking herself, 'am I doing the right thing?' The answer came at the closing ceremony, after the initial parade onto the arena and track. The national teams split from their regulated ranks and were free to mingle with the other teams. Shelley waited and hesitated; she was a little scared now, a depth of emotion like never before. *Jeez, I wish Mickey was here, he'd tell me!* And then Kaas was there by her side; he reached out and held her hand, smiled at her.

"Shelley, all that stuff before, I was a little immature kid. I so wish that…You know…Shelley, may I kiss you, kiss you properly? You can say no." Shelley smiled.

"Kaas, I say yes!" And as the cameras of the world panned the athletes, and then zoomed in on an orange tracksuit of the Netherlands and the red, white and blue of the British team, Kaas Prinz leant in and kissed Shelley Steele, and the watching world applauded and cried.

Part Seven
University

Chapter Forty-One
Council of War

"Are you sure you want to do this?"

"Never been surer."

"Why?"

"Because I love those kids…bloody eighteen-year-old kids! Chris, I honestly and truly believe that they—all of them—could do something at the London Games; I mean that. Me and you and Dan have seen them grow up; we've seen them keep their focus even when things weren't going great. Look at Lucy, can you imagine what it felt like after that bloody discus hit her! And did she give up? Never! And she must have felt so down sometimes. And Mickey, never have I seen a young man so loyal. You know when people say, 'I'd die for him', well, when I see how Mickey looks at Lucy, when I see how much he cares, then I know he truly would die for her. Sami, JoJo and Shelley gets back from the Games and all they wants to do is get together with her mates, TMRG rule!"

"Shelley believes it; they all believe that. Eric and Bobby came to me again and said, 'Any money those guys need, Gilly, you tell us and we'll get it for them.' They're eighteen years old, already running a successful business, and yet they're prepared to back their friends. Amazing! So yes, TMRG do rule, and yes, I'm very sure of what I'm doing. I've told Shelley, and now I've got to tell all of them. Oh shit, sorry, Chris…are you all right with it?" Mr Warren, sir, Chris grinned.

"Wouldn't dare to be not all right with it, Gilly, I think what you're doing is fantastic; it's brave, and if I could, I'd do exactly the same. I'll miss you, miss you all the time, but Bath's not too far, is it? All those weekends up and down the M4, I guess. And now I'm a HEADTEACHER (Chris deliberately exaggerated the word), I'm going to be busy. Four years in our lives? Don't know about going like a flash, but with the London Games to aim for, of course, you should do it."

"My lovely husband a headteacher." Gilly shook her head and smiled. "Always knew you would be, always knew…What really happened there?"

"Patsy McCarthy called me into her office for what she called 'a quiet chat'. She told me that she was retiring, that she'd recommended to the governors that I should be the next headteacher, and that if I didn't apply, she'd come back and haunt me every single day! So with Patsy sitting on the interview panel and the governors in her pocket…Well, what am I going to do? Say no? Don't think so. So, my angel of a wife, it seems that we start our new careers apart for a little while…Oh God, Gilly, I will miss you so much!"

All of them were there, all of them.

"It's a sort of debrief, I s'pose. Listen to me all posh, debrief, durrh!" And they all looked at Shelley, bloody fourth at the Olympics, our mate, fourth! "First of all, it was amazing, really amazing, and I was just so proud to be there. Second of all, I wouldn't have been there without Gilly…and Chris and Dan. That's right, guys, yeah?" And all the heads nodded yes. "And third of all—and this is important—it's doable; it really is doable. I did it, and you can do it."

Shelley looked at them one by one and said their names out loud, "Lucy, JoJo, Sami, Mickey, you can do it. If I went to the Olympics, you can go to the Olympics!"

Eric and Bobby, Alisha and Josh, Chris and Dan and Gilly were mesmerised. This was Shelley talking, their Shelley! Shelley had done it, and that made it real. "We've got uni coming up, only a week or so now, and I can't wait! I know we're not all going to be at the same uni, but a lot of us are, and I reckon that Bath will be the icing on the cake that gets us to the London Olympics, yeah?" Mickey was brave enough to speak back, speak back to his sister.

"Thing is, Shell, it'll be different there. We've been in a bit of a cocoon, you know. Mr Warren, Gilly and Dan; like they've always been there to help us out, always been there to support; like you said, you wouldn't have been there without Gilly. Ain't gonna be like that at Bath; like sometimes I wonder if, you know, we should just stay here and train with Gilly; we know it works…"

"Gilly?" Shelley smiled because she knew how the hell she'd managed to keep her mouth shut. Jeez! And she couldn't hold it in any longer, went over to Gilly and hugged her tight and whispered a big 'thank you' in her ear. "Gilly's got something to tell you."

"I told Shelley at the Olympics and made her promise that she wouldn't say anything, anything at all in case it didn't work, so this is it…" Gilly Warren drew a deep breath. "I've got a new job." The mouths dropped open. "So I'm moving…moving to Bath! Got an assistant lecturer's job in the education department, basically teaching the new teachers how to teach…But that won't take up all my time, so the rest of it is coaching the university athletes…that is, if you'll have me!"

"Really? You'd do that for us?"

Mickey unconsciously parroted Shelley's words and thoughts, while Gilly just nodded 'yes'. "What about you, Mr Warren, sorry, Chris."

"All of you know exactly how I feel about you lot, bunch of ruffians who almost destroyed me! I told you before, my first job in teaching and you made it an honour for me to be your teacher, so Gilly and I reckon it's worth a little time in our lives to put something back."

"We all think that you've already put back much more than enough." Mickey looked around at all of them. "That right, guys?" And the girls were more than close to tears, and in truth, so were the boys.

"Enough already! All this praising up Chris and Gilly, enough already!" The Speeding Bullet grinned and kept grinning. "You didn't think I was actually going to miss out on this big adventure, did you? Naah, not a hope in hell! Have you seen the pool at Bath? Right by the track and fitness centres, fifty metre pool, of course; great university squad there already…but they reckon they might be able to squeeze in just one more assistant swim coach, someone who's qualified, someone's who's had Olympic experience, someone who's started a swim club, based in an education environment, so 1 reckon that schools and academies count, yes? So, guess who they picked?" And Lucy couldn't hold it together anymore and rushed over to Dan, flung her arms around him and sobbed her heart out.

They were walking back to the estate now, quiet, not subdued, just thinking, each in their own worlds, with their own thoughts. *How did we get so lucky?* all of them thought. *Should I have chosen Bath?* thought Alisha. JoJo and Joshi were just a little jealous, no, not jealous, envious; pro football and a medical degree course but a little envious just the same. *Should I tell them the other stuff?* thought Shelley. *How can we help?* thought Eric and Bobby. Shelley started it.

"Listen, I need to tell you some stuff. I think a couple of you might hate me, but I have to tell you all the same."

"Never hate you, Shell, never hate you. Mind you if you, like, killed me, I'd be a little disappointed…is all," Mickey said.

"OK, here we go…but you might just change your mind." The good or the bad first? The good. "So, after my race—" And they all stopped and clapped and cheered, and Eric and Bobby got down on their knees and were giving it the 'we're not worthy!'

"Yeah, all right, all right, so me and Gilly were having a drink in the village bar, and this bloke comes up to us—"

"On the pull yet again, Shell?" Shelley hoped that she wasn't going to break JoJo's heart with what she had to tell her later. Shelley forced a smile. "No, not this time, should be so lucky! His name was John Smith, and he's an owner and a rep for a new sports clothing company." They waited. "And, like he's offered me sponsorship! It's a new company called Zig-Zag, and he said that's the name because it's how he'd be running down the home straight. He's a good bloke, I reckon anyway, pretty genuine, no, really genuine. Gilly thought he was gen…what d'you reckon?"

"I reckon you need an agent," Bobby said. "Maybe two agents…and I think I know who." Shelley realised that Bobby was only half-joking.

"You know what, Bobby? You might just be right." Bobby realised that Shelley was only half-joking.

"What's the deal, Shell? Did he spell it out, or is it all up in the air?" Mickey said.

"Pretty much all spelled out, Mickey. I've got copies of the contract. I'll let all of you have a look, of course. Zig-Zag will give me all the clothing and shoes that I want to race and train, and they have a whole bunch of leisurewear I can choose. Then they'll pay me on my results in races; it's a bit of a sliding scale depending on, you know, standard…like win a local race and they give me fifty pence…And—and this is for real—win the Olympics or Worlds, and they give me one hundred thousand pounds!"

"You for real, Shelley, you for real?" Lucy looked at her adoringly. "You so deserve that." Shelley felt her heart dissolving a little.

"And there's another bit as well." They waited. "Zig-Zag are going to pay my uni fees, so I don't have any worries about getting a job or anything to see my way through."

"Lucy's right, Shell; you do so deserve it." Mickey walked over to her and put his arms around her and hugged and hugged and hugged, and Shelley felt secure in his arms.

"So's that why we're gonna hate you, Shell, 'cause you got a brilliant sponsorship deal?" Lucy smiled at her again.

"No, that was the easy bit…this is the tough bit." Shelley inhaled and exhaled deeply three times through. "I met someone at the Games, someone I got to know properly and really liked."

"Yeah, we all saw you on telly, Shell; one of the Dutch guys, wasn't it? he did look lush!" Sami said. "Big old snog in front of about a million viewers and fans!"

JoJo and Mickey knew immediately whom Shelley had met at the Olympics immediately.

And Shelley knew that they knew.

"Told you you'd hate me, told you…couldn't help it. He's changed. Kaas has. Honest, JoJo. Honest, Mickey, he's changed. He's really nice, never tried it on at all, went back over…you know, all that stuff when we were kids, apologised properly, said that Marianne—and these are his words—had given him a real bollocking! He went to walk away…and then I gave in. Dunno why, just thought he deserved a second chance." Shelley stopped then and considered. "Listen, we all got a second chance from Mr Warren, didn't we? Can you imagine what we'd be doing now if he hadn't been our teacher?

"Certainly, wouldn't have gone to the Olympics, wouldn't be looking at uni in a couple of weeks' time. All of us, bloody all of us going to uni! You too, JoJo, if you weren't playing pro, you'd be there as well, you know that. Oh, JoJo, I truly am so sorry. I know how much you liked Kaas 'cause I did back then as well…and then he let us down. But even then, we both sort of forgave him, didn't we? You remember when he had the flowers for us, and we felt sorry for him, and we both kissed him after? JoJo, please don't hate me, please. I couldn't stand it; honest, I couldn't."

"Nothing to forgive, Shelley, nothing. That stuff when we were kids? Yeah, well, it wasn't great, but it ain't changed my life. 'Course I liked Kaas, made me laugh, made me feel good, and then he fucked up big time. But it's over; it's over. And if you like him a lot, then I reckon he must be a nice guy now; you're about the most non-stupid person I know, Shell. If you like him then, as far as I'm concerned, he's all right."

JoJo hugged Shelley tight and murmured quietly enough so that no one else could hear, "You hang in there, girl; you hang tough; you hang tough for me as well." And the tears came to Shelley's eyes, and she squeezed JoJo but didn't dare to try to say anything. Shelley looked at Mickey, questioning.

"Shell, we've known each other since...I dunno, always, I guess. Always loved you, always will, you know what I mean. Like everyone says we're like brother and sister, but you and I know it's more than that; we're not like brother and sister, we ARE brother and sister, yeah? So I reckon that if my sister has found somebody—at bloody last!—who she really likes, then I reckon I can be big enough to like him as well...if you'll let me."

And now it was Shelley's turn to whisper so quietly, "Mickey, you never let me down, never. It's gotta be my turn to do something for you...Actually, something for everybody." And in that instant, Shelley had just made a big decision. No, a huge decision.

Chapter Forty-Two
The Six Rules of Sponsorship

It was a fifteen-seater minibus, and even that wasn't really big enough. Bobby, Eric, Sami, Lucy, Shelley and Mickey, then Dan, Gilly and Chris. The six remaining seats were crammed with luggage, mostly clothes—training kit, of course—and a few utensils. The roof rack was similarly stacked. The atmosphere in the minibus was similar to that of going on holiday—going on holiday with your best friends. There was also an element of sadness because Chris, good old Mr Warren, wasn't going to be on the holiday with them. He'd stay overnight of course, but then he'd be driving back to London, back to his new post as the new headteacher. There was excited talking—not that far off hysteria, if truth be told—joined with silences as everyone reflected on how far they'd come, where they were now and where they were going. And that was the big question, wasn't it? Exactly where were they all going? They all knew where they were aiming for, but actually arriving at the destination? That was different.

They were missing Joshi, Alisha and JoJo. They had chosen a different path this time, but they knew that, somehow, they'd arrive at or near the same destination.

Through security at Bath University. Parking spot allocated by the apartments. Clear time limits placed on the vehicle remaining there. And then pure excitement! The six of them were moving into their own place—the six of them together. Mickey started laughing out loud as they began to unload.

"Dunno if you remember this. About a million years ago, we must have been about twelve or maybe thirteen, I said that one day we'd all be sharing a big mansion, and now look, we are!"

"You're so right, Mickey; it doesn't look too much like a mansion, more like a big flat, but you know what? It actually does feel like we're moving into a mansion...thanks, Mickey; thanks, bruv!"

Shelley smiled at him, and they were in the eight-bedroom apartment with the six of them, and the single bedrooms were about the same small size as their bedrooms at home, but they were together, and that was the difference. Chris, Gilly and Dan said their goodbyes, and there was a stillness as the new students realised that one huge part of their lives was going to be away from them, at least geographically.

"Mr Warren." Mickey was breathing slowly and deeply. "I have to say something, something important…and I haven't asked the others, but I know they agree." Lots of nodding heads. "Thank you, thank you from all of us; you changed our lives, and you're still changing them. I, we, cannot believe how lucky we are, right, guys?" And that broke them, all of them, the enormity of it. There were tears, lots of tears, hugs, lots of hugs, muttered and stuttered thank-yous; handkerchiefs were being surreptitiously taken out of pockets.

Chris Warren drove Gilly and Dan over to their temporary accommodation: a two-bedroom flat where new staff could stay while they were looking for something more permanent. A few more tears.

"Look after Gilly for me, Dan." And he knew, they all knew that Dan would. And then he drove back to London, alone, and only needed to stop once while he thought, thought deeply.

The folders and brochures were already laid out in the TMRG mansion, which they'd already decided to call their new flat that, 'the mansion'. The first week was called orientation week; lots of lecturers to see, lots of timetables, lots of seminars, lots of clubs to join, parties, drinking games, lots of coffees, lots of late-night discussions. And importantly, the start of structured training programmes and schedules. Lots of meeting the athletes and swimmers who had been at the university the previous year, two years. Shelley was known immediately, of course. Shelley was immediately hit on ('star-truckers and groupies, story of my life'), of course. Shelley immediately laughed it off, of course.

Four of the university swimmers and two of the track and field athletes had also been in Beijing, and through them and their teammates, Shelley was able to quickly introduce Sami, Lucy and Mickey. It was a great method of integration, a great way of feeling that they belonged—truly belonged. They deserved to be there; they'd earned that right.

Bobby and Eric took charge of the logistics of sharing the mansion. They set out timetables for coffee, meals, washing up; graphs were up on the wall for who was where in lectures and seminars. And then they called in Gilly and Dan and set about structuring the timetables for training sessions. The whole athletics and swimming set-ups were superb, as you'd expect from a university with the sporting reputation of Bath.

The four of them lived at the track; that's what it felt like. Four hundred metres, tartan surface, state-of-the-art, all the techno stuff on-site. Coaches for every event; Gilly already working with a middle-distance squad; Mickey, Lucy, Sami, of course, but other university runners attracted to Gilly and her reputation. Shelley joined in the interval run sessions but also had specialist hurdles sessions. The great Colin Jackson, multi-World champion and Olympic silver medallist was sometimes there coaching hurdlers, and the opportunity to learn from him was enormous. And Shelley took that opportunity, especially when Colin had come over to her at their first meeting and said, "Shelley, that was awesome watching you at the Olympics! You work on it, and you'll get gold!" Shelley did fall just a little bit in love then and became one of her own star-truckers. And Colin Jackson said another thing that made Shelley think, think hard: "I see you working with the middle-distance lot, Shelley; you thinking of moving up to the four hundred hurdles?"

And Shelley was having lots of thoughts of experimenting with the four hundred hurdles, lots of thoughts.

Eric and Bobby were often at the track too. Both of them with their pads and laptops, watching the training sessions, chatting and giggling, observing— observing everything.

Dan was an instant hero on the poolside; Olympic medallist coaching, of course he was. Dan was given responsibility for the distance squads and specialist butterfly swimmers. The swimmers warmed to him. There was no shouting, no bullying, no putting down of individuals. There was a lot of encouragement, a lot of humour, a lot of stories, a lot of self-belief instilled into swimmers. There was a phrase that Dan used a lot: "If I believe in you, you should believe in you," accompanied by a smile, often a hug. And after a session where a swimmer had felt down, defeated, low, Dan's comment and actions would leave that swimmer up, winning, high. In coaching, communication is everything, and Dan had that everything. Lucy still idolised Dan for all the reasons that all the swimmers did.

Dan had always believed, always cared, still believed, still cared. Still aware and cautious of her leg injury, Lucy made haste but slowly and cautiously.

Between them, Gilly and Dan monitored Lucy's training. Very rarely did Lucy do a double run session in a day, but she would substitute that second run with a swim session or an aqua-run. The fitness was returning, and Lucy was adamant that she would not allow herself to overdo it. Sometimes Lucy would hear the phrase 'no pain, no gain!' during a run training session, and she would just smile to herself. Complete trust in Gilly and Dan, complete.

Mickey was at the pool as much as possible. Running was priority number one, but he loved that feel of the water, loved swimming with Lucy or just wanted to be on poolside sometimes when Lucy was in the water. 'The other half of my being', and it was true.

For Shelley and Sami, swimming was becoming less and less possible. Sami had had no experience of swim training, and with the London Olympics in sight, Sami had committed to gaining selection, making the team. Sami's only dilemma was which event to go for? Shelley missed swimming; in truth, she probably missed the gentle banter with Dan but would go and observe the sessions whenever she could. Occasionally, she would join Lucy during one of the aqua-run training sessions, and the chat during the recoveries would be of: "Do you remember when?"

They would both get out of the pool feeling lucky, feeling special. Shelley had a problem similar to Sami's: which event? Everything pointed to the one hundred metres hurdles, fourth at the Olympics at just eighteen and with four more years to improve, but Shelley had already seen that luck—good or bad— could play a part in those two imposters, triumph and disaster, in the outcome of a technical sprint event. There was a lot of thinking, a lot of soul-searching. But there was only one thing to do: talk to Gilly, maybe talk to Mickey, Lucy and Sami. And Shelley knew that whatever was decided between her and Gilly, that she needed to talk with her brother and her now-adopted sisters. She needed to talk to them about that huge decision she had made. Now it was acting upon it.

*****

The parcel delivered to their mansion was huge. Inside was everything Shelley could have wished for: tracksuits, vests and pants, socks, trainers, racing spikes, and leisurewear. And all with the double overlapping Z stitched or printed on them.

"Bloody hell, Shell, look at you." Mickey was speaking for all of them as Shelley was putting on an impromptu fashion show, disappearing into her bedroom and then coming out preening and exaggerating her catwalk display before dissolving into laughter. And Shelley had no idea of what she looked like, no idea that thousands, make that millions, of teenage girls would envy her. And a large part of that attraction was that Shelley genuinely had no idea of the impression she was making—no idea of how the spectators at athletic meetings would see her.

"Lucy, Sami, try it on; go on. Probably won't be exactly the right size, but have a go, throw a flic, go posing." Sami and Lucy tried on the clothing, did the hands-on-hip pose, threw that flic. "Mickey, try on one of the sweatshirts, I asked for a couple of big ones." Mickey did as asked and took the girls' ribald comments on the chin with a smile. Shelley made the phone call to Gilly.

"Gilly, is it all right if I come over and see you? Need to ask you some stuff. and I don't want to do it down the track. And, Gilly, would it be all right if Dan sat in on it as well?"

"Well, just look at you, Miss Sponsor's dream!" Shelley blushed at Dan's words and looked down at herself wearing the new Zig-Zag leisure clothing.

"Is it OK? I don't look stupid, do I?" Gilly nearly cried, how wonderful to be so unaware.

"Shelley, sweetheart, you look fantastic, absolutely gorgeous!"

"Really, miss? Gotta stop doing that! Gilly, I mean. I s'pose it's when I get a little bit nervous, like a bit unsure of myself, I just go back to 'Miss'!"

"What've you got to be nervous about, Shelley?" Dan smiled and lifted his eyebrows.

"It's all the sponsorship stuff, you know? I'm so lucky, I know that as well, and I want to do myself justice and keep Zig-Zag and Mr Smith happy. He's coming down to see me next week, sort it all out…and I need to ask him something as well. Help me, Dan, Gilly. Dan, I know you had all this stuff when you were swimming. What do I have to do? Really have to do?" Dan smiled again; Gilly was waiting.

"Top lady, Shelley, top lady. A lot of sponsored athletes—all sports—don't realise how lucky they are, almost take it as a right rather than a privilege, don't even say thank you properly. And you're already planning it out; Zig-Zag are going to love you! What to do? OK, here goes, I got this from Speedo when I was swimming and wearing their kit but also a bit of a put-together from a whole bunch of swimmers, bit of an inside view if you like…Rule one: win! There's nothing sponsors like more than a winning athlete; if you're standing on the podium after every race, they will look kindly on your efforts. All those other athletes watching you, their rationale goes something like this, 'Shelley wears Zig-Zag, and she wins; therefore, I need to wear that brand.'"

Dan smiled again, leant back in his chair and took a sip from his teacup. "Rule two: if you don't win, be seen with the person who has won. When I was at the Sydney games, Ian Thorpe was the stand-out star. Ian won big-time…but there was always, always, always one particular Aussie swimmer in the photos, interviews, hugging immediately after. Good PR, I say! Rule three: always wear the sponsor's kit in races. Sounds obvious, doesn't it? But there is often that temptation to wear the 'favourite' pair of running shoes rather than the branded ones that you're obliged to wear. Don't! What goes around, comes around, and it will be on that particular race day that someone from the sponsoring company will arrive unannounced to watch you. Rule four: always wear the sponsors kit in training. 'But I want to save my 'best' kit for the race, I hear you say!'

"No, you can't. If you're lucky enough to be sponsored, then you have a professional and moral obligation to give back, and a big part of that is wearing your sponsor's kit whenever possible and appropriate. If you don't wear it, how are you going to persuade your training buddies to buy it? Wear it clean as well; you're promoting your sponsors, so do it professionally. Rule five: tell everyone how good the kit and equipment is. This is so obvious, but some athletes seem reluctant to do it. You're given you kit for a reason; the reason is that the sponsors want to sell more.

"As a very rough guideline, kit manufacturers need to sell six pairs of shoes to cover one pair of sponsored shoes to an athlete. If you can sell those six by telling your mates how good they are, you're earning your sponsorship. Rule six: Be realistic. Be different. Be nice. Be humble. Let's start with realistic. The big sports clothing companies—Adidas, Nike, Speedo et al.—have an average of twenty-five(!) requests for sponsorship arriving on their desks every single day. You've already gone past that stage, Shelley, so let's look at 'Be different'. The crowds already love you."

Shelley shook her head. "Yes, Shelley, they do; you're beautiful. Gilly, tell her! They see you on track, looking fantastic and they start having fantasies, so you play up to it, smile, wave, throw them a kiss and a wiggle, and then laugh at yourself; you'll break a million hearts, and Zig-Zag will love it. You're successful and articulate, so go with it. And be nice. If you're lucky enough to attract some support, be nice to the company. Give them weekly feedback of your races, send them photos of you winning and wearing their kit. Send them some training pics, tell them what you like about the kit, tell them why you enjoy wearing it.

"Maybe suggest what could make it a little better. Create a relationship with your support people. If you do that, then there is a much greater likelihood that the support will continue. And Shelley, it won't last forever, same for every athlete, so be humble. If and when it's all over, don't throw a strop. Write or phone the company, tell them what a pleasure and an honour it has been to have been involved with them. They're not going to ask for the clothing or shoes back, but if it's equipment, return it clean. You never know, they may think again..."

Shelley sat there quietly thinking, quietly thinking through what she was intending to do, what she was hoping for. And then she told Dan and Gilly. They looked at her, astonished. And then they weren't quite so astonished because they should have known, should have known what Shelley was like. They'd known her half her life.

The meeting with her sponsors, with Zig-Zag, with John Smith, was approaching.

Chapter Forty-Three
Heart of Gold and a Core of Iron

The training was getting tougher and tougher, and they adored it. The new members of Gilly's squad would say to Mickey, Lucy and Sami after a session, "Now we know why you made it; now we know, but it's good, innit?" And it was better than good; almost every session was better than good. The size of Gilly's squad was increasing. Shelley was still running with Gilly's squad twice a week. She suffered, suffered a lot on the endurance, but everyone gave her some slack because, well, because she was Shelley, she'd been to the Games and the boys on Gilly's squad already adored her and were a little bit in love with her. Except Mickey (well, Mickey did love Shelley but, you know, brotherly love), who gently teased her a lot of the time. Shelley would smile back at him, and the boys on the squad would be jealous because Shelley never smiled at any one of them in that way; she smiled at them, laughed with them, but they could tell the difference, and most of them wished just a little bit that they could be Mickey.

Lucy and Sami wore the Zig-Zag kit that Shelley had given to them. Why not? It was free, and it felt good, and they had got into the habit of wearing it for training sessions. Some of the other athletes in Gilly and Shelley's squad had also bought Zig-Zag running gear; after all, Shelley said it was good, and Mickey had his Zig-Zag sweatshirt on before and after sessions, during warm-up and warm-down. Shelley smiled. Shelley had a plan. And Gilly and Dan were in on it. Bobby and Eric had even taken charge of the washing in the mansion, and the kit was always clean and ready to wear.

"Can we meet at the track, Mr Smith? Something I sort of want to show you, maybe to talk about."

"Shelley, please, please call me John, yeah? Makes me feel like a sort of athlete still! Yes, would love to watch a session, time and place?" So, Shelley

348

told him and hoped, desperately hoped, that she was doing the right thing. But she knew she was. She asked Dan if he could take time out from swim coaching to be at the session as well. And with what Dan knew that Shelley was hoping and planning, how could he refuse?

When Mr Zig-Zag John Smith arrived at the track, Gilly's group were halfway through the training session. John Smith only noticed the group because there were so many athletes wearing Zig-Zag; he grinned to himself, brand making an impact! And then he saw Shelley, had been expecting to see her in a hurdles or sprint session, and so he was immediately intrigued to see her with the middle and distance squad. He watched intently. He immediately recognised Gilly and waved to her. Who was that black guy watching? Another coach? Seem to recognise him...where from? The big black guy with the big smile walked over.

"John?" A nod of the head. "We met briefly in Sydney; we were on holding camp together up in Brisbane."

"Oh man! Dan, Dan the Speeding Bullet! Sorry, Dan, how rude of me. 'Course I remember...What you doing here?"

"Coaching, coaching swimming; at last somebody recognised my hidden talents...Also, I'm here because of a certain young lady that you're sponsoring..."

"Shelley Steele?"

"Of course, Shelley; she is truly a very special young lady, heart of gold and a core of iron. Talented swimmer, started late and still could have made it in swimming, trust me. But she chose track, and it worked out pretty well for her, didn't it?"

John smiled and nodded. "See all those guys wearing your stuff down there? They're wearing it because of Shelley. They didn't all buy it, though. That kid leading the group?"

Another nod. "That's Shelley's brother...she'll explain, and the two black girls?" Another nod. "They're Shelley's two sisters; she'll explain that one as well. But all the others? They bought Zig-Zag because of Shelley; the boys and the girls, because of Shelley."

The Speeding Bullet exhaled strongly. "John, I know Shelley's got a proposition for you. I truly hope you hear her out; she's golden for you, absolutely golden...Don't lose her; please don't lose her; don't let her go." It was a big speech for Dan, and John Smith took it all in because he needed to and because it was the Speeding Bullet, the Olympic medallist, who was doing the pitch.

The training session finished, and the athletes started their warm-down. Gilly came over to John Smith.

"Hi, Mr Smith."

"Just John if that's OK, Gilly?" Gilly smiled. "So has Dan told you what Shelley's going to propose? I'm pretty sure it's only Dan and I who know; it has to be Shelley's pitch, has to be. Please listen to her."

With the warm-down ended, Shelley came over to the Zig-Zag group.

"Mr Smith." Shelley shook hands. "Fancy a coffee, Mr Smith?"

"Prefer John, Shelley, and yes, I'd love a coffee." Shelley smiled, and John Smith knew exactly why he and Zig-Zag had decided to sponsor her. Shelley had that inner-glow; the sun rose each morning merely to light the smile on her face and the warmth in her heart. She was magic, just magic. They sat around the table overlooking the track. Athletes and coaches passed by, waved and smiled and said hello.

"So, what are you going to ask me, Shelley? Can't give you any more money; we're stretched as it is, to be honest. I reckon you have a really good deal…What can we do for you?" Shelley explained everything, and then she explained why. She pointed out Mickey, Lucy and Sami.

"Me'n Lucy and Mickey grew up on the same estate, Mr Smith…John, we got lucky; we got very lucky. Gilly's husband, Chris, was our junior school teacher. Yeah, all in the same class. He told us that we could be anything, anybody that we wanted to be. Hadn't been for Chris Warren, I wouldn't have got to the Olympics; well, Chris along with Gilly and Dan Bullet, of course."

"Dan and I got to know each other a bit at the Sydney Games…lovely man!" And Dan had the good grace to look embarrassed; Shelley studied John Smith, was this a tiny piece of the jigsaw beginning to fit?

"And then we met Sami at the English schools; she really helped my sister Lucy, you know." John didn't question why Shelley called Lucy her sister; he'd worked that one out already. "And you've heard of JoJo Jackson?"

"Of course, Spurs and England regular. Hang on, you know her as well?"

"Yeah, she's my other sister, been through quite a bit with JoJo, so JoJo's from our estate as well, same class at school as us, and she'd say exactly the same about Mr Warren; wouldn't have made it if it hadn't been for him." Dan and Gilly were smiling now. They'd just watched a crash orientation into TMRG.

And those other three members of TMRG were sitting and chatting at a separate table, and they had no idea of what Shelley was about to ask.

Shelley laughed out loud, and John Smith's heart jumped. "Thing is, John, I've just realised what I'm about to ask, and I know how stupid it'll sound. Anyway, here goes! My brother Mickey is going to get a medal at the London Games, not sure what event yet, 5K or 10K or maybe even the marathon…and those two sisters of mine, Lucy and Sami, are going to get medals as well, probably same distance as Mickey, not quite sure yet…and JoJo will be there with the GB football team…So, what I'm asking is whether Zig-Zag would consider sponsoring them? Not JoJo, of course; she's a lot richer than us already!

"Not suggesting money, John; that wouldn't be realistic, but helping out with kit, you know, would save a load of money for poor students…so what d'you reckon on Zig-Zag sponsoring not one but four Olympic Games medallists…'cause I'm gonna win gold next time. I'm gonna bust a gut!" John Smith was stunned. Here was an eighteen-year-old athlete who'd barely been with Zig-Zag a month and she was asking for her friends to be included! Not a chance, not a chance in hell. But then… what if? What if those promised medals really happened? Zig-Zag would join the big boys in the sports clothing industry. John smiled at Shelley.

"You've got some bottle, Shelley, some bottle! And you're more than brave even asking. Listen, I need to really think about this, need to talk to the head office guys, can't promise anything. Listen, I'm staying in Bath tonight, catching up with a few guys from Sydney; we'll all be telling each other how good we were…how about meeting up tomorrow?"

"Thank you so much, John. How about coming to watch Gilly's session tomorrow? I'm not doing it because I have an early hurdle technique session with Colin Jackson. I can sit and watch the session with you if that's OK? And, I haven't said anything to Lucy, Sami and Mickey—not a thing." And the only answer was yes as Shelley's smile and eyes drilled into his heart.

It was a very long and very complex phone call with Zig-Zag's head office. John was waiting for an out-and-out 'no', but it didn't come—not quite. "You've been there, John; you've done the Games; you've seen what it takes; and you should know the difference between those who talk the talk and those who walk the walk. Have a think, and then come back to us."

Chapter Forty-Four
This One for Me

It had been a great evening. John and his old running friends had indeed told each other just how good they used to be. Food had been eaten, beer and wine supped, but not too much for John Smith because he was interested, make that intrigued, by Gilly's upcoming run session and was also looking forward to hearing Shelley's thoughts and watching her brother and sisters' efforts.

It was a big group—a very big group—almost thirty athletes warming up, stretching, going through the strides on the all-weather Bath University track. Shelley was warming down after her technique session, when she saw John, smiled, looked down at her watch and indicated five with her hand and fingers outstretched. She joined him on the bench, put out her hand and then thought better of it and kissed him on the cheek. John smiled. Shelley smiled back.

"Gilly calls it the 10K acceleration session; she was telling us about how she found it. She was on the internet and looking at some old East German training sessions. So easy to translate now, isn't it?"

Mr Zig-Zag nodded his agreement. "And then Gilly found out that Liz McColgan and Paula Radcliffe had used variations of these sessions. Then Gilly told us that she was a CASE coach; CASE standing for Copy And Steal Everything. We all thought that was pretty good, y'know? And then when Gilly explained it, we were blown away. Hurts like hell, but you dig deep, really deep towards the end, and you see the improvement so quickly. OK, this is how it goes; the slowest that you run is your best 10K pace, and that's the recovery phase."

John Smith listened carefully as Shelley went through the session. This was his area of knowledge as well, although maybe—just maybe—this particular session wouldn't have been appropriate for his eight hundred metres event. But then he started thinking back to his weak areas and started wondering, 'what if?'

"So, John, I bet you probably know this already, but anyway, you start off with a 400 metres at just faster than best 5K pace, then directly into a 400 metres at best 10K pace—that's the recovery phase, yeah, racing pace for a ten! Then straight into a 300 at 1500 m race pace, into a 300 at 10K race pace again, nearly there…then we go 200 at best 800 metres pace, 200 at 10K race pace and finally into a one hundred at 99% full sprint effort."

"Wow, that's a toughie!" Shelley burst out laughing.

"John, that's only the intro! We go straight back in with the 400 at 5K pace and repeat the whole sequence."

"Jeez, now that is tough!" And Shelley laughed again.

"And then we go through the sequence one more time, so three times in all, although I'm pretty sure that Gilly may well move us up to four times through fairly soon—not all the squad, not all. So that's six kilometres, just under four miles, yeah? Then it's a three-minute jog and we go again but only twice though, another three-minute jog and go again but just once. So, if you do the lot, and all our guys; Mickey, Lucy and Sami all do the three reps, then you've covered twelve thousand metres plus warm-up and warm-down, that's seven and a half miles in old money…and if Gilly does start increasing the distance, then our guys are going to be pretty tough to beat!"

John Smith was sitting, thinking, considering. Gilly called the group together, some last-minute instructions, and then a 'two, one, hup!' It was a very short time before the group started splitting. John was focused on Shelley's three proposals, the possible Olympians, the possible Zig-Zag-sponsored athletes.

"How do these guys know what times to aim for, Shelley?"

"Well, Gilly has a sort of formula that gives you equivalent times for middle-distance, you know, if you can run a ten in whatever time, then you should be able to run a five in whatever. But you see those two guys sitting on the grass over there?"

John saw the two black youngsters with a laptop and pads of paper. "OK, they're Bobby and Eric; they're part of our group as well. Yeah, that group, same estate, same junior school and secondary school, same old Mr Warren as teacher, even sharing our flat down here at uni. We call it 'The Mansion'. Anyway, Bobby and Eric do all the paperwork for us, keep all the times, the splits, work out equivalent times; they've really bought into the challenge; they want to be a part of it, and I reckon it's brilliant. I reckon they're brilliant. We'll probably all have a coffee after the session. Fancy it?"

"Shelley, I've seen a lot of national squads less well-organised than what you have here. I'd love to meet all these guys after." Twelve minutes had gone since the start of the session; the athletes were spread all around the tartan track, all working to their individual time targets. It took less than a minute to work out the leaders, and he was less than surprised to see Mickey way in front of the men and Sami and Lucy tied together by an invisible cord for the women. Going over the distance points, John Smith could see the barest check on the watches, a glance down and continue the run.

Mickey Honey crossed the line for the end of part one. Gilly waited until Lucy and Sami had crossed (only three other men in between them and Mickey), then blew a whistle. Mickey jogged to Lucy and kissed her; Sami looked at him questioningly, put her index finger onto her cheek, and Micky grinned and kissed Sami as well. Sweatshirts on and a one lap jog for all the squad; lots of laughter, lot of chat, more laughter. Thumbs-up to Eric and Bobby as they jogged past.

"Ready, you guys, come on." Second phase and then third, some of the athletes instructed by Gilly to miss one rep or two, no arguments; he knew there wouldn't be.

Session over...almost. "Lucy, Sami, Mickey (three other names called out), fancy impressing me? Just one more, two more reps through, another two and a half miles...of pain!" The six athletes ran through the starting line, four hundred done, the next, three hundred, two hundred, sprint the next and repeat...and hurt. "Nice one, guys, very nice; big time shoot a dime!" Mickey looked at Gilly.

"Just one thing you forgot, Gilly…"

"Mickey?"

"That stuff about 'this one for me'; you forgot that, Gilly."

"Didn't forget, Mickey; didn't need to say it; the one you're doing is for you, always. Me? I just go along with the deal!" Gilly and all the athletes laughed because they knew that it was a lot more than that. Shelley looked at John Smith; John looked back at Shelley; they both grinned; they both nodded, and Shelley wondered if a deal might just have been struck.

Eventually, they all staggered up for coffee.

"Listen, you guys, this gentleman is John Smith; he's the man responsible for me looking like 'cool as a mule' on the track in all the Zig-Zag gear. I asked him to come down and look at the session. John ran at the Sydney Games...knows Dan as well, so can't be a bad 'un, can he?" Smiles and shaking heads indicated that no, John Smith couldn't be a bad 'un.

"Lovely to meet you guys; loved the session—glad I wasn't doing it, though!"

Appreciative laughter. "OK, reality check, Shelley here"—he nodded over at Shelley—"came up with this ridiculous idea that Zig-Zag might like to sponsor you guys purely on Shelley's say-so, so I told her it was impossible, but sometimes the impossible happens." He exhaled a big 'phew'. "Yes, sometimes the impossible happens. Shelley sold me a dream, and although I don't believe in dreams, sometimes dreams do come true, so…Lucy, Sami, Mickey, Zig-Zag would be willing—make that 'happy'—to supply you with kit, shoes and leisurewear up to and including the London Olympic Games. What d'you reckon? And Eric, Bobby, sounds very much like you're important members of the support team, reckon we can kit you out with a few sweatshirts and leisurewear as well, sound reasonable?" They all stared over at Shelley, who blushed and looked down at her feet…and then looked up.

"Shelley? Shell?" Mickey said. "Shell, you'd do that for us? Put your own stuff at risk…For us? Bloody hell, Shell, just bloody hell!" Mickey got up from his chair, lifted Shelley up from hers and hugged and kissed her. Mickey wasn't too far from tears, real tears. Lucy and Sami didn't even have that pretension, they were straight into the floodgates. Eric and Bobby just stared at each other. Gilly was smiling, smiling, smiling. But now, Shelley had another thing to do, and she really wasn't too sure—wasn't too sure at all what she wanted to do about it.

Chapter Forty-Five
Sealed with a Loving Kiss

Back in her room, Shelley opened up the laptop and looked at the message again; this would be the fifth time that she'd read it and wasn't sure, wasn't sure at all, what she was going to do about it.

'My dear Shelley,

It was so lovely seeing you again in Beijing. I loved being able to spend time with you and get to know you properly, so much better than when I thought I was the coolest kid in town and just had no idea of how to behave. I think and hope that I've improved my behaviour. And I loved kissing you. There, I've said it!

Shelley, I have something to ask you, and I will understand totally if you say no or that you don't think it's a good idea. OK, here goes. Marianne Deussmann and I are at the same university in Amsterdam. Like you and Mickey, I think of Marianne as my sister; she keeps me on the straight and narrow (is that how you say it in English?) and properly behaved! We wanted to be around each other and also thought that the training facilities for Marianne's running and my swimming would be excellent. Sad to say, they are not. There are not enough structured sessions, not enough pool time and experienced coaching staff. And now, I think you know exactly what I'm going to ask you. Yes, I know you do. We would both like to attend Bath University; we have asked for transfers and for overseas student status. Also, Bath has seen our sports careers and CVs. And they liked them. I know that Dan Bullet is coaching swimming (I read all the swimming magazines), and he's already getting rave reviews for his training sessions and also for the rehab he is doing with athletes from all sports. Marianne does exactly the same as me but for running, of course.

Shelley, I want to be at the London Olympics. I have unfinished business, and that unfinished business is a medal. Marianne is improving all the time. I know that she will be with the Dutch team for London, and I also believe that she has the hunger for a medal. So, my question, Shelley, is: would it be all right for Marianne and I to come to Bath? I know I don't need your permission, but I wouldn't want to put you under pressure in any way or pressure your friends. Marianne and I can start immediately, as the lecturers at Bath tell us. We are both registered on the sports science course in Amsterdam, and we are able to transfer to Bath's sports science course. If you say yes, I promise that I won't bother you at all, but if you decide best not to, then I will totally understand and respect your decision. I have now (as you say in England, I think) my fingers tightly crossed.

With much love and respect.

Kaas, X

*****

"Mickey, Lucy, need to talk to you, right now, if that's all right?"

Two nodded heads, two okays. And so, Shelley showed them the email, didn't say anything, just waited, then Lucy said, "Shell, you like him? You really like him?" Lucy smiled at Shelley, reached out and took her hand. "Really like him?"

"Think so, Luce, think so, Mickey…all the star-truckers, you know, just pretend, smile and walk on by…Kaas is different, so yeah, really, I really do like him…but you know…all that stuff before, oh shit, Mickey, what am I gonna do? What if they do come over and it all goes tits-up?"

"Right, I'm gonna talk to you like I've never talked to anyone before, not even Mickey…'cause, well, 'cause it's all about Mickey…and me. See, Shell, I can't imagine my life without this bloke beside me, and I don't even tell him that, but I'm saying it now. I'm saying it because I want you to have what I've got…and like you've been different since you got back from the Games; yeah, I know, Olympics and all that, 'big time, shoot a dime', but it ain't just that, Shell; it certainly ain't just that. You been thinking of him, haven't you?" Shelley nodded a big yes. "Then you go for it, girl; you one hundred per cent go for it! Mickey, what you reckon?"

"Gotta do it, Shelley, you just have to. Listen, if it all goes tits-up—oops! Sorry! Well, you know, if it does, then you'll know that you tried and it didn't work…but if it does—" Mickey stopped talking and, together with Lucy, held Shelley.

"Dunno what I'd do without you guys; no, honest, you've saved my life a million times, so I write back and tell him 'yes', yeah?"

"You have to, Shell; you know you have to. You know what, ladies? I think I need to treat you to a drink. Glass of wine, fancy it? Yeah, I know, athletes in training, restricted area! But not this time; no, not this time." And the three of them retreated to the university bar while Mickey was ringing Sami, Bobby and Eric to join them.

And the email was written.

Less than a week and they were there. Shelley was nervous, so nervous but hoping that she'd done the right thing, not just for her but for all of them. The bus from the train station slogged it up that long steep hill to the university, and the six members of TMRG plus Gilly and Dan were waiting for the two newbies to get off the bus. A lot of faffing about to start with as Marianne and Kaas struggled with the three large kit-bags holding pretty much all their worldly possessions; waiting, waiting, waiting…

It was Marianne who broke the silence, broke the not-quite-knowing-what-to-do; walked over to Gilly, held out her hand, broke into a smile.

"How lovely to see you again, Gilly; you must be very proud of Shelley…and very proud of being an Olympic coach!"

Marianne looked at Bobby and Eric, and smiled again. "Ooh, you two look lovely! I think I'm going to like getting to know you two properly. It's Bobby and Eric, I think? Mickey told us about you all those years ago, and now I think you help Gilly with keeping all the records and statistics, yes?" And poor old Bobby and Eric couldn't speak; they were entranced, entranced with Marianne. Marianne, Shelley and Lucy embraced.

"Thanks, Marianne, that was brilliant." A walk over to Mickey and a hug, then a hug for the Speeding Bullet and for Sami. And now it was Kaas's turn.

"Shelley, Mickey, thank you, thank you so much." Shelley kissed him on the cheek. Mickey held out his hand and smiled.

"Good to see you, Kaas. We're going to be fine; we really are." The other introductions were made, a few embarrassed silences but only a very few, and the atmosphere was gradually lifting.

Marianne's and Kaas's apartment was located in what was called the 'International Zone' of the flats and halls of residence, and they very swiftly adapted to the lectures, seminars and, most importantly, the training regime at Bath. They fitted in quickly; they were hard-workers, pleasant, spoke excellent English and had the necessary sense of humour. That Marianne was extremely pretty and Kaas a very good-looking young man were, of course, added bonuses!

And now a lot of things started to happen, a lot.

After a cautious week where they were both checking out the ground rules and each other, Kaas and Dan hit it off.

"Trains hard, never complains, always cheerful and pleasant, encourages the others if he sees them having a hard time. And he's an Olympian; he's been there, done it and got the T-shirt, so the other swimmers will listen to him; couple of them know him already from Beijing of course." Dan was impressed.

Gilly introduced Marianne to the sprints coach, and there was an almost identical connection as there had been between Dan and Kaas; work hard, never complain, encourage, be cheerful, be nice. Occasionally, Marianne would ask if she could join in with Gilly's middle-distance squad; Gilly never asked why, always allowed until.

"Gilly, I love your sessions and hate them at the same time!" Gilly waited. "And you don't ask me why…"

"I reckoned that you'd tell me when you were ready…"

"So, I want to go to the London Olympics, yes?" Gilly nodded. "And I look at the athletes, the girls I think I will be running against, and I wonder…will I be good enough? Will I make the team? Will I make the final? And I wonder again. And then I think, 'So I used to run cross-country a little, and it was OK, so maybe I should try the four hundred as well as the two hundred metres…Gilly, what do you think?" Gilly thought that was a very good idea. Gilly was impressed.

They'd been sitting on the bench on the poolside, stopwatches in hand, pads on knees, writing, chatting, watching. Dan had his 'A' squad, including Kaas in lanes three and four, and then Lucy, Shelley and others in lanes one and two.

"Get all the stuff, guys? All the times?" Bobby and Eric nodded 'yes'. Dan waited, he sensed there was something coming.

"Dan, dunno if this important, probably isn't, but, you know, thought it was worth checking it out with you." Dan waited. "You know like we're a bit techie, yeah?"

Dan nodded. "So we were timing the individual stroke of all of the swimmers, you know, entry of the right arm into the water and then next time and so on and the same with the left. So pretty much the guys in the top lanes were hitting identical or near identical splits on left and right, and then we had a look at Lucy. She was about three tenths different on left and right. Like we don't know if that's important or if it means anything at all, but thought we'd mention it just in case." Kaas was listening as well.

"Mr Bullet."

"Dan, Kaas, or Coach Dan, please."

"Sorry, Dan." Kaas grinned. "Don't want to disrespect you, Dan, that's all…" A pause. "Dan, when I was doing my level one and level two swim coach's stuff in Holland, we had one of the speakers who was really into sports science—maybe as a techie as Bobby and Eric—and he talked about that as well. Said that it was really difficult to see, a bit of 'I know something's not quite right but can't put my finger on it' you know, and so I did use it a little bit with the youngsters coming through; easier to adjust things early, isn't it? Once we'd got it sorted out and then the timing and stroke length, we really did get results, speed of course but also feeling less tired during the long sessions and races…" Dan waited. *Please, please, please say it!* "So, Dan, if it was all right with you, maybe I could do a little bit of work with Lucy? If she'll let me, of course…" Dan thought, *Yes! Yes! Yes!*

"I think that would be perfect, Kaas. You sure you have the time?"

"Got lots of time, Dan. Maybe it's a tiny way of saying thank you to everyone; me'n Marianne are so grateful, you know." Dan knew that in Kaas, he had a good'un. Lucy agreed, a little hesitantly, but Lucy agreed. After just a couple of technique sessions ("Kaas, d'you mind if I watch?" Dan asked), Lucy started improving. And kept on improving.

The word spread quickly. "That kid who's a runner, yeah, Lucy, that one who does a load of swimming, even though she's not really a swimmer? Yeah, Lucy. Well, you wanna see her now. She's getting a bit of coaching from that Dutch kid, the pretty one. Yeah, I know he's a bloke, but he's still pretty. Kaas something went to the Games, but he can coach as well." Shelley listened and smiled and kept on smiling.

"Kaas, listen…do you want to make it official?"

"What d'you mean, Dan, official?"

"Official as in if you're doing some coaching, then you should get paid for it. Sound reasonable?"

"Dan, I'm fine, honest. It's a pleasure and a privilege to be on the poolside with you, and if you think I'm doing OK with the new swimmers coming along, then that's good enough, truly."

"I'll take that as a 'yes' then." Dan grinned at Kaas, who grinned back. "I'll make sure that your coaching doesn't interfere with your own swimming, and I'll get a couple of notices put up, something like 'improve your swim technique with Olympic finalist and current Bath University student, Kaas Prinz; sound reasonable?"

"Thanks, Dan, thank you very much." And both of them were forced to turn away from each other, just in case, you know, just in case...

And then one day, Lucy arrived for her swim session, dived in, did the warm-up as set by Kaas, and then held onto the pool edge while she waited for everyone in the two squads, the senior elites and the stroke improvers, to finish and settle. Dan and Kaas were on the poolside, and to Lucy, it looked as if they were whispering and laughing, almost as if they were conspirators. What was going on?

"Listen up, swimmers." Dan set out the two different sessions, his and Kaas' and wrote them on the whiteboard. "Lucy, jump into lane three, please, put all your equipment on three as well...let's see what happens, yeah?" Kaas winked at Lucy and even dared to blow her an air kiss. And what happened was that Lucy coped with the new harder session, actually did better than cope, did well, extremely well. By the end of the session, Lucy was no longer the final swimmer going off reps in her lane; she had already moved up in the pecking order, and every swimmer there knew what that meant.

Over at the track, Shelley was preparing for one of her few endurance sessions with Gilly and was going through the motions of warm-up, laughing and joking with Mickey and Sami as always, with Marianne also choosing to run endurance. Didn't notice the five hurdles set out on the second two hundred-metre stretch out in lane five. Why should she? It had nothing to do with her when she was with Gilly...until...

"Shelley, Shell? Shelley, I'm springing something new on you, OK?"

Shelley nodded. "Of course." Always trust Gilly, always.

"So session is ten by four hundred with these guys looking at race pace for fifteen hundred, two hundred jog recovery. What I'd like you to do, Shelley, is ten by two hundred hurdles, you're out in lane five as you can see." and Shelley took in the spaced hurdles for the first time. "Let's see what happens; you're only going two hundred while these guys are running four hundred, so maybe aim to keep up with them, that's some target! Marianne, I'd like you to run three hundreds rather than four hundreds, but keep with the pace! Go lane six, please; give Shelley something to chase!"

The first rep was a mixture between comedy, farce and humility. Shelley had little idea of stride pattern and even less idea of expected pace. As the main pack came past, she moved into action mode with them and then came the first barrier, a sort of clearance, and then almost before she knew it, the next barrier was there and the next and the next. Somehow managing to keep in contact, over the line, "Fifty-nine, sixty, sixty-one."

Jogging back with Marianne, the first half a grin, the second half embarrassment and semi-shame. The second rep was better, the third better still; Marianne was hanging in there and suffering. Mickey and Lucy were looking over at her, smiling and encouraging. Three to go, you can always hang on for the last few. One or two of the girls in the main pack were beginning to drop a couple of seconds, but hanging tough. "Hang tough, girl, just hang tough," Shelley said to Shelley but also to Marianne.

Sweat, sweat, sweat cascading down the faces, into the eyes, cascading down the bodies. "Just hang tough!" Into the final rep, Gilly's voice in self-parody, "This one for me!" And for all the athletes there who knew it to be self-parody, this one WAS for her.

Over the line, "Fifty-eight, fifty-nine, sixty," half a stumble, onto the grass, sprawl rather than sit down. Gilly was quietly moving amongst them, a word here, a pat there, a squeeze, a hug, all deserved, all happily received. "Trackies on, guys, let's go." Easy, very easy jogging down, then a little easier, then the smiles, the chats, the jokes; final stretching, the occasional fart. "Someone's bottom just coughed!"

Appreciative chuckles, more giggles and laughter. "Maybe you stay behind me on the next rep!"

More giggles and laughing. Gilly thinking, *I love this; I absolutely love this...and they pay me!?* Kaas arrived, funny how he seemed to arrive from his swimming session just as Shelley was finishing her track workout or still going through it. He waved and smiled over at her, hoping for a smile returned. It was. Next level? Maybe, just maybe.

"Bit of a mess, eh, Gilly?" Shelley smiled but wasn't that far from tears. Gilly squeezed her arm and looked over at Eric and Bobby.

"Got Shelley's splits, you guys?"

"Sure, Gilly; Shelley, you went a thirty-two on the first rep, but after that, you were splitting a fraction under thirty, final one a high twenty-eight."

"Got the variations for lane five?"

"'Course, we make it around one point five, looking at somewhere around nought point four for each lane out, so probs coming in at a twenty-eight five average…"

"So maybe not too messy, Shelley, gives you a fifty-seven for four hundred—and that's in training, ten times through; you'd probably need a fifty-five to make UK finals, and that's on a single run…so maybe not quite as messy as you think, Shelley. We didn't talk about number of strides between hurdles, didn't talk about possibly having to alter number and then lead leg as well. First ever proper long hurdles session, Shell, not the tiniest bit messy. And Marianne, great session. Shelley was knocking twenty-eight five; you were squeezing on a twenty-eight flat plus the hundred in; reckon you're ready for a sub fifty-five right now, maybe sub fifty-four." Shelley and Marianne high-fived each other, embraced, embraced Gilly and walked to the changing rooms with arms around each other. Kaas looked at Gilly and smiled.

"See what happens, Gilly? I get these two together, and what thanks for me? Zilch, absolutely zilch!" And they both burst out laughing. Mickey, Lucy and Sami came up to Gilly.

"Coffee?"

"You buying?"

"Us? Poor students…'course we're buying! Loved the session, Gilly, absolutely loved it. How you got Shell and Marianne involved, totes brill, really totes brill."

A silence, then, "Gilly, serious question, like really serious…Can we make London? Really, can we make London?" Gilly smiled back at them.

"No, you can't make London…" The silence and crushed look told a million stories. "It's not about making London; it's about doing something there. Look, I can't say you're going to win or medal; 'course, I can't. but what I can say is that if you keep working like you're working now, then I don't think anybody is going into the London games—still over three years, guys—better prepared.

There's lots to do; of course, there is, but yes, you can make London, make it big-time." And three more athletes walked away even more determined.

*****

Meanwhile, back in London, another member of TMRG was making her own push. With the local elections for the Borough of Newham councillors fast approaching, eighteen-year-old Alisha Buzdar was learning her trade, doing the rounds, knocking on doors, lots of doors. And once the shock of seeing a kid ("How old is she? Looks about fourteen to me.") pitching for their vote had subsided a little, they listened. They listened to a local girl making her case, age seemed to matter less and less as Alisha explained why she wanted to be on the council, why she couldn't wait any longer, where she lived, where she had gone to school, the difference that teachers and education had made to her, to her life, why she had chosen to continue her education locally in London despite the many offers she had had.

It was the single statement of, "I want to make a difference to kids' lives and that will make a difference to their adult lives," that got them. They asked around, discovered more about the prospective candidate, liked what they heard and read, liked the stories about her schools, her friends; local kids doing good. It impressed them. "She might look like a bit of a kid, but bloody hell, does she speak well and makes sense. Yeah, I think I'd like her sticking up for me in those bloody council meetings rather than someone who sounds like they love the sound of their own voice."

*****

And the improvements kept on coming. Eric and Bobby (the others had started to call the two of them 'Stats', as in Stats Eric and Stats Bobby), had every single session recorded and monitored. Copies were given to Gilly, the swim times to Dan. The two coaches kept researching world leading times, various university, under-twenty and senior team qualifying times. A first minor sensation when Lucy recorded a fifteen hundred metres time in training that would have qualified her for the British Swimming Nationals. Dan and Kaas just smiled at each other. Lucy hugged them both, then ran off to tell Mickey, Shelley and Marianne. The group grew stronger. Times recorded in training kept dropping.

That first year at Bath University with all the happenings, all the surprises, all the improvements was coming to an end. Up to Loughborough University for the British University Championships. For most of the students taking part, the most important event of the year. For some, a stepping-stone. A five-day meet that included both swimming and athletics meant that there could be heats where necessary.

For Lucy, one of the very few students who had qualified for both a swimming and a track event, it was essential. Sami and Mickey were content to compete in just one event, while Shelley had entered both the hundred and four hundred hurdles, which entailed four races if she made it through to the finals on both. Shelley had also managed a qualifying mark in the long jump but was holding back from making a firm commitment in that.

There was a big contingent from Bath of swimmers and athletes. Bath was seen as one of the 'big four' sports universities along with Leeds, West London Institute (previously Borough Road) and Loughborough ("They all call it Lufbra," Dan told them.) and were expected to compete well. Gilly had been talking to all her charges in the coach and then chatted with Kaas as well; Kaas listened and nodded his head 'yes'. The coach pulled into the Lufbra car park, and Gilly stood up at the front of the coach.

"OK, listen up, you guys, want to show you something and then a couple of our guys are going to say something as well." Gilly was well-respected, well-liked by everyone, so they settled back in their seats and listened. Gilly held up a DVD, twirled it around in her hands and smiled. "I've got a DVD here, and by my magic powers, it already has this meet for the next few days, taped and recorded."

There was appreciative laughter. "Yeah, I know, stupid…but what if it did? What if I did have those magic powers and all your races were already recorded, what would you like to see when you play it back at Christmas?"

Then there was a silence that went on…and on. *Yeah, I know exactly what I want to see. I want to see me winning.* Same thoughts from different brains. And Gilly's words did exactly what she hoped they would; they focused the attention of every swimmer and athlete there. She smiled again. "Makes you think, doesn't it?"

The smiles and the laughs and even a few hand-claps showed that the demonstration had made them think. "I've asked a couple of people to say a few words, couple of first year students at Bath, couple of guys who went to the Olympics last year, you know them, of course, Shelley and Kaas." And now there was real cheering, Shelley and Kaas were popular with everyone; clapping, shouting out, whistling. Shelley stood up, slightly blushing. Kaas squeezed her hand and winked at her; Shelley squeezed his hand back and smiled.

"Kaas is going second 'cause he's prettier than me." Much laughter and protestations. "No, no, never!"

"What Gilly just did made you totally get it, didn't it? Can you imagine sitting and watching that old vid and knowing that you didn't do your best, didn't give it everything? But that won't happen now, will it?" And the heads were shaking and eyes were catching other eyes.

"Listen, I'm gonna be a bit flash now, so forgive me, please?" And everybody there would have forgiven Shelley anything. "Me, the Olympics, I got fourth, fourth. So, is that any good? Well, depends, doesn't it?"

Absolute silence now; they were all imagining, 'Me, could I get there?'. "I didn't get a medal so maybe it was a failure." Heads shaking no, no. "Or maybe I made the final, so it was a success." Heads nodding yes, yes.

"So maybe it was a bit of both, success and failure…Anyone remember that old poem from Kipling?" Heads turning and looking around; some nodding yes. "Kipling called it *Triumph and Disaster*, and he said that the important thing was to treat them both the same…Makes pretty good sense to me, guys. So, all I can say is this, go out there and do your absolute best, and whatever happens, be proud; Triumph and Disaster, yeah, different ends of the same stick, that's all." Shelley sat down to rapturous applause, another ten or so broken hearts and dreams. Kaas stood up.

"So, I'm the pretty one, am I? What d'you reckon, all you blokes? Me or Shelley the prettiest?" There was little doubt that Kaas had just lost his beauty top spot, and now he was even more popular.

"You know what, guys? I can't really add anything to what Shelley has just said. I made two finals at the Games, didn't get a sniff at a medal, nowhere near…but I did give it everything, absolutely everything, and I'm proud of that. And I promise all of you that I'm going to give it everything here at Lufbra as well…and also at the London Olympic Games!" And there were as many flutterings in the girls' hearts for Kaas as there had been with the boys for

Shelley. It was a good meet for Bath University, a good meet for the coaches, swimmers and athletes. It was a very good meet for TMRG and their two new associate members, Marianne and Kaas.

Kaas did exactly as he had promised. Competing in the two individual medley events, the two and four hundreds, he gave it everything and finished with two gold medals in times only just outside what he had posted at the Beijing Games. And while still in a period of heavy training and little taper, that was excellent. Shelly had watched both events and, after the second final, had leant over the barrier and beckoned to Kaas as he walked past with the spectators still applauding.

Kaas went over to Shelley, and she leant forward and kissed Kaas on the mouth while the crowd—as they say—went wild. Shelley, along with all of TMRG, stayed in the pool to watch a very nervous Lucy Newton swim in the fifteen hundred metres. No finals, eventual positions decided on overall times. And on overall times, Lucy Newton in her first-ever competitive gala finished in eighth position. With everything geared to technique, Lucy flipped into the final three lengths and brought in her powerful legs for the final one-fifty metres rather than just using them for balance and passed three other swimmers. Dan and Kaas were ecstatic, and Mickey, if anything, even more so.

"First swim, Lucy! First swim, little one, and you were superb! Eighth, and if there had been finals, I have absolutely no doubt that you would have moved up at least a couple of slots...keep the dream alive, Lucy; let the pot simmer, but keep it there!" And then Dan hugged her and turned away in case she saw the tears in his eyes. And that gave Lucy hug-time with the other half of her being, who also had those leaky eyes. And it was just twenty-four hours before Lucy Newton was due to appear again, joining up with Sami, in the five thousand metres on the track.

It was a straight final for the women's five thousand metres. Twenty-eight athletes poised and ready for the starting pistol and all of them thankful that they wouldn't have to go again. Sami and Lucy next to each other on the curved line, "Take your marks." Lean forward. "Crack!"

There was a surge to the front, and when the surge calmed down into what the majority of the runners thought would be the pecking order for the first couple of thousand metres, two athletes kept on, holding that fast pace from the gun. Sami led from Lucy, as they had planned and going through the first two hundred mark ('thirty-three, thirty-four'), Sami moved slightly out, and Lucy took over at the front. At four hundred ('one nine, one ten'), the movement reversed itself with Sami retaking the lead and the pace as Lucy eased over. Only three runners were sticking with the pace-setters, all three senior or under twenty-three internationals.

Every two hundred metres, Lucy and Sami switched; two runners with them, then one, then just the two of them as they passed five laps, the two thousand metres mark with the timekeeper shouting out, "Five fifty-five, fifty-six." Mental gymnastics were juggling the numbers; they had set out their target time as seventy-two seconds for each lap, which would bring them in at fifteen minutes exactly (World qualifying is fifteen-ten but it's a fairly soft mark compared to most), but they were under that schedule, and unless they blew up—which was always a possibility—a flat fifteen was on! To the other runners in the race, the pace was relentless, and the more experienced athletes who had been anticipating a swift payback from the early fast pace were seeing their hopes quickly vanish.

On and on and on, never moving from their own half-lap turnaround pacing plan, Lucy and Sami reached the bell—one lap to go, in fourteen forty-four. They looked at each and smiled, touched hands (Gilly saw and had a sharp intake of breath) and ran side by side through the final lap with the crowd on their feet and chanting out their names; across the line together with clasped hands held high. Jogging the victory lap together, clapping back at the crowd, going to the barrier by the Bath Uni contingent, two quick kisses for Mickey, more crowd cheers, over to the electronic scoreboard, seeing their names as joint first, time of fourteen minutes, fifty-two point nine seconds. Stadium announcer going quietly berserk. "With the fastest time in Great Britain this year and Senior World qualifying time, representing Bath University, please put your hands together for Lucy Newton and Sami Richards!"

Marianne was nervous; she'd time-trialled a couple of four hundreds in training, but racing was different; you brought a different mindset to a race. She was placed in the inside lane, lane one in the first heat. Anticipation, a little fear and relief were jostling each other in her mind. Looking forward to it, bit afraid of the distance, relief to be actually doing it at last. Out of the blocks, very quick to rise, cutting down on the stagger very quickly...*Jeez, this is easier than I thought!* Payback started as Marianne entered the home straight, three hundred done, last hundred to go.

It felt like a bear jumping on her back, like needles were pricking her legs, like her stomach was about to disgrace itself, with sheer guts and pure determination, Marianne held on and finished second; the winner almost five metres ahead and three other athletes within the thickness of a vest behind her. Marianne managed to go through the reciprocal 'well-dones', walked away from the track and promptly burst into tears. Up in the stands with laptops and notebooks in hand, Eric and Bobby looked at each other.

"You go, Eric. If it's both of us, Marianne will feel threatened, I reckon."

"Then we'll cheer her up, won't we?" Marianne finishing her warm-down, saw Eric approaching and tried to smile but lost that particular battle.

"Marianne, OK if I talk to you?" A nod 'yes' of the head. "Well, you know me and Bobby are pretty much stats freaks?" Marianne smiled a little. "So we've got just about every time you've done in training, all the splits, everything...including your race today."

Marianne waited. "So in training, you pretty much do even splits, if you're repping four hundreds, you'll split a twenty-nine and a twenty-nine, maybe a couple of tenths difference but usually evens, even in the time trials you split even, but that didn't happen today." Eric opened his laptop. "Have a look, see? You went out like a scared bunny rabbit and paid the price in the last hundred...make sense?"

Marianne nodded, smiled properly this time and agreed that, yes, it did indeed make complete sense. "So me'n Bobby watched the rest of the heats, and if we've got our sums right—and we always get our sums right—then you're in the final tomorrow, probably the last qualifier on time, but your second place got it for you. Now tell me to shut up if you like, but this is what me'n Bobby reckon if you want to medal."

Eric went through what he thought should be Marianne's race plan, went through it again, answered all the questions, gave the rationale for the answers and even wrote figures and numbers down on the notepad. Marianne smiled with her whole face this time, whispered a very quiet 'thank you', leant in and kissed Eric on the cheek, then thought better of it and kissed him again very briefly on the lips and then again on the lips. "One's for you, the other kiss is for Bobby...Don't forget to give it to him!" And old Epic Eric wasn't too sure if he was going to share that kiss with Bobby or not.

The final. Lane eight. All competitors inside Marianne. No one outside to pace and to feed off. Calm now, collected. Race plan set. Nerves gone, 'nought to fear but fear itself.' Out of the blocks fast! But not silly fast. Eric had explained that there was an adrenaline surge so that you could carry the first fifty or so

369

metres almost at one hundred per cent but not much further. Focus, focus, focus. My lane, my lane only. My pace. My race. Holding steady, fast but steady, in control, through two hundred, halfway, nobody yet showing in front, it would be that second bend where it would happen.

But nobody came through. More confidence now, it worked! Eric and Bobby's race plan was just fine. Tired, sure. But a tiredness that she could deal with and fight off because she was in control. Tape bursting against her chest, Marianne carried on running straight to Bobby and Eric in the crowd just beyond the finish line, two more kisses, two more hugs. Then back to the group of finishers all with the 'what happened?' look on them. Marianne Deussmann had just come of age in the four hundred metres. Eric and Bobby smirked at each other, then the high five. Gilly Warren just smiled and mentally ticked off another milestone achieved.

Shelley opened her account in the sprint hurdles, heats and final on the same day. Disappointingly for Shelley, there was no one of her class in the line-ups, and she won convincingly. At the back of her mind, the mantra she'd talked about in the coach, 'always do your absolute best', and that was Shelley, the absolute best. Even in the final, she was four metres in front as she breasted the tape, four metres that could have been a mile.

It was the four hundred hurdles that played on her mind; Shelley hadn't raced or done a full four hundred time-trial over the barriers although the indications from the quality two hundreds and three hundreds in training were good. A day's rest and recovery after the sprint hurdles and then into just three heats of the four hundred.

"Pace and stride pattern, Shelley, get those right, and the race will come together," Gilly said. They'd worked on that stride pattern a lot. "Hold fifteen as long as you can, maybe even to eight hurdles, and then come down to sixteen and remember to focus on the other leg leading in."

Seemingly calm and collected, Shelley entered the zone, heat three, lane five. The other athletes were looking at her; 'unknown quantity, still a kid really, different world stepping up to the four hundred, sure she can hurdle, proved that at the Games, but four hundred is a different world, still so young, welcome to the world of suffering, superstar.'

Out of the blocks and total focus, get the stride right before even looking up at the first barrier; nine, ten strides, look up, over on fifteen, felt good, felt comfortable, a little stretched but that was because of the first short strides coming out of the blocks. More comfortable now, second, third, fourth barrier, girl in the lane outside Shelley was passed, another one on the barrier five, into the second bend, concentrate and focus, concentrate and focus! Off the bend and leading over hurdle eight, into the straight (Shelley could hear Mickey calling it 'the stretch'), legs tired now, stomach tightening, almost a stumble, 'get it back, girl!', down to sixteen strides and that was tough, over the ninth, beginning to fall apart, sensing the others closing, hold that sixteen strides and I'm over on the left leg, yes, better!

Hanging tough as always, tape broken but more effort than anything like the hundred hurdles, that was over in a flash. Hands on knees, breathing ragged, athletes coming over, pats on shoulders, murmured congratulations, maybe even a little jealousy that the new kid had made the transition from sprint to four hundred. Or maybe a little admiration. And the new-made memories that they'd raced against an Olympian and had done pretty damn well. Electronic scoreboard displaying: '1st Shelley Steele, Bath, 55.9 seconds.' Qualified for the final, two other athletes faster than Shelley, and that wasn't a surprise, the newbie in her first race, just qualifying was a bonus.

They were eating dinner together, just the two of them, Shelley and Kaas, the night before Shelley's final. Did she dare say it?

"Kaas? Kaas? Listen, are we going out, like going out properly? Boyfriend and girlfriend?" Kaas' eyes opened wide.

"That's what I want, Shelley; that's what I truly want."

"So, no messing about, no sneaking some bird in on the sly, no cheating on me, not ever. You do it once, I'll cut you out of my life…yes, I would. I'd cut you dead."

"No, I wouldn't do that, Shelley. You gave me a second chance; I wouldn't blow it for a silly quickie…is that how you say in English?"

"Yes, Kaas, that's pretty much exactly how you'd say it in English…but how would you know that?" Shelley grinned at him. "Go on, tell me."

"Maybe I hear it with the bad boys when I'm trying to show them how to be good, I think, yes." Shelley burst out laughing, properly laughing.

"Kaas, at the end of term, I'm going back to London. I miss my mum. All of us are going back…would you like to come with me?" Kaas wouldn't have wished for anything more.

"And meet my mum, Kaas? Meet my mum?"

"Shelley, I would adore to meet your mum, maybe I tell her what a bad girl you are?" Shelley laughed again.

"Kaas, you need to know some stuff, me and, well, all of us, we don't come from the posh part of London...actually—and you can learn this—it's a bit of a slum, and the correct English is, 'a bit of a shithole'." Kaas howled out loud and took a pretend pen and paper out of his pocket.

"So you can maybe tell me what this means?"

A long pause, then he said, "OK, Shelley, I have to get serious now. I think and I hope that I want to be with you for my whole life; no, I'm not being silly, not being melodramatic, Shelley. Maybe you can think a little on this. So, yes, please, I want to meet your mum. I think maybe I want to say thank you to her because without her, I wouldn't have met you." Shelley melted, and just a few tears squeezed out, but they were happy tears.

And then it was Shelley's final, the final of the four hundred metres hurdles. There was nobody who could have beaten Shelley that day. If it had been the Olympic final, she would still have won because Shelley Steele, Shelley Jelly Belly, Shelley from the estate, Olympic finalist, was high on life. And she was in love!

There was an aura about Shelley as the athletes walked out onto the track. All seven of them sensed that there was something different about the new girl. A confidence? Maybe something more than that? Whatever it was, every single one of them wished that they possessed it!

Shelley saw it in herself, seemed that she was looking from the outside at herself ('that Shelley Steele girl') and saw an athlete brimming with confidence. She didn't assume that she would win but knew beyond doubt that if anyone did beat her, they would have had to look deep into their soul because Shelley was prepared to search her soul to the deepest level. Shelley was smiling—inside and out—waving at the crowd, as she blew kisses to her little group, TMRG all stood together. A special blown kiss for Gilly ('owe her everything, everything'). Then, on to talking to her fellow-hurdlers as they all struggled out of their tracksuits, and she wished them all luck.

Lane six this time, a couple of high leaps then settled in the blocks, lift and anticipate on "Set." Out of the blocks, body rising to upright on the first six strides, feeling good, no, feeling awesome. Lean in and snap down. *Oh God, I feel good!* Second hurdle cleared, already lane seven coming back to her, along the back-straight, fifth hurdle cleared, lane seven and eight both taken, on the bend. Spectators were actually gasping at the space between the leading girl and her chasers. Was she going to blow up? Was she going to die on her feet? Not this time—certainly not this time. Into the finish straight and Shelley's lead seemed even bigger.

Over number eight, can I hold that fifteen stride pattern, yes! And again, flying over the final barrier, break the tape, and then just like Marianne those couple of days before, kept on running towards her group, looking for Kaas, Mickey, Gilly...and then, yes, it's him! It IS him! Mr Warren! Mr Warren's here! Shelley just ran into him, put her arms around him and then burst into those happy tears.

"You came to watch me; you came to see me, Mr Warren, sir, shit! I mean Chris. Thank you, sir, thank you so much!"

"Wish I could have been here for every day, you know, but someone has to keep the British education system going!" And for some reason, that just broke them all up. "In first place in the women's four hundred metres hurdles in a time of fifty-four point three seconds—incidentally an Olympic qualifying time—representing Bath University, Shelley Steele!"

And now there was just one remaining TMRG member to run: Mickey Honey, the Duracell Bunny. Mickey went over to Chris Warren.

"Thank you, sir, thank you for coming to watch."

And very quietly so that only Mickey could hear him, "Couldn't and wouldn't have missed it, Mickey; you know all you guys are more than just a bit special to me." And if Mickey had needed any more motivation (which he didn't), then those few words from good old Mr Warren would have supplied it. Mickey held out his hand to Chris Warren.

"Thanks, Mr Warren...Chris, look I need to warm up now." As Mickey started his easy jog around the outside of the track, Shelley eased alongside him, wearing her tracksuit but still flushed from her efforts.

"All right if I do a couple of laps with you, Mickey?" Mickey grinned.

"'Course." They jogged in silence for the first lap, then Mickey asked, "So, go on, why you doing my warm-up with me?"

"Don't need a reason, do I, Mickey? Maybe I just like running with you."

"Yeah, right...and the real reason?" Shelley burst out laughing. "Really is like brother and sister then...Look, one of the guys in your five thousand is Charlie Marx; he was in Beijing with us, didn't make the final, but he's pretty good. He's up here at Lufbra doing a Master's or a PhD or something, so he's got a lot of experience…in Beijing, everyone called him 'Skid'; you know as in 'Skid Marks'."

Mickey roared. "Well, old Skid really does think he's a bit special, been to the Games, 'big-time-shoot-a-dime', all that stuff, yeah, actually a bit arrogant; he's got a great sprint, so a slow race really suits him…what he can't handle is big pressure, anyone following his break; when he can't get away from the pack, basically it's the big hurt he can't take, just thought I'd mention it to my brother…No, no, need to say thank you. I'll take it as said." Shelley squeezed Mickey's hand, gave him a quick brush kiss on the cheek and slowed to a walk while Mickey carried on running…and thinking.

"Athletes in the men's five thousand metres to the track, please." Mickey was still thinking as he pushed off his tracksuit bottoms carefully over his spikes. "Best tactics? Yeah, I know the best tactics…couple of options, I think. Plan A or plan B?"

"To your marks." Very tight on the line, shoulders nudging shoulders. The gun cracked. Caution on the first lap, and the second, everyone looking around; everyone waiting. Mickey Honey decided that he'd live up to his nickname, so the Duracell Bunny moved away from the large pack, didn't sprint but gradually increasing his pace and the pressure until he was ten metres ahead of the pursuers. The pack closed, of course, and Mickey waited until they'd settled back in and did exactly the same; pulled away to another ten-metre lead, waited until the gap was closed and did it once again. By the two thousand metre mark, the pack was split to an extent that there were only eight runners (including Mickey) in the lead group.

Skid was there, an Olympic athlete; he should be and needed to be. This was the start of his launch onto the London Games and a medal…so Skid thought and intended. And Skid knew, just knew, that Mickey Honey's efforts would tire him to the extent that he would fall apart. What he didn't know was how much the Duracell Bunny was prepared to hurt and suffer, how much he would give, how he needed to emulate the efforts and results of his group, his group.

Just over half the race done now, at six and a half laps with six to go, Mickey accelerated again; there was a group (now down to five athletes), a sigh almost, 'here he goes again, bloody idiot!'. But the bloody idiot got to his allotted two hundred metres, and this time didn't ease back. The group looked at each other, then focused on Skid Marx, 'Your call, Skid, you're the one with the experience and all the bloody chat, C'mon, what do we do?' And while the group hesitated,

Mickey Honey increased his lead to almost fifteen metres. 'He'll die the death, fall apart; 'course he will, bloody idiot!'

But Mickey Honey had absolutely no intention of falling apart. Five laps to go, still at fifteen metres; Skid had to make a move and increased his pace, trying to hold it as manageable because he knew that the stupid kid in front of him would pay for the audacious attempt and the race would be his, Skid's. Gradually, the pack with Skid leading closed on Mickey; the effort was more than Skid intended, but, 'You know, Olympic athlete, I'm prepared to suffer.' And so, Skid suffered, but Mickey Honey was prepared to suffer more, much more. As the group closed (now down to just three members) on Mickey, he raised his pace again; in truth, it wasn't that much of a raise but a raise it most certainly was, and as soon as the door was shut, the Duracell Bunny opened it again.

Now an audible groan from the three chasers; this wasn't in the script! Kid was supposed to die! Two and a half laps, one thousand metres; hurting, hurting, hurting, Mickey focused on his technique, focused on his leg-turnover, and a photo image of Lucy and Shelley seared his brain; his other half and his sister. Without realising, he strode out longer and stronger, raising the pace once more. And this time, nobody closed the gap; nobody got near. The hurt was everywhere, leading athlete and chasers.

The bell sounded, final lap, Mickey dared to snatch a look over his left shoulder as he entered the first bend. *Fucking hell, that's a big old gap! Hang tough now, just hang tough.* And Mickey Honey did indeed hang tough, more than tough enough. Skid didn't, not quite enough, with the exertions of gap-closing taking its toll, Skid was out-leaned on the line and took third behind a delighted Bath student who had been training with Gilly and Mickey for the last year.

Mickey didn't manage to emulate Marianne's or Shelley's triumphant run-through to his group; he was just too shattered. Bending over, hands on knees, chest pumping and pounding, clouds of sweat steaming up from his body. The other kid from his training group came over, hugged him.

"Thanks, Mickey, thanks for a great year's training."

Mickey managed a, "Tell Gilly, Freddy; Gilly's the mastermind." Freddy considered.

"Yeah, you're right, 'course she is…But thanks anyway, you lead the reps so much, learnt a lot this year, a lot." Mickey Honey felt pretty damn good.

"Just outside thirteen, Mickey! Just outside thirteen minutes, BUSF record easy, fantastic!" Gilly put her arms around the still-steaming shoulders, kissed him on the cheek. "Go and warm down, easy as, yeah." Mickey did as he was told, an 'easy-as' warm-down.

And it was over, the BUSF Championships were finished for another year. Gilly, Dan and two further coaches stood up as the team bus drew into Bath University car park.

"I have to say, team Bath, that you were fantastic, absolutely fantastic; a lot of wins, a lot of medals—huge amount of medals in both swimming and athletics." Gilly looked over at Dan, and track coach Jimmy Ruddle and swim coach Melissa Hugback, who all nodded. "Guys, anything to say?"

Three shakes 'no' of three heads. "OK, then, day off tomorrow, I think, yeah? Anybody who wants to have a chat about anything, literally anything, Me'n Dan, Jimmy and Melissa will be pretty much in the café by the track most of tomorrow; spin by or, if it's easier, give us a call or even check a time with us right now." And a whole bunch of students checked their meeting time with their coaches as they got off the coach. TMRG got together immediately.

"Drink anyone?" Mickey said. "Really think we deserve it, yeah." Everyone agreed. "Gilly, Dan, would love you to have a drink with us; we know that you must be shattered, but we all would love you to have a drink, maybe we might even say thank you!" And even though Gilly and Dan were more than shattered, they happily nodded their agreement.

Chapter Forty-Six
A Thousand Days

The drinks were collected and paid for; glasses were raised. "Cheers!" Thanks to Gilly and Dan, thanks to Eric and Bobby. Sighs and smiles, lots of grinning and nudging each other, lots of laughter, lots of reflection. And then a sudden silence as they all looked at Gilly and Dan. Lucy spoke. Lucy had a foot in both camps now, the running and the swimming.

"Gilly, Dan, me'n Mickey, well, me'n everybody just want to say how much we appreciate what you've done for us all, me especially as I've had a double dose of the training!" Appreciative hand-claps and smiles happen. "Without you guys—and we're not forgetting you two, Eric and Bobby for what you've done as well—we know that we wouldn't be anywhere near what we did at BUSF, so huge thank-yous; you're stars!"

"And I guess that we're supposed to say something now, are we?" Gilly smiled at the Speeding Bullet. "Well, even if we're not supposed to, we're going to talk." And they waited while Gilly took another sip of her wine. "Three years to go to the London Games, a thousand days, actually a bit more than a thousand, but let's say a thousand, yeah?"

Heads nodding agreement. "Can you imagine how good you'd be if you improved just one per cent every day till then?" Lips pursed, brains thinking… "But that's not going to happen, is it? Your times'd be down to zero… so how about one per cent every ten sessions? And that's not gonna happen either, is it? That'd be a ten per cent improvement every hundred sessions, so at the end of a thousand days, your times would have disappeared to nothing. OK, next step, one per cent improvement every hundred days? No again…or could it be? That would mean a ten per cent improvement over that thousand days' lead-in; you'd be running a sub-fifty seconds four hundred hurdles, Shelley—that would possibly make the men's final!

"Mickey, you'd be going an eleven and a half minutes, so sub-four-minute miling three times through with no rest or recovery; no, isn't going to happen either. Lucy, you'd be dropping three minutes on your most excellent swim time, so sadly, no, again. But what if we aimed for a five per cent improvement, what about that? One per cent better every two hundred days, what about that indeed? Could you improve that tiny bit—let me work it out." And they were all pretty sure that Gilly and Dan had already done all the working-out necessary. "Three seconds for every minute, that's five per cent; Shelley gives you a fifty-one something, better than current world record! Far better, Mickey, so three seconds off each of those thirteen minutes, how about a twelve thirty-five or thereabouts, puts you right into contention!"

Gilly stopped and looked at them while their minds were running away with them, imagining, imagining it all. Then she said, "Dan, help me out here."

"Gilly's so right, you guys. It's the finest of fine margins that does it. Can you imagine just how many swimmers and runners are dreaming about the Games, their Games? Loads of them hoping they're going to win. And there will be dozens, literally dozens who think they can win. But they won't, not if they just think they can win. And in those dozens, there will be some, some who don't think they can win; they KNOW they're going to win—absolutely know it beyond a shadow of a doubt...The Olympic Games Champion will be one of them." And every one of them—Shelley, Lucy, Sami, Mickey, Marianne, Kaas—every single one of them was asking deep within their souls, 'Do I have that belief? Will I get that belief?'

Dan went on, "Now I'm not saying that you need to have that belief right now, that would be crazy...but what I am saying is that, as the Games get closer, then you have to, you must, get that 'I will win' belief. That belief will make the difference of winning gold and not medalling at all." Dan looked at them and then smiled. "Big call, isn't it?"

Nods and smiles. "Yeah, huge call, now I've known you guys for, what? Eight years since you were eleven years old—and that's a lifetime ago! But— and I hope you'll take this and believe me—I knew immediately that there was something different about you all. Chris had told me about you all—sorry, Marianne and Kaas—but you're the same, even though I didn't get to know you till the Holland trip and not properly even then, but this last year...You have it; you have that magic spark, that spark that makes the difference, the big difference between being an Olympic medallist—hopefully gold—or an also-

378

ran…and you guys are NOT also-rans, never in a million years." Dan smiled over at Eric and Bobby. "You gonna do the stats for me, you two? Don't need to ask, do I? I know you love crunching those numbers!"

Eric and Bobby smiled right back. "And then there's tactics, race strategy, if you like. Maybe not so much in swimming—but there definitely is—maybe a little less in the sprints on the track compared to you distance guys—but again, definitely. Even pace throughout? Sprint to start and try to blow the opposition away? Sit in and hope to outsprint everyone? All worth thinking about. Big old cliché now, 'race to your strengths but train to your weaknesses', three years to go, guys, three years that will go like three weeks; believe me, I've been there." Dan turned to Shelley. "Shelley, anything about your Games? Any tips from the top?"

"Dunno about tips from the top, Dan…for me, it all happened so quickly. One day, I was this little girl dreaming about it; the next, I was there, actually there. I got a bit nervous, but if I'm honest, it was so quick that it was all excitement and thinking how glad I was just to be at the Games…and then, after the final, then it was a bit of a comedown, but Gilly got me through it…and then Kaas." Shelley smiled over at Kaas. "Go on, superstar, what about your Games? Tell us about them."

"Swimming's a bit different to athletics, in as much as you can get there a bit younger than you guys running—that right, Dan?—but it's changing. Nearly everyone who's class is a pro-athlete now; pro-athlete as in pro-swimmer. So, no one's going to need to pack it all in because they have to get a 'real' job, not like it used to be back in the day. If I can be as honest as Shelley, then I think in my heart I knew it was my apprenticeship, like learning on the job, and boy, did I learn! Come London, I'll be in a much better place…"

Kaas turned to the Speeding Bullet. "Dan, you've taught me so, so much this last year. I'd think I was letting you down if I wasn't totally focusing in getting a medal." And Kaas had the good grace to blush. "You guys letting me and Marianne come over and join you, can't thank you enough, all of you…changed my life, you know, that right, Marianne?" Marianne didn't, couldn't look up but nodded her head 'yes'. And then Kaas said, "A happy place isn't just geography, you know? A happy place is the people in it."

"Wow, that's pretty impressive, Kaas; might have to use that."

"One last thing, if I may, sort of something that worked for me, yeah? Every day, every session, whenever the doubts start surfacing, this is your mantra to repeat, 'This is who I am; this is what I do', sort of helps to keep focused, helps you to know exactly who you are…enough, I think I need bed."

And every head was spinning with the words, 'This is who I am, this is what I do', again and again and again.

Part Eight
Breakthrough

Chapter Forty-Seven
Back in London,
Back to the Estate

"Mum, this is Kaas; we're at uni together. Mum, is it OK if Kaas stays for a few days? He's from Holland and never been to London before." Shelley's mum was smiling with eyes that knew everything as she took the bunch of flowers that Kaas presented to her.

"'Course Kaas can, Shelley. I'll make up the sofa as a bed…Kaas, we don't have too much room here; hope you'll be OK on the sofa?"

"Thank you, Mrs Steele. I'll be absolutely fine; thank you for having me…Mrs Steele, may I say something?"

Shelley's mum nodded. "Mrs Steele, I don't mean to sound rude…but…you look more like Shelley's sister than her mum. I'm sorry, is that rude?"

"Not rude at all, Kaas, not rude at all." She smiled. "And flattery will get you absolutely everywhere!" And Shelley knew that it was all going to be all right.

*****

"Mum, Dad, this is my friend, Marianne; we're at university together. Would it be all right if Marianne stayed with us for a few days? She's never been to London before. Marianne's training for the London Olympics, same as I am, even though she's going for either the two-hundred or the four-hundred. We do a lot of sessions together at Bath. Please mum, dad, would that be OK?"

"Height of luxury here, Marianne; we'd love you to stay with us. Maybe you can teach Lucy to speak English as well as you do?"

Marianne and Lucy laughed out loud, and Marianne hugged Lucy's mum… and then her dad as well.

"Lucy, Marianne in with you, OK? Can you sort out the bedclothes and everything?" Nodded 'yeses' and then into the bedroom.

*****

They all met the next day; all of TMRG, Alisha and Joshi, even JoJo made it to get together with the Bath contingent. An anxious Kaas waited to see how JoJo would approach him. JoJo walked over, put her arms around him, kissed him gently on the cheek and whispered, "It never happened, OK? Nothing happened…we're not going to talk about, not one bit; it was a different life then. One thing Kaas, just one thing…you be good to Shelley." Kaas sighed with relief.

"It's a bit weird, innit? Being back in London like…don't get me wrong, really nice to be back, see everyone, 'specially my mum, but still a bit weird, you know?"

"It's called growing up, Mickey. I come back from uni all the time, Imperial's only just down the road, but, yeah, it feels like I'm growing out of it." Joshi looked over at his sister.

"Alisha, that about right?"

"Yeah, it is, but right now, I just want to share time with my best friends…and my best new friends as well!" Alisha went over to Marianne and Kaas. "Hello, you! Hope Shelley told you exactly what our estate's like. Did she mention the very English word 'shithole'?"

"Yes! First thing she told me." Kaas looked over at Shelley and smiled, and her heart was singing. "Listen, I know I'm the new boy here, but are we actually going to do what we said we'd do?" And there was a group hesitation because they were going to look at their future. And that was pretty scary. Alisha took charge.

"Yes, we are because I'm now a council member for the London Borough of Newham, and I'm incredibly important!" This broke them up as well.

It was a short bus ride, and then they were there, Stratford, site of the 2012 London Olympic Games. It was still very much a building site, but a site that already had a structure, already had some of the event venues finished. They showed their passes a little self-consciously, the Bath contingent with 'Olympic contenders' printed and the others, courtesy of Alisha and her Borough position ("See, told you I was important.") and now wearing their bright yellow safety jackets and hard-hats, were free to wander around. There were only two venues they wanted to see: the athletics stadium and the swimming pool. All the Olympic football matches would be played at the various Premier League grounds, which pleased JoJo greatly.

"Jeez, man, look at that!" Mickey spoke for all of them, mouths wide-open, gazing from high up in the stands. "Jeez…can you imagine running here, really imagine it?"

"This is who I am; this is what I do, so yes, I can totally imagine it. This is my dream, always been my dream; now all I have to do is make it come true." Shelley spoke the words, but any one of them could have said them.

"Better close your mouths, you lot, gonna breathe in a lot of flies if you don't, and you'll get ill," Joshi said. "It's a medical condition known as 'tene os clausum', and I should know because I'm almost a doctor. I'm at Imperial College, London University, don't you know?" Sami took the bait.

"All right, Dr Joshi, what the hell does 'tene os clausum' mean exactly?"

"Good question, Sami, loosely translated it means 'keep your mouth shut!' See, told you I was almost a doctor!"

"Missed you, Joshi, you too, Alisha, and you, of course, JoJo; don't get me wrong, Bath Uni is great; it really is…Kaas, OK if I repeat what you said?" A nod from Kaas to Mickey. "Kaas said that a happy place wasn't where you were, Kaas said that a happy place was actually the people in it. I reckon I'll go along with that!" They were smiling and laughing, a few hugs, even a few kisses. How lucky to be in a happy place! How lucky to be surrounded by good people!

And then just a short walk to the pool. This was Kaas' territory. Lucy was looking on and wishing and hoping, and she knew that it was a mixture of both, and she knew that Shelley's 'dream come true' was a big call. Could she do it? Could she? Truly? Black girl swimming? Role model? Could she really do it? She laughed at herself, laughed at herself inside; she hadn't even bloody qualified for the track, and she was dreaming about swimming! Get real, girl, get real. Kaas was pointing out details of the pool that nobody else had even realised were important.

"Ten lanes, no one swims the outside lanes, cuts down turbulence; no deep end or shallow end, every swimmer has same stuff to deal with, rebound from bottom can be significant, see the lane ropes? How thick they are? Cuts out wash and turbulence even more." Tiny, tiny details, all adding up to the correct answer.

"Guys, coffee time? I'm ready, this thing just got real." And it was very real, indeed.

Gilly and Dan were back in London the following week. Gilly—happily back with Chris—wasn't seen by anyone for the first few days as she relished her time with her much-missed husband. And when they did all meet up again, it was down at Vicky Park track in the shadow of the new Olympic stadium.

"Time to get started, I think; a few of those thousand days gone already." Gilly smiled at them all, including the seven watchers, Joshi and Alisha, Kaas, Eric and Bobby, the Speeding Bullet and Mr Warren. "Altogether today, nothing desperate, just re-establishing the habit. OK, easy jog warm-up, everyone." Around the track on the grass inside, lots of laughing, lots of jokes.

Lots of teasing and mickey-taking, the occasional fart. Mickey said, "How dare you fart in front of my girlfriend!"

The group responded, "Sorry, didn't know it was Lucy's turn!" Shrieks of laughter. Everybody loving it. Going past the observers who all joined in with the mickey-taking, and they all knew that it was a badge of honour, an earned tribute. Lots of stretching, individually, then with a partner, lots more laughter. Spikes on, bottom of the home straight, six strides with a jog back recovery.

It felt good to be back. 'This is who I am; this is what I do.' A steady interval session suited to all of them. Shelley and Marianne were hanging tough on the final four hundred metre rep. Warm-down. "Guys, a quick word." They all waited. "It's the Vicky Park Club Champs at the weekend. The club would absolutely love you to take part; they're so proud of you all…Sort of heroes and role models, reasonable?"

There was a subdued silence. Gilly had been anticipating it. "And the other thing is, I think it would be a good idea, a really good idea to not race your specialist event; it takes the pressure off of you, and it takes the pressure of the club guys, sound reasonable again?" Lots of smiles now; the pressure was lifted.

"And what events do you reckon, Gilly? I'm more than sure that you have suggestions," Mickey questioned.

"Well, what I think is that all of you should race the eight hundred metres, tough move-up for you two." Gilly smiled at Shelley and Marianne. "Oh, Marianne, I've got you guest membership of the club, wouldn't want you to miss out, and then a step down for you three," a motion towards Lucy, Sami and Mickey. "Chance for doing some serious speedwork. Now look, I know you've all done an eight hundred before either in training or in racing, but when you're on the line for an eight hundred, it can be the toughest event. A lot of the old middle-distance run coaches, Harry Wilson, Frank Horwill and others, reckoned that everybody should race an eight hundred at least once a season just to feel the hurt...all OK with that?" Nodded agreements. "Oh, and Shelley? One last thing, the club are putting on a heptathlon on the same day, a few invited athletes, thought maybe, just maybe, you might want to enter, to give it a go, nothing to lose...and you still get to run an eight hundred."

Lots of comments, lots of 'Oh, you're my hero, Shelley. Shelley, did you really go to the Olympics? Oh, you must be famous, and you're a sponsored athlete, that's really famous!' Shelley took the ribbing, and knew that yes, she had to enter the heptathlon. It was settled.

There were just ten days between that first session back and the Club Championships. Shelley was desperately aware that she knew nothing—absolutely nothing—about the heptathlon.

"Gilly, need your help here...please, feel a bit out of my depth to be honest. 'Course I'll do it, but need to know a bit more."

"OK, seven events, Shelley, three runs and two each of jumps and throws. There's a set order of events, and it's a two-day event, except in the case of the club competition, which is all in one day. The order goes like this: first off is hundred metres hurdles, so you'll get a flying start, then high jump, shot put and two hundred metres—that would be the usual first day—then long jump, javelin, and finish off with an eight hundred metre run when everyone's shattered, even more so if it's just one day. Does that make sense?"

Shelley nodded, already repeating the order to herself and committing it to memory. "And then, the important bit, you get points for each event, the better the performance the more points. Whoever it was who sorted the points table out originally wanted the events to mirror each other, so an average performance in, say, javelin and hurdles would get the same points. Make sense, Shelley?"

Another nod and a grin this time. Shelley was just getting used to the idea of a heptathlon, and it wasn't too bad, not too bad at all. "So let's look at your best event, hurdles and one of the throws, javelin, yeah? To get a thousand points, you'd need a 13.85 for the hurdles so you'd be way above that to start, but for a thousand in the javelin, it'd take a throw of over fifty-seven metres...Reckon you'd make that?" Shelley burst out laughing.

"To be honest, Gilly, if I got over twenty metres, I'd be dancing in the air!"

"Oh, I think we may be looking at double that distance, Shelley. I really do. You pick up techniques and skills really quickly. I'll never forget the first time you went over the hurdles and look where that led." And now Shelley did start remembering…the way she'd learnt high and long jump technique, by watching and then practising it while the memory was still sharp, even the shot put with the metal ball tightly into the neck and a fast straightening of the arm with the elbow out high and wide and using the rotation of the body to get some strength and power behind it, and now the memories were razor-sharp. And so was Shelley's brain.

"Gilly, this for real, isn't it?" The realisation was hitting home. "You think I can, don't you Gilly. You really think I can…me, heptathlon, London Games, really?"

"Yeah, for real, can you imagine? Hundred thousand spectators in that stadium, everyone willing you on, everyone getting behind you, local girl, London girl, very pretty London girl with a little bit of attitude, everyone thinking back on Beijing, remembering Denise Lewis in Sydney, half the crowd already in love with you and the other just about to be; yeah, I'd say this is for real, wouldn't you? Shelley, I'm going to introduce you to the guy who looks after the throwers at the club; he's a bit old-fashioned, bit straight, to be honest, but you know the old 'heart of gold' thing?"

A smile and a nod. "Well, Justus has that heart of gold. He came over from the old East Germany when it was collapsing and fell in love with London, fell in love with the whole country, actually, gives all of his time to the club; it's his life. Respect him, Shelley, and he can give you the world; he can give you the world that you'll want to live in for the rest of your life." And that was it for Shelley. How could so many people be kind to her? How did she ever get so lucky…but she knew that; it had all started with Mr Warren, and then Gilly and then Dan. And now she was here, and now she was very, very close. And not unnaturally, Shelley Steele, girl from the slums, had tears in her eyes and hope.

"Justus, can I introduce you to Shelley? This is the girl I told you about. I know you will have seen her on TV at the last Games, Justus; she's got something special, and you know I never say that unless it's a hundred per cent true."

"Ah, so, Shelley, my name is Justus Brandt. I know your name already. You are famous, me, not so much." Shelley smiled, uncertain how to react. "Shelley, my name is Brandt; you know the meaning in English?"

Shelley shook her head 'no.' "Brandt means 'fire' or 'burn'. I have that fire within me to try to make athletes realise their talents. I burn with that desire. My good friend Gilly here tells me that you have that fire, Shelley; Gilly tells me that you are special. Are you special, Shelley?" Justus Brandt's stare was piercing. Shelley felt that he knew all about her.

"No, sir (the 'sir' was instinctive), I'm not special, not special at all, but...the people who've helped me, the people who've coached me, advised me, believed in me, they're the special ones." Justus Brandt's face was wreathed in smiles.

"So, Shelley, now I think that you are special, very special. You put others before yourself; you are grateful, so yes, you are special...And for you, Shelley, my name is Justus, not sir. Most people call me Mr Brandt to begin with, but for you, I think that Justus is good." Shelley knew that she had passed some unwritten test.

Shelley spent a little part of most days' training sessions with Justus Brandt in those eight remaining days before her first heptathlon. Justus didn't attempt to do too much; he knew that wouldn't work, that boredom would set in. He worked on one, maybe two points of technique only, and the next day, he would reinforce that before introducing another point, and so it continued, day after day. There was a little jumps practice as well, reminding herself of stride number on the long jump, curved run-up and hip-lift on the high jump. And then it was time, heptathlon time. There was more of a crowd than expected; it was only a club championship, but rumours of invited athletes and the opportunity to see some home-grown stars attracted the curious and the journalists. One in particular, David Caxton of the Times. Sixteen athletes in the heptathlon, including two under-twenty-three internationals looking for a run-out without too much pressure. Quite possibly a wrong assumption.

Chapter Forty-Eight
A Day Out in Vicky Park

Kaas had got back to the flat just after eight that morning; he'd been to the local swimming pool and talked his way into the early morning club session; he unlocked the door and let himself in.

"Good morning, Mrs Steele, may I make you a cup of tea or coffee?"

"That would be lovely, Kaas, thank you." They sat in the tiny kitchen, a comfortable happy quietness between them. "What are you doing today, Kaas?"

"Going over to Victoria Park to watch Shelley and the others in their club champs. Marianne's racing as well, so I'd get thrown on the rubbish pile if I didn't go. Mrs Steele, why don't you come with me? It would be my pleasure and honour." There was silence that seemed to stretch almost to eternity but was a few seconds only…

"I don't know, Kaas; I really don't know. You know I've never seen my little girl race, not in real life, seen her on the telly, of course, and that was magical. But in real life…not sure if I'm honest. I don't want to be, I dunno, the bad luck mum or something. She's done so well, and I don't want to take the chance of me being the one who breaks the angel's good luck charm. You know, if Shelley sees me and gets all nervous…Kaas, Shelley isn't as confident as she gives out, you know; there's still a lot of little girl insecurity in there…Kaas, you won't hurt her, will you?" Kaas leant over the small table, reached out and took Shelley's mum's hand, smiled at her and squeezed her hand.

"Mrs Steele, I would never, never in a million years, hurt your daughter. Shelley means the absolute world to me; in fact, Shelley is my world. I can't imagine being without her…Is that all right, Mrs Steele? Mrs Steele, please don't cry. I didn't mean to upset you, honestly. Are you OK?" Mrs Steele wiped her eyes.

"Sorry, Kaas, just an old lady being silly and sentimental." Kaas interrupted.

"Stop right there, Mrs Steele; stop right there! You are most certainly NOT an old lady. I was serious when I said that you looked like Shelley's sister. OK, it may have been flattery, but I said it because it's true. And as for being silly and sentimental, well, if you're not allowed to worry about your own daughter…"

"Thank you, Kaas. Kaas, if I did come along, would I be able to find somewhere to watch from where Shelley couldn't see me? Now I really think about it, I would love to see Shelley race!" The deal was done. They walked out of the estate, a few of the hoodies were there, not early-risers, rather stay out-all-nighters. They watched Shelley's mum with Kaas. Not one of them said anything; they'd learnt not to mess with Shelley's mum.

*****

"Gilly, Dan, Mr Warren, sorry, Chris! May I introduce you to Mrs Steele, Shelley's mum."

Handshakes, words of congratulation, a murmured, "I did meet you at a junior school parents' evening, Mr Warren; seems like an eternity ago," and then a "Thank you all for everything you've done for Shelley." Shelley's mum was very, very close to tears then. Kaas explained what Mrs Steele wanted to do, how she wanted—needed—to watch without being noticed; they were sworn to silence—a silence with a few giggles. Dan sat with her.

"Thought you might like a bit of company, Mrs Steele?" He smiled. "Bit weird being out of your comfort zone, isn't it? I'm still learning about all this track stuff…Mrs Steele, I have to tell you that Shelley is a wonderful girl, quite honestly one of the nicest people I've ever met; she's an absolute credit to, you must be so proud." Mrs Steele was close to tears again.

"Thank you, Dan; she adores you, you know…Dan is it all right if you call me Angie, as in Angela? Would make me much happier."

"Angie…done deal!" And they shook hands for the second time in ten minutes. "Look, there's Shelley!" Whistles blowing, marshals marshalling, organised chaos as the sixteen heptathletes assembled near the hurdles start. Shelley was in heat two, and everyone was watching the girl who'd come so close to an Olympic medal just one year ago. Lane four, 'set', lift, bang, go.

"Oh my God!" Angie Steele's mouth dropped open. *My little girl streets ahead! How can she be so good?* As Shelley crossed the line a full five metres in front, Angie turned to Dan, "I had no idea, absolutely no idea…how can she do that? How can she be so good?"

"Talent, of course, an amazing amount of hard work, training when others are dropping out, listening, learning, never giving up…and also having a mum who cares." And the tears were very close again.

"It's called 'Sisu', Angie; it's a Finnish word; all the kids know the word. I think it was Gilly who taught them it, or maybe the teachers at secondary school. There's no real translation into English; it's a mixture of guts, determination, bloody-mindedness, never even thinking of giving up."

"Yes, that's my Shelley, especially the bloody-mindedness!" And now the tears were long gone. "What's next, Dan?"

"High jump, I think." Dan checked his programme. "Yes, it's the high jump." Then over the tannoy, "Leading the invitation heptathlon after one event is our own Shelley Steele, in her specialist event, the one hundred metres hurdles. Shelley's time of 13.45 gives her one thousand and fifty points on the Ubrich International scoring table. This is Shelley's first ever heptathlon; we wish her well in her new events to come. For those spectators following the heptathlon rather than the club championship events, we draw your attention now to the high jump."

There were two high jump fans side by side. Two groups of athletes acknowledged their names when called and shuffled to the appropriate sides.

"Hey, Shell, nice hurdling, girl!" said Denise Smith ("Call me Denny, please!") and Flossie Saintiemme ("Call me Florence just once and I'll suck you in and blow you out in bubbles!"), the two under-23 GB heptathletes. Shelley had been on a couple of trips with them as she was coming through the ranks and had watched them gradually move from their original events, Denny long jump and Flossie shot and discus, into heptathlon.

Quick kisses and hugs, Shelley had had a laugh with them, loved their sense of dark humour. Shelley had also intervened when a drunken athlete from an East European country had got into a rant about black girls representing Great Britain, and when the white girl had fronted up to him in front of Denny and Flossie, they'd been friends ever since.

"So, this it, giiiiirl? Gonna move into our territory?" Flossie gently edged her hip into Shelley's, as if to move her away, and then her face broke into smiles.

"Dunno 'bout that, Flor-ence," Shelley emphasised the correct name and broke it into two separate syllables.

"You'll do fine, Shelley, just fine." Flossie rubbed Shelley's arm. "Yeah, you're gonna do just fine."

"Ladies, please, starting height one metre twenty, going up in five centimetres to one-forty and then three centimetres from there on. Come in at whatever height you want, and let me know if you're going to pass a height." There were only a couple who came in at 1.20m and then both opted out of 1.25m and 1.30m. At 1.40m, eight athletes opted to jump, two failed all three attempts. Shelley came in at 1.43m cleared easily, high arch and into the crash-mats; opting out at 1.46m, Shelley watched three more jumpers fail. Denny and Flossie entered the competition at 1.49m and cleared easily along with Shelley while a further three athletes watched the high jump bar crash to the ground.

Eight remaining, bar set at 1.52m, first time clearance for Shelley, Denny and Flossie—high-fives all around—now down to just five. Up to 1.55m, Shelley nervous now, personal best height if she managed and she did, easily. One more failure; the three favourites still in along with Andi Solomonides, a clubmate of Shelley. At 1.58m, Andi and Flossie found the mountain too steep, now just Denny and Shelley, first time clearance for Denny, second time going over for Shelley.

Shelley felt no pressure at all; none. This was all bonus, first ever heptathlon competition, no one expected anything...or, did they? Already seven hundred points in the bag with the 1.58m jump, Shelley started her curved run-up, lifted her right arm high...and watched the high jump bar crash to the ground. Following her, Denny cleared first time. Second attempt for Shelley, same result, bar settling on the pink take-off area. Oh well, not bad. Denny came over.

"Shelley? Listen, you're lifting your guide arm just a tiny bit too slowly. Trust me, you need to be more dynamic; it makes a big difference. Final jump at this height, what's to lose?"

Denny smiled and squeezed Shelley's shoulder, then demonstrated her words. "Trust me, all right?" Ninety seconds before her final attempt, Shelley was simulating her final approach and steps, bringing that right arm more quickly with each practice. "Thirty seconds, Shelley," said the jumps judge. Total focus now, run fast but controlled, into the curve, so close to the bar, hip swivel, thrust that right arm high...and clear! Clear at 1.61m! Over again at 1.64m on second attempt and finally failure at 1.67m but not far off eight hundred points in the bag. Two events done, five to go. Shelley Steele leading.

"Denny, Denny…how come? What if I'd beaten you? Why did you help me? Never had that before in a competition."

"Heptathlon's different, Shell; we all think that we're in a special club, you know? Not quite us against the world, but we definitely have attitude…and you have attitude, Shell, and I mean that as compliment. We help each other even in competition; it's what we do. You stay in heptathlon and you'll be doing exactly the same…and Shell, me 'n Flossie will never forget the way you stood up for us and fronted that idiot back in Belgrade…that was guts, pure guts."

"Twenty minutes break, ladies, then shot put." Shelley drank some water then went over to Justus and Gilly.

"Any last-minute tips, Justus?"

"Yes, Shelley, there are. I think you must mentally rehearse before you get into the circle. You must see yourself with that shot, see yourself as if from the outside, and then you must go through one by one in your mind the techniques and the skills that we have worked on, you understand?" Shelley nodded. "And then there is a second part. I want you to get into the circle without the shot and I want you to do everything that you would do but do it without the ball in your hand, you understand?"

Shelley nodded. Sometimes it was good to have someone whom you trusted to tell exactly what to do. Shelley went and sat in the little shade that there was. Closed her eyes and visualised her action and technique. She saw herself go through the correct motions, everything as perfect as she could make it. She could even sense the atmosphere, saw the scenario in colour, could even smell it, felt her hand touch the iron, the pressure on her fingers as she moved it into her neck, watched herself rotate and explode. And visualised it again and again. Three times through.

"What's she doing, Dan? Why isn't she warming up with that metal ball thing like everyone else is?"

"I'd bet a lot of money that Shelley knows exactly what's she's doing, Angie. She's going through it in her mind. This stuff is pretty new to her, and she will have checked it out with Gilly and the throws coach, Justus…just trust her…Angie. Would you like a coffee?"

"Thanks, Dan, that would be lovely." Angie thought, *What an absolute gentleman.*

Shelley walked over to the shot put circle, stepped over the rim, closed her eyes for an instant and then opened them, went into the semi-crouch position, moved her spread hand into her neck, checked that her elbow was parallel to her hand, powered the imaginary iron shot onto the grass and checked the imaginary distance. Shelley went through the same procedure once again and finally did it for real, watched the landing between the chalk lines. 'Hmm, just over ten metres, so be it.'

Two pools each of eight athletes, the two shot put circles just ten metres apart, every athlete immediately aware of what her competitors were doing, the distances they were achieving. Claps, whistles and cheers following each attempt ('yeah, like an exclusive club, want to be a part of this').

Shelley into the circle, total focus now, hearing nothing, correct position checked, go! Tapes out, measured, ten metres seventy-two, OK improvement on warm-up. Focus on next effort.

Repeat whole procedure, already have a distance, so can go a little harder, ten ninety-eight, better!

Last try, go for it? Try what Justus had said? Why not? Everything a bonus. Trying for the rotation technique, done it a couple of times in training, nothing to lose, concentrate, concentrate, concentrate! Full spin done, follow through hard, stay inside the circle! Stay inside! Eleven twenty! Yes, bloody, yes! Three bloody PBs, good on you, Shell! Even made six hundred points on that last one! Three events done, four to go, Shelley Steele with two thousand four hundred and thirty-six points maintains her lead.

Two hundred metres now, how quickly was this day going? Shelley was caught in the atmosphere. All the girls to chat with if she wanted, but nobody would interrupt if they could see you focusing on the event. *I love this, I really love this!*

"Two hundred, heat one, ladies, please." Shelley in heat two with the eight leading on points at this stage. Denny and Flossie there as well, of course. "You are under starters orders."

"Take your marks." The concentration was second nature now. "Set." Lean on fingers, press back against the blocks, lift that butt, girl, don't wait for the gun, anticipate it! Out clean, throw those arms back, lift on first eight strides, lengthen out now, into the bend so quickly, outside lanes coming back, into the stretch, nobody in front as the lanes unstagger, just focus on you, other lanes don't matter, crowd noise somewhere in the distance, final fifty, five seconds, lean, break, over, yes! Denny second, Flossie third, and their shared delight for Shelley was equal to what it would have been had they won.

"Heptathlon two hundred metres heat two, Shelley Steele, twenty-four point two, Denny Smith, twenty-four point eight, Florence Saintiemme twenty-five point one."

*****

Dan looked at Angie Steele and smiled.

"Glad you came, Angie? Happy to see your little girl run?"

"Dan, I honestly had no idea; this is amazing…Thank you so much for looking after me; look, I'm sure you've got better places to be, I'm fine now." Dan smiled again.

"Got nowhere else to go, Angie, love to sit with you if you don't mind?"

"That would be lovely."

*****

"Nine hundred and sixty points, Shelley! Nine-sixty! Great performance, that'd be the end of day one in most competitions, grab a rest while you can, long jump's up next," Gilly said. "Got to run, Shelley, eight hundred's up next, men and women. Let's see how our novices get on." The four of them, Lucy and Mickey, Sami and Marianne, were warming up together on the inside of the track, then spikes on and strides on the back-straight.

"Thoughts, Mickey?"

"All these guys will have loads more basic speed than me, so the only thing I can do is to make them hurt so much that they won't be able to use the speed, gonna have to run it out of them right from the start…might die the death big-time, but I sure ain't going down without a fight." Lucy and Sami were nodding in agreement. Marianne was quiet, working out her own race tactics.

"Men's eight hundred 'A' race." Names were checked, lanes had already been allocated. Mickey Honey in lane one staring at the seven vests in front of him, 'Let's do it.' "To your marks." Lean forward, right elbow pushed back ready to thrust forward. Off! No pacing now for Mickey Honey, go out at ninety-nine per cent, see who breaks, see who hangs on. Off of the stagger into the back-straight and Mickey had a seven or eight metre lead; the pursuers were glancing at each other. 'This isn't meant to happen! Bloody distance runner leading.'

396

But the bloody distance runner kept on leading, through the first lap, hearing the bell, hearing the 'fifty, fifty-one' through the blurring hurt. 'Jeez that's fast!' hang tough, Mickey; c'mon you can do this; you're good at hurting. And the pursuers were catching but only a little. Trying now to draw on their speed, they found that a large part of that speed had been run out of them, and with still two hundred metres to run, the spirit disappeared along with the speed. Mickey Honey broke the tape in a lonely splendour with a fifteen-metre gap.

Gilly, Eric and Bobby all looked down at their stopwatches. Gilly shook her head slowly. 'One forty-eight four, never even done a competitive eight hundred before', Eric and Bobby looked up and smiled.

"Ladies, eight hundred, please." Every athlete had watched the men's race, seen what had happened and now looked at Lucy and Sami; history about to repeat itself? Both distance runners like Mickey, even trained together, same coach, but what do we do if they do go out silly fast? And that was always the question, any place, any time, any situation, the unanswerable question, 'what if?', and it only became answerable when it happened. Marianne had already made her decision, nothing to lose…Tracksuits stripped off, onto the track, too much doubt, too much wonder in five runners' heads, no doubt at all in Lucy, Sami, Marianne.

Off from the gun and it seemed as if the field waited for Lucy to take the lead, which Lucy did but only because the pace was ridiculously slow. At one-fifty, Lucy nudged Sami and started to stride out. Sami tucked in behind her, and Lucy gradually upped the pace, faster and faster as lap one fell away, still accelerating, still Sami tucked in behind. Marianne was sitting in the middle of the pack some five metres behind the two leaders as they took the bell, "Sixty-three, sixty-four," Sami went past Lucy and accelerated further and gradually pulled away from Lucy; Marianne sat tight, watched the gap open and knew she didn't have the stamina to even think about closing down with four hundred metres still to run.

Two hundred metres to go now, Sami leading by three metres from Lucy, Lucy six metres in front of the pack, into the bend and Marianne starts to use her base speed, moves into third and so it stays as they cross the line; first, second, third.

"Nice running, ladies." Gilly is all smiles. "Two-eleven, you guys, and a superb two-fifteen, Marianne, not bad for a sprinter!"

"Had a good coach, Gilly, thank you." Marianne laughed. "Lucy, Sami, warm-down?" And the three jogged off throwing a wave at Shelley measuring out her run-up for the long jump.

*****

"They only get three jumps in a heptathlon, Angie; if it were a straight long jump competition, then everyone gets three, and the six best get another three, so six in all. So, they don't need so much energy, maybe a little less stress, but if you make a mess of the first jump, then the pressure's really on, even seen it in major games."

"But Shelley'll be fine, yeah, Dan? There's no pressure on her in a heptathlon, is there?"

"I don't think Shelley's competitive mindset would allow there to be no pressure, Angie; she'll want to win, believe me." They were very comfortable in each other's company, the mum and the coach brought together by the athlete, and Angie Steele was so happy that she'd allowed Kaas to persuade her, and so happy that Dan had given his day to calm her nerves.

*****

"Couple of run-throughs, ladies, need to get going." Two long jump pits almost side by side, athletes checking their strides, moving their markers backwards or forwards, and then checking again…and again. Whistle blows, runway clears, first athletes up. 'Safety first, get a legal distance, then go for it.' Every one of them was thinking it, but Shelley more than most; it was still so new to her. She thought back to the competition in Amsterdam; was that really eight years ago? Where did that time go? Where did that little girl go? She'd made mistakes there, but she'd learnt a lot as well. The little girl was all grown-up, but inside, Shelley was still very much that little girl. On the run-up now, level with her marker, focus on the run, accelerate through, good take-off…yes, good jump! And then Shelley looked back and saw the red flag. Foul! No, impossible! She went back to the judges, ready to question and then saw the scuffed plasticine just half a centimetre over the take-off board, shit!

Waiting for her second attempt, Shelley moved her marker back a centimetre, then a further centimetre—better be safe. Here we go! Phew, made it! Not a great jump, 4 metres 95 centimetres, maybe 540, 550 points, not good enough. Third and final attempt, this one we go for! Still holding the same marker, Shelley accelerated away, feeling good on the run, on the take-off, in the air…and land, fall forward, that's got to be near six…yes! Yes! Over six! And then the inevitable red flag lifted and elation descended to despair. *I'll never be a fucking heptathlete, let me stay with hurdles at least I'm good at that, messed up four hundred points there, fucking hopeless.*

"Everyone gets it some time, Shelley." Denny had her arm around Shelley's shoulders. "D'you think me'n Flossie haven't mangled it? 'Course we have. Lift yourself up, girl, two events to go."

"With just the javelin and eight-hundred metres remaining, Denise Smith has taken the lead, Shelley Steele now in second place and Florence Saintiemme in third."

*****

"What does that mean, Dan?"

"It means that Shelley has to lift herself, has to think forward and not backwards; she lost a lot of points; she'll be feeling down…could be interesting." Dan looked over and softly squeezed Angie's wrist. "Angie, if you keep watching Shelley at these events, you'll have to get used to the ups and downs. I've been around international sport for almost a couple of decades now, competing and coaching, and my stomach still gets knotted when I watch my swimmers, and Shelley, of course…it goes with the territory. Still want to watch?"

"You know I do, couldn't walk away now…Dan, thanks for being with me today; explaining everything made it OK." Dan smiled.

"My pleasure, you're very welcome…" He hesitated, as if he were going to say something else, but no.

*****

High elbow and fast arm, and as you release, throw your hip forward, Justus' advice was resonating in Shelley's brain. *Don't overcomplicate it.* Shelley's first throw was safe, target achieved, albeit twenty-two metres, twenty-four on the second and a big increase to twenty-nine on the final throw. In a way, it was an

399

awakening for Shelley; she knew she was a novice, but those two performances on long-jump and javelin reinforced it. She knew that she had a lot to learn—change 'a lot' to 'massive amount'—but she was dispirited, down. The hill seemed a lot steeper than a couple of weeks ago. Flossie and Denny were great, supportive, understanding, but it wasn't enough. Three years to the Games? Forget that for a game of soldiers, fucking heptathlon, hate it!

"With just, the final event to go in the heptathlon, the eight hundred metres, the lead board has changed again. After her superb javelin throw, Flossie Saintiemme leads with Denny Smith in second and Shelley Steele in third. The current points standing is…"

There was a hesitation on the tannoy. "Flossie Saintiemme 4452 points, Denny Smith 4412 points and Shelley Steele 4321 points. With the points counting at around seven seconds for each 100 points in the eight hundred metres, it looks a very tall order for anyone to unseat the two front-runners. Heptathlon eight hundred metres goes in one hour at five this afternoon."

*****

"Dan, what does that mean, please? Please, tell me."

"OK, Shelley needs to run the eight hundred around seven seconds quicker than Denny and eleven seconds quicker than Flossie if she's going to win, and that is such a tough call." Angie Steele made a tough call, a really tough call…

"And I bet she's dying inside; she'll be thinking of everyone she thinks she's let down and she hasn't let anyone down. Oh shit—sorry, Dan—I'm going down to see her…Dan, will you come with me, please, please?"

"Of course, I will."

*****

"Mum, Mum! I didn't know you were here, oh, Mum…I'm so crap at this, dunno why I started it." Gilly smiled and stayed silent. "Mum, how come? How come you're here?"

"It was Kaas, darling, Kaas. We were having a coffee this morning, and he sort of persuaded me to come, Shelley. I've loved it, every second. Can't believe I haven't come to see you properly before. I'm not going to miss you again…Shelley darling, you're certainly not crap. Dan's been telling me all about

400

this heptathlon stuff, couldn't believe it! No, you're not crap, first time out? Shell, you're amazing. Last race, isn't it? Tell me again, four hundred metres or something?"

"Mum." Shelley smiled. "It's eight hundred metres, and I really ain't too good at that."

"No, darling, you'll be fantastic, trust me." Quite ridiculously, Shelley did trust her mum. Dan Bullet had just one thing to say.

"Just be you, Shelley, just be you." And Shelley Steele was just that. *This is who I am; this is what I do.*

All sixteen athletes on the line, final event. Fatigue, satisfaction, shared endeavour, shared hurt and pride, shared humility. *I don't give a fucking shit! Shit or bust, shit or bust!* Tensed, bang! Straight to the front, Shelley Steele was on a mission, a mission from God. *Yeah, I can hurt a bit; watch me now.* The established heptathletes reigned back; they'd seen this before, glory girls and boys. Flossie and Denny looked over at each other, shoulders raised, shrugged, what can you say? You do your apprenticeship first. They waited for Shelley's initial surge to come back to them; it didn't. Running a mid-fifties four hundred hurdles gives you an appreciation of how much you can hurt, just how much you can take. Shelley Steele went through that first four hundred in a sixty-two; she was already five seconds in front.

My mum's here to see me, my mum! Relentless into the second half, spectators already on their feet, something special was happening. No holding back now, no holding back, hurt upon hurt, welcome it. *This is who I am; this is what I do.* Angie was screaming, on her feet, of course, as was everyone. Everyone on the rails, willing, willing, willing, no surrender. Shelley crossed the line in two minutes and six seconds; no one was close. As she collapsed on the floor, Gilly, Kaas, Angie, Dan rushed out to her.

She was laying there, laughing. "Fucking look at me, silly little me!" And the sweaty little girl giggled as her four biggest supporters embraced her, and she kept on giggling for the next thirty minutes.

"Please welcome to the podium the medal winners for the heptathlon. In first place representing Vicky Park, Shelley Steele!" Denny and Flossie bowed in mock appreciation on the presentations, but it was in respect rather than anything else. They'd been there; they'd done it.

*****

"Mrs Steele? Angie, do you fancy going out for a meal? Nothing too fancy."

"Are you hitting on me, Mr Bullet? Are you hitting on me?" Dan Bullet smiled.

"I believe I may just be doing that, Mrs Steele…"

"In which case, I say most definitely yes!"

*****

David Caxton Writes in the Times

Around four years ago, I wrote about some up-and-coming athletes, possibly the ones to watch for the London Olympic Games. Two of those names you will remember immediately: Shelley Steele took fourth at the Beijing Olympics just one year ago at the tender age of eighteen, and JoJo Jackson is a regular starting player for Spurs ladies and for England. The other names were Lucy Newton (you may recall Lucy suffering a horrendous injury being struck by an errant discus at the European Under-18 Athletics Championships after taking gold in the 3000 metres), Sami Richards and Mickey Honey. And now these kids have truly come of age. Just a couple of weeks ago, they swept the board at the BUSF Championships—Lucy also finishing eighth in the women's 1500 metre swimming event as well as taking joint gold with Sami on the track—and earlier today, I watched them support their club, Victoria Park Harriers, in the Club Championships.

It is sadly rare for top athletes to do this; time, commitments, training, sponsors and major race schedules all conspire against this. But not for these young athletes; encouraged by their coach, Gilly Warren, they stepped away from their main race distance and entered the eight hundred metres. All acquitted themselves perfectly. All except hurdles specialist Shelley Steele. As a total novice, Shelley took part in the heptathlon and won. She won because she doesn't know how to give up. Shelley Steele doesn't know when she's beaten. Shelley Steele fears nothing and nobody. This ragged old journalist has seen many, many track and field championships and many heptathlon and decathlon events.

What this ragged old journalist has never seen—before today—was the pure guts and determination of this young lady. In third place on the points table before the final eight hundred, Shelley had no chance—absolutely no chance—of winning. She needed to win by at least eleven seconds, and that, ladies and gentlemen, is almost the distance of the home straight. It's impossible. But nobody told Shelley that. Shelley doesn't understand the meaning of impossible, and so the impossible becomes possible.

When I spoke with Shelley after her final event, she was surrounded by her friends and her Dutch boyfriend, Kaas Prinz, a finalist in the pool in Beijing. The interview was one that I so enjoyed. The happiness radiating from group is contagious; they feed off of each other; they support each other; they make each other feel good about themselves. Towards the end of our chat, Shelley told me that they have a mantra. She started to quote it, and every single member of this happy band joined in before she had even got to the second word. And the mantra?

'This is who I am; this is what I do.'

The London Olympic Games is three years away. Victoria Park lies in the shadow of the new stadium. These young athletes will be in nobody's shadow when the time comes. David Caxton saying, 'I have seen the future, and the future is bright.'

Chapter Forty-Nine
The Trials

Time's weird, isn't it? You can't change time; it just ticks on. But it doesn't just tick on, does it? Time goes by so fast sometimes, and sometimes it goes by so slowly. Mickey remembered one of his dad's so-called friends (on one of the rare occasions when his dad was there) talking about doing time—being in prison when one day could stretch on forever. And Mickey remembered so many sunny summer days with TMRG when the day would go by in a flash; they'd just started and already they were getting the calls from out of the windows to 'get your backside in here now!' and it was getting dark. How did that happen?

Three years now, three years gone since their first BUSF Championships, and those years had accelerated. The training had been fierce in Bath and in London, the athletics and the swimming. The mansion in Bath now had eight occupants rather than six; it had just seemed to be the right thing for Kaas and Marianne to move in. They'd crossed the milestones, made the England and Great Britain senior teams (Holland for Marianne and Kaas). Lucy and Shelley had even made the England team for the Commonwealth Games in India in 2010. Shelley had taken silver and bronze in the two hurdles events, and Lucy had made the final in the five thousand metres, finishing fifth behind three Kenyans and one Ugandan. And now it was the Olympic trials.

"There are only two important races for the Olympics," said Gilly and Dan so many times. "The trials and the Games themselves, and we are preparing for those. We look forwards, not backwards." But of course, they looked backwards as well; you need to look back and consider the mistakes you've made and use that experience to not make the same mistakes again. All of them had needed to make the decision—the big decision—which event? Or do you dare to try and qualify for two? Double medal or double failure? The Olympic Games timetable was already out, and the seven of them had pored over it, looking at all the possible combinations: heats, second and third rounds, if required by the number of athletes, and finals. For Kaas, if he made the Dutch swim team, the heats and finals would be on the same day for the four hundred, heats in the morning, final in that same evening and for the two hundred individual medley event, heats and semis the same day and the final on the following evening. For the two weeks of the Olympic Games, the swim events take precedence in the first week; there is an overlap during the middle weekend and athletics comes into its own for week two. But for all of them, first you had to qualify.

*****

Alisha didn't have to qualify; she'd already done so. Mayor ("Don't call me Mayoress! I'm not the wife of a mayor, OK!") of the London Borough of Newham, the youngest ever mayor of a London borough. She was already assured of getting into any event, any sport, and she planned to use that privilege, perhaps more than use it. Alisha had very definite plans for the Games. Getting onto the council, doing the groundwork, paying her dues, taking on a lot of the dirty work, she'd earned the respect of everybody, not just for the hard work but also for not taking any shit from anybody however important, however much older or more experienced. And now Alisha was confident in her role, graduating with first-class honours from university she had applied to be a social worker in her own borough, and that had gained her even more respect. She was hands-on, and anybody who wasn't, Alisha was very quick to tell them. Several of the time servers moved on, the social work group grew stronger, their clients grew happier. After that first year, Alisha was the leader, and becoming mayor, well, who was going to argue with her?

*****

JoJo Jackson was already in the Great Britain football team for the London Olympics. No trials for JoJo. And JoJo was in as captain. Captain of Great Britain. All those years, all that hard work. Frequently, the captaincy would go to the single overaged player allowed, but not this time; JoJo was captain because she'd earned it and deserved it, and there wasn't one single British player who would have disagreed. Messages had come into JoJo within minutes of the team names being announced, not just the players in the women's league but players from all over the world, players whom JoJo had worshipped, tried to emulate, played against. And now it was JoJo's time.

*****

Eric and Bobby were going through the names and the numbers, checking and cross-checking. They'd built up their import agency to the extent that it almost took care of itself and added another venture by representing the athletes whom they'd been watching and timing those four years. It only took one athlete to approach them initially and then that trickle became a stream and became a torrent. Managing and helping athletes became a vocation for them; they wanted to share the good fortune they'd experienced as youngsters. Some of Gilly's group had risen to represent their country; England, Scotland, Wales, Northern Ireland, Great Britain and several European Countries with their athletes and swimmers being attracted to the coaching at Bath University.

Sponsorship for an athlete is never easy, especially at the start, but Bobby and Eric were able to point the athletes in the right direction, starting small, not attempting to approach the big-name companies but rather local businesses to gain a foothold. Lucy and Mickey now had contracts with Zig-Zag, not on the same level as Shelley but a steady supply of essential kit and expenses for travel and training made a big difference. Eric and Bobby were becoming very well-respected in the sports community and were well-respected by Mr Zig-Zag, John Smith, and John had plans for Eric and Bobby.

*****

Joshi had applied for the post as soon as he'd seen it advertised. Joshi was a smart cookie, and smart cookie Joshi the Doc had been given the whisper that the British Olympic Association would be getting the adverts into the medical specialist papers. Joshi had impressed the board at the interview; his youth, his being a local boy, his obvious intelligence, the fact that he'd gone to university early, gone to medical school early, graduated with honours early and that his sister was the mayor of Newham helped in no small way as well. As did his knowledge of the athletes, going to junior and secondary school with four of those athletes and his friendship with Gilly Warren, the British squad distance coach. It all helped, and the whole became bigger than the sum of the parts. Dr

Joshi Buzdar was on the medical advisory panel for the British Olympic team, Team Great Britain.

*****

A thought. *Am I good enough? Am I? I know I shouldn't be having any doubts.*

"Be positive," Gilly says.

As soon as she's said it, "I'm up for it. But, like, when I start thinking, really thinking about it…me? Olympic Games? How can that be? You know what? I'm gonna talk to Shelley; she understands; she's been there," Marianne said.

*****

And another thought. *Am I good enough? Am I? I know I shouldn't be having any doubts.*

"Be positive," Gilly says, and then as soon as she's said it, I'm up for it. But, like, when I start thinking, really thinking about it…me? Olympic Games? How can that be? "You know what? I'm gonna talk to Lucy; talk to my little adopted sister. She understands; she's been there," Sami said.

*****

"I never knew my dad, Kaas. Well, to be honest, I never had a dad; he scarpered before I was born. But I was so lucky with my mum; I didn't properly realise when I was growing up just how lucky. D'you remember the London bombings? All that extremist stuff? Well, that was when I did realise, could've lost my mum, wrong place, wrong time—shit happens, you know? But I didn't, and then I did know how lucky I was. My mum gave me everything, everything, and I just took it for granted. She never went out, worked two or three jobs just to get me by, make sure I had decent clothes and enough food. She never had a boyfriend, never! And my mum's really pretty." Kaas nodded his head.

"Shelley, your mum's not pretty, your mum's beautiful…Shelley, you really do look so much like your mum." Shelley smiled back.

"And now I'm so happy for her. I've never seen her happier; she's been with Dan for three years, three years! And you know what? Well, I'll tell you. She's never—not once—had Dan stay over when I'm home, not once, and that's because of me. Bloody hell, Mum, me! You know her and Dan started when she came along to watch me down at Vicky, yeah? Remember that first heptathlon? Me too! It was my mum being there that got me through that bloody eight hundred. You know what, Kaas? I sort of didn't really feel any pain until it was over…you ever had that swimming?"

"Just the odd once or twice, I suppose…and it's always been when something outside the swimming has come along, something brilliant, and you feel"—and Kaas struggled for the word—"euphoric? Shelley, is that the right word? Euphoric?"

Shelley nodded yes. "When you came to see me swim at those BUSF Champs, I didn't feel any pain when I was in the water; it came and bit me on the bum when I'd finished." Shelley laughed out loud.

"Your English slang is impressive, Kaas."

"I was so happy that you were there; I just felt so lucky that I was with you."

"We gonna make it, Kaas? Me and you, we gonna make it?" Kaas kissed her hard on the lips.

"Yes, we are going to make it, me and you together."

And finally, Shelley said, "You know what I said about never having a dad? Well, I was wrong there; I've had two dads, real dads, Mr Warren and Dan Bullet…they've been my dads …yeah, they've been my real dads."

*****

"Mickey, am I mad? Am I stupid?" Mickey put his arms around her.

"Why stupid, baby girl?"

"Like thinking about the swimming, even thinking about it makes me feel a bit dopey; I've scraped qualifying for the trials, and it's bloody eight hundred freestyle, not fifteen hundred; it's not right, you know; all the athletics is the same now for men and women, thank God! Can you imagine back in the sixties there wasn't even a fifteen hundred on the track for the women, let alone five and ten thousand? Athletics got their act together; 'bout time swimming did."

"What does Dan think? He thinks you've got a chance?"

"You know Dan, he's always so positive—realistic as well—lovely man. Dan says that if there's even a sniff of getting to the Games, you gotta take it."

Mickey smiled at her. *You know what? I think I love her more every day, yeah, really.*

"Think you got your answer right there, Lucy, right there…"

"Mickey, I don't want to mess up any chance I've got of a medal on the track. I'm hitting the same sort of times as the Kenyan girls now, just don't want to mess it up, you know; heats of the five thousand are the day after the swim final…as if I was going to make it!"

"So you do the trials on swimming and then make a decision, easy-peasy, lemon-squeezy!"

"So you made your decision yet, oh, wise person? Five or ten or both?"

"Three full days between the ten final and the 5K heats…so in theory, possible. And could always do the marathon the day after the 5K final…yeah, right!"

They both smiled; they'd both qualified for the marathon at their first attempt at the distance, the London marathon back in April. Third fastest Brit for both of them, nowhere near the Africans heading up the field, nowhere near at all, but it had been a magic training run; the papers had gone mad, of course. 'The Golden Couple Head for the Games! Double Gold for Lucy and Mickey!' Not a hope in hell…but yet…

"But maybe the marathon for the next Games, what d'you reckon?"

"So, we're getting ready for Rio in four years' time and we haven't even qualified for London yet…" They both realised that yes, yes, they were.

*****

"We haven't done too badly, have we?" Chris was down in Bath for the weekend.

"Not too dusty, my long-time friend, not too dusty at all." Dan punched him lightly on the shoulder, and Chris pretended to cringe away. Gilly was used to them and just smiled.

"You started it, Chris, you. Eight kids from your class, eight kids from the bad side of town, add in Sami and Marianne and Kaas, it's a bit of a legacy, you know. If it hadn't been for you, those kids wouldn't be where they are now. All those care-worn cliches can't do you justice; they still worship you. You know, when they're warming up or warming down and they're all chatting together, they still call you 'Mr Warren' sometimes, even 'sir' when they forget. It's all about 'do you remember when' and then they'll come out with a story and start smiling, grinning, laughing out loud. They know, Chris, they know exactly what you've done for them, that self-belief they had, but they didn't know it; it took you to light the fire inside them.

"I know we're focusing on the Games; well, obviously, I so hope they make the team, but it's the others as well; can you believe that Alisha is mayor of Newham, Joshi already qualified as a doctor and Eric and Bobby are going to be the biggest sports agents ever—the uni athletes are flocking around them—as well as coining it with their import business…so I'd say that, yes, we haven't done too badly at all, but you started it, Chris, you. Don't put yourself down; you deserve a medal. I honestly don't think that Dan and I would be in this position of working with, coaching, Olympic hopefuls if you hadn't been their teacher…changed their lives, Chris; you changed their lives, my lovely husband."

There was a long silence, one of those silences that actually feels comfortable. And then, "So Mr Bullet, what about you and Shelley's mum?" Dan made a show of checking his watch.

"How long did that take you, Gilly? So, me and Shelley's mum, Angie. Well, to be honest, it felt really weird to start with. It was just that day down at Vicky Park, you know? We were just sitting together pretty much all day, and…well, it just happened. Never felt so comfortable before. It was strange obviously because of Shelley, had no idea how she'd react, really worried me to be honest. I adored Shelley, still do.

"She's been an absolute diamond, still treats me exactly the way she's always done, still comes up and hugs me, still kisses me after the odd session that she's able to do with us. And if she does see me and her mum together, no phasing at all, just normal, as if it's always been like that, love her to bits…wasn't sure, you know? The black and white thing. Yeah, I know, for all these kids, it's normal, but it's not so normal when your mum hitches up with a black guy, so it was a bit of a worry, but not anymore. By not saying anything, Shelley tells me it's all good with her…I feel very, very lucky; I honestly do. I know getting married is a bit of an old-fashioned idea, but after the Games, when it's all over, I'm going to ask Angie to marry me. There, said it. And if she says yes, Chris, would you be my best man?"

*****

And then it was the trials; six weeks out from the Games, the only other race that mattered. And you needed this race; you needed to ace this race because if you didn't…then bye-bye Olympic Games, bye-bye for four more years.

And the trials went well, went really well except for one athlete.

Back in Holland, Kaas made both individual medleys, broke the Dutch record in the four hundred and was close in the two hundred. Shelley went with him (of course, she did). Ranked in the top eight in the world, Kaas was on a high. As was Shelley because Kaas had whispered to her, "I do love you; I truly love you," straight after his second race.

Marianne made it…just. She'd qualified for the final in the four hundred—just—and then Gilly sat down with her and gave it to her straight—absolutely straight. In the final, Marianne was a different athlete: positive, dynamic, assertive, ran her own race, finished third, made the team. And thanked Gilly again and again and again.

Mickey was just brilliant. Took first in both the five and ten thousand…and then started thinking about what was best to do. And so did Lucy, won both fairly easily, took control mid-race in both and controlled the pace and the pack. Sami opted just to race the five thousand, sat behind Lucy right the way through, made no moves, took second and burst into tears all over Lucy past the tape.

And then it was Shelley. Sitting in the stands, her mum, Dan and Kaas. Three events and two of them the toughies: the four hundred hurdles and the heptathlon along with the sprint hurdles. There was no way that Shelley was going to compete in all three at the Games because the timetable made it impossible, but qualifying in all three and with firsts in all three gave her the options. It was only the third heptathlon of her life, just one in between Vicky Park, and these trials and Shelley's improvement—particularly in the technical events—was phenomenal. And now she would have to sit down with Gilly and decide.

Lucy stood on the blocks in the Olympic pool, heat one of two, lane one, so ranked fourteenth out of sixteen, eight fastest times to make the final, two to make the Games. And Lucy didn't make it, didn't make the final, didn't make the Games. Dream over. First black girl to represent Great Britain in swimming, not this time. The dream was over, really over. She sat with Mickey and Dan, didn't cry, what was the point? She'd given it everything and—bottom line—wasn't quite good enough. Mickey didn't know what to say, anything would have been useless. He felt lost, unable to help Lucy. Mickey felt like he'd failed. Later that evening.

"Mickey, I'm going to see Dan, that all right?"

"'Course it is. Want me to come with you?"

"Just go by myself if that's OK, yeah?" Mickey kissed and hugged her and Lucy left.

As she knocked on Dan's door, she knew, just knew, that he had been waiting for her. The door opened immediately, and then any pretence of holding it in vanished. Lucy was sobbing, sobbing out loud, and all Dan could do was hold her.

"Oh, Dan, I've let you down! I'm so sorry." And her sobs continued. "All those mad dreams, should have known, shouldn't I? Just not being realistic…Dan, I feel like I'm broken, broken inside and out." Dan hugged her tighter.

"Reckon I need to unbreak you then, don't I?"

"Don't think you can, Dan, not right now; my heart's aching. I so wanted to, you know, black girl swimming, all that stuff…"

"So shall we give it another go, then, what d'you reckon?"

"I reckon that I'd love to, but for a start, there's no more swimming, and for a follow-up, I'm not good enough, oh, Dan!"

"Well, we'd better change it, then, hadn't we?" Lucy felt the tiniest ray of hope, but only the tiniest.

"Dan, not being funny, but I'm not hanging on four more years to the next Games. C'mon, let's be realistic. The standard's only going to get better, you know that."

"Lucy, I need you to think outside the box now, throw all the old stuff away; can you do that?" Lucy nodded her head.

"But what, Dan, what?" Dan breathed in deeply and slowly and even more slowly breathed out.

"Open water, Lucy, open water, listen, it's ten kilometres, just over six miles, now that'd be playing to your strengths, wouldn't it?" And Lucy dared to dream again.

Questions, questions, questions, so many questions.

What was different? What was the same?

What do I need to do? Will I be able to get a trial?

"Yes, your eight hundred and fifteen hundred times qualify you."

"When is it? Two days' time?"

"Do you want to do it?"

"Yes, of course!"

"Then we need to get you out in the open water tomorrow, Serpentine, Hyde Park, same venue as the Games."

"You sure about this, Lucy?"

"Never surer."

And Lucy was unbroken.

Dan swam with her, talking all the time, talking about drafting. "What's drafting, Dan?" Talking about legs for balance and then powering the legs for the finish. "That'll be your strength, Lucy, your legs." Talking about being in a pack, a tight pack where the experienced swimmers would use that experience to intimidate you, how to get out of that pack, talking about dealing with the cold, how your mind could control that, talking about the need to slap the board at the finish line, miss that and it was definitely over. And Lucy learnt six months' experience in a ninety-minute swim.

There were a lot of the trialists going through their paces in the Serpentine. Dan knew most of them and was known by most of them. Lots of handshakes and hugs and lots of hooded eyes sizing up the new girl, sizing up Lucy.

It wasn't a huge field for the open water trials, twenty-two in total including four of the girls who'd swum the eight hundred in the pool just those couple of days ago. Lucy jumped in for the deep water start; she had a game-plan; she had Dan's game-plan and intended to follow it one hundred per cent.

"On the start, Lucy, it's treading water, and the way you do even that can make a difference; now what you have to do is use both arms and legs almost as if you're running before the gun goes off. If you're using both together, then you're going to be dropping and rising in the water, and if the gun goes when you're dropping down, you're going to be half a yard down already, and believe me, that can and will make a difference." The advice was seared into her brain, *I have another chance, a second chance!*

Treading water, sculling with her hands, anticipating, bang! Sprint, sprint, sprint! Get on those feet, chase them. Chase! Yes! Establish position, look around, front pack, hold, hold, hold! Anyone moves up, follow and get right on their feet, and if you can't get their feet, then right alongside their hip. You've got to get that draft! One swimmer away, Dan said there probably would be, don't be tempted, save energy, save it and get ready to use it when you have to. Pack splitting, some swimmers out of their depth, and absolutely no pun intended. Lucy feeling comfortable, distance playing to her strengths, she doubted if anyone in the water had a better or stronger engine than she did, all those years of running distance, running intervals.

They might be better swimmers, but could they hurt as much as she could? Doubt it—really doubt that. Legs just for balance now, hold position. Watching some of the swimmers taking on drinks as they passed the feeding station. Dan had said no; it was a new skill, and there wasn't time to learn it. But it was magic even watching, hand goes up, takes the bottle, turn over on back, drink, bottle goes. Gotta learn that soon as! First mile gone, pilot boat ahead, pack splitting more, lead group down to eight now, two miles gone. I can do this! I really can! I'm comfortable. I can hold. Three miles gone, halfway. One more swimmer dropped away, cold? Exhaustion? Who knows? I feel OK, bit cold but nothing desperate, those bloody bitter evenings down the track at Bath.

Four miles now, six holding, early leader back in the pack. Just got to stay here and get ready, get ready early, Dan said. Got to be ready to cover the break, someone will go early, cover. Last mile, twenty minutes. I can do this; yes, I can. Kick a little just to check the old legs can still do it, relax back...Someone's gone for it! Gone early, wants to break! Cover, kick, get those fucking legs turning over, please, legs, please! And Lucy's legs responded, on the feet of the lead swimmer, sighting the finish board, hundred yards, into overdrive, sprint, all out sprint. Sight the board, hand up, bang! Touch, yes! Yes, fucking, yes! Second, I did it! Lucy ripped off the goggles and looked up to see Dan, Gilly, Chris, Mickey and every single one of TMRG jumping up and down on their seats.

David Caxton Writes in the Times

History will be made at the London Olympic Games by runner Lucy Newton who has qualified for both the five and ten thousand metres on the track. Indeed, Lucy has also qualified for the marathon run. Actually, Lucy has qualified for two marathons. How so? Because Lucy Newton has qualified for the marathon open water swim as well. Ten very damp kilometres in the Serpentine. But runner and swimmer, Lucy Newton, will be making history for another reason, and to this poor hack, it is quite extraordinary that Lucy will be the first black girl to represent Great Britain in a swimming event. Can you believe that? The first black girl. And the reasons are multitude, and I'm sure that somebody somewhere will have written a doctoral thesis about it. When I spoke to Lucy, she was adamant that she knew the reason.

"We don't have a history in swimming, Mr Caxton; black girls don't have any swimming role models…But I want to be a role model for any little black girls out there. Black girls can swim. Black girls can represent their country. Maybe I'm the first, but there will be hundreds now. There're lots of little girls just like me out there, just like me; you wait and see."

David Caxton feeling humble and thoughtful.

Chapter Fifty
The Greatest Show on Earth

The world had come to London. And London was ready. In particular, seven young Olympic athletes, four supporters and three coaches and teachers were prepared and ready. It didn't always feel as if they were, but the hard work, the hard miles, the technique, the self-doubts, which almost always came in the middle of the night, were done. Nervousness was present, but not always; the athletes had three supportive adults to calm them. They were sitting together in one of the several lounges in the Olympic village. The athletes and coaches all had beds here, but, mostly, they preferred to stay at home. They were out of the melee, out of the hustle and bustle, out of the spotlight. Gilly was centre-stage, going through the outline schedule with all the possibilities that they would face. All fourteen of them had the written schedule on a clipboard in front of them. Mickey was thinking, *These are the days of my life*. And most of the others echoed those thoughts.

"OK, take a look through, you guys, nice and slow, and then we'll take comments." They looked down, searching for their particular event or events.

Friday, 27 July: opening ceremony

Saturday, 28 July: swim men's 400 metres individual medley, heats and final

Wednesday, 1 August: swim men's 200 metres individual medley, heats and semi-finals.

Thursday, 2 August: swim men's 200 metres individual medley, final.

Friday and Saturday, 3 and 4 August: Track, women's heptathlon.

Friday, 3 August: Track, women's 10,000 metres final.

Friday, 3 August: Track, women's 400 metres heats.

Saturday, 4 August: Track, women's 400 metres semi-finals.

Saturday, 4 August: Track, men's 10,000 metres final.

Sunday, 5 August: Track, women's 400 metres final.

Sunday, 5 August: Track, women's 400 metres hurdles heats.

Sunday, 5 August: Road, women's marathon.

Monday, 6 August: Track, women's 400 metres hurdles semi-finals.

Monday, 6 August: Track, women's 100 metres hurdles heats.

Tuesday, 7 August: Track, women's 100 metres hurdles semi-finals and final.

Tuesday, 7 August: Track, women's 5,000 metres heats.

Wednesday, 8 August: Track, women's 400 metres hurdles final.

Wednesday, 8 August: Track, men's 5,000 metres heats.

Thursday, 9 August: Hyde Park, women's marathon 10-kilometre swim.

Friday, 1 August: Track, women's 5,000 metres final.

Friday, 10 August: Track, women's 4 x 400 metres relay heats.

Saturday, 11 August: Track, men's 5,000 metres final.

Saturday, 11 August: Track, women's 4 x 400 metres relay final.

Sunday, 12 August: Road, men's marathon.

Sunday, 12 August: Stadium, closing ceremony.

It was a long hard look at the schedule, taking everything in. Eventually, the athletes looked up at Gilly, with Dan and Chris alongside. How Joshi had got into the village along with Eric and Bobby, only Alisha knew, and she was keeping quiet.

"Busy times, ladies and gentlemen, busy times indeed ahead." Gilly smiled at them all and had the smile returned. "OK, let's take it in order…Kaas, you'll want to talk to Dan, of course, but opening ceremony is the night before your four hundred IM; I know you'll want to do the opening but, well, you know."

That was decided. "Shelley, you've got a head-on collision, heptathlon on 3rd and 4th, then four hundred hurdles heats on the 5th, semis of that on the 6th along with heats of the hundred hurdles, and then semis and final of the sprint hurdles on the 7th, and then final of the sprint hurdles on the 8th. Something's got to give, Shelley; otherwise, you could fall right down the middle, yeah?"

Shelley nodded and waited; she was ninety-nine per cent sure what her decision would be, but she needed Gilly to spell it out for her. "Now first two days heptathlon, that's eight events right there, and the day after four-hundred hurdles heats, you'll be tired, but you're right up there, so qualification is there. You just need to run smart. Go onto the sixth and you have four hundred semis and hundred hurdles heats, and if you went for sprint hurdles, its semis and final on the seventh, but four hundred final is the eighth, so a day's rest…but only if

417

you opted out of the hundred. You try for all three, Shelley—and I know you want to—you're going to be shattered." Everyone sitting there was waiting.

"Four hundred hurdles, Gilly, four hundred hurdles and heptathlon, I HAVE to go for those two." Gilly smiled back at her.

"Good girl, pick the toughest two! Knew you would!" And the applause from everybody was heartfelt, and then Gilly murmured quietly to herself, "And there's always the relay…" Then louder again, "Sami, Marianne, JoJo, a little bit easier for you guys. One event to focus on—and I know it's heats and finals, you two." Gilly smiled at Sami and Marianne. "Well, semis for you as well, Marianne; three rounds will play to your strengths, trust me, and never trust anyone who says 'trust me', especially a coach!" Cheers and boos from the athletes. Gilly always seemed to have the right knack for putting them at ease. "JoJo, it's not my business, I know, but I—no, we—all want to wish you the absolute best of luck, six games if you get to the final, six games. Jeez!" And JoJo stood up.

"I need to say something, something from me, but I reckon it's something from every single one of us." JoJo took a deep breath and then another, and then looked directly at Chris Warren. "Sir, yes, I know, but I absolutely HAVE to call you sir right now because without you, Mr Warren, without you then, I would most certainly NOT be here now. I would not be playing for Spurs. I would not be earning the sort of money that my mum and dad could only dream about, and I would not be at the Olympic Games. You see, sir, it's not fair that the athletes get all the attention, not fair at all." And the heads were bowed in the room, looking down at their feet. "It's about the support team, the coaches, of course, but also it's about the people who set you on the right path, who told you what you could achieve, who taught you to believe in yourself…and that's you, Mr Warren, that's you. And it's you, Gilly, and you, Dan. There's not one of us kids in this room—and we're still kids when you're here—there's not one of us who doesn't owe everything to you, everything."

A slight pause, then JoJo said, "'S right, guys, yeah?" No one dared to speak; no one trusted themselves, but every single head was nodding 'yes', and there were a lot of hands covering up a lot of eyes. "So there's one more thing I have to say, sir, really is from the bottom of my heart, yeah? If I win a medal—and I know it's a big if, a really big if, 'cause no one expects us to even get one out of our group—but if I do, then it's your medal, sir…Is that all right, sir?"

And Chris Warren, tough old Special Services, tough old headmaster, couldn't hold it together any longer. He walked over to JoJo, hugged her tight and just stood there, speechless. And he knew that a long, long time ago, he had made the right decisions. And they all needed a break before Gilly continued.

"Mickey, you've got the ten thousand first, straight final on the first Saturday of track, then the five heats four days later—loads of recovery time!—then the 5K final three days after that on the last day…apart from the marathon, that is."

"I won't be running a marathon the day after the hardest five thousand I'm ever likely to run, Gilly, not a chance in hell." And Gilly thought, *If there was one person who I'd put money on to be able to do it, it'd be you, Mickey, you.*

"Lucy, your schedule is pretty similar to Mickey's, straight final for the ten, four days later the 5K heats, then you have that little water massage with the marathon swim two days after and the final of the 5K on the Friday, all good?" Lucy nodded her head.

"It's all good, Gilly, all good. I'm ready for this…honest, I'm ready. I reckon the swim'll be a bonus, like you said, 'water massage in between the running'. I know marathon's out of the question, comes right in between the ten and the five, and I'm not that stupid…well, I don't think I am…Thing is, with the swim, I have literally nothing to lose, nothing. My aim was to make the team; I've done it, me, little Lucy's gonna swim for Great Britain, black girl swimming, me! Shelley said it, you know, 'shit or bust'. That'll be me, 'shit or bust', I promise."

*****

"Can you believe that, JoJo? Can you believe her?" Chris, Gilly and Dan had been joined by Angie Steele. Angie was a little nervous but happy to be there. Dan related to Angie what JoJo had said. Angie smiled.

"Mr Warren, they all think about you like that, honest. My Shelley worships you, you know? She worshipped you as a little kid at junior school, and she still worships you now…Dan, true story?" Chris Warren interjected.

"Angie, can we make a deal? If I call you Angie, can you call me Chris?"

"Yes, I know…but it still feels a bit weird, you know? Never thought I'd be hob-knobbing with you guys; never thought I'd be with this lovely man beside me!" Dan Bullet just sighed happily. Gilly nodded in total agreement.

"These are the kids that would have been written off, Chris. These are the kids that people would have said, 'Why bother? Not worth the effort, only let you down.' But they'll never let you down, never. Don't know whether they'll win medals or not, you can never know, but I think there'll be some. But I'll bet a million dollars that they'll die trying; they'll die trying because you taught them to believe, to believe in themselves." Gilly had said it, but Dan and Angie believed it as well…because it was true.

*****

And now it was time, time to put it on the line, time to show yourself to the world, to prove that you were the best. They'd all marched in the opening ceremony, all apart from Kaas and JoJo, who'd already opened her account in Cardiff with a one-nil (scorer Ms. J. Jackson) win over New Zealand, but as soon as they were able, they hurried away to rest, to rest, to think and to plan.

Day 1. Saturday, 28 July

Kaas was seeded fourth in the four hundred metres individual medley. He took his place in the final heat, lane five. First seed next to him in lane four. "Take your marks," and the klaxon blared. Into the butterfly, extend, push back hard, lift and breathe, again and again and again, into the second turn, one hundred metres gone and into backstroke, stay down as long as you can, more, more, surface and reach back, work the hips, look over, lane four fractionally ahead, flip into turn and stay down again, reach and stretch, reach and stretch, two hundred down, flip turn onto breaststroke, weakest stroke, need total focus now, slipping back, slipping back, hold; you must hold! Into final hundred on front crawl, work hard, let's get it back, c'mon! Inch by inch, closing, closing down, final fifty, so let's really bring the legs into this, super kick! Stretch and touch! Look up, immediate feedback from scoreboard, second by just two tenths, no worries, will make it up this evening in the final! Swim-down in the training pool and meet Shelley for coffee.

"You happy with that, Kaas?" Shelley gently kissed him.

"Yes, be fine for tonight; fancy a bite to eat? Then I'm going for a massage and lie-down, just need to think about my pacing right the way through, but, yes, I'm going for the big one."

Lane five again for the final; same American in lane four as Kaas had battled against in the heats; first and second head-to-head in the middle lanes. The crowd was waiting for this one; after all, Kaas was almost a Brit! Out a little harder on

420

the butterfly, let's try to get a couple of tenths up, turn equal first, really stay down on backstroke, double leg-beat and up at twelve metres and super stretch, last bit of the push-away really go for it, into the breaststroke, and 'I'm leading, I'm leading!' Now really go for it, c'mon now! Working, working, working, the whole field gradually drawing closer but turn into the final freestyle, and now watch me…and the crowd watched, and Shelley watched as that hard-won lead was gradually eclipsed; one, two three swimmers slipped past…fucking fourth! Might as well have been nowhere! Shelley was crying as Kaas limped past her, reached over the barrier and hugged her to him, hugged her tight.

"My fault, Shelley, my fault totally. I got sucked in and went with their strengths and my weaknesses; should have had the confidence to swim my own race…but I've learnt from that; oh, yes, I've learnt." Dan was there nodding his head.

"Kaas, that was a brave swim, but you know that it wasn't a good one…You're totally correct, you didn't swim your race; in the two hundred you need to do that—swim your race, swim your strengths—and then the medal's yours, yes?" Kaas smiled a sad smile 'yes' and was already planning the three races: heat, semi and final of the two hundred metres individual medley.

✶✶✶✶✶

Day 5. Wednesday, 1 August

There had been a lot of thinking for Kaas in the three days before his two hundred IM, a lot of thinking, a lot of discussion with Dan, a lot of work in the training pool; technique, pace, turns…and Kaas was ready, ready to die for it, or as Shelley and Lucy had so eloquently put it, "Shit or bust." Six heats, sixteen to qualify for the semis, Kaas was in the fifth out of the six heats and knew exactly what he needed to do to make the semis, and he did, fifth fastest qualifier with a lot in hand. Swim-down, eat, rest, warm-up. Second of the two semi-finals, lane three, again knowing exactly what was needed to make the final eight. He reflected on what Dan had told him, looked up to the gallery and smiled and waved at Shelley and Dan, both wearing their team GB tracksuits, and then laughed as he watched all the spectators gawping at Shelley rather than the pool. *But she's mine, you jealous buggers. Shelley is mine; we're together forever!* And that made him feel good, feel lucky, feel privileged.

On the blocks now…and bang! Stay down, double leg kick working hard, stretch out, extend long for that first stroke, establish the rhythm…and that set Kaas up for the entire race, just as Dan had said it would, worked the technique on breaststroke and qualified for the final the next evening in fourth place, lane six it would be, and Kaas felt more confident. He looked up at Dan and Shelley again, saw Dan give the double thumbs-up, and Shelley blew him a kiss… Olympic final, yes!

"You made me feel so good, Shelley." She half-frowned, puzzled. "When I looked up at you and all I saw was everyone staring at you; honestly, all the other swimmers and the spectators didn't care about the race; all they cared about was looking at you, you beautiful girl, and it made me feel so happy…and in a way, the race was that little bit less important because I'm the one who's with you, me, just me. And you know what? It gave me that freedom to swim exactly my own race…and it worked, worked a treat…I really do love you, Shelley Steele; I truly do." And when they stood up to walk out of the Olympic village restaurant, there was a little hand-clapping, a little applause, and then the other diners stood up and clapped and cheered, and Kaas knew that he was even luckier than he'd believed. Shelley held his hand and smiled.

*****

Day 6. Thursday, 2 August

"This is the one; this is the one, no excuses, had something in hand…did I? Yes, I did…I can do this…do I really believe it? Yes, I do. I do."

"Ladies and gentlemen, in lane eight, representing…" The announcer went through the swimmers; lane eight, one, seven, two, Kaas in six, three, five, and finally four, the fastest qualifier. The whistle blew, tracksuits off, goggles adjusted, swimmers kneeling down, throwing water from the pool into their faces…the most important two minutes of their lives. A second whistle, swimmers now on their blocks, Americans in four and five, an Aussie in three. "Take your marks." Total focus…and Shelley, always Shelley.

Explosion from the blocks, Kaas knew it was good, better than good, final downbeat, lift and rise and holding position, turning third into backstroke, work on the body rotation Dan had said, gives you a longer pull, checking the lanes inside him, great turn from back to breast, out of the turn, big kick, up to second, hold this, hold this! But losing one place, back to third, long and low out of the turn, stay down as long as legal will let you, up at twelve metres and now explode, every single fucking arm pull and leg kick, fucking explode! Inching back, inching back, level now; I must be level, c'mon, Kaas, c'mon! And level with the red lane ropes just five metres out, Kaas took the lead for the first time in this Olympic final, judged the finish perfectly and knew he had won, Olympic gold! Thank you, God; thank you, Dan; thank you, Shelley. He looked up at Dan first, held his hand to his ears and Dan thumbs-upped back, picked up his mobile phone and said, "Shelley, Kaas won! He won!"

Shelley, watching on TV at home with her heptathlon first day competition tomorrow, was lifted as high as the proverbial kite and hugged her mum...

"I won't let you down, Mum. I promise, I won't let you down."

*****

Day 7. Friday, 3 August

Shelley didn't have to walk to the Olympic Park, nor a bus or taxi; the British Olympic Association sent a car for her. *I'm happier sleeping at home; I like my mum near me.* Straight into the warm-up area in the stadium, greet the other girls. "Hi, Flossie, shame Denny didn't make it." Waves and smiles, a few kisses. What Flossie and Denny had told her was absolutely true: heptathletes were a bit different. Even in an Olympic final, Shelley sensed that. Of course, they'd be busting a gut trying to win, and there probably wouldn't be any helping tips, coaching and corrections from other competitors in this one...*Oh God, I'm so glad I chose this one. I'm so glad I'm here.*

Marianne and Lucy weren't here; they were racing later. But everyone else were all just behind the barrier, along with Shelley's mum. Even early in the morning, the stadium was full; sure there was the women's ten thousand metres final later on, much later on, but the majority of the spectators had come to see one athlete, Shelley Steele, Great Britain. The stadium announcer introduced the heptathletes to the crowd; when Florence Saintiemme's—"It's Flossie, Flossie, right!"—name was read out, the crowd erupted, but it was nothing compared to Shelley's welcome; they really did go wild; there was chanting of Shelley's name...'Local girl, you know', 'Yeah, even went to school in the borough, not one of those posh schools', 'Still lives with her mum on the estate where she grew up', 'Should have got a medal in Beijing, you know' and 'She is absolutely gorgeous, isn't she?'. Shelley waved, circling around, smiling, blew a few kisses.

The two USA athletes were looking at each other. *OK, she's a Brit, a local girl, but she doesn't have any real pedigree in heptathlon, not like she's gonna medal or anything.*

Shelley was in the middle lane, lane four of the second of the two hurdles heats by virtue of having the fastest hurdles time amongst the athletes. *Time to put a marker down, must get over a thousand points, make them think a bit; I've done everything I could.*

"To your marks, set...bang!" Flow, flow, flow, lift and thrust and lean and snap-down; second, third barrier, over the ninth hurdle and sprint over the last...look up at the electronic scoreboard...Yes! Yes! Yes! Shelley Steele, GB, 12.65...*Same time as I did at the last Games, that's well over a thousand points, well over!* And the two USA girls were looking at Shelley just a little bit differently now; hold that level or a one-off?

Two pools for the high jump, two bars and stands, two landing pits, semi-circular and take-off areas side by side. Names read out; pools allocated; starting height, one metre forty-three centimetres. Shelley missed out the first three heights and came in at 1.52, cleared easily, missed 1.55 and then cleared 1.58. The Fosbury flop came easily now, all that time spent on technique, all that time spent on strength work and mobility in the gym...all worth it. The sixteen athletes were down to twelve, to nine. Up to 1.64 and the number down to six, 1.67 height worth just over 800 points, and it was just four remaining; Flossie Saintiemme was out. All clear at 1.70; Shelley, the two Americans whom Shelley knew (she'd done her homework) were Chantelle Beaugrand and Cisse Tellier, and the Dutch girl was Dafne Hoeven, who had moved—like Shelley—from hurdles. All four over at 1.73, again at 1.75, and at 1.77, Dafne failed all three attempts. Just the three attempting 1.79, and it was a triple failure, the bar going down each time.

"Nice jumping, girl; nice jumping."

"Shelley, it's Shelley...and you're Chantelle? And Cisse?" Smiles from both Americans.

"Man, it must be great in front of your own spectators, just great."

"And my mum's here as well...and my boyfriend; he got gold in the pool last night, two hundred IM." More smiles, then Shelley said, "OK, just going to see my mum and friends; see you at shot put."

Shelley stood in front of the crowd barrier, smiled at everyone and then listened attentively to Justus reminding her of the important points in the shot.

Shelley absorbed and nodded, turned to go to the throws area and saw Marianne walking out for her four hundred metres first round.

"Hey, Marianne, good luck! You feeling good?"

"A bit nervous, but a good nervous. Can't wait to run; still can't really believe that I'm at the Olympic Games!"

"Because you deserve it, Marianne, because you deserve it." And whether it was Shelley's words or not, Marianne qualified easily for the semi-finals, fifth fastest out of the twenty-four that went through.

Two pools of athletes again at the shot put; two concrete circles, two grass throwing areas. Shelley was much stronger now, much more confident, maintained her balance and composure throughout. The rotation had been practised so many times under Justus' supervision, Shelley could have gone through it blindfolded, and indeed, she had gone through it as if blindfolded with eyes shut and building that confidence each time. First effort, 13.70; good, but not yet good enough; second put 14.20; that's better! Worth over 800 points. Final chance now, everything into this one, oh yes! Scoreboard flashes 14.81, got to be around 850! Both Americans half a metre ahead, and Dafne Hoeven the golden girl in the shot circle with over sixteen metres.

Back over to the barrier, an air kiss from Kaas; actually, air-kisses from everyone. Last-minute points from Gilly, all positive, no fear, no fear at all. Second of the two heats, leading eight athletes together; Dafne, Chantelle and Cisse there, Flossie just scraping in. "Set...Crack!" Get to full height, pull those feet off of the tartan surface, lean in, hold the curved lane-marker.

Use your bloody arms, girl! Elbows back hard each time, off the bend into the straight, where am I? Close, close, close, moving away...I think, moving in front; c'mon, c'mon, c'mon! Chest out, break the tape, me! And then the self-doubt...did I? Did I get it? And the scoreboard flashed the electric truth; 1st Shelley Steele, GB, 23.39. Oh God! Personal Best, PB at the Games.

"And at the end of day one, Women's Heptathlon standings are, currently lying in 3rd place with 3710 points, Dafne Hoeven, Netherlands; in 2nd place with 3838 points, Cisse Tellier, USA; and leading the women's heptathlon after day one with 3985 points Shelley Steele, GB!" It had been a good day; it had been a very good day. Shelley immediately went to the warm-down area, then to the massage unit, and before going home to rest, Shelley had one more important thing to do; Shelley had to watch her sister race, the women's 10,000 metres final.

Lucy was sitting in the call-room with warm-up finished, quietly thinking, quietly contemplating her race. Looking around at girls doing as she was, sitting and thinking. She knew all the girls at least by reputation if not personally. Lucy knew their times, their favoured race tactics. The three Kenyans would run as a team, Lucy was sure; the Ethiopians, maybe. She'd planned her tactics and race strategy; she'd planned out a second strategy if things went wrong. The three Kenyans Lucy did know as Zahra Kamau, Nafula Ochieng, Kabisa Kibruto; they had all beaten Lucy at the Commonwealth Games. They'd warmed down together after their event, when the three Kenyans had welcomed Lucy.

Lucy had improved more than they had since the Commonwealth Games...but improved enough? The Ethiopians had had tremendous pre-Olympics performances. Faizah Tadesse was leading the world rankings but could be inconsistent. Zala Abebe had medalled at Worlds and was a great one-off runner, and Mazaa Mulugeja very much an unknown quantity...but she'd achieved the Olympic qualifying time.

Lucy was entirely realistic; the Olympic ten thousand metres winner was going to come from one of seven: the Kenyans, the Ethiopians and Lucy herself. There wasn't another European nor an American who would be able to live with the pace when it kicked in...and Lucy believed that, yes, she would be able to live with the pace...whatever it was...*I'm good at hurting. I'm good at putting myself on the line. I'm good at believing in myself. It's London; it's my hometown. This is where I grew up; this is where I belong. My whole life is here...Mickey is here; Mickey is my life.*

"Ladies, please, to the track." And there was an almost audible sigh as the twenty-four athletes rose as one and started to shuffle in a most unathletic manner to the gaping opening onto the track.

As Zahra Kamau came alongside Lucy, Lucy smiled and whispered, "Hello, quiet warrior." Zahra put her hand to her mouth to hide a smile; she, Nafula and Kabisa had told Lucy the Kenyan tribal meanings of their surnames, 'quiet warrior' for Zahra Kamau, 'born when the sun shines' for Nafula Ochieng and 'she who likes to travel' for Kabisa Kipruto. When the Kenyan girls had asked Lucy the meaning of her surname, 'Newton', Lucy had at first been at a loss and then with a smile had replied, 'she who suffers in silence', and the three Kenyans had nodded wisely as if it made total sense. They had become genuine friends, genuine friends who were about to make themselves suffer to the utmost. Yet still remain friends after.

Ten thousand metres is twenty-five laps of the track, thirty plus minutes of running for the best female endurance athletes in the world. On the curved start line, shuffling, edging, squeezing, pushing…And away. Everybody cautious to begin, aware of legs, elbows, flying feet, spiked shoes, and with that caution, nobody fell. First lap in 77 seconds as the pack fell into a semblance of order, Lucy's mind immediately translated it into thirty-two minutes plus finishing time, and that pace was most definitely not going to stay that slow. Second lap 75 seconds, third lap 75 again, and the fourth and the fifth similar; Lucy's translation a thirty-one fifteen, and Lucy knew that it was going to be much faster than that unless the sprinters could dominate and hold the pace down. Already the rabbits were disappearing from the back of the pack, twelve laps gone—three miles in old money—and the pace was still holding 75s, Lucy put plan A into operation. From seventh position, Lucy accelerated to the front, past the Kenyans and Ethiopians and a lone USA athlete and kept acceleration.

That lap went in 68 seconds, and the next and again and again. Sixteen laps down, nine to go. *Hurting now, hurting, but it's OK. I was born to hurt.* With Lucy taking the brunt of the pace-making at the front, the six athletes shadowing her anticipated either Lucy breaking or falling quickly off of her-imposed suffering…the next four laps followed in an almost metronome 68 seconds, and 'She who suffers in silence' was holding that lead with just two thousand metres to go. The lead pack now was down to four, Lucy plus Zahra and Nefula and Faizah Tadesse. The backmarkers were already being lapped, most moving out so as not to slow down the leaders, just one or two unknowing of track etiquette and staying on the inside lane. *Deal with it, girl, just deal with it.*

Suddenly, Faizah was gone, dropped five metres in a hundred, and then another five metres before recovering slightly, but her chance of victory was gone, and she knew it. Four laps, three athletes, three medals, but only one gold. Lucy's searing pace had fallen off slightly, but she was still holding 70s and 71s, four laps remaining, then three. The London Stadium had been quiet when Lucy had launched her attack, waiting to see what would develop, but now London found its joint voice, "C'mon, Lucy!"

"You go, girl!" But the only voice that Lucy could hear was Mickey, her Mickey telling her that he loved her, her Mickey who had been there forever…and at the Olympic stadium in the Olympic Games in her hometown, there really was nothing that was capable of stopping Lucy.

Two laps remaining and the gap opened, almost imperceptibly to begin with...One metre became two, three, then five and, on the bell, a full ten metres with Zahra getting ahead of Nefula. Crowd on their feet, every single one of them, just one athlete in their eyes and mouths, "Lucy! Lucy! Lucy!"

Lucy Newton, Olympic champion, gold medallist, broke the tape and crossed the line in solo splendour and miraculously managed not to fall but waited to congratulate Zahra and Nefula as they took silver and bronze. A Union Jack was thrust into Lucy's hands, and with spikes gratefully taken off, she ran on her lap of celebration with Zahra and Nefula on each side. And in the stands, one tight group of spectators sobbed their hearts out.

"Ladies and gentlemen, girls and boys, I believe we have just seen one of the epic races!" said Jeff Harrington, the stadium announcer. "In first place representing Great Britain—and to my certain knowledge, a young lady who lives just a few bus stops away—Lucy Newton in a time of"—a quiet hesitation—"thirty minutes and 18.77 seconds!"

*****

Eight of them went out for dinner in the village: Lucy, Mickey, Shelley, Kaas, Gilly, Chris, Angie and Dan. Of course, they were noticed, but the majority of the athletes and coaches there didn't intrude; they were looking at two Olympic gold medallists and two who would be fighting for that gold the next day. They deserved their privacy in the busy restaurant. But the rumours were already starting, 'They all went to the same fucking school, you know', 'You're kidding me, don't talk trash', 'Got to be on something', 'And that's bollocks, not one of them's ever tested positive, never', 'Got the same coach', 'All at uni together.' And the voice of reason: 'Any proof? Any proof at all? Any other athletes stitched them up? No, maybe they're just working their arses off, and they got what they deserved.' The jealousies of the professional losers, those who weren't prepared to do what TMRG had done.

*****

"I'm nervous, Kaas, really nervous. You did it, and now Lucy's gone and done it...My turn now, Kaas. What d'you think?"

"What I think, Shelley, is that you make it three out of three, and then Mickey makes it four out of four this evening…that's what I think." They were both in the village after celebrating Lucy's victory the previous evening. Shelley was aware that she was going to be in the firing line, under pressure and attack immediately. Just three events to go and the difference between a gold medal and not getting on the podium as easy as a bad slip or take-off or stepping over the line or misjudging pace; as easy as that. Kaas spoke again as they showed their passes to enter the stadium. "You have three things that will make the difference, Shelley, three things…First of all, we have each other. I would die for you; truly, I would die for you, not that I want to, of course!"

Shelley smiled. "And second, you're the local girl, the London girl; you're the one that everyone's in love with, the one that everybody in the stadium will be cheering for, and you have a third asset, which is huge…you know exactly who you are, and there are very few people who know that. Keep repeating the mantra, our mantra, 'This is who I am; this is what I do'." They hugged, kissed, and Shelley was into the changing and preparation area.

Warm-up completed with Gilly, Shelley joined with the others and entered the stadium.

"Ladies and gentlemen, girls and boys, please welcome our competitors in the Olympic heptathlon." Jeff Harrington on the microphone went through the names, the nationalities and the athletes' high-spots from the previous day.

And when Shelley's name was announced and she did the Shelley wave and the Shelley wiggle and the Shelley blow-a-kiss, the crowd erupted, "Our girl! Gonna win!"

The two long jump pits side by side, athletes split into their two groups of eight.

"Great first day, Shelley." Dafne Hoeven kissed Shelley on the cheek, and then Chantelle and Cissie did the same, the same kiss and the same words of congratulations. "So, we ready to rock, ladies?" said Dafne.

The four of them knew two things: that one of them was going to be Olympic champion, and one was going to miss a medal entirely. Run-throughs completed, jumping order given, markers moved back and forth on the runways. All four of the favourites jumping well, only a few centimetres between them. No fouls for the big four.

"And after their third and final long jumps in the heptathlon, Dafne Hoeven wins with 6.78 centimetres; Cissie Tellier and Chantelle Beaugrand tie with 6.74;

and Shelley Steele with 6.66." *Shit! Lost forty points to Dafne and thirty-odd to the Americans, but I'm still leading. I'm still in the driver's seat.*

To the javelin. Shelley was aware that this was her weakest event, although so much improved with the input of Justus, and she could not—absolutely not—lose too many points…If she did, then the Olympic dream was over. And Shelley Steele most definitely did not want her Olympic dream to be over.

The javelin was always going to be tight; what none of them realised was just how tight. There were no dramas, no catastrophes, no tears. The contest was enough. After they had all thrown their third and final, there was a group hug. 'So true, really so true, heptathletes ARE different.' The entire crowd had been silent watching the run-ups and throws and then exploding as the javelin hit grass and the automatic measuring kicked in and the electronic scoreboard revealed the secrets. Jeff Harrington called the distances and the points.

"And in the javelin discipline in the heptathlon, we have in fourth place Shelley Steele with 51 metres flat; in third Dafne Hoeven 51.49; second is Cissie Tellier 52.24; and taking first place with 52.31 Chantelle Beaugrand." A pause, then he said, "And with just the final event, the 800 metres to go, the points situation in the heptathlon is as follows, Dafne Hoeven leads with 5830 points, in second Shelley Steele 5828 points, third Cisse Tellier 5821 and lying in fourth Chantelle Beaugrand with 5815 points. Ladies and gentlemen, as you can see the points are ridiculously tight. Ladies and gentlemen, on the international scoring table for heptathlon, one second in the 800 metres is worth approximately fourteen points; we have just fourteen points between first and fourth. I think it's fair to say that there will be no prisoners taken in the 800 metres in just forty-five minutes' time!"

Shelley almost didn't see Marianne coming out for her 400 metres semi-final, lane five in the second heat of three, first two to qualify from each heat plus two fastest losers.

"Shelley, Shelley! How we doing?"

"I've dropped three places, Marianne, three places. You know what I said before…shit or bust, shit or bust. I did it before, and I can do it again…because I have to."

And Marianne took that 'shit or bust' attitude into her semi and qualified in third place to be sixth overall, as that third place made her the fastest loser from the three heats. And when the qualifiers were announced, she whispered to herself, "Thank you, Shelley, thank you."

"Gilly, Dan, what does that mean?" Angie Steele was as nervous as she'd ever been; she was pretty sure she knew the answer to her question but needed to hear it from the experts.

"Unless it's a blanket finish—and it could be—whoever wins the 800 metres in thirty minutes time is going to be Olympic heptathlon champion, and if it is a blanket finish…then anyone of the four." Gilly smiled at all of them. "And my money's on Shelley; she's been there before; your little girl is very special, Angie…but you know that."

There had been two withdrawals from the 800 metres with injuries, so fourteen athletes came out onto the track. Just one final race all together, one athlete in lanes one and five, two in the remaining six. Very steady at the gun, who wants to get taken out in the last event? Shelley was shattered, but she knew that everybody would be. She'd put herself on the line before in the eight hundred and was more than able to do it again…but she knew that putting yourself on the line was a prerequisite in the Olympic final, and she knew that every other athlete on the track with her was capable of exactly the same.

Through the first lap in sixty-five seconds, all of them watching each other knowing that the bell could signify a long sprint out, no one went, a slight relaxation because they know that the next trigger point was with three hundred to go. Everyone knew that except Shelley…Right on the middle of the bend, three hundred and fifty metres out, Shelley Steele unleashed the most magnificent acceleration when least expected and was running free with three hundred left; they chased but in vain. 'Shit or bust', Shelley had stated, and this was most certainly that.

As she ran into the home straight with a fifteen-metre lead, she allowed herself a look over her shoulder, saw she was clear and gave the crowd—her crowd—the Shelley wave. And the London crowd responded with a tsunami of cheering, clapping and shouting. She'd won! Olympic champion! She stood and congratulated everyone else home; lots of kissing, hugging and tears and then the fourteen heptathletes took their joint lap of honour, clapping back at the crowd. And in one corner of the stadium, TMRG celebrated again.

"Lord Coe, may I speak with you?" Alisha was in her mayoral robes.

"Madame Mayor, my absolute pleasure; what a tremendous job you and your team have done for the Games, and I know just how much stress and work you've put in, really super job! One thing, Madame Mayor, would it be OK with you to call me Seb? When I hear the words 'Lord Coe', I look around to see who they're talking to."

"On one condition, Seb…"

"Which is?"

"That you return the compliment and call me Alisha." Lord Sebastian Coe roared with laughter. And the laughter turned to amazement when he listened to what Alisha Buzdar, mayor of the London Borough of Newham, was suggesting. But he didn't dismiss it out of hand. No, he considered it very seriously indeed.

"Tell me more, Alisha." And Alisha told him the whole story.

*****

And now it was his time. Mickey had dedicated his life to this; he wouldn't have used the word 'dedicated', but it was true nevertheless. Gilly kissed him as they walked from the warm-up track to the holding room.

"Gilly, cannot thank you enough; I know I wouldn't be here if it wasn't for you…and for Chris, of course." Gilly didn't reply, didn't trust herself to speak, instead squeezed his hand tight, kissed him again and then managed to whisper a 'good luck' and turned away before he could see the tears. Gilly adored Mickey Honey, had for a long time. Adored him for everything he had done, overcome all the obstacles, all the 'given at birth' drawbacks, his love for Lucy, the way he had taken TMRG with him. He truly was the glue that held them together, and every one of them knew and acknowledged it. And now it was his time. He saw the American Mickey Winzenreid as he entered the call-room; they'd always got on well, took the mickey out of each other usually by one of them singing softly, "Oh, Mickey, you're so fine, you're so fine, you blow my mind, hey, Mickey!" After the Toni Basil song.

As Mickey approached Mickey, they both started to sing the refrain softly and then had to stop as the laughing began. The other athletes, more subdued, watched them and looked away. How could they not care? How could they not be worried? The American had only recently moved up to the ten thousand metres; he'd started as a handy eight hundred metres runner and finding he didn't have quite enough basic speed to make it at world and Olympic level had gradually moved through fifteen hundred, then five thousand and now the ten. Had he given himself enough time? Mickey Honey wasn't sure; he hoped not…

"Gentlemen, to the track please." Walking out to the crowd, the noise, the applause, the introductions; breaking into nervous strides and sprints. The whistle blows, tracksuits are stripped off and stashed into the kit boxes. A big field, straight final. Athletes separated into two groups, marshals directing them to the white lines, arranging them into order; nerves, nerves.

Nerves…Introductions from Jeff Harrington again, huge cheers for Mickey Honey, hands raised, waves given. "To your marks…Crack!" Super-cautious to begin with, every runner wary, lots of jostling, elbows, even pushing; as the two start lines merged, a communal sigh, no one had fallen. Now it was serious time. First lap in seventy flat, no problems with that; it was the sorting-out lap, but it needed to get faster or the sprinters, the hangers-on, would take it. Next two laps both in sixty-eight, no excitement yet, a couple of the backmarkers struggling already. The Ethiopian world-record holder, Taya Ambassa, was leading his teammate, Hakim Cherebet, and controlling the pace. Every time someone challenged, they would ease the pace up slightly and cause the challenge to evaporate.

Twelve laps gone, almost halfway, the sense of frustration in the crowd was almost palpable. And Mickey knew that if the Ethiopians' strategy continued, there would be only one thing to do. And the strategy did continue, so Mickey did exactly what he needed to do. 'Carpe Diem' flashed through his brain as he accelerated to the front and refused to fall back when the two Ethiopians picked up the pace. That four hundred went in sixty-two seconds with the Ethiopians refusing to give way; why should they? Two more laps at that same pace, and then again. Winzenreid and Atticus Mwangi, the Kenyan who'd taken silver at the previous Games, were the only athletes who could take the new pace. Behind the leading five, the pack was already spreadeagled around the track.

A further lap and suddenly Ambassa cracked, cracked completely. Now just four of them: Ethiopia, Kenya, USA, Great Britain. Just six laps remaining, the pace eased a little to sixty-three, sixty-four. Still four together at the front, four laps to go, the crowd screaming for the home athlete, "Go, Mickey, go!" But it wasn't Mickey who went; it was Hakim Cherebet…and he went backwards…quickly. Three still there at the front, three medals to chase, the backmarkers pursued and lapped, and another and another and another. Two laps, Mickey Honey knew that he had to go now, the leaders were hanging tough by sheer grit and determination, but the hurt was immense. Mickey lifted the pace, a small gap opened and then closed just as quickly as Mickey Winzenreid and Atticus Mwangi responded immediately to cover.

That penultimate four hundred went in just fifty-six seconds. The bell! Crowd on its feet, TMRG jumping up and down, one of them, one of their own leading! Speed increased once more, last two hundred, Mwangi to the front, Winzenreid covering, Mickey now in third. Into the home straight, last hundred and the pace lifted into an all-out sprint. Absolutely level now, absolutely level, Mickey in lane three, Winzenreid two, Mwangi on the inside lane. Throwing themselves at the tape and the line.

Collapse on the tartan track, exhausted, shattered, finished. Who won? Who won? Who won? The three fighters now with arms around each other's shoulders, looking up at the scoreboard, Jeff Harrington for once speechless. Who won? Who's won? And the scoreboard sprang into life...triumph and disaster.

3rd Atticus Mwangi, Kenya. 27.30.77

2nd Mickey Honey, GB. 27.30.73

1st Mickey Winzenreid, USA. 27.30.72

Triumph and disaster indeed; four hundredths of a second and one single hundredth of a second. That was the difference between triumph and disaster. But Mickey and Atticus didn't feel as if they'd been in a disaster; they felt as if they'd contributed to an epic conflict and Mickey Winzenreid had taken it. He beckoned to both of them, and together, they jogged around the track, and the entire crowd stayed on their feet. Lucy and Shelley were both crying and rushed down to the barrier as the three champions came past. Mickey.

"Hey, hey, c'mon you guys. No tears for us, not ever. Did my best, honestly did. My best time in a weird-paced race...still got the five to go; you'll see; you'll see."

He kissed them both and re-joined Atticus and the other Mickey. Eyebrows lifted, questioning, Mickey grinned. "My girlfriend and my sister...and my best friends."

Day 9. Sunday, 5 August

Lucy and Mickey were having a leisurely breakfast in the Olympic village restaurant, interrupted frequently by the congratulations offered to both. Marianne and Shelley had had coffee with them before going off to prepare for their events; first round of the four hundred metres hurdles for Shelley and final of the flat four hundred for Marianne. Shelley was very tired and needed her pre-race massage and a peptalk from Gilly. Marianne was calm; she'd made the final and whatever happened from now on was a bonus. It was a good place to be. The ever-present television was tuned to the women's marathon.

"Wish you were doing it, Luce?"

"Well, yeah, sort of…but there's no way to double with the 10K, is there? My legs are still feeling it from a couple of days ago, and it's only two more days to the five heats…and that'll be interesting with Sami as well. But in the future? Definitely, love to see what I could do…maybe have a think about the Rio Games…if I'm still racing." Mickey grinned. 'What else would they do with their lives?' Then Lucy said, "Mickey, you all right with…you know, getting silver and not gold? We all know how hard you worked for it."

"Lucy, my little angel and love of my life, there's a lot worse things than getting a silver at the Olympic Games, you know!" Mickey smiled.

"Like what, for instance?"

"Like finding out that the people you really care for don't care as much for you; that's a lot worse, and you know what? I ain't got that; I've got you, Shelley, all the guys in TMRG and Gilly, Dan and Chris of course, and I know without a doubt that you all care for me as much as I care for you…fact!" Lucy kissed him hard on the lips and did it again, and her heart soared.

Shelley certainly didn't feel great or rested for her heat but followed Gilly's race-briefing exactly. She knew what times would be likely from the other girls, and there were twenty-four to qualify for the semi-finals. Holding an exact stride pattern, Shelley made it through comfortable in 12th position overall on times but happily had a couple of seconds in hand. She knew she'd be more rested and ready for the semis.

It was Marianne's time. At the warm-up track, no one thought it was remotely strange that an athlete wearing the Dutch colours was going through her preparation under the guidance of a coach wearing a Great Britain tracksuit; the best people gravitated towards the best people, it was understood. The pre-race routine was finished, and they started the walk towards destiny.

"It's funny, isn't it, Gilly?" Marianne linked arms with her coach. "How we got here, all the stuff that happened. A lot of chance, a lot of luck and a lot of nice people. If you hadn't come to Holland on that trip—how long ago was it? Eleven years or something? If Kaas and Shelley hadn't gone to the last Games, hadn't met up, Kaas and I hadn't talked our way into Bath, I hadn't gently leant on you to coach me—I would never have made it at two hundred metres, you know—well, I know I wouldn't be here…Thank you, Gilly, thank you for everything." Marianne inclined her head into Gilly's shoulder and uttered a huge, long sigh. Gilly had been hearing a lot of nice words at the Games; Lucy, Shelley, Mickey and now Marianne.

"Wouldn't have missed it for the world, Marianne; loved every single minute…Marianne, it has been a privilege and an honour to work with you, to work with all of you. Coaching is my dream—my absolute dream. If it hadn't been for you guys, I think I'd still be teaching—not that that's a bad thing, but this is the Olympic Games, and I'm—we're—here! OK, go and have the best race; that's all you can do."

And Marianne did have the best race, ranked sixth going into the final; she was in a blanket finish with Caroline Hogarth, representing Great Britain, and Dixie-May Tarquine with the red, white and blue of the USA, although all three of them were a metre behind the winner and gold medallist Sonya Rees-Derek of the USA. Sonya had clocked a 49.550, and the three pursuers looked anxiously at the flashing scoreboard, then:

4th Dixie-May Tarquine, USA, 49.750

3rd Marianne Deussmann, Netherlands, 49.720

2nd Caroline Hogarth, GB, 49.700

1st Sonya Rees-Derek, USA, 49.550

From 6th in qualification to a place on the podium, and a personal best time by over half a second and her first time under fifty, all of Marianne's dreams had come true. The, by-now usual, reunion with all of TMRG, the hugs, the kisses, the tears. And resolve hardened even more in Lucy, Sami, Shelley and Mickey.

Day 10. Monday, 6 August

Shelley was watching the heats of the women's hundred metres hurdles event on television in her room; she hadn't trusted herself to go to the stadium; she had her four hundred hurdles semi-final later in the day, and she couldn't afford to get emotionally involved in the event that had brought her that fourth place back in Beijing. Shelley surprised herself by not thinking of missing out on a possible medal. She had made her choice and moved on. Now there were fresh targets to be met, one of which had already been achieved. As Shelley walked into the stadium along with the other twenty-three semi-finalists, she was spotted by the spectators sitting near the entrance, and they erupted. The cry was quickly taken up by the entire stadium; on their feet.

Shouting, cheering, name called out and Shelley responded; first the wave, then the smile, then the blown kiss and, finally, the Shelley wiggle. The crowd were happy, and Shelley was happy.

"Shelley Steele attempting to do the double, the heptathlon and the four hundred metres hurdles," Jeff Harrington said in the commentary box. "I don't think that this particular double has ever been done in the Olympic Games, although Wassana Winatho of Thailand did it back in 2007 in the South East Asian Games—she also took a gold in the four-by-four metres relay—but with all due respect, the Olympic Games are totally different."

The crowd's roar of approval had lifted Shelley. *They like me; they really like me! They want me to win! No pressure there, then.* Shelley waved again at the crowd, and the response lifted her that little bit more. Lane three in the first of the three semi-finals, and as with Marianne's four hundred flat, first and second through by right and then two fastest losers overall. The Hungarian Zuzana Gabor and Larissa Knox-Hooke USA, the ones that Shelley had deemed to be her main threats, both on form, both posting wins in the pre-Olympic circuit of races. Zuzana in four, Larissa in five. *Good! My two pace-setters.* Crowd silent, then exploding, "Shelley's running! Our Shelley, golden girl, ain't she? Lives up the road; no, honest, really does live just up the road. Go on, Shelley!"

Focused on the two lanes outside her, Shelley was feeling comfortable, in control of herself; she couldn't control what Zuzana and Larissa would do, so she was self-examining herself, head steady, look forward not down, two barriers cleared, closing on Larissa, four barriers, lean hard, five barriers, level with Larissa but Zuzana still ahead, through the top part of the bend, seven barriers, Zuzana coming back to me, concentrate, you silly bitch! Eight barriers, I'm leading, into the stretch, snap down hard, I'm free. I'm free! Feel the tape snapping on the chest, waving at the crowd, automatic qualification for the final. Look up at scoreboard, 53.33. Jeez, that's good for a semi! Turn back, embrace Zuzana and Larissa. Will Larissa make the final? Don't know; it's tough running in the first semi; everyone knows the time they need to get to beat the third placer. Who knows? We shall see. Shelley waved once again and disappeared to warm-down.

JoJo was ecstatic in her phone call to Chris Warren, took Japan in the final minute of added time, final minute! Result Japan nil, Great Britain one.

437

Scorer…Ms Joanna Jackson. Great Britain was in the final, a medal guaranteed. The all-conquering USA were waiting.

Day 11. Tuesday, 7 August

The semi-finals of the women's hundred metres hurdles were in the morning session. Again, Shelley was watching on TV, luxuriating in a day's rest before her final tomorrow. She had a massage and a short session with Gilly, where Shelley knew she would focus on pace and technique and that Gilly would get inside her mind, would talk about visualisation and mental attitude. Gilly had given the chat before, and she was an expert at it. Shelley welcomed it—all of it.

Gilly said that you had to be outside of yourself and watch yourself race; you had to see it in colour; you had to check out all the other stuff that was going on, and Shelley hadn't really understood that at first. What did the race smell like, what did it taste like, was there a feeling of touch? Shelley had got it, the smell of your own body and the sweat, the feeling of the nerves, the taste of your fingers when you licked them as you got down into the blocks, all the feelings, all the anticipations. See yourself winning, go through every single stride in real time, check the hurdles clearance. All positive, all clear; everything you've worked for, you deserve it. Dream a little because if you can't dream, then how do you know when your dream comes true?

Shelley noted the times in the three semi-finals, decided that she would have made the final if she had been running half-decently, and then she switched off her mind to focus on her preparations for her race, her final, her very much hoped-for medal. A sleep, one more chat with Gilly—Gilly had that fantastic ability to relax people, to make themselves not take anything too seriously, even if it was the most serious thing in life—then Shelley watched the sprint hurdles final, saw that the times of the three medallists were faster than her personal best, decided that if she had made a different decision, she would have been able to beat them, but who cared now? You can't look back, only look forward, and Shelley was most definitely looking forward to her final. A double in the heptathlon and four hundred hurdles…was that even possible?

But there was one event that Shelley was going to watch, was going into the stadium to watch because Lucy and Sami were running in the five thousand metres heats.

Lucy and Sami had warmed up together. Lucy sensed that Sami was nervous and was gently trying to draw her out, "Lucy, I'm only here because of you, you and Gilly, of course. But you, if you hadn't persuaded me, I don't think I would even have gone for it, never would have thought that I could make the Olympic Games, never thought I'd got the talent, so thank you, little one, thank you from the bottom of my heart. Just being here is enough, you know? 'Course I'm going to give it everything, 'course I am, make the final, why not? Look at us old ladies! You were eleven and I was thirteen when we met at London schools, you remember? 'Course you do! Then that fabulous English schools cross-country up in Washington, fabulous times…They're here, you know? That lovely family we stayed with. You know both the girls have made GB junior teams; can you believe that? Without being flash, little one, we did something good up there; yeah, we really did. So, I'll say it again, thank you, thank you from the bottom of my heart."

And Lucy and Sami both qualified for the final. In Lucy's heat, the other athletes were watching Lucy; they'd seen her in the ten thousand, and she was able to run the race pretty much as she wanted. Sami ran a cautious race but had the confidence to go when it was needed, covered all the breaks and finished in the top five to comfortably make the final. Fifteen in the final in three days' time…but the day before that, Lucy had another appointment to keep, a somewhat wetter appointment in the Serpentine in Hyde Park.

Day 12. Wednesday, 8 August

They were on the warm-up track together, Shelley and Mickey. Both were racing in the evening session, Mickey in the five thousand metres heats and Shelley immediately after him in the final of the four hundred metres hurdles. They were comfortable in each other's company, Shelley and Mickey; brother and sister, brother and sister who got on unlike many blood brothers and sisters.

"Gonna win again, Shell? Gonna be the Games golden girl; actually, reckon you're golden girl already. Being in the crowd when you were racing, it was amazing, Shell, just amazing…they're all a little bit in love with you, you know."

"Yeah, blow them a kiss, wiggle my bum, 'course they're gonna love me…Mickey, seriously, aren't we just so lucky to be here? Me and you, wrong side of the tracks, weren't we? And look at us now. You know what, Mickey? Not one day goes by that I don't thank Mr Warren, honest, every single day. We got so lucky, me'n you, and all of TMRG, changed our lives, didn't he? So now I reckon it is a bit of payback time, like JoJo said about giving Mr Warren her medal, me too, honest again. Even if I don't get on the podium for the hurdles—

and it'll be bloody hard to do that—I'm giving him my medal from the heptathlon, I promise."

They stopped and looked at each other. Mickey nodded. Shelley hugged him. "Shit or bust, Mickey, shit or bust! Go out there and give it to them!"

Mickey in the first of the two heats; Mickey Winzenreid and Atticus Mwangi in the second. The heats of the longer distance events tend to be tactical affairs; athletes are focusing on conserving as much energy as they can for the final. First five in each heat and five fastest losers to qualify for the final on the last track day of the Olympic Games. Mickey knew it was going to be a tactical race, but he was confident in his own ability, proud of what he'd done in the ten thousand.

OK, so if it's a slow pace, I know now that I do have the speed. I can lift and cover, done it once, do it again. And they were off, a big field, twenty-two athletes, maybe too big. Mickey was cautious, watching everyone around him, staying towards the back, just waiting until the field spread a little, and there was more room, less danger. First lap through in 68 seconds, very slow, too slow; if it had been the final, the sprinters would have been happy. Little increase on lap two or three or four; sixteen hundred metres covered in four minutes thirty seconds. A little increase in pace now but only a little, up to 66 seconds per lap, and it stayed like that until eight laps were gone, and now the athletes were preparing for the finish, down the finishing straight and into the final four laps, and they all knew it was going to take off, take off very soon.

And it was Taya Ambassa who took it on. Quietly seething that his tactics hadn't paid off in the ten thousand, he was determined to make amends here, but despite his speed, Taya couldn't put a big gap between himself and the chasers, that initial very modest pace meant that two-thirds of the field felt that they had a very good chance of making the final. That four hundred in sixty seconds flat, three laps only now, another sixty second split, twelve athletes remaining, a slight drop off to sixty-two, the bell, the bell, 'give it everything', and at last, the gaps started to show, the twelve became eight, became six, final two hundred, off the bend into the straight, 'make the first five, can't take chances', and that was when Mickey Honey clipped the foot of the athlete inside him, also making his move at the same time. In the most undignified manner of a genuine fall, Mickey Honey was down on the track.

Immediately up and chasing hard now but getting those few seconds back in less than one hundred metres was too much. Mickey Honey finishing sixth and now qualification in the lap of the gods...or rather in the times of the second heat. And it wasn't to be. All five fastest losers came from the second heat, knowing exactly what they needed to do; they played it to perfection.

And Mickey Honey was out, down and out. The dream was over. Protests went in from the Great Britain team managers, but Mickey and everyone knew there was little chance, and there wasn't. Four years to wait now for a second chance, four very long years until Rio. Within seconds, Mickey was up in the stands with his supporters; no one really knew what to say, so Mickey said it.

"Shit happens and you deal with it; no one's fault, no one meant it."

Mickey had his arms around Lucy and Gilly had her arms around Mickey, and they thought that the world had ended. There was a stir in the crowd near TMRG, spectators were turning around as four track-suited athletes came up to Mickey; Taya Ambassa, Hakim Cherebet, Atticus Mwangi and Mickey Winzenreid were all standing there. Atticus was the spokesman.

"Mickey, we are so sorry; we were looking forward to fighting you to the death again on Saturday..." And Mickey Honey felt lifted, not much but enough to be able to smile.

"Aah, thanks, guys, I'm going to miss you too." Atticus smiled at Lucy.

"Look after him for us; he is a good man, a good man." And that was when Mickey lost it, lost it completely.

*****

"What's happened? Something's happened?" And one of the officials filled Shelley in on the fall, the protest, the judges' decision. And something happened to Shelley; it was something both good and bad. She was filled with a white heat, a white heat of anger. *Mickey's my brother; he's always been there for me, always; it just ain't fucking fair; no, it's not. Well, my brother's going to get a gold medal anyway, you bet he is, so I've got to get two, one for Mickey and one for Mr Warren.*

Shelley drawn in lane six, she'd qualified third fastest. Ireland's Siobhan Poldark the fastest, then Irena Klatchlikova, a blast from Shelley's past from Russia. ("Shelley, you made me change, you made me realise I could be a clean athlete, I'm here because of you") with Zuzana Gabor and Larissa Knox-Hooke as fourth and fifth fastest. Realistically, all five knew it was going to be between them; there was almost half a second difference before the sixth fastest qualifier. Jeff Harrington in the commentary box.

"Ladies and gentlemen, girls and boys, we come to the final event of the evening, the women's four hundred metres hurdles final. We've already had enough drama this evening, but now we have some more, Shelley Steele from Great Britain is going for a golden double, never before achieved in an Olympic Games, the heptathlon and the four hundred hurdles…can it be done? We shall see."

Staring down at the tartan track, hips high, anticipating and away! First steps to rise out of the blocks and Shelley was already focusing on Larissa Knox-Hooke one lane outside her. By the first hurdle, Shelley had taken two metres away from Larissa; there was no thought of pacing now, Shelley was burning inside. By hurdle number three and into the back-straight, Shelley was level with Larissa. The entire stagger had been brought back in one-third of the race. The crowd could see the margins over all seven of Shelley's pursuers. With two hundred metres to go, just five hurdles remaining, Shelley's lead was ridiculous, and the crowd were waiting—make that 'anticipating'—for her to pay the price of going out too fast, far too fast. But if Shelley could hear their combined thoughts, she was taking no notice of them.

One-fifty now, halfway around the final bend, holding that stride pattern, no drop down, stretch and go, stretch and go, totally in control, final hundred, nobody sitting now, the entire stadium on their feet, barely any noise, everyone's focus was on the athlete leading, Shelley Steele, Golden Girl, was running herself into a place where very few people in the entire sports world wouldn't know her name.

Over the final hurdle, aim for the line, who was second? Who was third? Who cared. And as Shelley crossed the line and lifted her hands high, she turned and waved to where she knew her own particular groupies and star-truckers would be; she put her hands to her mouth and sent the air-kisses upwards to them. Larissa, Zuzana, Siobhan and Irena all over to Shelley, group hugs, of course, and then the mock-bowing, which wasn't really a mock, it was real; it was respect.

"I will grow old telling people that I was in this race, Shelley…unbelievable, unbelievable!" Irena spoke for all of them. They looked up to the electronic scoreboard, waiting, waiting, and then it flicked into life:

3rd Irena Klatchlikova, Russia 52.81

2nd Siobhan Poldark, Ireland 52.75

1st Shelley Steele, GB 51.35

And the magic letters 'WR! WR! World Record! World Record!' were flashing brightly.

"Ladies and gentlemen, a new world record for Shelley Steele. Shelley has absolutely smashed the previous world record by ninety-nine one-hundredths, almost a full second, quite remarkable." Jeff Harrington spoke for all.

Into the drug testing centre, all negatives, Irena thanking Shelley once again. And then Shelley did what she wanted to, she joined up with her friends, her extended family; she joined up with TMRG.

And just before they left to go their separate ways, Gilly received a most interesting phone call, so interesting that she excused herself to take it.

Day 13. Thursday, 9 August

Every one of them boarded the event bus going from the Olympic village to the Serpentine in Hyde Park; everyone except JoJo. JoJo had other business to attend to. JoJo would be at Wembley Stadium that evening, playing in the Olympic football final against the United States of America. Mickey was surprisingly upbeat.

"How can you be like that, Mickey?" Lucy was snuggled into his shoulder.

"Lucy, it's no one's fault; you find out a lot about yourself when you're dealing with stuff like this…I'm not dead. I'm not even injured. I could run again today. I'll be back; yeah, I'll be back." Gilly took notice of Mickey's words. Mickey went on, "Look at us, Lucy, well, look at you! One gold already, swimming in the Olympics! Bloody hell, Lucy, everyone's watching you…but I'm the lucky one; I've got you."

Lucy whispered to herself, "No, I'm the lucky one; I've got you."

At the Serpentine now, Dan was with Lucy by the edge of the water. Up in the stands, Gilly whispered quietly to Chris. Chris nodded and grinned and passed the small packages along the line. And now everyone was smiling; everyone was in on the secret. As the announcer called out Lucy's name to step forward, there was a huge round of applause; everyone knew Lucy, everyone. How many athletes represented their country in two different sports in the same Olympics? A few maybe, but not many. Lucy's fan club stood up together. Lucy looked up and waved…and then saw them holding up the T-shirts from all those years ago, from the English schools cross-county.

'GO. LUCY. GO!'

Lucy just burst out laughing, good old Mr Warren! Lucy knew that he had sorted it all out, good old Mr Warren! And Lucy resolved to give it everything, in the immortal words of Shelley, 'shit or bust!'.

Twenty-five swimmers in the water for the six laps, and Lucy was under no illusions at all; if she didn't finish last, then she'd achieved something…best swimmers in the world…and me! She laughed at herself again…*but I did it, I did it! Black girl swimming, me, I really did it!*

The klaxon sounded, immediate panic and confusion over that initial two hundred metres as the pecking order sorted itself out. Lucy was sprinting, all the world's best open water swimmers were sprinting, and the sprint stretched out for four, five hundred metres until a semblance of order. Lucy was feeling it already, but as the pace eased slightly, she regained a little breath and a little composure. 'It's bonus; it's all bonus.' Two swimmers already off the back, Lucy on the outside of the pack, breathing to the right, taking a draft off of the hip of the swimmer to her right, holding her position, first lap gone, Lucy picked up the drinking bottle, so happy that she'd worked on the technique of taking and drinking; heard a whistle blowing and saw a flag waving, someone getting a warning, maybe an accidental touch of the boat? Three further swimmers off of the pack now, two laps gone, another drink and halfway. Halfway done already! What happens to time when you're swimming? Accelerates or something?

A movement at the front, three swimmers making a break, Lucy lifted her head and sprinted flat out to get back on, she managed…just. Hanging tough now, can I? Can I? The lead three revolving, taking turns in leading, fifteen or twenty strokes, taking turns in drafting off of each other with that fifteen per cent less effort required than being in front. But Lucy couldn't take the lead, she was at one hundred per cent effort just to hang on in fourth. Final lap, final drink, another whistle, another flag wave…but no disqualification. Half a lap, the final two hundred metres. Suddenly, the pace went wild, flat-out efforts from everyone. And Lucy could see the gap open, flailed at the water, but no fairy-tale ending this time.

Lucy Newton, already a gold medallist in the ten-thousand metres on the track, took a magical fourth in the ten-thousand metres in the water. And in the stands, Dan Bullet, Gilly Warren, Chris Warren and Mickey Honey stood and applauded. Lucy had missed out on a medal by just three seconds…but three seconds in a swimming event can be an eternity.

Lucy stayed and congratulated the three girls in front of her, Hungary, Italy, USA, and looked at the times. Wow! One fifty-seven! Me as well! And then she literally ran up to her group; a huge hug for Dan, her coach, another hug for Kaas, also her coach, and then hugs for everybody, Shelley and Mickey the last. Shelley and Mickey both looked at Lucy, wanting to ask but a little scared. Lucy smiled again and then laughed.

"You guys look like you're at a funeral, honestly! Look, I'm obviously a bit disappointed, but I'm certainly not unhappy, fourth in the Olympics. Me, fourth! Never thought I'd make it in swimming…well, I hoped but didn't really think it was realistic…but it was, and I did it! You wait and see now; there will have been lots of black kids out there watching on TV, and the papers will make a big thing about it. You just wait and see how many black kids get into swimming now because they know that they can!"

It was back to the village for a rest before they were all heading out again; this time to Wembley to cheer on JoJo. But first a conversation was needed and Gilly wondered which way it would go…But she thought that she already knew.

"Shelley, Mickey, fancy a coffee?" And they both knew that it might be something important because the others hadn't been invited. "So, I had a call last night; you might remember I took it outside?" They nodded. "Well, it was Mark Blatchford, GB manager for athletics. Remember him?"

Two nodded 'yes'. "He had a proposition for you both…didn't want to say anything earlier because of Lucy racing…"

"Gilly, c'mon please," Mickey was pleading. Shelley thought that maybe, just maybe, she knew. And when Gilly explained what Mark Blatchford was suggesting, it took almost one tenth of a second for Shelley and Mickey to agree. Perhaps 'Agree' wasn't the strongest word, they were both ecstatic. Gilly went through the timetable. "Maybe worth writing it down?"

For Mickey, it was a chance of redemption. For Shelley, it was a possible chance of lifetime fame…and maybe fortune.

"Listen, guys, don't say anything before JoJo's match this evening; it's her night, but after the match, I think you should tell everyone. I haven't even told Chris yet. Is it OK if I confirm with Mark Blatchford?" Shelley and Mickey were jumping in the air, amazingly hugging each other with the very real chance of falling flat on their faces and negating everything that Gilly had just told them.

*****

There was a big crowd at Wembley that evening, home team Great Britain against reigning world champions and superstars USA. JoJo was in charge in the dressing room.

"They think they're going to win; they think it's going to be a pushover for them; they think they're going to rub us into the ground…But you know what I think? Actually, you know what I know? They're wrong; they're one hundred per cent wrong. Look at us, first time ever there's been a GB team, ever. Nobody expected us to even get out of our group, but we did, and we're here in the final, in the bloody Olympic final! We can make history here, you guys. Do you believe that?"

The players, starters and subs, stood in a circle, hands went in. JoJo started chanting, "GB! GB! GB!" It got louder and louder; every player now chanting, almost shouting, believing, believing that they could. And they were hoping that team USA in the dressing room just down the corridor could hear them.

Out on the pitch now, waving at the crowd, listening to the chants, the individual names called. Into the centre circle, the coin was tossed, Alicia Smith, the USA captain, makes the call and gets the call right. USA for the kick-off, short pass, diagonal pass backwards and across half the pitch; midfielder holds, then passes back again, eight USA players massing on goal area, ball goes high, Alicia heads it down, onto the goal-line, takes the high return, and it's in! Less than one minute gone, USA one, GB nil. The American players running back, even more confident now. That confidence showing in the ball staying on the USA feet, pass after pass, twenty minutes gone, USA dominating, totally dominating.

JoJo growing frustrated, urging GB to lift themselves…and they tried. An interception, ball high into the USA goal area, goalie claws it down from the sky, holds, looks up, the twins, Domino and Davinia Kennedy, running free on the left, throws out, ball received, the old one-two, GB full-back left floundering, thirty minutes gone, and it's USA 2-0 GB. JoJo is trying desperately to hold her focus, to maintain concentration. *This isn't supposed to happen! We're playing like fucking muppets!*

"C'mon, girls, we're ten times better than this! Time to believe!" And the words did lift team GB. The passes became more accurate; the confidence of holding the ball growing, team GB were coming back! And on the stroke of halftime, JoJo from way out took her chance and volleyed for goal; it was going in! She was just about to turn and run back celebrating when she saw her shot ricochet off of the goalpost out to left-field. Domino receives the ball, sees her chance, volleys up to her sister close to the GB goal area, jinks around the keeper, USA 3, GB nil. The referee's whistle blows, and a disconsolate white-shirted GB with heads and shoulders drooping trudge back to the dressing room.

"Three-nil, three-nil, ladies! OK, we might lose, but I'm not going to be a loser, and there is a huge difference. We can go out there and just play out the time, or we can go out there and attack, attack, attack! There are about a million little girls out there in the crowd, and they want to be like us; they want to be you, and they want to be me! All they want is to pull on an England, a Scottish, a Welsh team shirt, are we going to let them down? No, never in a million years." The heads were gradually lifting.

"I will die trying not to let those little girls down; they deserve better; we deserve better! I was one of those little girls; every one of you was one of those kids." JoJo was pointing now at all the players one by one. "It was my teacher who believed in me to start with…and he's out there now with those million little kids. I will not, I will NOT let them down!"

It was a different GB team that started the second half, and the Americans knew it immediately. Every tackle that went in was hard; every challenge was ruthless, but it was almost on the hour that USA broke. JoJo took the ball just in her own half, looked up and saw the USA defence backing off, reluctant to commit, so JoJo took off, dribbling, dribbling, dribbling, the Americans covering, waiting for the pass, but there was no pass, as space kept uncovering, JoJo advanced on the edge of the area with team USA close to panic. JoJo watched the keeper come off her line, come off just a little too far, and, without hesitation, chipped the ball high, and it dipped just under the bar with the keeper scrambling back but unable to do anything. Now three-one, and the game was on!

Team USA knew it was on now; team GB was attack after attack, and when the ball was lost, the British girls were fighting back. *How could this happen? We're team USA; we're world number one.* The thoughts were going through heads, and the self-doubt was starting. Alicia Smith was desperately trying to lift her team but to little effect. She recognised herself in JoJo and gave grudging respect.

GB possession again, the ball flies out to the left, a measured cross not to the middle but directly to the right wing, a fast cross to the goal area and to JoJo…but JoJo is facing away from goal, caught wrong-footed. A sigh of relief from the

American defence, which immediately turned to despair as JoJo—without turning—took the pass on her right foot and sent it into the bulging net with an overhead shot; Three-two, twelve minutes remaining.

And a million little girls in the crowd screamed their heads off and swore to themselves that one day, one day soon, they'd be doing exactly this.

"We can do this! We can do this!" But time was running out, running out very quickly. There were only three minutes remaining, and the ref was looking at her watch continually. Jodie Spear in the GB goal saw JoJo standing unmarked on the halfway circle and threw a long ball. Team USA panicked; they'd seen what JoJo could do. Three defenders rushed at her. She's not going to do that again! And JoJo did something different. As they neared, she turned away from them, played the ball back to the unmarked centre-forward Annie Hope, who screamed the shot into the net. Three-three, less than two minutes to play.

And a million little girls in the crowd screamed even louder.

Alicia Smith was onto her team, lecturing, pointing, almost shouting but then lowering her voice to ensure that the team, her team, had to concentrate to hear what she was saying.

"We play it out, play the time out, our kick-off and we hold possession, got that? We are still the best team in the world; let it go to extra time; let it go to penalties if needs be. We're stronger; we're better; we have never—let me say that again, ladies—we have never lost a match in added time or on penalties. So, we hold possession, go to the line; two, three players on the ball, turn your back, stick your backside out...do NOT give this ball away!"

JoJo was thinking, *What would I do in this situation? What would I be saying to my team?* And JoJo knew, well, she thought she knew, and she was prepared to gamble on it, exactly what Alicia would be saying and exactly what team USA would need to do to reclaim the match. *Left or right or down the middle? Who's the best shielder? Yes, Tanya, Tanya Brown; it's gonna go to her...I hope.* A huge decision from JoJo, probably the biggest she had made on the football field, and very fleetingly, Shelley's words came in her mind, 'Shit or bust!' and JoJo smiled inside. *Shit or bust, then!*

When the ref blew for the kick-off, JoJo didn't even follow where the ball was going; she'd made that decision, and now she had to go with it. Running at Tanya Brown, flying towards Tanya Brown...'Yes! Yes! Yes!' Tanya saw JoJo flying at her and panicked, got the ball—just—but couldn't control and saw JoJo take it off of her feet and watched her run and run and run towards the USA goal;

no defender near enough to take her out, straight at the goalie, wait for the attempt to dislodge, wait for the attempt to foul even, sidestep, keeper on the ground, the USA players on the ground, it was over. JoJo Jackson side-footed the ball into the net and ran back, screaming, screaming, screaming to her adoring teammates. The ref blew the final whistle. USA still on the floor, weeping sobbing, shaking their heads how? How did this happen?

"Show some class, you guys." JoJo was speaking to a celebrating group. "Show some class; it could have been us; could very easily have been us." And team GB did indeed show some class, a lot of class. JoJo was over to Alicia immediately, no words, just a huge hug. And then onto every USA player, hugs and a few words, no gloating, just commiserations: 'Great team', 'Played brilliantly'. The players linked arms and walked and jogged around the pitch, waving, smiling, blowing kisses to the millions of little girls out there. And a million dreams were born.

*****

"Mr Warren…here's your medal. I promised you. I promised you." And then she threw herself into Chris Warren's arms and thought back to all those years ago when it had started, when it had felt safe, when she had started to believe. This man had done it, this man who was still here. *Thank you, God, thank you.* Very close now, very close to tears, Chris Warren drew a deep breath.

"Oh, JoJo, thank you so much. I will treasure this medal; it's my first Olympic gold, you know?" They all laughed.

"But, JoJo, may I ask something from you?" JoJo nodded her head, 'yes'.

"JoJo, would you look after it for me? I'm hopeless with taking care of stuff, just ask Gilly." And they all laughed again.

"Could you do that for me, JoJo? Could you look after my Olympic medal somewhere safe? Could you show it around for me, please? Would that be all right?" JoJo really was speechless; she nodded her head 'yes' and put her arms around Chris Warren once again.

"But it is yours, sir, your medal, I promised…and yes, I'd love to look after your medal. Thank you, sir; thank you for everything."

"Down to you now, Sami, Lucy, last chance tomorrow in the women's five thousand; our little gang has got five golds already plus a silver and a bronze; I reckon that would put us up in the overall country rankings!" Dan was grinning. They looked at each other; something was up.

"Well, maybe." Gilly was grinning as well, definitely something up. "Shelley, Mickey, got anything to say? Maybe to wish Sami and Lucy good luck for tomorrow?"

"I'd like to wish them good luck, but something's come up for tomorrow. I might be a bit busy."

"Shell, you've got to come and watch us!" said Lucy and Sami together.

"And me too, please, Shelley. I have the four-by-four hundred relay," Marianne said.

"Oh, I'll be there, guys. I'll most definitely be there, and I'll be watching you particularly closely, Marianne. I've been added to the relay squad. I'm running the relay heats for Great Britain tomorrow! I'm a total novice in relays, but Mr Blatchford was impressed by my hurdles, said I was faster than some of the girls in the flat four-hundred, said he'd put me on the first or last leg, so I didn't have two takeovers to worry about—almost certainly the first, I reckon. And then hand over to the real four-hundred runners if we make the final for Sunday." And there wasn't one person there who believed that Shelley would be dropped from the team for the final.

"Shelley, I think it is how we met, racing against each other?" Marianne said.

"Is OK, Marianne? It's OK?"

"Perfect, Shelley—absolutely perfect." Marianne walked over to Shelley and kissed her, and they were both thinking of all the possible scenarios.

"Mickey, you'll come and watch me 'n Sami and Shelley? Mickey, what's going on? Please be there, please be there for us. I run better when you're watching." Lucy was close to tears, and Mickey was smiling as he walked over to her.

"I would never not watch you run, Lucy…and you guys, all of you, but Shell and Sami tomorrow, of course I'll be there, but I just hope the timetable is right, can't stay up too late, need a bit of a rest on Saturday, got something to do on Sunday…" And they all knew immediately.

"Mickeeeeeeeeeey! You're doing the marathon! You're in the marathon on Sunday, oh my god!"

Day 14. Friday, 10 August

Last event of the morning session and everyone was in the stands, everyone except Shelley and Marianne, who were warming up together, giggling together, striding out together. The golden girl was watched by everybody and so was Marianne. Lots of stories had leaked out about how they'd got to know each other, lots of stories about them training together, same coach, Kaas as Shelley's boyfriend. The British Press loved the stories, and the British public loved reading the stories from the British Press.

"Ladies, please." Two heats only, first three teams in each heat and two fastest losers to make the final. Marianne in lane four, heat one; Shelley in lane eight, heat two. Marianne was on glory leg, fourth runner, and Shelley was lead-off merchant. An elongated stagger for the relay, lead-off athlete in each team staying in lane throughout and the second athlete in each team required to stay in lane until the five hundredth mark was passed. The first takeover would be clean, but as soon as the runners came together, takeovers between second and third, and third and fourth runners could be very hairy, seven athletes jostling on the line, watching their incoming runner and moving inwards and outwards accordingly.

"Set..." and off! Shelley watching intently, very aware that she was the novice here. The marshals moved the second-leg runners onto the track. Some of the staggers gradually being eaten up but difficult to check the leaders; it seemed to Shelley that USA and Holland were making inroads. First takeovers and second-leg runners were off. That hundred around the bend done and the athletes now in order, USA leading, Marianne's Holland second. Clean takeover for USA and Holland with so much space between them and their chasers, Ukraine and France desperately working hard to close.

Third runners on the line jostling, USA inside by right, Holland next, a few movements outside them as teams saw their incoming runner go up or down the rankings. Field spreading out now as the third runners got into their rhythm. USA ten metres in the lead, Holland with five metres over Ukraine, and that's how the order stayed until the finish. Marianne making slight inroads on team USA, but USA comfortable in control.

Shelley had learnt a lot by watching, and to her, it was evident that, for her as the lead-off runner, there was only one thing that she could do, go bloody fast, give team GB the lead, and then there wouldn't be any messy takeovers. No fear for Shelley settling in the blocks, this was a bonus, a bonus for which she was very grateful, another race in the Olympic Games, and what if GB did get a medal in the final? Then Shelley even not running that final, would get a medal because she had run in these heats. *Pace it like the hurdles and I'll be fine. I'll be fine.* And Shelley Steele was a lot more than fine. Shelley Steele split a 49.99 to give team GB a five-metre lead over Jamaica and straight into the final as heat winners.

"What d'you split, Marianne?"

"49.99, only a couple of tenths off my individual. You, Shelley, what did you split?" Shelley burst out laughing.

"49.99! What are we like? Same bloody everything as usual!"

"I see you in the final tomorrow, Shelley."

"No, they only needed me for qualification."

"Trust me, Shelley, you'll be in the final tomorrow; you'll be on the start line." And in a blinding flash of awareness, Shelley realised that it was very likely true.

*****

It was their time—Lucy's and Sami's. Sami had lost that fear and nervousness; it was still there, but Sami kept it under control. Gilly had done what Gilly did best, she had got rid of the fears…rather, she'd taught both Sami and Lucy to accept them for what they were.

"I'm pretty scared, coach…" Sami said.

"Yeah, I would be too—really scared! You know, Olympic final and I'm one of the best distance runners in the world, running at my home stadium, a hundred thousand people cheering me on, willing me to win…yeah, I'd be terrified!"

Sami and Lucy laughed out loud. "Makes it a bit more realistic like that, doesn't it?" Sami was smiling now.

"Sorry, Gilly, sorry. You know…"

"Know what, Sami? Sami, Lucy, you were at Wembley with me last night? Well, I think you were. What was the loudest noise you heard all night?"

"That's easy, easy-peasy, all those kids, all those little girls screaming for GB and for JoJo. Oh my god, that was unbelievable!"

"Except it wasn't unbelievable, was it? All those kids wanted to be playing at Wembley, just as tonight there will be another hundred thousand little girls wanting to be on the track, wanting to be running…wanting to be you."

"You remember those two twins in Northumberland at English schools?" Sami interjected.

"Yeah, Lucy told me; they both made it to GB juniors. Fantastic! Just fantastic!"

"And they did it because of you, because of you guys, because of what you taught them, because of how you made them feel…you made them feel good; you made them believe in themselves…I would bet a thousand pounds, no make that a million pounds that those twins are in the stadium tonight. Actually, I know they are. Alisha made sure they got complementary tickets to watch you. Alisha's another one who believes in you; we all believe in you. It's been a long journey, ladies; it's been a great journey, not all sweetness and honey along the way, but—for me—the little bit of hurt has been worth it, worth it a million times over. Let me say one more thing and then I'll stop because I'm getting boring; I'm actually beginning to bore myself!

"OK here we go, 'There's nothing to fear but fear itself.' How about that, ladies? And the thing is, it's true. What if you don't win? You going to be thrown out of your house? No! Your parents going to disown you? Don't think so! Can you believe how proud they are? TMRG, all those wonderful friends that you have, they gonna walk away? No! Never in a million years. So, go on, go for it, what d'you have to lose? Absolutely nothing—nothing! Get out there, girls; get out there and show the world what London kids are like; get out there and show them that London kids are the best!"

It was a night and a race that nobody in the stadium or watching on TV would ever forget. There were only ever going to be nine athletes in the frame; seven had raced to the ten thousand: the three Kenyans, three Ethiopians and Lucy. Add in Sami Richards (GB) and Namazzi Kizza (Uganda) and the field was set. Lucy had told Sami how she intended to race, her strategies, the pace she was intending, and Sami had listened, nodding her head again and again and again. It was simple really. Lucy remembered what she had told the three Kenyans her surname meant, 'she who suffers in silence', and tonight, she intended to show them that her self-appointed tribal name was absolutely true.

"You going to give it a go with me, Sami?" Sami nodded 'yes' because Lucy had decided what was needed and what they had to do. "Ladies…" Fifteen athletes in the final, just the single start line needed. Introductions, waves and smiles from the athletes, special cheers for Sami and Lucy, the London girls.

"To your marks." Lean forward and ready. The explosion from the gun, immediate reaction and the field settled down to see how this one would work out, what pace? What tactics? For the sprinters or for the even-pace guys? They all knew that it would take at least a couple of laps to sort itself out; after all, this was an Olympic final, so no one was going to go mad early on, too much to lose.

Except two athletes had decided not to conform with conventional wisdom for championship races, two athletes had made the decision to be different, to go for it. Lucy had told Sami exactly the pace that was required, "That's the time, Sami, set a few years back now, no one's got near it; no one in tonight's line-up can get near it...except us."

Lucy went straight into the lead, Sami just inches behind, almost a sigh from the pack. *Great! Someone's gonna lead; don't have to worry about it now.* Lucy glanced at the clock as she went through the two hundred metres mark, '34'. Perfect! Four hundred in 68, eight hundred in 2 minutes 16 seconds. Thoughts from the pursuers, *OK, OK, you've proved your point; let's not be stupid; world record pace ain't going to carry on, not in an Olympic final.* The gap was ten metres already; she who suffers in silence and Sami were expressionless. Four laps gone, sixteen hundred metres. "Four minutes, 30, 31, 32..."

The stats guys, the commentary team, the knowledgeable spectators were doing their sums, working out the options. "Naah, ain't gonna happen; that's a world record pace, and it was Tirunesh Dibaba who set it; ain't nobody running tonight who can get near that."

But there were two athletes who weren't only near world record pace, they were on it and showing no sign of slowing down. It was close to panic in the pack. *What if they don't come back to us? Twenty metres, they have to come back to us; can't keep that up, no way!* Zahra Kamau made her decision, moved to the front of the pack, now in third place and focused on trying to cut into the lead. A gap opened behind Zahra as she matched the pace of the two leaders but couldn't close down.

Through the halfway point, two and half thousand metres, the twin metronomes still on pace. "Seven minutes 1, 2, 3..." Sami was hurting like never before. *Does Lucy feel like this? I have to keep going. I have to.*

In the stands, Mickey was smiling, checking out the others and smiling; he knew. Lucy hadn't shared her race plan with Mickey, but he now knew exactly what Lucy and Sami had planned, and now it was coming to fruition. Nine laps gone, less than four to go; the metronome...68, 68, 68, 68, every lap give or take the tiniest of margins. Lucy still leading from Sami, Sami going into a dark place that she'd never visited before but still hanging tough. Zahra in no man's land between the leaders and the pack, and the pack fifty metres back. Two laps to go, the spectators could see a gap opening between Lucy and Sami and then saw why as the lap timer came up with 66 seconds. And the final lap now, everyone on their feet, Jeff Harrington going ballistic in the commentary box, the spectators going equally ballistic. "She did the bloody marathon swim yesterday! Did the ten-kilometre swim—got fourth, you know—and now she's smashing the entire field here; bloody hell, kid's a legend!"

Mickey was still smiling because he knew. Lucy didn't dare wave to the crowd, didn't dare to break her rhythm, final two hundred, waves of sound, 'focus, focus, focus!' Into the home straight, Sami twenty metres back now, Zahra closing hard, the pack in despair; it wasn't meant to be like this! Break the tape, over the line, collapse, total collapse. *I have nothing left in me—nothing.* Sami was hanging tough to hold that second place. *Me! A bloody Olympic silver, me!* And Zahra Kamau took third. The three medallists lay there, then were joined on the floor by every athlete as they crossed the line. Lucy looked up, searching the scoreboard...flashing now, flashing, times ready to come up.

3rd Zahra Kamau, Kenya 14.14.01

2nd Sami Richards, Great Britain 14.12.22

1st Lucy Newton, Great Britain 14.07.35

WR! WR! WR! NEW WORLD RECORD!

The three medallists couldn't even jog around the arena to take the rapturous applause from the crowd; they were just too exhausted. They walked, arms around each other's shoulders, smiles and kisses to each other and to the crowd. They stopped by TMRG; of course, they did. Mickey raised his eyebrows, waiting. A huge sigh from Lucy luxuriating in Mickey's arms.

"Sometimes you have to go beyond...sometimes you have to go to places that you didn't even know existed, not 'til you get there...think me'n Sami visited that place this evening; yeah, we did."

"You got me there, Lucy...to be honest, I didn't even have a race plan...it was just sort of, 'well, I'm in the Olympic final so that's it', so it was you, little one, you, and Gilly. All that 'nothing to fear but fear itself', you were right, weren't you, Gilly?"

"Yeah, the race..." Gilly was smiling now. "It was all right...I s'pose..." And that really did crack them up.

Day 15. Saturday, 11 August. Final Track and Field Day of the London Olympic Games

Shelley's mobile rang.

"Shelley, Gilly here, just had it confirmed that you're definitely running in the final. Yeah, I know that Mark Blatchford told you last night, but he's definitely confirmed now; team names have gone into the officials and media. Shelley, you know warm-up and takeover practice times? Yeah, good. See you there then." Gilly, who had already done a lot of smiling in the last week, smiled again. She was wondering how Shelley would respond to the news down at the warm-up track.

*****

"Mickey, you all right with not running the five today?" Lucy was lying back in Mickey's arms, her legs as sore as she could remember. She looked over at the gold medal next to her bed. Mickey considered his reply.

"To be honest, Luce, I don't really know…it was like after the ten, I honestly thought that I could win the five. I learnt so much in that 10 K…so, yeah, I'm disappointed, but I'm not going to let it spoil my life forever, am I? I've got a bonus in the marathon tomorrow…yeah, I know the Kenyans and the other Africans will close it out, but I'll be learning again; maybe Rio in four years' time, what d'you reckon?" Lucy didn't reply directly to Mickey's question but answered with questions of her own.

"You're going to watch the five, though? Shelley's definitely in the four-by-four, and Marianne, of course, for Holland." Mickey had been diverted.

"You see all the papers this morning, Lucy? They're all bigging you and Shelley up as the golden girls of the Games; 'bout right too, four gold medals between you, pretty bloody awesome, I reckon."

"And how many medals has Gilly got? Seven, seven! Me'n Shell's golds, your silver, Sami's silver and Marianne's bronze, not forgetting JoJo's gold as well. Can't be another coach out there with that many…how lucky are we?"

*****

For Mickey, it was an anticlimax watching the five thousand metres. He knew that he should have been there, but the fall had taken that possibility (make that 'probability') away. Nothing he could do about it. Atticus won it, won it fairly easily, put the big boot in four laps out and actually ran way under four minutes for that final mile. Micky Winzenreid missed out in fourth place but was stoic about that; he already had his gold medal.

And then the final event of the evening, final track event of the Games: women's four-by-four hundred metres relay. Shelley had taken in the news from Mark Blatchford and had gone through the different preparations that she now needed with Gilly and the relay coach. She was jogging around with Marianne and knew that she had, just had, to tell Marianne the news. The phrase 'moral obligation' didn't appear in her mind but the meaning of it did.

"Marianne, have to tell you something…"

"So, they're putting you on anchor leg, is that correct?"

Marianne smiled. "Of course they are, Shelley; you're their best runner, so maybe we carry on as we started, running against each other. You remember that two hundred metres back in Amsterdam? So now we run again…I think it is good that I can run against one of my best friends. I also think that without you, I would not be here."

"Oh, Marianne! Thank you so much; thank you for understanding!"

"So now I tell you a few more things, OK? The Americans and the Jamaicans are the favourites, best in the world for a long time now. But for all the other teams, it is not so clear, and I believe that Holland and Great Britain have the chance to take a bronze medal. Be careful on your baton change, Shelley, no dropping and no disqualification, promise me?" Shelley promised.

Thirty-two athletes in the holding room, the whistle blew, the marshals gathered them and walked out on the track with them. The final track event of the London Olympic Games, and there was a British team in with a chance. Had to be in with a chance because they had the golden girl; they had Shelley Steele in their team.

The home-grown experts in the crowds knew it all; reading about Shelley in the papers meant that they thought they knew her, knew what she was capable of. And they had no idea that a little knowledge can often be a dangerous thing. Holland in lane three, Great Britain in six, Jamaica and the USA in four and five. The crowd absolutely silent now…the starting pistol explodes; the athletes explode; the crowd explodes.

The middle lanes with Jamaica's Sharisha Brown and USA's Dixie-May Tarquine look to be leading, but with the extended stagger, no one is sure. Into the home straight and Jamaica and USA have a slight lead, less than expected. The handover is clean for all teams, second athlete on the first bend and then the break into the back-straight, still Jamaica and USA battling it out up front with Ember Williams and Florence Freeman, a three-metre gap and Holland, France, Russia and Great Britain's Caroline Hogarth, who had taken second in the individual four hundred vying for third.

Into the stretch and the incoming runners spotting their team member, shoving and moving in the mass takeover…but it's clean, clean again! Jamaica and USA still neck-and-neck, lead now up to five metres, Zekia Johnson holding the inside line with Jenny Rudolph alongside her. Holland move slightly ahead of Great Britain. Shelley waiting on the final takeover smiles at Marianne inside her, the gap now seven metres for Marianne to chase and a further four metres for Shelley behind Marianne. Fifty metres to takeover, USA's Jenny Rudolph tries to move in front of Zekia Johnson, can't quite make it, drops back…and their elbows clash. The two leaders now stumbling, almost falling, trying desperately to stay on their feet, speed dropping away. The gap closing, Holland now level, twenty metres only, Great Britain slightly closing on Holland.

Clean takeovers for Marianne and Shelley, and they go out shoulder to shoulder with a three-metre gap to USA's individual four hundred winner Sonya Rees-Derek and Jamaica's Jamie Campbell, who took gold in the two hundred metres. Marianne on the inside, Shelley level and a silly thought flashed into Shelley's mind, *Read this in a book and you wouldn't believe it.* Shelley and Marianne, best friends, *I have to win, give it everything!*

Anything less would be a lack of respect. Final two hundred, Sonya Rees-Derek moves level; Jamie Campbell has dropped a couple of metres. Sonya forced to run in lane three around that lung-screaming bend. Into the stretch, too much for Sonya, those extra three or four metres have taken her out of contention for gold. Can she hang on for bronze? Marianne and Shelley still locked together. *How can something so short hurt so much?*

Fifty metres…twenty…ten…throw themselves at the tape, collapse on the ground, roll over and embrace each other and burst into hysterical laughter, laying on the track, just laughing and laughing and laughing. Eventually stand up, still giggling, still holding onto each other. Kiss and hug Sonya and Jamie.

What the hell's happened to the scoreboard? Who won? C'mon, who won? "Ladies and gentlemen, apologies for the delay in posting the results of the women's relay; you will have seen Great Britain and Holland locked together at the finish. The teams, Holland and Great Britain, have been given the same times. The judges now have to check the digital super-slow-motion replay and the pressure-sensitive digital timers. Please bear with us."

It seemed like an eternity but was actually less than a minute. The scoreboard started flashing. Marianne and Shelley grinned at each other. "Who won?" And then up came the numbers…

3rd United States of America 3.21.111

1st Holland 3.20.661

1st Great Britain 3.20.661

And they were face to face, still screaming at each other, fairy-tale ending, of course it was! The other six runners from Holland and Great Britain were on the track with Shelley and Marianne, and it was the perfect lap of honour to close the final track day of the Games.

Day 16. Sunday, 12 August. Final Day of the London Olympic Games

Mickey was thinking on the words from the previous evening. Shelley, JoJo, Lucy and Gilly had sat down with him away from the stadium, away from the crowds of well-wishers, groupies and star-truckers. There had been lots of words spoken. Mickey didn't really remember them properly, if at all. But he'd taken the sense of them. "If we could do it, you can. Give it everything, Mickey, and if you don't get there, it doesn't matter because you tried, because you gave it everything."

And then, "We're the kids who nobody thought could make it; we're the slum kids, the no-hopers, and we proved them wrong. We're TMRG, and we proved them wrong."

And the Duracell Bunny hoped that he could prove them wrong as well, but if he didn't, he knew that he'd go close to dying, trying. He'd looked at all the comparison times and tables, knew that on paper he couldn't even light a candle to the Africans' times, but he had something special that they didn't have; he had Mr Warren and Gilly on his team; he had Lucy and TMRG. And he knew that he hadn't touched his potential on the marathon, but he was going to see exactly what his potential was in a couple of hours' time.

It was a very different marathon course from the usual London marathon: one short lap of just over two miles and then three laps of eight miles, giving the classic marathon distance of twenty-six miles and three hundred and eighty-five

459

yards. The start and finish were in the mall, and Mickey was disappointed that the finish wouldn't be in the London Stadium, but that was out of his control. The laps were taking in Buckingham Palace, St Paul's Cathedral and the Tower of London. *London, my London*, thought Mickey.

It was a small field, just over a hundred athletes, and Mickey thought back to just those few months ago when he'd run his first and only marathon with over forty thousand spread through the streets of London. Out of his competitors today, Mickey knew only a very few: Taya Ambassa and Hakim Cherebet, his Ethiopian rivals from the ten thousand metres final, and the three Ugandans, Akiki Kato, Joseph Masika and Moses Ajot. He'd even written their best times on his arm in biro, and he'd also written on the back of his hand the various pace times he could check each mile as he went past.

The whistle blew, marshals marshalling, athletes assembling in the mall. The introductions to the crowd, ten athletes only, Mickey the first to be introduced and only as a sop to the largely British crowd because he'd medalled already and wasn't expected to feature in the marathon, then through the big names, Kenyans, Ethiopians, Ugandans, one American and one Mexican.

"Gentlemen, the final event of the 2012 London Olympic Games, the marathon. Gentlemen, you are in the hands of Mr Starter." And they were off.

There was one article that Mickey remembered reading about the marathon, and it had stuck with him because it rang true. It was that you could divide the marathon up into three sections if you were a serious contender: the early stages—maybe four or five miles—where you established your position in the leading group, checking out your rivals and not letting anybody steal off of the front; the mid-race—fifteen, sixteen, seventeen miles—where you held your position and were able to relax just a little bit; and the final three, four, five miles when the pace would up, and if you weren't serious, you'd be spat out of the back in bubbles. Mickey didn't know what was going to happen towards the end, but he was very sure that he was going to go with the early pace, whatever it was. The race started off slowly; Mexico's Jose Garcia broke away once, twice, three times but was dragged back by the pack.

Mickey checked the pace, looking at his hand. *I'm comfortable; I'm fine.* First small lap completed, and the runners headed out on the first long lap towards the Tower of London. A lead pack of fifteen athletes had formed, everyone running cautiously and within themselves. At the tower were Mr Warren, Dan Bullet, Eric, Bobby, Shelley, JoJo, Joshi, Kaas and Marianne. Lucy,

Sami and Alisha were with Gilly in the mall. The six-mile marker and board showing 29 minutes and 30 seconds ('Sub two ten pace and I'm still feeling good…'). Back past St Paul's Cathedral, Big Ben, down Birdcage Walk, past Buckingham Palace and the leading pack still together as they went through the ten-mile mark back at the start. Mickey's four supporters cheering for him, "Looking good, Mickey, looking good!"

Through that ten-mile mark in 49.10, holding that same pace. On the second big lap taking them through eighteen miles in 1 hour 28 minutes and 30 seconds, five athletes fell away as the pace increased just that little bit. Ten now, ten remaining. Akiki Kato went to the front, Roger Hill of USA immediately followed, and the two put daylight between themselves and the eight chasers…but it didn't last; the faster pace wasn't quite fast enough and the ten were together but only a short while, and Roger Hill fell off the pack. The turnaround at the Tower of London for the final time, twenty-two miles gone (1.48.10), just over four remaining, and Mickey heard Shelley shout out to him.

"C'mon, Mickey! C'mon, bruv! Shit or bust!" Mickey made a decision…it was time to turn it on; he owed it to himself; he owed it to TMRG, to Gilly, Dan, Mr Warren. *Four miles is nothing, not even twenty minutes.* A quick glance at the back of hand, even quicker calculations, Mickey upped the pace; he knew—or he thought he knew—just what pace he could hold for the last miles. The pack had to follow, had to. If they didn't go with him, they were out completely, so they followed…at least six of them did, three dropped back within two hundred metres. Seven remaining, seven in with a chance of an Olympic gold medal. That four fifty-five miling had dropped to four forty pace, and Mickey held strong, another mile, another three rabbits got burnt.

Two miles only now, along the embankment; Mickey, Joseph Masika, Mose Ajok, Hakim Cherebet. Mickey could hear the harsh breathing. All of them? Just one? *Don't know…can't allow myself to care. This is who I am; this is what I do.* And Mickey Honey, the Duracell Bunny, opened the tap a little further and allowed the speed to flow; he heard a groan and knew one had gone, guaranteed medal! *Don't care a left-handed fuck; there's only one medal I want.* Birdcage Walk, one last mile. *This is who I am, this is what I do.* There was no pain now; he was outside himself, watching as if from the skies. He moved away from Joseph and Hakim, five metres, ten, in a flash it seemed he was one hundred metres ahead. And as he broke the tape, Lucy ran out to throw her arms around him, and millions upon millions of TV viewers cried.

Alisha was there, also in tears; she was on her mobile phone…ringing, ringing, ringing, and then a pick-up.

"Lord Coe? Sorry, yes, it's the mayor…no, it's not, it's Alisha, yeah, I know. Seb, you remember our conversation? You do? Have you watched the marathon just now? Of course, you did. What do you think?"

Lord Sebastian Coe had some very serious thinking to do, a lot of phone calls to make and some very big favours to call in.

*****

The final podium presentation of the Olympic Games is made just before the closing ceremony. There is only one event, one presentation remaining: the men's marathon. Mickey, Joseph and Hakim were waiting in the shadows of the stand, waiting to be called. The announcement was made; the scoreboard flashed up the results:

3rd Hakim Cherebet, Ethiopia 2.08.09

2nd Joseph Masika, Uganda 2.08.02

1st Mickey Honey, Great Britain 2.07.53

Seb Coe walked out with the medal winners; he was smiling inside; he'd managed to call the favours, no feelings hurt.

"Please welcome your marathon medallists, third, then second, then first onto the podium." Seb smiled up at the medallists, and then he did a most unusual thing; he winked at Mickey, very slow and very exaggerated.

"Presenting the medals this evening, I'd like you to welcome a local teacher, a local teacher who has had the most influence on some of his pupils' careers. One of past pupils is the mayor of the London Borough of Newham, and four of them have won gold medals at this Olympic Games, including our marathon winner, Mickey Honey. Please welcome Mr Christopher Warren."

And Mickey, Lucy, JoJo and Shelley really did sob their hearts out.

*****

They were all in the mayor's parlour at Newham townhall the day after. Mayor Alisha Buzdar had organised a celebration. A private celebration for TMRG, Marianne and Kaas, Sami, Gilly and Chris and Dan, and Shelley's mum Angie. It had been a long, long journey, a journey of twelve years, but the team were still together. There were two more invited guests, David Caxton of the Times newspaper and Mr Zig-Zag, John Smith.

Angie and Dan had spoken to Shelley about what they were going to do—it was as if they were asking permission—and Shelley had burst into happy tears and couldn't stop hugging both of them. Alisha gave them each just one minute to say a few words; in truth, they were all happy with that restriction because they feared there would be lots of tears if they spoke too long. There were lots of thank-yous in the few words; of course, there were. Olympic medallists thanking their coaches and mentors, how could there not be? Shelley was the last to get up to speak. After her thank-yous, she took a deep, deep breath.

"OK, I have three Olympic gold medals, and I thank all of you. Cliché time. Without all of you, I wouldn't be here saying this. I know I'm being flash ("What, you, Shell? Never!" Lots of giggles), but I don't care because something even better is going to happen, something that makes me happier than any number of medals could do." And she looked over at her mum and then Dan and caught the smiles and the nods. Shelley smiled and managed not to cry. "You see…my mum and Dan are going to get married, and I honestly couldn't be any happier…for both of them…actually, for me as well!"

Everybody applauded and cheered, smiles and blushes from Angie and Dan. "You see, I used to tell people that I didn't have a dad, well, maybe I didn't, but these two gentlemen here, Dan and Mr Warren, have been more than dads to me, much more." More cheering and applauding, more blushes from Chris and Dan. "And I don't know if my mum is going to change her name…and obviously, I'm not…but if I did, if I did, then I'd be Shelley Steele-Bullet, and I really would blow everyone away!" Shelley walked over to her mum and Dan, hugged and whispered and cried a little, and sat down emotionally exhausted.

David Caxton Writes in the Times

Eight years ago, I was privileged to meet some extraordinary young athletes at the European under-eighteen track and field championships. I have followed their careers with interest. More than interest, I have somehow become involved with them, and last night, I was honoured to sit with them to celebrate their Olympic triumphs. Between them and their shared coaches, Gilly Warren and Dan Bullet, they have won nine gold medals, two silver and one bronze; that is better than all but four nations in the Olympic Games. Four kids from the same class in one junior school! Add their three accomplices and that is truly amazing, and I try not to use that word too often because I believe it is often misused.

But on this occasion, I believe that I have used it wisely. Their coaches I have mentioned, and now I mention their junior school teacher, Mr Christopher Warren. Because it is Mr Warren who set this ball rolling, Mr Warren who instilled in these young people the belief that anything is possible—as long as you want it hard enough and as long as you are prepared to work hard enough. Teachers can change lives; teachers can open the doors of opportunity by giving their pupils the imagination to see those opportunities. Mr Warren did exactly that, and I am truly humbled. Many people are honoured for many different things in the country; if there is one person who deserves the highest honour for services to education, it is Mr Christopher Warren.

*****

It was a very special assembly on the first day of the new term at Riverside Junior School. The headteacher, Mr Christopher Warren, stepped onto the stage and introduced eight ex-pupils to the school; one was the Mayor of Newham, one a medical doctor, two very successful businessmen, and four of them were multiple Olympic medallists. All eight of them spoke to the school children about what they had achieved in life, how they had achieved it and how much they owed to Riverside School and to their old teacher—now headteacher—Mr Warren. They spoke about how proud they were to have attended Riverside, how proud and lucky that they were taught by Mr Warren, and how all the children in assembly should be proud that they were pupils at the best junior school in the world.

Every child listened and every child vowed that one day, they would be standing on the stage and talking to the children in assembly about what they had achieved.